Home Front

Annie Clarke's roots are dug deep into the North East. She draws inspiration from her mother, who was born in a County Durham pit village during the First World War, and went on to become a military nurse during World War Two. Annie and her husband now live a stone's throw from the pit village where her mother was born. She has written frequently about the North East in novels which she hopes reflect her love and respect for the region's lost mining communities.

Annie has four adult children and four granddaughters, who fill her and her husband's days with laughter, endlessly leading these two elders astray.

Also by Annie Clarke

Girls on the Home Front
Heroes on the Home Front

ANNIE CLARKE
Wedding Bells
on the
Home Front

arrow books

1 3 5 7 9 10 8 6 4 2

Arrow Books
20 Vauxhall Bridge Road
London SW1V 2SA

Arrow Books is part of the Penguin Random House group
of companies whose addresses can be found at
global.penguinrandomhouse.com.

Penguin
Random House
UK

First published in Great Britain by Arrow Books in 2020

www.penguin.co.uk

A CIP catalogue record for this book is available
from the British Library

ISBN 9781787462595

Typeset in 10.75/13.5 pt Palatino by Jouve (UK), Milton Keynes
Printed and bound in Great Britain by Clays Ltd, Elcograf S.p.A.

MIX
Paper from
responsible sources
FSC® C018179

Penguin Random House is committed to a
sustainable future for our business, our readers
and our planet. This book is made from Forest
Stewardship Council® certified paper.

For Cass and Ben with so much love

Chapter One

Fran Hall sat on the back seat of the bus that carried her brother Stan, his bride, Sarah, and half the wedding party. With Bert at the wheel, they were travelling from St Oswald's Church to the wedding tea in Massingham pit village. She could see Cyril's bus carrying the other guests just in front of them.

Fran grinned because she knew that Bert would be right fed up that he'd been slow off the mark and Cyril's passengers would be first at the food and drink. Oh aye, she thought to herself, they'd be clustering around the buffet table like gannets.

The buses were travelling slowly, as snow had come out of nowhere just as they'd left the church. It was beginning to lie on the road. She looked through the window, seeing the flakes tumbling, then speeding up into flurries, blocking the view of the fields where sheep would be huddled in the lee of the drystone walls. The snow was blocking out Auld Hilda's slag heap, too. It didn't matter, for she knew exactly where their village pit was, and the pithead, and Massingham itself, all of which were as permanent as – well, Davey.

Davey who was even now sliding his arm around her, kissing her cheek and saying, 'By, I'm right pleased Stevie finished the photos quick, so we could get on board and not end up like snowmen.'

1

'Aye, but look what it's doing, bonny lad.' Fran nodded towards the front of the bus, where the snow was settling on the windscreen, making the wipers labour and screech. In an instant the chatter was stilled, and everyone watched, and waited. Fran grinned along with the other passengers.

Davey squeezed her closer, and then breathed, 'Wait . . . Wait . . .'

It took a few seconds, and then she heard the clearing of Bert's throat. Any minute. Any min—

'You keep yourselves going, you bliddy wipers,' Bert shouted. 'I've a bliddy beer waiting at the bliddy wedding tea, you bliddy hear me?'

She cheered, along with everyone else, for here, on this bus, was her world, strong and sturdy, and aye, permanent. These were her family, friends, neighbours, fellow munitions workers, and pitmen. She pressed into Davey, aching with the need for him to stay and not return to Bletchley Park and the code-breakers. Stay. Stay. For he belonged here, with his pitman scars, his blue eyes, his soft lips. Davey kissed her and she pressed harder against him, not caring that her cracked ribs were not completely healed, nor her fractured arm. Not completely, but enough, and she was home, working at the local munitions factory, not the Scottish one to which she and Sarah had been temporarily transferred, only to be injured in an explosion.

Davey was whispering and pulling her back from the accident, to the bus, to him: 'I do love you, Franny Hall, sister of Stan and Ben, and soon to be me missus. And as me missus, you'll have to do as you're told. Clean the windows, scrub the step—'

She slapped him. They smiled, and kissed. Around them the easy chattering and bursts of laughter continued. She was safe, but the memory of the pain still seeped back, the explosion . . . She chanted in her head: Stan had just married

Davey's sister. They were squashed together on the other side of her. Beth sat alongside Davey. Viola was jammed in next to her. So, all three bridesmaids were together.

She had given the words a rhythm and Fran continued chanting: Viola, whom they had brought back from Scotland. Viola, who was without her parents. Without half a hand. With half an ear and a scorched scalp. From that same accident.

Davey whispered, 'Makes me feel good, pet, being home amongst them all.'

His words resonated – *home amongst them all*. She clung to them, finding a laugh. 'And with me, of course?'

Davey kissed her temple. '*Them*, I said, so no, I don't care whether you're here or not.'

She poked him and this time they laughed together, as they had since they were small bairns, and all right, and the cries of those trapped beneath the debris had no place in this moment, and no place in her dreams. She touched his hand, so warm, rough. Davey, her Davey, was being a pest, and that's as it had always been and she loved him for it. She dug him in the ribs. 'Then maybe don't come back in a month for our own wedding, eh?'

Davey grew serious, and he lifted her hand and kissed it again and again. 'I would crawl on my knees from the south to marry you, my dearest lovely Franny. Besides, everyone would be right irate because they'd miss not having pheasant sandwiches for the wedding tea. Mr Massingham sent birds down from the Hall, didn't he, so he'll likely do the same for us?'

'Oh aye, I reckon so. He's a good man. You might have heard that the bridesmaids' mams and the marrers have been up before dawn making them into sandwiches, but I've done a few spam as well. It's them I've put aside for you.'

3

'Best not do that for the wedding tea, or it's out into the cold you'll go.'

Fran laughed, pinching his hand just below a pit scar. 'Ouch.'

'Serves you right,' she said, looking past him to Beth and Viola. 'I reckon Davey thinks if he doesn't turn up for our wedding you'd be right cross because you'd miss the tea, not because he'd left a lonely bride waiting in tears at the altar.'

Beth raised her eyebrows at Viola. Together they nodded. 'Aye, that'd be right,' said Beth. 'Canna have enough wedding teas, or them with a bit of pheasant on the menu anyway.'

Viola smoothed her dress. 'Will you wear Sarah's dress, and will we wear these?' She pointed at their summer frocks.

Fran raised her eyebrows. 'Depends if we can find any more discarded curtains at Massingham Hall. There's not enough left of the nursery ones we found for Sarah, so maybe I'll just swan down the aisle in me pinny and little else. What d'you think, our Sarah?'

Sarah was far too busy listening to Stan's sweet nothings to reply.

'Come here, Franny.' Davey eased Fran closer to him, and she kissed his hand better, but saw Beth peering past them to the bridal couple, squashed together at the end of the back seat. 'Sarah's going to look as though she's been dragged through a hedge, with all this hugging.'

Viola sniggered. 'It's a brocade curtain, so I reckon any creases will drop out with a bit of a shake.'

Sarah heard. 'No one's shaking me or my dress, or I'll set my husband on you.' There was more laughter, this time from the seats in front of them too, the sound rippling down the bus.

'Calm yourself,' Fran muttered to Sarah, 'and get back to

being squashed, eh. But I reckon the wedding photos will be quite something. There'll be you, blonde and blue-eyed, looking like a queen in your finery, wondering who these three lasses are cluttering up the place in their mams' summer dresses. There'll be me with hair as dark as Ben's and Stan's, Beth red-haired, and Viola a dark auburn, all with munitions chemicals streaked through. Howay, a line up of right beauties.'

'What about me, I'd like to know,' huffed Stan, 'the bridegroom in his best bib and tucker, shiny boots, no chemical streaks, and a come-hither smile?'

Sarah laughed. 'Don't forget your blue pitman scars, you daft apeth.'

' 'Tis your *only* bib and tucker,' called Ben, who was sitting in front of Stan.

Stan flicked the lad's cap. 'Enough from you, little brother.'

Viola sighed. 'I couldn't get over the confetti – all that colouring and cutting by the evacuees up at Massingham Hall. Must have taken an age.'

The bus crawled around a bend and Fran saw that though the snow was easing, it hadn't quite stopped yet. A few flakes were still falling, and somehow it made the day even better, because everywhere was so white, clean and magical. She looked down at her hands, tinged yellow by the explosive chemicals. It was daft to have to be so secretive about what they did when half the women on this bus were walking posters that declared *We're working in munitions, helping to win the war*. But all they could actually say was that they worked in a factory, making – whatever lies they came up with.

Davey covered her hands with his. 'All right, lass?'

'I'm always all right,' she said.

The bus crawled around another bend, skidding on the icy road, then straightening. Fran smiled at Davey, responding to the tightening of his grip. He murmured into her hair, his breath warm on her skin, 'It's so grand being here, and look, the snow's on the point of stopping, bonny lass, and there'll be elderberry wine any minute, which'll make you sweetness and light. Makes me think that while you're rushing about gathering up my posh sandwiches—'

She slapped him. He laughed and continued: 'While you're doing that, I'll have a bit of a word with Bert, because I noticed the front off-side tyre is bald, and could be dangerous. I'm not having me girl at risk, for I need her fit and well to look after me.'

Viola peered along at him and said, 'You are bliddy joking. A bald tyre dangerous? And our work at the Factory isn't, you daft pitman?'

'And the snow's just about stopped,' called Beth, 'so Bert can give over swearing at the wipers, for I reckon he still is.'

Beth's husband, Bob, who was sitting in front of her, asked, 'How can you tell?'

'He nods his head when he blathers away driving us into the Factory. Have a good look – he's doing it now. Enjoys it, I reckon. Likes any old excuse.'

They all sat back as the wipers jettisoned the last of the snow and began to sweep cleanly across the windscreen to reveal the smouldering Massingham slag heap, and the pithead standing against the grey sky. Aye, thought Fran, and that's just as good as the magical, dancing snow. Davey was hugging her again and whispering, 'You know, lass, since you told me over the phone about our mams nursing Ralph Massingham up at the Hall—'

She nodded as Beth cut in: 'Aye, the pus from his pit cut got into his blood – near killed him. Right grand the mams' proggy-makers' co-op were, for Sophia Massingham couldn't manage to nurse him on her own, what with the evacuees as well. Day and night them women slogged, took it in shifts – with Sophia taking her turn, mark you. Fore shift, aft shift and night shift, saved his life they did, using the sphagnum moss to suck the pus out.'

Viola pulled a face. 'Must you keep saying pus? I've gone right off eating.'

The call was taken up by the next few rows.

Over the complaints, Davey took up where he'd left off. 'Well, I reckon they performed a miracle, for it not only drew the poison, but something deeper that were making him the beggar he's always been. He's paid towards the booze, hasn't he? Not his da, but the whelp? And he's different – spent time talking to people at the church.'

Beth wagged her finger at him. 'Don't let the co-op hear you calling him the whelp. They got fond of him when he were poorly, and reckon the change in him could well last. Me mam said there's just something different about him.'

'But what I say is, can we trust the turnaround?' Davey muttered. 'Can the stuck-up owner's son switch to be some-one human?'

Fran couldn't understand the change either, except that her mam could charm the worst into being angels, and Ralph had been the worst. Always a bully, right from a bairn, lording it about the village. Nothing like his da at all.

Bob dragged out his Woodbines and threw the packet to Davey. 'Pass them along – and put your hand down, Ben.'

'It's not fair,' Ben moaned.

Stan swatted him. 'It is – you're still a bairn.'

'I'm twelve,' Ben protested.

'Aye, still a bairn,' they all shouted.

Ben sulked as Stan lit everyone's cigarettes.

Bert ground the gears. Near the front of the bus, Mrs Oborne broke off from her chat with Fran's mam and yelled, 'Been on the booze, our Bert?'

'Chance'd be a fine bliddy thing. Even when I get to the

Miners' Club I can only have a bit, since I have to get the old besom back to the depot after.'

'You're not taking me to any depot, you dirty old man,' yelled Mrs Oborne.

Davey spoke over the laughter: 'Some things never change, thank the Lord.'

Bob had taken off his naval cap and was fanning his laughing wife. 'Calm yourself, Beth. You and all, Viola, or you'll do yourselves a mischief.'

Bob's 'Ouch' as Beth clipped his ear was loud enough to make Sarah shout, 'Man up, Bob, she's only a bitty lass—'

Just then there was a screech of brakes and they were flung forwards, then back. Bert bellowed, 'Bliddy hell, it were a cat. It ran across in front.'

'Black one?' boomed Mrs Oborne.

Someone who had a window seat yelled, 'Aye, it were an' all.'

'That's all right then,' shouted Mrs Oborne, 'for it's good luck for us all. So come on, Bert, stop making a meal of it and get your bliddy foot down. We need to get to the victuals before Cecil's busload eat the whole bliddy lot, for it'll be gobs open and no holds barred.'

'Aye, and you could do to shut yours an' all, Tilly Oborne, or I'll turf you off.'

The passengers were sniggering, and Bert's tirade ended on a great guffaw as he drove on.

Sarah felt Stan so close to her they could have been just one person, and didn't think she could be any happier. She linked her arm carefully through Fran's strapped one, and as the bus trundled along she couldn't hold in her joy any longer. 'Here I am, Sarah Hall – yes, Hall, not Bedley any more.'

She stopped as those in the nearest rows turned round, smiling. 'Aye,' she called, not caring what anyone thought,

'I'm the wife of Stan, one of the best hewers in the pit, and a scholarship lad who's been to Oxford an' all.'

Fran leaned against her. 'Aye, Mrs Hall, my brother is one of the best.'

Sarah just grinned. 'Well, in a month you'll not be Fran Hall any longer, but Fran Bedley. It's like a roundabout, isn't it? Hall, Bedley, Bedley, Hall, and if you don't have a black cat running in front of your bus, then you'll share mine. Oh Franny, it's all so wonderful.'

Stan was laughing, and Sarah kissed his cheek. He was so strong, so brave, so certain. Well, he was a pitman, so of course he was. What's more, she was strong too, especially after the dreams – or perhaps nightmares would be a better word – had faded. Night after night they'd come, the dreams of lying beneath the debris in Scotland, only stopping when they'd left hospital and finally returned to Massingham.

Aye, Massingham, with its back-to-backs, the clop of pit-men's boots in the early morning, and Stan, wonderful Stan, who had soothed her and put her to rights. She snatched a look at Fran, who was too pale, too short of sleep, and who still heard the cries from under the rubble. Night after night Fran dreamed it, and Sarah had told her it were just plain daft for they had not made a noise, but the lass seemed not to take it in.

There was another screech of brakes, and they braced themselves as Mrs Oborne yelled, 'For pity's sake, Bert, get a bliddy grip.'

'Aye,' came Bert's reply, 'and the grip'll be round that big gob of yours. Open your eyes, lass. We're here.'

Everyone had been too busy talking, but now they looked out of the windows and saw that they were parked behind Cecil's bus, about twenty yards from the Miners' Club.

'All off the *Skylark*, and last one in's a cissy,' yelled Bert.

'And I'll have no more cheek from you, Tilly Oborne, or I'll lock you in the luggage hold and your old man'll not stop me, so you can settle back down, our Steve.'

Steve sat down with a thump, laughing. Then he was up again as his wife shouted orders to join the queue and be sharp about it.

Fran and Davey slipped into the aisle on the heels of the bridal couple, Davey's breath warm on her neck as he said, 'I know you're still having them dreams, lass, but don't fret, the dreams are your mind's way of shifting the thoughts. Stan and I were the same in the pit when the coal came down and buggered our legs. Best to ignore them.'

Fran nodded as they shuffled forward. The coal that had fallen on Stan and Davey was a natural fall, but the explosion at the Scottish factory hadn't been natural at all. That had been the result of a kirby grip falling into a machine on which one of the new girls was working. The metal grip had caused a spark, which had ignited the explosives in the machine. The whole lot had gone up and the ceiling had come down, and it was her – Fran Hall's – fault. She had been too slow in calling out a warning as she walked along to take her place at the workbench, too unsure that it really had been a kirby grip she'd seen glinting in the girl's hair.

Fran moved down the aisle. She, Fran Hall, was moving down the aisle. She could move, smile, talk, kiss the man she loved because she was alive. Four others would have been if she hadn't waited so long, peering forward to make sure, really sure.

Fran had already told her friends and her mam that she hadn't called the warning in time, but all of them just interrupted and wouldn't let her say she felt so guilty. Instead, they just said it wasn't her fault, stop going on about it. Even Viola had shouted, just as Sarah had, 'Don't be daft, it's not our job – we check our marrers, not the whole bliddy shift. And no one else saw the glint. And no one screamed, or cried beneath the bricks, bonny lass. Pull yourself together.'

Her mam had said, 'Hush, Franny, these things can happen in a munitions factory. It's not your fault.' But she felt it *was*. So, what do I do about that? she wanted to scream. Let someone tell me what to do about it, because I can't stand the dreams, but I canna stop them – or the guilt.

Ahead of her the bridal pair were laughing at something. Davey murmured, 'Cheer up, lass. Dreams aren't real.'

She felt rage sweep her – for if he didn't know her mind, who would?

'Come on, down with you,' he said. They had reached the bus steps and Fran eased herself onto the ground. Davey followed, slipping his arm around her waist, careful not to jog her. She looked ahead to the club, where bunting hung over the doorway, each triangle of cream wallpaper coloured red, white and blue by the evacuees. Some of the red had smeared as the snow had fallen and it looked as though it had been weeping.

Beth followed Viola along the bus and waited while the lass eased herself down the steps behind Davey and Fran. Aye, and I'd ease myself if I'd been hurt as Viola has, for it will hurt for a while yet, poor lass. Once down, Viola called after Fran and Davey, 'Wait for us.'

Beth was about to descend with Bob close behind her, when Bert muttered, 'Leave a spam sandwich for me, pet.'

'No spam for you, lad. I reckon it'll be the best for the man who drove us in the snow squall, eh?'

He smiled, tiredness dragging at his face. Well, she thought, he was about fifty, perhaps older, and drove the bus to and from the Factory, delivering and returning the shift workers at all hours, so of course he was tired. But then there was a war on, and everyone—

Bob tapped her on the shoulder. 'Howay, lass. Let's get going or there'll be nowt left, and I need to be gone by midnight or I'll turn into a pumpkin. See you in there, eh, Bert?'

'Aye, you will, lad. Be rough at sea today, so 'tis best you're here.'

'In refit, so we'll be calm as a millpond, but still busy as hell.' They set off, reaching Viola, who had almost caught up with Fran. Ahead of them, beyond the allotment, snow lay on the hills, with just a scattering left on the shed roofs.

As they walked, Bob said to Beth, his voice low, 'Hurry yourself along, pet, for I need to eat. Tommy'll pick me up at midnight from the telephone box. He's been up near the Scottish border on his motorbike and we're to get to Grimsby and the minesweeper by dawn. But I'll have to kill you if you tell anyone that's where I'm headed.'

She squeezed his arm. 'I'll not say a word, as long as you swear to take care, eh? Besides, everyone who's anyone knows where you're off to, daft beggar.'

They reached the warmth and light of the Miners' Club hall, where the food was laid out on trestle tables. The women of the Proggy Rug Co-operative, led by Mrs Bedley, Mrs Smith and Mrs Hall, were bustling about, whipping the greaseproof paper off plates of sandwiches and pouring wine into the glasses Stevie had loaned them from his pub, the Rising Sun. It always made the girls laugh that he doubled as a photographer, turning the small bedroom into a darkroom, having shoved Mildred's sewing machine onto the landing. She had not been pleased. She still wasn't.

Beth knew exactly where the pheasant sandwiches were, since she, Fran and Viola had helped sort out the victuals at dawn. Sid and Norm, Stan's marrers, had been there too, putting up the bunting, which had been a grand effort, given the hangovers they both had. Sid had said, winking at her, 'Had to commiserate with the groom over a pint or two, for it's not every day we get to offload a marrer into the wedded state . . . Poor devil.' Beth had pulled his hair, which wasn't quite as red as hers, and his eyes were blue.

As they headed for the tables, Bob yawned, tired after his dash to get to the church, and though he'd been a bit late he'd been there to throw confetti, and Beth loved him for it. She stood on tiptoes and kissed his cheek. 'By, I love you, lad.'

He jerked round. She said, 'Don't look so surprised. I'm just so pleased to see you, bonny lad.'

Fran and Sarah, standing close by, nodded. 'Aye, Bob,' said Sarah. 'It's a grand effort, and one that's brought a big grin to our Beth's chops.'

Bob laughed and Beth squeezed his hand. 'We can just sit, not dance, eh?'

He shook his head. 'Dancing's part of a wedding. Just like the cake.'

Beth saw that the co-op had put the magnificent cardboard cake on a table in front of the stage. Underneath it was the small cake Beth's and Sarah's mams had made with ingredients supplied by everyone in the village who had a twist of sugar or flour to spare from their rations.

Coming to stand alongside, Viola wondered aloud, 'The cake is so huge – is it real?'

'Things are as real as you want them to be, Viola,' Bob answered. 'You can pretend them into being real, if you choose to. That's what you need to remember.'

Beth put her arm around Viola and whispered, 'You see, the cardboard one lifts up and there's a tiddler underneath, and I reckon my lad is wrong, for you canna make pretend into reality – you can play along for a bit, but the truth is always there, nudging for attention.'

Viola smiled as Bob wandered off just as young Ben clambered onto the stage and put a record on the gramophone player. It was a waltz. 'Coats off,' Ben yelled. 'Let's warm the place up with a bit of a dance while the mams get the urn on for tea, or a bit of the other.'

'Watch your language, lad,' yelled Sid.

Ben smirked. 'First waltz for the new Mr and Mrs Hall, but no kissing. It's disgusting and too much of a shock for a young lad. Come on, all of you, get yourselves sorted, 'tis bliddy freezing, and Sid, that's bliddy enough from you.'

'Language,' shouted everyone.

Ben scowled and gestured them all to be quiet, or that was perhaps how the gesture could be interpreted. Beth muttered to Viola, 'Thank heavens nothing changes.'

Viola looked from Beth to Fran, who had just joined them, and smiled. 'I'm beginning to see that.'

Quietly, Fran added, 'But let's hope some things do.' No one heard.

They watched now as Stan and Sarah took to the floor. Bob returned and tried to get Beth to dance. She smiled. 'Let the newly-weds have their moment, lad.'

Bob nodded. 'Oh aye, of course.'

They watched the bridal couple, Sarah's brocade dress shimmering against Stan's dark suit. It reminded Beth of her parents' wedding photo on their mantelpiece and she murmured to Viola, 'Howay, lass. It must be hard, both your parents gone in the Newcastle bombing, along with everything you had. At least we three still have our mams, and you must remember your home's in Massingham with us now, so never think you're alone. See, as long as we girls stick together, nowt can break us.'

Behind them, coats were being thrown over the chairs lining the room or hung on the pegs along the wall and on the backs of the double doors. Though the walls were painted a dull green, the usual noticeboards were festooned with bunting, creating instant cheer. At the back of the hall stood the Massingham Colliery banner, which was another splash of colour. Beth glanced at the dance floor to see Stan leading his new wife into a turn, his hair black against Sarah's blonde chignon. With a glance at Ben, and a wink, the only kiss he gave his bride was one on the forehead, and there was as much love in that as there would have been in anything more.

At Ben's urging, a steady flow of couples joined them. Among the first were Fran and Davey, as in love as the other two, and then Norm, Stan's marrer, escorted Viola into a dance, holding her wounded hand as gently as if it were cut glass. Following them were Sandra Young from the top end of Leadenhall Terrace, who also worked at the Factory, and her lad, Andy.

Beth looked on, loving the sight of her friends and neighbours, and then she felt Bob's arm slide around her.

'You all right, lass? Must be strange to see your old boyfriend wed to your marrer?'

Beth was so startled she pulled away from him. 'No, you daft thing, no stranger than Stan being at our wedding. You listen to me, Bob Jones – you know that I love you, deep through to me core.'

He drew her closer. 'I know you do. But this bliddy war makes things so difficult, such a bliddy mess, and changes so many things.' He paused, then repeated against her hair, 'Aye, all such a mess.'

'There's a way to go before the war's done with, lad, so we just have to get on with it,' Beth whispered.

'Oh, I know, but . . .' he started to say. 'You see . . .' He stopped, and began again. 'I look around and I'm right glad you are here in good old Massingham, with your marrers, and your family. I heard you tell Viola she'd never be alone, and neither will you, here.'

She kissed him, saying, 'I know, and I have you, even when you're away, and that's enough.'

He sighed, looked around, and gave a small shrug. 'Give us a dance, pet. Then I'll have a chat with some of me mates from Minton pit. It seems an age ago I were there.'

Beth murmured, 'Well it is. It was in a different world – peacetime, it's called.' They danced for just a moment, but then Beth saw Bert enter and groaned. 'His sandwiches.' She flew to the buffet and gathered up several pheasant and a couple of spam. She hurried to the hatch and passed the plate across to her mam and Sophia Massingham, Ralph's stepmother. 'These are for Bert. We promised.'

Sophia laughed. 'Then he has two platefuls, for we sorted it earlier. Lucky him.'

'Well, guard 'em both with your life,' said Beth, 'for if they go walkies he'll make our lives a living misery tomorrow, tearing round corners.'

She left the two women laughing and almost banged into Ralph, who stepped to one side. 'So sorry, Beth.'

She smiled uncertainly for Ralph never said sorry. This was a bliddy miracle.

'It was a lovely service,' said Ralph, and leaned in closer. 'But did I hear a mouse? There was a definite squeak.' He winked.

She laughed, surprised, and looked around to check that the organist, who was the Reverend Walters' sister, was nowhere near. 'Ah, Ralph . . . Sometimes there's a problem with the organ – wind in the pipes, it's said – resulting in a squeak.'

They both looked at one another, then burst out laughing. His mouse-coloured hair flopping over his right eye, his light brown eyes alight with amusement.

'Well, not quite like that,' she said, and could feel herself blushing.

Ralph nodded. 'But something similar, no doubt?'

Beth scurried off to dance with Bob again and told him of the conversation, and when Bob had stopped laughing, he said, 'Aye, well, the pit's a hard taskmaster, and perhaps our whelp met his match working on the face and has had to grow up.'

Beth turned to watch Ralph, who was wandering amongst the villagers, talking, smiling, nodding, being friendly.

'Come on, lass.' Bob was jigging to the music of a foxtrot and she forgot all about Ralph as she danced in his arms, knowing that one day the war would be over and they'd be together every day.

'Hang on to your hat,' Bob murmured. 'I'm about to sort out a turn.'

As he manoeuvred, she saw the dithering and doddery professor who had mentored Stan at Oxford. He was chatting to his old friend Reginald Massingham, who had set up the Massingham scholarship that Stan had won. But as she watched, the professor tapped Reginald on the arm and began to wend his way through the tables and the chattering groups of guests towards Ralph, who was taking his coat down from one of the pegs near the door.

What? she thought. It's only just started. But then the lad had been ill. And he was really pale. She shrugged and turned back to Bob, kissing his cheek.

Chapter Two

'Going already?' Professor Smythe almost whispered to Ralph Massingham. Ralph had to lean close to hear him over the music, the clatter of plates and the chatter of the guests. Smythe continued: 'I had hoped I might have your answer before I left as to whether you are prepared to work with those of us in counter-espionage, focusing on your very own Fascist cell in particular?'

Ralph wanted to beat away 'your very own Fascist cell', for it made him want to vomit. Suddenly the weight of his coat over his arm felt too much. He glanced around, frightened someone might be close enough to have heard, but he should have known Smythe was much too experienced to make such a mistake. He replied, just as quietly, 'I need a bit more time. I'm not sure I can do it.'

'Well,' the professor said, under cover of coughing into his hand, his pale blue eyes sharp as tacks, his white hair thinning in a way that Ralph had not noticed before, a million miles from the dithery professor he purported to be. For Professor Smythe was not just an academic, but a guardian of their country, or so Ralph had confirmed while talking to him in the shadow of St Oswald's. Ralph glanced across at his father. Was he more than a businessman too?

'I understand,' the professor was murmuring. 'Counter-espionage is a dicey task.'

Smythe lifted his head and his eyes were now as cold as steel as the two men exchanged looks, then stood together surveying the room. 'Smile, lad. Look as though we're enjoying a few pleasantries, eh?' Smythe laughed and Ralph managed to produce the semblance of one too.

The professor continued. 'The point is, dear old thing, you are the one who approached me outside the church – once I'd dropped a few openings, admittedly. It was apparent then how desperate you were to make amends for setting the fuse that blew out the props and caused the roof fall. Not that you intended to snaffle the Hall and Bedley fathers, of course, just halt production like the good little Fascist – or perhaps we should say Nazi? – that you are—'

Ralph cut across him, his voice harsh. 'Like the good little one I once was, until I came to my senses.'

Smythe smiled and turned to him. 'Do keep your voice low, Ralph. Yes, as you say, like you were, or so one might believe. May I continue?'

Ralph nodded and smiled, gesturing around the room. 'Lovely to see everyone together.'

'That's better,' Smythe replied. 'Now, I know that the deaths were unintentional. I know that they grieve you, and I hear you when you say you have had a change of heart.' He paused for a moment, waving towards Reginald Massingham, who was sitting at a table with the evacuees. 'I accept that neither Fran's nor Sarah's father was expected to be surveying Bell Seam that morning. The overman was too damnably keen, but there we are, two men dead, a seam blocked. I accept your telling me just a few hours ago that you had to get out of the whole damned traitorous Fascist mess you have created for yourself.'

Professor Smythe's voice was little more than a breath, but his laugh was hearty, and he patted Ralph's arm as he raised his voice. 'Yes, those sandwiches do look scrumptious.'

Ralph forced himself to nod and smile. 'You really should try the pheasant. Father's gamekeeper hung it for just long enough, and the co-op roasted it to perfection. Not that I've tried the sandwiches yet, but we know that whatever the co-op turn their hands to is a success. Lord, they even made me better, in more ways than one. Best tuck in, Professor, since you have a way to go, but delightful to see you, not to mention catch up on the news from Oxford. It seems so long ago.'

He looked around. It was what he found himself doing a lot now, for who knew who might be a member of Tim Swinton's Fascist cell, which he had joined while a sixth-former at home for the holidays. Back then it had been so different from anything else, a little gang of rebels intent on opposing the Communists. So many meetings, so many taking opposing sides – until war was declared. Ralph Massingham, a fool unto himself, had somehow stayed involved, but never, ever again.

He stared at these people sitting, dancing, chatting, some on leave from fighting. God, he was a bastard, but worse, a traitor and a fool, and he had to make amends even if it killed him.

Professor Smythe was still talking and Ralph made himself listen: '. . . sandwiches, so delicious. I can hardly wait.' Smythe lowered his voice again, though no one was in the vicinity. 'I do hope you *do* decide to work with us, for I repeat, it will put me in the most dreadful bind if you don't, dear boy. One thinks of the monitored calls from Massingham Hall to and from your handler, Tim Swinton . . . They prove beyond all doubt that you committed treason by virtue of your act of sabotage in time of war.

'Now, one should, of course, choose the spam, but . . . Pheasant was your idea, your father tells me and what matter if it's out of season? Reginald is quite entitled to bag what he wishes on his own land, especially when it's off ration. God bless the man is what I say. And the beer and wine paid for by your good self. The Rising Sun's best—'

Ralph interrupted, and he too was speaking quietly, so terribly quietly. 'No, you don't understand when I say I'm not sure I can do it. I mean, how can I go on being one of them, or pretending to be so, when I am . . .' He looked around as he whispered, 'I fear my loathing will show. I don't want to be near the bastards, to be a part . . . The shame I feel . . . The kindness of the women's co-op, the goodness of their daughters, and sons, the burden of guilt . . .'

Professor Smythe nodded. 'Indeed. But what option have you? Restitution or disgrace, possible exoneration or the rope.' He laughed, clapping his hands as a dance ended. 'So wonderful to be young.'

Ralph followed the professor's lead, though his mouth was dry with terror at his words. 'Well, Professor, I should get myself onto the dance floor too, but instead I must sleep. I find I get easily whacked after this septic cut, and I *am* on the fore shift tomorrow.' He waved to Mrs Hall, who smiled as she left a plate of sandwiches on one of the tables. She mimicked drinking a tankard of beer and Ralph pointed to the door. She nodded and he murmured to the professor, his voice shaking, 'I so need to reclaim some honour. I have been mad for too long – selfish, self-pitying. My mother died, and I used it but I need to know—'

Smythe put up his hand and whispered a warning: 'Wait.'

Davey was weaving between the tables, heading towards them with Fran, feisty Fran, daughter of Mr Hall. Mr Hall, now dead. Mr Hall, loved by Mrs Annie Hall, the co-op's leader, whom he, Ralph Massingham, adored for her guts, her kindness. Oh God.

Fran seemed pale, and Ralph remembered hearing Annie Hall talking to Beth's mother in his bedroom after they'd dressed the wound everyone believed was a pit injury.

They had been worried about Fran blaming herself for not spotting the kirby grip sooner, blaming herself for the four deaths. They had agreed then not to let her speak of the dreams in which she heard them crying out in the rubble, or of her sense of guilt, in the belief that it would help her put it all behind her. Ralph suspected that, like him, she probably wouldn't. What she needed, for it was what *he* needed, was for someone to understand, and to forgive. For him that was impossible, but not for her. She had tried to call a warning, her mother had said as she and Mrs Bedley sat knitting by his bedside, but felt she could have done it sooner.

Ralph stepped to one side as Davey shook Professor Smythe's hand. 'Good to see you, Prof. Thought you'd like to know young Ben's doing some crosswords for the London magazine that commissioned mine, on your recommendation, of course. How's your RAF son? Promoted to instructor was the last Stan heard. So, more or less out of it, I suppose?'

Professor Smythe's face changed, just a fraction. 'Sadly, the dear boy went back to flying sorties and failed to return. We wait for news, or rather, I wait for news, as his mother is, also sadly, no longer of this earth.'

There was silence between them, and Davey flushed. 'Oh, I'm so—'

Fran reached forward and gripped the professor's hand. 'You wait, he could well be found in a prisoner-of-war camp. You just wait, d'you hear me?' Her voice was low but fierce.

While the music flowed and the dancers swirled, Professor Smythe covered her hand with his own and nodded, for a moment appearing unable to speak.

Ralph noticed his father beckoning him over to the buffet table, where he was chatting to Annie Hall, who had just filled another plate with sandwiches. As Ralph reached them, Annie nodded at the coat over Ralph's arm. 'Glad to see you being sensible, lad, and heading home. Don't you keep him long, Mr Massingham, he needs his rest. You nearly lost him, but you know that.' She headed towards a different table.

'So, Ralph, we've had our orders,' his father winked, adding, 'Nice to see our Stan and Sarah married. Heartfelt service, eh?'

'Yes, yes, of course it was. Well, it would be with those two.' Ralph paused. 'But, Father, I need a word later this evening, if it's convenient?'

Reginald Massingham studied his son, then nodded. 'Yes, that would be good. Auberon Smythe has apprised me of your brief discussion outside the church, dearest Ralph.'

That was all, but 'dearest Ralph' was too kind.

Ralph walked back, skirting Smythe, who was in earnest conversation with Davey. Fran stood listening. Ralph shrugged himself into his coat and reached for the door, but paused, listening to the warmth of the music and laughter. He spun round for a last look, almost knocking into Fran, who had moved away from her fiancé and was looking at nothing – or perhaps at all the horror that consumed her – her face drawn and strained. Ralph stepped nearer.

'The cries are a manifestation of a sense of guilt, Fran,' he whispered. 'You mustn't go down that path. I heard your mother, you see, in my sickroom. You did all you could. You might think you didn't, but you did. You tried, but it was too late. Frances Hall, the dead don't want your sorrow, your guilt. They want you to live – for them. It was an accident. You tried to stop it. That's what's important. So face it, look back at it, see the truth, then give yourself permission to move forward.'

He turned and stepped towards Smythe, interrupting his chat with Davey. 'Yes, do telephone me tomorrow, Professor. Does three o clock, after the fore shift, sound a good idea? Always good to chat about whether to return to finish my degree one day.'

Smythe hadn't suggested three, but it felt good to take back a bit of control when Ralph's life had been spiralling out of it for far too long.

The professor held out his hand and shook Ralph's. 'I will,' he said, his eyes searching Ralph's as if hoping to see a decision. Against his palm, Ralph felt a slip of paper. 'The number to telephone.'

Ralph pocketed it and slipped from the hall, still fearful that he could never be one of Swinton's people, when he so abhorred the mere thought of it, of them, of himself. Even as he dragged on his gloves and pulled up his collar against the biting wind, he knew he should – but if Tim Swinton suspected he was in opposition, he would kill Ralph's family. It was what he had promised would be the fate of any turncoat when Ralph was recruited into Tim's wartime group – though who his fellow members were, God knew, such was the code of secrecy.

He hesitated on the path, for Davey had interrupted just as he was about to request the family's protection. Should he return? He shook his head at his expectation that others would sort out his problems, and walked on, deciding he'd just have to arrange a codicil to his Will paying for someone who would. So, there it was, done and dusted. All that was left was to do his duty to his country. After all, what did it matter what happened to him after that? Smythe and his merry men could hang him from the rafters, for it was what he deserved.

He walked on to Main Street, heading for home. The early evening gloom gave just enough light. The sounds of the pit workings carried on the wind, and nearer Massingham Hall he would be able to hear the owls in full voice. As he neared the phone box he heard the telephone ringing. He hesitated, chilled, fearing it would be Tim Swinton. Had someone been watching him? Was one of Tim's group a wedding guest? He breathed deeply and hoped that it was a prearranged call from someone's son or daughter. He looked around. No one was waiting, but there was someone just turning into a back lane. Who? The ringing continued.

He stood for a moment longer. It could be Tim, for this was one of their contact telephones, but contact was usually by arrangement. Again he looked around. No one was hurrying to take the call. He hesitated. What would happen if he left it for someone else to pick up and it was that bugger? Would Tim just put the receiver down? Or did he always know where Ralph was? Had he eyes everywhere? He waited another couple of rings, and still no one else came. He swallowed, braced himself and pulled open the door. He reached for the receiver. 'Hello?'

'Well, Ralphy . . .' It *was* Tim Swinton. 'How was the wedding tea?'

Ralph broke into a cold sweat, but managed to answer. 'How do you think? It's just one of those things the Massinghams have to do. I'm still not quite well. Well, not nearly well, in fact, so I'm on my way home.'

'Yes, so I gather. Amazing that Fran Hall can still work at the Factory with that strapping on her arm.'

Ralph sighed. 'Tough people, the Halls.' Thinking – who the hell was reporting?

'And a lift back from St Oswald's with that doddery old fool Smythe, eh? So, long time, no speak. How are you after that nasty bout of septicaemia?'

Ralph sighed a second time. 'As I said, Tim, not too good.

A bit knife edge, in fact. I caught my side on the broken fence around the Factory when I attempted the break-in. I rubbed coal in it when I was shoving a tub to the main seam, to disguise it as a pit injury. It went septic.'

'Devious sod, aren't you? So, Ralphy, we'll make something of you yet, for you know the penalty if you backslide.'

'Why would I do that? I'm on the surface on the fore shift tomorrow, which I should be able to manage, and will keep my ears open.'

'Yes, I heard that, so eyes as well as ears, eh,' Tim said. 'As always, I need information, any snippets, especially from the old dears who nursed you, or your delightful parents with their army of evacuees, the Factory girls, and anything swirling around the pit. Any news from anyone at all, because what seems trivial to you might mean something to me. Beth's naval husband arrived, for instance. Based where?'

Ralph stared out at the moonlit street. Along the road was the bus stop where Bert picked up the Factory girls for their shifts. 'Lord knows. No one talks about these things, you know . . .' Of course Tim knew that, but he also knew that somehow information seeped from some people. Look at that Amelia, blabbing after a drink or two about the perimeter fence being down around the munitions factory. Yes, she had been useful, but he just hadn't been able to subject himself to her any more. Or was it she who had given him up? He rubbed his forehead. He couldn't remember clearly.

Tim's voice was sharp. 'I know no one's supposed to talk, but you and I know they do. Surely the wife said something?'

'Wife?'

'For goodness' sake, Ralph – Beth.'

Ralph's mind raced, looking for an answer that meant nothing. 'All I know is Bob has to return tonight.'

'Now, the surname is Jones, isn't it? Beth Smith became Beth Jones, so hubby is Robert Jones. You see, that's the sort of information that can be useful if we ever find out where and what his ship is. So, stay on that, and anything like that. Remember, we're not working alone, Ralph. What might be useless to us won't be to others. Sharpen up, eh.'

Ralph knew damned well that Bob's ship was a minesweeper, but that was for him to know and not for Tim to find out – not from him, at least.

'The Bedley boy is back for the wedding. What's he up to these days?'

'Again, I don't know.' Of course he knew.

'Then find out.'

'I'll keep my ears open.' But not for you. He would report to Smythe that there were 'others' interested in information, and that questions had been asked about Bob Jones. But perhaps this was a chance to glean more.

'So, you run another cell, do you?' he asked.

Tim snapped. '*You* don't ask the questions. You just do as you're damned well told.'

Ralph knew he'd gone too far. There was movement outside and he peered through the taped glass. But it was only a dog sniffing at the snow in the gutter.

Tim spoke again. 'Just listen. The priority is the Factory. We need to slow down supplies to the troops. I know the perimeter fence is up again, so it might be worth resurrecting your flirtation with Amelia. She seemed to be a fount of information, and could find out about the transportation of munitions from the Factory.' Ralph's heart sank. 'But,' Tim went on, 'any girl will do. A few drinks, flattery, get them talking when they're in their cups. The Factory is unfinished business, Ralph. One pathetic attempt to damage it isn't enough, it really isn't.'

Ralph closed his eyes, keeping his voice level. 'All right,

Teacher. I will try to do better. It's just that I've been out of action.'

Tim said nothing.

'Hello, hello?' Ralph said.

'Don't just try,' muttered Tim, '*do* better. So, I'm pleased to hear that you are being pleasant to people, which is a good move. It'll get them onside, make them relax. They might not share information with you, but you could over-hear it. Don't forget, I have ears on the ground and will know if you slouch on the job. Information, information, information.'

There was a click as the line went dead. Ralph replaced the receiver. He pushed open the door and jumped as an old lady said, 'Thank you. Got to ring my daughter. If I don't, she worries, but nice to have someone who cares, eh?'

Ralph looked hard at her, examining her words. Was she who she said she was?

He forced a smile. 'It is, really it is, good to have someone who cares.' He could hear his father saying 'dearest Ralph'.

He walked off along Main Street, thankful for the moonlight, though he'd know his way to Massingham Hall blindfold, after all he had been coming and going there all his life. He carried on, turning off for the road to the Hall, thinking of Tim and how that beggar's father, a fore-man at the Factory, would curl up and die if he knew who his son really was, just as Ralph had thought his own father would. He stopped. Perhaps his father didn't know it all, just thought he did. How much had Smythe actually told him?

Well, his father would know soon enough, and would also know that Ralph was Smythe's newest recruit.

His legs still felt weak, so the walk home seemed long. He headed along between the drystone walls, hearing Massingham Home Farm's sheep on either side, and the lowing of the cattle higher up the slope. Farmer Thompkins was a good tenant who was pleased that his lad was working with him and not in the pit. Who could blame him? Ralph slid on a patch of ice, but steadied himself, keeping to the centre of the road. With fuel rationed, there was little chance of traffic.

On he went as the wind grew fierce, and he wished it was behind him, not fighting him every step of the way. Finally, he turned into the Massingham Hall drive, and ploughed on, head down, his homburg pulled low, his collar up. 'Nearly there, nearly there,' he kept repeating until he crossed in front of the porticoed house, passed under the arch into the cobbled garage yard and went down the steps to the basement kitchen. He found the key on the hook, then, making sure the blinds were drawn, switched on the light before hurrying to the range to warm himself. Home. He was home.

He hurried up the stairs to the sitting room, lighting the fire for the evening, then into the study, but the fire there was banked up from this morning. He went up the next flight of stairs to the first floor, lighting the fires in the children's bedrooms, where they slept two to a room, except the second of the girls' rooms, in which there were three beds. Five girls and six boys, although the girls were more than a match for the boys, especially little Eva, who could rule the world. He grinned, for ruling the world made him think of the three, no, four Factory girls, Fran, Sarah, Beth and Viola, not to mention the co-op. So was it any wonder these children were as feisty, for they were all from the same stock, Geordies one and all.

In each room, their pyjamas – sewn by the co-op and Sophia – were folded on the ends of the beds. In each room he drew back the bedclothes to get some warmth to the sheets, then went on to his parents' room, where he did the same. For they *were* his parents, and Sophia was his mother, though he had never in the past accorded her that right: Sophia had been his nanny, the woman who had married his father and taken his dead mother's place like a cuckoo – or so he'd felt. How stupid, how self-pitying, for it was Sophia's arms that had hugged him goodnight while his mother had merely presented her cheek to receive a kiss, for to do more would disturb her clothes and hair. Of course, that was only between her jaunts abroad, which had been varied and often. But at least she had left him an inheritance.

He stopped then, looking down at his parents' fireplace, making sure the guard was firmly in place, as he had done in all the rooms. He knew the old Ralph would never have considered it his place to light a fire for anyone.

Finally, he settled on the sofa in the sitting room, waiting for Sophia, his father and the children to return, which they did as the clock moved on to 10 p.m., all of them bundling into the hall, the children talking nineteen to the dozen. Ralph went to the door, watching, wanting to feel the energy, the life, to be part of it. 'Everyone have a good time?' he asked.

Eva spun round. 'Bliddy marvellous, Mr Ralph. I had a bit of bird in me sandwich, a peasant someone said.'

Abraham pulled her pigtails. 'Pheasant, Eva. Peasant's a person. Best not to eat people, less'n you're a cannibal. Makes you burp.'

Eva pulled a face. 'Leave me plaits alone, and stop being a know-all, Abe.'

Abraham just laughed and Tommy said, 'Well, he's clever. Boys are.'

Melanie pushed Eva. 'Hit him, Eva.'

'You and whose army?' jeered Marty.

Sophia was shooing them to the stairs. 'That's quite

enough of that. Anyone would think you'd all been at the wine.'

Suddenly the children fell quiet, and Ralph looked across to his father, who was removing his gloves, and placing them in the drawer of the hall side table. His father grinned and raised his eyebrows, acting out lifting a glass to his lips. Ralph laughed quietly.

Sophia turned. 'Do not in any way, shape or form think this is amusing, you two. Go back to the warmth, Ralph. You shouldn't have walked all the way. I should have asked Alfie—'

Reginald Massingham interrupted. 'It was I who should have driven him, but I was rather taken up with the co-operative's discussions on how many more proggy rug hangings Briddlestone's might want, and whether the general, Annie Hall, could negotiate an increase in the price. Such businesswomen – so sharp they could cut us all into strips and put us in their rugs.'

Ralph grinned, thinking of the co-op and their no-nonsense attitude when they had given him bed baths to cool his fever. The first time, Beth's mother had yanked down the sheet after he'd clutched it to his chin, saying, 'Divint be daft, young man. I've seen it all before a million times. And let me tell you, there's nowt special down there.'

Even now it made him laugh, just as he had laughed then. Mrs Smith had hummed as she washed him, while Mrs Hall came along after, drying. Mrs Bedley, not to be left out, had ordered, 'Turn over.' He had submitted and turned, thinking of England, as the joke said.

He realised then that his father was pointing to his study. Ralph followed, and now he wished he'd had more than just a measly sip of elderberry wine, for his heart was beating too fast, sweat was rolling down his back and his hands were trembling. He filled his mind with trivia, telling himself he should have taken the poker to the banked-up fire after all, and at least added a lump or two of coal.

'Sit yourself down, Ralph.' His father was leaning back in his armchair to the left of the fireplace. 'So kind of you to light the sitting-room fire. Did you manage to do the same in the children's rooms?'

Ralph lowered himself into the opposite armchair. 'Oh yes, and yours. The fireguards are up.' He could feel the beating of his heart right up to his ears now, because here they both were, and he had to tell his father that he was a traitor. A traitor to whom Professor Smythe had offered restitution. His father had said he knew, but how could he know it all?

His father's cigar ash was more than an inch long and seemed about to fall, but just in time Reginald tapped it into the ashtray balanced on the arm of his chair, saying, 'I drove the little blighters home with my cigar newly lit and they coughed all the way, just to make the point that it wasn't to their liking.'

It was so unexpected that Ralph burst out laughing, and it broke the fear, because his father was saying now, 'I suppose you don't remember how you used to be the same. Sometimes I'd sit you on my knee and you'd steer the old Rolls-Royce down the drive. You hated the smell of the cigar smoke, so one day I didn't light it and as we reached the bottom of the slope you said, "Daddy, I do after all like it when you smoke. The smell is safety." Perhaps one day the evacuees will think the same. Some are rather like you, Ralph. Melanie, Eva and Marty are without parents, and two others without a mother. The bombing, of course – it brought down their terraced houses. They were all pulled out – well, obviously – whereupon the rescue team called, "Who claims these bairns?" Answer came there none.'

32

He inhaled, withdrew his cigar and looked at the glowing tip. 'I understand that you felt abandoned when your mother died and I married Sophia. I am so sorry, because into the vacuum of abandonment crept other things, and it was I who created that vacuum. I should have been here for you more often, not away on business. I should have convinced your mother to remain in Massingham more often. I should have waited longer before marrying Sophia. So many things I did, and others I did not do. So many things you have done that you should not have done. If for no other reason than that, I understand, and my dearest boy, I am here to help you.'

It was the banked-up fire his father looked at, its ash, its grey embers, as he continued: 'It's most extraordinary, isn't it, Ralph, how one can bank up a fire in the late morning and yet here we are, ten o'clock at night, still feeling a vestige of heat. I wonder . . .' He placed his cigar in the ashtray, reached forward, took up the poker and, with deft sure strokes, pierced the embers and ash to create air holes.

He propped the poker against the coal scuttle, then picked up the bellows and gently squeezed, once, then twice. Slowly the embers brightened. 'There,' he said, 'you see. It appeared dead, but in reality the embers, when helped, came back to life.'

He looked at Ralph. 'A bit like people. They can be subsumed by something that ultimately renders them grey and defeated. They just need help to allow them to live and thrive again.'

They looked at one another and after a long moment Ralph whispered, 'You really know it all, don't you?'

His father nodded. 'As much as you have told Auberon. Is there more?'

Ralph told him all of it. The lies about the British Union of Fascists uniform that his father had found hanging in

Ralph's wardrobe just before returning to school. He had said he was keeping it for someone else and would return it. Now he explained it had been his. While Reginald absorbed this news, Ralph wondered what he'd—Then he remembered exactly what he'd done with it – hidden it with a load of stuff he'd outgrown in a trunk in the attic. But who'd look? Surely no one. He'd sort it out, after he'd spoken to his father. No, that wasn't right, for what could he do with it at night? He'd have to do it tomorrow instead, bring himself to touch it, take it out without anyone seeing, and turn it into ashes.

Ralph came back to the present with a start as his father said, 'Carry on.' He was adding kindling and coal, so that the flames leapt and curled. On and on, Ralph talked – of Tim Swinton, once a lad from the backstreets of Sledgeford, but now in charge of a Fascist cell, and also in charge of Ralph Massingham.

His father's grip tightened on his cigar, which he had been about to lift to his mouth.

Ralph continued describing his act of sabotage that had killed Fran and Sarah's fathers. Reginald merely nodded. Ah, so he knew. Ralph drove on, and ended with the deliberately failed attempt to break into the munitions complex, and the sadness he had felt when Mr Swinton had asked at the wedding if he knew where his son was and he had lied and said no.

'But of course it wasn't quite a lie, for I don't know where he is, but I do know *what* he is. But how could I tell Mr Swinton that?' Ralph drew out a packet of Player's, offering them to his father, who declined, waving his cigar at him. Ralph lit one for himself, blowing the smoke up towards the ceiling, but, smelling the cigar realised it was indeed the scent of safety.

'There you are, Father. You have a traitor for a son, and

Professor Smythe has offered me a chance to make some of it right, but only some, for I have the deaths of two good men to bear. For a while I was scared that I couldn't pretend, couldn't carry on with Tim as though I don't hate myself, and him, and the whole damnable ideology.'

His father was still staring at the fire and Ralph, too, watched the flames as they licked the coal. He added a few more lumps, replaced the tongs and resumed his seat. Together they watched the coal as it eventually glowed redhot. Ralph said, 'Daddy, you didn't fail me. I failed myself. I was all that was wrong in a son, and I am most heartily sorry.'

His father threw his cigar onto the fire. 'No, you are my son. I love you, Sophia loves you. You have been misguided. But I should have realised when I found that damned uniform. You were a boy, and boys do stupid things. There were Communist meetings too, and many went to both to see what was what. Such a shame you didn't—'

He stopped, shook his head. 'No, we must draw a line and it must be put right, but only you can do that, though I will be there beside you all the way, Ralph.' He paused. 'Sophia will know nothing of this.' It was not a question, but a command.

Ralph nodded, unable to speak, because he was not alone, though he deserved to be. No, his father was with him. He threw the remains of his cigarette into the fire, as the gulping sobs came. He heard the door open, but his father said softly, 'Not now, my dear.' The door closed again and then Ralph heard his father rise and felt his arm around his shoulders as Reginald sat on the arm of the chair. Ralph leaned into him, and his father said, 'Hush, my lad, hush, I'm here.'

Eventually, Ralph dragged his handkerchief from his pocket and wiped his face, still leaning against the rock that was his father. 'I need to make a phone call, Father. I'll just have to be good enough.'

He stood, told his father the details of Tim's telephone call to the box on Main Street, then made his way to the desk, drawing from his trouser pocket Auberon's telephone number. His father said, 'Auberon is in Newcastle and will be with us tomorrow morning. Albright has been told you are on urgent Massingham business and will report on Tuesday. When you telephone Smythe, best you tell him that "Barkis is willin'." That's all, just in case others are listening. I do so enjoy Dickens, don't you?'

Chapter Three

Monday, 2 March

Sarah stirred in her mam's front room, now a bedroom, and whispered, 'Sarah Hall, née Bedley.' She smiled, reached up and ran a finger down Stan's face. He woke, gripped her hand, kissed her palm. 'I love you, pet, more than I did yesterday, but not as much as I will tomorrow.'

She kissed his mouth. The sheet fell from her, and he held her to him. She ran her hands over his blue-ridged hewer's scars and breathed in the scent of his skin. 'I can hardly believe we're really man and wife,' she murmured, remembering the night, the passion, the sense of really coming home. Aye, she thought, well, she was doubly home, here in the front room of her mam's house, with her husband who made her feel safe as houses.

She had expected it to feel strange, being downstairs, with him, but it wasn't because her life was so glorious, Stan was so wonderful, and . . .

They kissed. The knock on the door startled them. Her mother called, 'No rest for the wicked, 'tis three thirty in the morning, there's a working day ahead of you and if you divint get a wriggle on, you'll be late for the bus, pet. And I reckon Bert's sore head will make him worse'n a bear, and Mrs Oborne won't be any better. I'm keeping Viola here with me, for she's not up to the sewing room, no matter what the Labour Exchange people said when the co-op went to complain. War is war, they said, but needed a good

37

slap for them words. So, no, she's not going in, and that's that.'

'Right, Mam, be there in a minute.'

Stan was kissing her neck, but she threw off the bed-clothes, dragging herself from him. It was still dark and for that she was relieved, for she might love him, might have lain with him, but him seeing her naked was just . . . There was another rat-a-tat on the door. It was Viola.

'Whatever your mam said, I'm up and coming to work. 'Tisn't fair on Mr Swinton, who's expecting me, and any-way, he saw me playing the saxophone in the service and even if it were far from perfect because I'm missing a couple of fingers on one hand, I reckon me mam would have said, "If you can do that, you can get into work, bonny lass." Besides, I need the money. I can't live here for free.'

Sarah gripped Stan's arm. 'She can't go in.'

He was reaching for his work kegs. 'Best let her make up her own mind, pet. It's what you would do, and don't even think of telling me you wouldn't, or I'll have to deal with you.' He was laughing as he reached for her.

She stood, dodging his arms, and whispered, 'Oh no you don't, or we'll end up in mischief, so we will.'

Viola and Sarah ran along the back lane of the terrace, Viola pulling her woolly hat over her hair, Sarah tying her head-scarf, though why she bothered she didn't know, as strands were already escaping. But when didn't they? They had to dodge the groups of pitmen clomping in their boots towards Auld Hilda, and as she ran, Sarah looked over her shoulder and saw her man in the moonlight, her husband, her Stan, leaning against the Bedleys' back wall, Woodbine in his mouth, his cap tilting to the left, waiting for Sid and Norm to come along. He waved to her and shouted above the chatting and coughing of the pitmen, 'Be safe, bonny lass, and you an' all, Viola.'

Sarah stopped, turned, and walked backwards for a few paces. 'Be safe, lovely lad.' She spun round and ran on, for she could hear Bert tooting, and then Auld Hilda's hooter drowned out all else. It was as it ever was, even though *she* was different, for she had been with her husband for the first time. The word 'husband' echoed in her head as the two of them slowed, turned into Main Street and saw Fran and Beth loitering, watching for them.

Viola laughed. 'Come on.'

All four broke into a run and tore towards the bus stop and the queue that was fast disappearing inside the idling bus. Fran panted as they arrived, 'Howay, girls, get a move on, for it's all aboard the Factory charabanc with its laughing joking driver.'

Mrs Oborne stopped, one foot on the bus, the other on the pavement, her headscarf tied round her grey hair. She grimaced. 'No shouting's the first order of the day, our Fran, and it's all your fault, Mrs Sarah Hall, for getting wed yesterday and putting on a good spread, then forcing that Stevie's beer and elderberry wine down our throats.'

Bert's voice boomed from his cab, 'Get your big arse on this bus, Tilly Oborne, and shut your noise, or you are walking to work, missus. Me head's known better days.'

Beth was shrieking with laughter. 'Serves you right, our Bert. A right load of beer went down your throat and I divint see no forcing involved.'

'Aye, well,' shouted Bert, 'one more word and you're another who'll be walking.'

As they waited, all Sarah could think of was being called Mrs Hall. She played it through her mind – Mrs Sarah Hall, Mr and Mrs Stanhope Hall – and already it seemed more natural than Bedley. Would it be the same for Fran when she became a Bedley?

Bert hooted again. 'On you get, girls, quick, quick.'

But Sid and Norm were running towards them, looking pale and sweaty even in the moonlight. They slowed, finally stopping when they reached them, Sid bending over, his hands on his knees, coughing. He groaned. 'You and our Davey had better break my arms if you see me pouring Stevie's special brew down my throat at your nuptials, our Fran, for I'm not going through this hangover again.'

Norm tipped his cap. 'Me an' all, but I reckon we might drag your Stan out to the club tonight – what d'you think of that, Mrs Hall? Hair of the dog, eh?'

The lads set off at a run again.

It was Sarah laughing now as she called after them, 'I'll be waiting with a rolling pin, you see if I won't.'

Bert was revving the bus as Fran yanked Sarah up the steps and dragged her down the aisle, to the cheers and claps of the women as they drove off. Mrs Oborne shouted, 'You got that tyre sorted, Bert? Davey said it were bald, but then so are you at the back, so I reckon you'll like the company.'

'One more word,' yelled Bert, 'I promise you, one more word, Tilly Oborne, and out you go. And aye, the depot is getting one sorted today. Just need to go steady and miss any ice in the meantime. That suit you? And while we're about it, leave me hair out of it.'

Tilly Oborne blew a raspberry, then said, 'That'll do nicely, Bert. I like to know I'm safe.'

She conducted while the girls all laughed and called out, 'Then best get off the bus now.'

Viola, Sarah and Fran followed Beth to the back seat. Once there, the other passengers called, 'A grand wedding tea, lass.'

'I had a couple of pheasant sandwiches, and too many elderberry wines.'

'Lovely scones and all. Spread with honey, eh?'

Maisie stood, looking towards the back seat. 'Shame you'll be back too late to wash his back in the tin bath, Sarah.'

Sarah blushed, but whispered to Fran, 'Aye, it is too.'

It was Fran's turn to blush as she whispered, 'Oh, our Sarah, what in the world's come over little old you.' She put up her hand. 'No, on second thoughts, don't tell me, please, please.' This was followed by more laughter from the bus.

At last they left Massingham and sank back, relaxing. As they passed the Hanging Tree, Sarah said, 'Shouldn't have run with our bruises. Hurts like a right pig, it does. But Viola, it's worse for you. Are you all right?'

Viola nodded. 'Course I am, I'm with you all, and I'm only in the sewing section, so that's canny.'

'No, it isn't,' muttered Fran. 'You'll come back off shift with that bandage seeping blood again from guiding the material. We need to find you something else, something outside the Factory, and ignore the Labour Exchange.'

The others nodded while Viola covered her damaged hand with her other one and shook her head. 'Stop fussing, for there are no chemicals to get into it, and in time . . .' She drifted to a stop.

Bert was driving along lanes overhung with sycamores struggling to produce buds, and in the fields the snow had almost disappeared, with just the shady areas harbouring remnants. The verges beneath the sycamores were dotted with dirt-stained clumps, and ice still coated the pools of water lying on the road.

Sarah stared out at the snowdrops huddled in the lee of some of the stone walls. 'Spring's on its way, girls, and if in a few days that hand doesn't start healing proper, Viola, we'll have something to say, and the mams'll too.

The Labour Exchange had better batten down the hatches, for they'll be stormed, right, girls?' The other two nodded, along with Mrs Oborne.

Sarah turned to Fran. 'Me bum's getting numb from all the jolting on these slats, and my ribs are getting a workout, too, but I haven't heard you complaining yet. What's the matter with you? Cat got your tongue?' She whipped off her headscarf and her short blonde hair flew about in the draught from an open window above Maisie's seat.

'I just wish me head was numb too,' Fran replied. She called down the bus, 'Shut your window, Maisie, for the love of Mike. That draught's cutting into my hangover like no one's business.'

'It's broken,' Maisie yelled back, 'and I canna, that's why I've got my muffler up over my head, not because I think it's a good look. Isn't that right, our Sandra?'

Sandra Young, who was sitting next to her, groaned. 'Just stop your shouting. Me head's about to explode.'

Just then, Bert called down the bus, 'While I remember, you three – or should it be four, with Viola? Anyway, it's The Factory Girls singers I want—' The girls heard this much, but the noise from the others escalated and drowned the rest. Bert sounded the horn, twice, and yelled, 'A bit of hush, if you don't mind.'

The women fell silent until Mrs Oborne called, 'Out with it then, our Bert, and we don't take kindly to you hooting when we've heads fit to burst. Bliddy Stevie and his elderberry wine.'

Bert steered the bus carefully around the long uphill bend before Sledgeford. Over to the right the Sledgeford slag heap stood guardian, and near it was the pithead with the cages working, bringing up coal and taking down miners. 'Aye, well, it's the lad Stevie himself I'm on about. He needs the lasses to sing for him at the Rising Sun on March fourteenth. Not a lot of notice, but he says it came to him at the wedding that it were time for another sing-song. Let me know on your way out, our Franny, if you and the lasses can do it. And don't you go getting left out, Viola.'

The girls on the back seat listened with glee. Viola opened and shut her hand, wincing.

Fran whispered, 'It would help the three of us to have a bit more money to pay the bills, but you don't need it for that, Viola, because you can stay at Sarah's or mine, or Beth's, for free, just like you're doing now. If you want to come, just sing – divint tax your hand.'

Mrs Oborne butted in, swinging round in her seat: 'Or, do a bit of singing, bit of playing?'

Beth leaned forward, smiling past Fran and Sarah to Viola, who nodded. 'She says yes,' said Beth, 'so you give Bert that answer, Fran. Don't want "you know who" snapping it up if we dither.'

Mrs Oborne, who had ears like a bat, stood and shouted, 'Aye, that's a yes, Bert. Viola'll do a bit of both, so that's all four.' Looking about the bus, she added, 'Howay, we're coming into Sledgeford, so if that Amelia gets on, keep quiet about it, everyone. You know how canny she is and'll grab the booking for herself and her group, given half a chance.'

Bert shouted, 'Took them words right out of my mouth, Tilly Oborne. Why d'you think I said it afore we got here? So, keep your traps shut, and I'll let Stevie know.' He was reducing speed as he approached the bus stop.

Talk began again as Fran called, 'Why would she be on the bus? She's nine to five, for heaven's sake.'

No one replied, for Bert had stopped outside the Miners' Club, where there was now a bus shelter, built by the women's menfolk. The girls and women piled on, their noses red from the cold, contrasting with the yellow of their skin. Yawning, they slumped onto the slatted wooden seats.

The four girls watched their friend Valerie make her way down the bus, raising her eyebrows at Mrs Oborne and grimacing. Then they saw why. Amelia Cartwright from the Factory office was following along behind. There she was, the girl who had been going out with Ralph Massingham until recently. The girl whose mission in life seemed to be to get up everyone's noses, with the three, now four, Factory Girls her particular target.

Valerie, in whose house Amelia lodged, ducked into an aisle seat in front of Mrs Oborne, while Amelia headed nearer to the back. Brenda and Rosie, part of Amelia's singing trio, followed.

'But why?' whispered Sarah. 'Their villages are on a different bus route.'

Mrs Seaton, who was sitting in front of Fran, turned. 'Them two started lodging in Sledgeford while you and Sarah were in Scotland – don't you remember, Beth? Something about it being on a shorter bus route. Them three'll be in early to smarm up to Brown, the office boss, or do overtime, I reckon. Whatever it is, it'll be something to benefit themselves.'

The three girls had not been invited to the wedding because by no stretch of the imagination could any of them be considered the Factory Girls' friends, not after snaffling a New Year's Eve booking at the Rising Sun whilst the girls had to remain on shift to get up to target when a conveyor belt broke. Amelia had refused to step in and had instead taken the booking with Brenda and Rosie. Fran pushed it from her mind and concentrated on Bert as they approached the bridge over Cod Beck, the drovers' bridge that was very narrow.

She listened now, everyone did, and as always she heard Bert's voice: 'Don't you bliddy take my wing mirrors, don't you bliddy dare.'

It was as though hands were going to come out and grab them. Up and over they went, and were soon roaring along between high hedges, scattering the nesting birds.

Beth explained to Viola: 'That Amelia sent an anonymous note to Davey's mam to forward on to him, accusing Fran of messing about with Ralph, all because The Factory Girls were chosen to sing when *Workers' Playtime* were broadcast from the Factory.'

Viola looked suitably shocked and there was some satisfaction in that, Fran found, but didn't want to think of it, or feel the missing of Davey, so settled back, her head worse, if that was possible. She wished she had only had one glass of wine, but she had been so happy to be with Davey that she'd drunk without noticing. She wondered how he was, because he had sunk far too many beers before taking the night train down south, and would probably go straight into work when he arrived at Bletchley Park. She hoped he'd slept, for he needed his brain sharp for decoding the Nazi messages.

As the bus travelled on, Fran listened to the singing, the chatting and the laughter and joined in, but only superficially, for now she was remembering the cries beneath the rubble that had, as usual, woken her throughout the night. She pushed them from her as she thought of Ralph, and how he'd seemed to understand. She hoped he was right, that the dead didn't want her sorrow or guilt and that all she could do was to go on. But it was easier said than done. She closed her eyes, but within seconds opened them again, for in that darkness the cries had grown louder.

She looked out of the window, up at the big sky, at the slag heaps dotting the landscape, the pitheads, the farms they passed, and the hamlets and pit villages, the smoke from the chimneys of the terraced houses, the skylarks lifting from the fields, the sheep . . .

She shook her head, then stopped because it felt as though her brain was actually throbbing. Water, she must have some water. If it helped to sluice the chemicals, it would do the same to the wine. She felt for the glass bottle in her bag, nestling there with her gas mask. As always, that made her tut – a gas mask when they worked with explosives? It was daft. She replaced the bottle, noticing the other three taking sips from theirs too.

They smiled at one another, drifting, chatting and listening until at last they neared the Factory. Fran snatched a look at her watch – five twenty. Perhaps she'd slept, for the last half of the journey had just disappeared, but surely not – there had been no dreams, or cries, and what's more, she felt rested. Beth leaned towards her. 'You were snoring, bonny lass, and dribbling.'

Fran gasped and wiped her chin. Sarah called, 'Don't be so daft, Franny, course you weren't. Well, not dribbling, but the snoring would wake the d—' She stopped as Beth poked her, frowning. Sarah began again. 'Aye, you were snoring, but not a dribble in sight, thank the Lord, or we'd have to get Mrs Oborne to cut out and sew a bib for you, not a wedding dress.'

Fran, who had not sweated or shaken at the word 'dead', which was what Sarah had been about to say, allowed herself to begin to thank Ralph. For even if his niceness wasn't as real as it seemed, she had indeed slept without dreaming for the first time since it had happened. He had said to face it, but no, not today, not yet, because it might just be the hangover that had made her sleep. Just that.

She stared out of the window at the scenery, which looked as though it was rushing by when it was actually they who were doing that. Things sometimes weren't as they seemed.

But actually, now she came to think of it, the bus wasn't rushing either, for Bert was driving cautiously. She snatched another look out of the window. Again, she thought of Ralph, his eyes so intense, his voice so urgent. His understanding was so surprising that perhaps she should look back as he had said. Fran was gripping her hands together, the yellow skin stretched across her knuckles, and she made herself breathe in for four and out for four, and again. She repeated the two times table to calm herself. Finally, she made herself think about the workshop.

There she was again, walking in front of the workbench, the girls, the machines, a man, elderly with dark hair, rather thin. Where had the security officer gone? Oh yes, he was the elderly man, just behind the new girl. She, Fran Hall, was heading for her own workstation, but now someone spoke, called out. Who? She had, she realised. She had seen the glint, looked again – seconds it was, only seconds – because she was shouting. Yes, she had shouted, just seconds after seeing the glint. Then it fell, then darkness.

She blinked, her hands were still clenched in her lap, on the bus, but her knuckles weren't as white. She looked out of the window. She had seen it, heard it, and she hadn't been quite in time, but almost. And she *had* tried. Yes, Ralph was right. She really *had* tried and she must cling to that truth, just as it was true that it was the bus passing the scenery, not the scenery on the move. Would she remember, though? she wondered, shutting her eyes, feeling her shoulders hunch, but that hurt. She straightened, smiling. Of course she bliddy would, for she would just hunch her shoulders and they and her ribs would remind her. She hunched and rolled her shoulders. And then again, to remind herself. Then looked out of the window. 'There,' she muttered. 'That's really the truth of it.'

'The truth of what, bonny lass?' asked Beth.

Fran laughed now, really laughed. 'Oh, that we're passing the countryside, not the other way round.'

Viola leaned forward. 'Oh aye, Fran, I know what you mean. Beth, remember what you said to Bob about the cake? It weren't real, it was the little one that was, and truth would nudge out the pretence.'

Beth looked puzzled. 'I divint remember, not really, but it sounds bliddy good, as though I have a brain.' They smiled, though their headaches were still just as bad. Beth folded her arms, leaned back and nodded. 'Aye, has there ever been such a happy time, eh? Three of us will be wedded women by this time next month, with only Viola to sort out, eh? And sort her we will, for there's a bloke somewhere who will deserve her, and we'll root him out.'

The four of them looked at one another and nodded. Fran said quietly, 'Aye, a happy time.' She meant it for the first time since the explosion.

Bert pulled into the Factory siding. 'Off you go, ladies. Time for me to take the night shift back, and maybe get me head down, too. Keep your minds on the job – don't want you coming back in little bits. Especially not you, Mrs Stanhope Hall.'

Mrs Oborne sat waiting for everyone to disembark, beckoning the girls to go ahead, but they waved her on because they knew from her grin she was up to something. Up she got, huffing and puffing. Her headscarf had slipped to her shoulders; she yanked it up, and then down the aisle she swept, all thirteen stone of her. She stopped at Bert's cab and cuffed him lightly on the head. 'Keep your mind on your driving, you old fool. No letting your lids droop till you're in safe harbour, and I don't mean Cod Beck with the wing mirrors wrapped round your neck.'

Off she got, roaring with laughter, as was Bert, and the four girls were hysterical too, and the five women hurried towards the guards at the gate. Dawn was beckoning as

Harry Bishop and Barry Evans – 'the unholy twins', as Mrs Oborne called them – checked their passes, then searched their bags in case they were full of sabotage materials, grinning at their bottles of water. 'One day it'll be beer,' Barry guffawed.

Beth groaned, her head throbbing. 'Don't mention alcohol, if you don't very much mind.'

'Or laugh so loud,' ground out Maisie, standing to one side, fumbling in her pocket for the pass she so often mislaid. 'At last,' she muttered as Barry checked it before lifting the pole for them.

'Alcohol?' he queried. 'Oh, aye, I'd forgotten we had a blushing bride with us. Keep your mind on your work, pet, not on your man.'

Sarah smiled weakly and hurried on, whispering to Beth and Fran, 'I do wish people would stop going on. Not only have I a head on me like the rest of you, but me private life's me own.'

Beth grinned. 'Since when is anything private round here?'

They followed Maisie and Mrs Oborne along the wide roadway between the single-storey brick buildings that housed numerous workshops. In these the women filled munitions with explosive chemicals. Over to the left were the semi-underground shell-filling workshops where any explosions would put all others to shame. Had the women in these heard the detonator explosion in their sector a while ago?

In the distance was the storeroom, close to where there had been a thwarted break-in when the fences had come down during a vicious snowstorm. Who the hell had tried to do it?

At the wedding, Bob had asked Beth just that. She had played dumb, for to be heard chattering about such a thing would mean a warning, or worse, the sack. She had said, 'I canna possibly comment.' This was what her da had told her a union official always used to say whenever her da had wanted information about anything.

Bob had just looked at her, and she slowed now as she remembered, because he'd said, 'I suppose a traitor makes a choice, a bit like love. Sometimes people have to choose . . .'

Looking back, she couldn't understand why he'd kept going on about truth, pretence and love. As she headed for their section, Fran slipped her arm through Beth's. 'Penny for them?'

'Keep your money, Fran,' Beth said. 'I'm just thinking about our Bob.'

'Ah, love, eh?'

Beth nodded, and squeezed Fran's arm. Viola and Sarah linked arms in front of them, and they turned left, down a narrower path, while Amelia headed for the office.

Their section, like all the sections, was brick-built with a flat roof. They hurried in through the double doors, down the corridor and into the whitewashed changing room. Here they stepped out of their boots, put on their day shoes and overalls, and took headscarves from their pockets to wind into turbans to keep their hair safe from the machines. But first they must be checked, and listen to the safety and security rules – again. It had become the norm after the detonator explosion to have them read out daily. Within two minutes the foreman, Mr Swinton, and the one-handed senior security officer, Miss Cynthia Ellington, commonly known as Cyn, arrived.

But where was the other security officer? Beth wondered, for there should be two.

Both Swinton and Miss Ellington were pale and clearly also had hangovers. Well, thought Beth, why should they be any different to every other wedding guest? She wondered if

Stan and his marrers were suffering as much as they were, but they were pitmen so should be used to it. Bob had barely drunk at all and she was glad, for otherwise he'd probably have fallen off the back of Tommy's motorbike.

The girls were putting all metal items into their individual boxes and then checking one another. Miss Ellington began to pass amongst them. 'Silk, nylon – anything likely to cause static?'

As always, Maisie groaned. 'Silk? Chance'd be a fine thing.'

Sarah asked, 'Where's Mrs Raydon?'

Mr Swinton heard. 'She's been transferred to another section. We're expecting someone from Head Office any minute. Some sort of investigator, 'tis said. Happens from time to time, when there's been, well, when things have gone awry. He's in this sector to begin with, but'll move on to the others. He's said to be thorough, so let's be on our toes.'

'Oh aye,' whispered Fran to Beth. 'As though we aren't always.'

'Indeed, Miss Hall.' But Mr Swinton's voice was quiet and friendly, which it had been since her da had been killed. He'd even spoken up when Mr Bolton had ordered Sarah and Fran to Scotland, saying to the deputy section manager that it wasn't fair that these two should go so soon after their tragedy. But Bolton had pointed out that Fran and Sarah were by Swinton's own admission his best girls, and that's who had been requested from someone on high. He'd meant Head Office, where many tin gods lived, Miss Ellington muttered later.

At that moment the door opened and a man of about fifty, roughly Mr Swinton's age, entered, his hands bunched in his white overall pockets. Mr Swinton clapped his hands. 'I'll read the rules good and quick, for 'tis already five forty-seven. The first is, we need to keep alert because yesterday was a grand time, but the wedding is over. Work, work and work *safely*, eh? Those working with detonators, remember there will be, as always, no music from the tannoy, no talking, or singing. Elsewhere, yes, you may hum, talk quietly occasionally, but always concentrate.'

The man turned to Mr Swinton and said something. Mr Swinton flushed. 'My lasses are extremely responsible, and there's no need for that, thank you, Mr Gaines.'

Sarah nudged Fran, whispering, 'No need for what?'

Mr Gaines heard and snapped, 'Young woman, I don't approve of workers arriving with headaches, hangovers or any such thing, for we work in danger, and I'm not having flibbertigibbets causing mayhem or worse.'

Mrs Oborne stepped forward. 'And just who are you to say these things, Mr Gaines? Mr Swinton is in charge and there's no one more demanding of safety procedures, or so I'll have you know.'

There was a general shuffling of feet and Beth snatched a quick look round, thinking how extraordinary it was that a few months ago they'd have been cheering Gaines – anything to get back at Swinton for his wretched bossing, which, they had only lately realised, made them efficient and careful workers.

Mr Gaines did not reply, but looked around, his hands still deep in his pockets. The girls all jumped as he suddenly bellowed, 'I am the investigative security officer, that's who I am, and you need to remember your place, my good woman, as do all of you.'

He swivelled to look at Miss Ellington, the workers and then Mr Swinton, whose colour had risen. Gaines then glared at Mrs Oborne.

'Oh dear, bad Mr Gaines,' muttered Beth as Mrs Oborne took a step, her chin thrust out, but Mr Swinton and Miss Ellington also stepped forward, in tandem, their hands up, as though stopping a runaway carthorse. Well, thought Beth, they weren't far wrong.

Miss Ellington began to speak over Mrs Oborne, but it was Mr Swinton whose roar stunned the room. 'Thank you, Miss Ellington. Last time I looked this was *my* section, and it is for me to reply.'

It was now that he bunched *his* hands in his overall pockets and rose on his toes as he always used to when vexed. This time, though, he whipped out his hand and pointed at Mr Gaines. 'You, my good man, might be an investigative security officer from London's Head Office, but I am foreman and responsible for the care of these women, and of the product. Product without which the war will not be won. You can sling yer hook if you are rude to my girls, you hear. I'm not having any more jumped-up arses taking my best workers to some ungodly Scottish site and sending them home hurt. Neither am I having jumped-up arses telling me my bliddy business here, in my own sector. You've got that, have you? For if you haven't, you joyless lump of Head Office namby-pamby, I'll find some written notes and stick them up your bliddy arse.'

There was utter silence. Mr Swinton shoved his hand back into his pocket, Mrs Oborne stepped back, nodding, probably thinking, guessed Beth, that she couldn't have put it better herself. Miss Ellington drew in a deep breath as Mr Gaines's colour changed from brick red to white. She coughed, then said, 'Time for the rules, I think, Mr Swinton. We don't want to keep the night shift waiting for this fore shift to take over.' She nodded at the clock.

Mr Gaines turned on his heel, swishing out, only to be called back by Miss Ellington. 'I think not, Mr Gaines. While the rules are repeated, we will need to continue checking that the lasses have missed nothing that will impinge on their safety. That is our job, even if *one* of us is an investigative security officer and the other is not. What think you?'

Their foreman cleared his throat and ran through the rules, which everyone knew by heart; for safety had become second nature to them all.

'Any coughing, step away from the bench. Felt shoes for the detonator section. No metal, no silk or nylon either, anywhere. Concentration, absolute obedience. We've covered singing and the tannoy. No gossiping around the neighbourhood, no loose talk.' On went Mr Swinton, and at the end they all clapped. Mr Swinton looked surprised, as well he might, but, thought Beth, there was a first time for everything.

Mr Gaines and Miss Ellington continued their search. Mr Gaines had taken the left-hand side of the room, poking his fingers through the girls' hair, checking their legs for nylons.

Mrs Oborne looked down at Mr Gaines as he lifted her hem. 'No touching me pins, mind,' she said. 'Any of that, and you'll get me foot in your face, or your arse, whichever's to hand. If it's your arse it'll be right busy, what with Mr Swinton's notes paying a visit too.'

Gaines straightened, scarlet, his greying hair so short you could see that his scalp had blushed too. 'It's my job,' he said, strutting around everyone, then making for the front of the room.

'Right,' said Mr Swinton, 'these are the stations for today, ladies. Mostly, the same as last week, but Fran, Beth, Sarah – to the pellets. You're sure your strapped arm is up to it, Fran?' Beth groaned at the thought of the sticky chemicals as Fran nodded. Mr Swinton went on. 'Viola, sewing section.'

He was ushering Gaines and Miss Ellington before him into the corridor. The women followed, but headed to their various workshops as Mr Swinton said, 'Mr Gaines, you are going to Mr Bolton's office with Miss Ellington as escort. I want this fracas reported. Once I've set up the shift, I will be along.'

As Sarah and Fran passed the poster calling on them all to Be Like Dad – Keep Mum, they heard Gaines's voice, high-pitched with fury. 'Yes, and we'll find out then, just who is in charge.'

Surely he can't be?' said Fran. 'Not after Mr Swinton has worked so hard, and is now so reasonable?' They looked at Swinton, striding past them. Sarah shook her head. 'It's a madhouse.'

Beth muttered, pulling on her turban, just as the others were doing. 'Pellets and Mr Gaines. What a bliddy start to married life, our Sarah, eh. But it's worth it, just to have heard Mr Swinton, and Mrs Oborne.'

They walked on past the propaganda posters, towards the pellet section. The tannoy was playing music quietly as they headed for the workbenches. Dora raised her eyebrows, sighed and stepped back from the bench. 'By, am I glad to see you. Met our ray of sunshine, Mr bliddy Gaines, have you, with a mouth like a sparrow's bum? He joined yesterday. Jumped-up little squirt. He's been drafted here after the "incidents" to check we're all up to scratch. I reckon we're stuck with the beggar for a while, but not for ever, I hope. Still, it's a living, till we're blown up.'

They laughed as Dora led the night shift out into the corridor, then they stepped up to the workbench, ready to wrap the inch-long fuse pellets designed to charge detonators and send shells and bullets on their way. Beth smiled and whispered, 'Aye, well, she's right, it is a living. Plus, I have Bob's navy allotment, and Stan'll help with his mam and you, Sarah. Fran, you'll soon have Davey's help with your mam and Ben, so as long as we work in the dangerous sections, the expenses are more'n paid.'

Fran whispered in return, 'The singing bookings will build, and the co-op's proggy rugs bring in a bit, so we'll all be right. Then we can all start to put some aside for our das' headstones.'

Sarah leaned forward. 'And your mam's little Betty's, Fran.'

'It Had to Be You' was playing over the tannoy as Mr Swinton handed over to Patrick, the deputy foreman, and removed himself from the workshop. Fran muttered, 'While Viola's in the sewing section she won't be getting as much, but it doesn't matter, for we can all chip in for owt she needs, and at least there's no rent to pay.'

The girls agreed, and on they all worked, pasting the fluted paper pellets. They tried to ignore the chemical mixture coating their fingertips, knowing that by the end of the shift their fingers would be a deep yellow, and that the chemicals would seep deep into their skin, and aggravate the rashes that covered their bodies. But howay, that was part of their lives now.

They pasted another, and another, blessing the mams' sphagnum-moss dressings that soothed and prevented the rashes from becoming septic if they scratched too hard. On the whole, though, they preferred the lavender grease because it smelled good, and helped them sleep. But the key was to keep drinking water whenever they could.

'I can almost feel the rash getting worse,' grumbled Sarah.

'Aye well,' called Maisie, 'your Stan can scratch it for you, but don't let it go to pus. Nowt pretty about pus.'

Beth placed a pasted pellet in the stand on the workbench. 'Aye, well, that's just put me off me dinner – please will everyone stop talking about pus. Bad enough on the bus yesterday, and here we are, at it again.' She looked up at the clock. Seven o'clock, was that all? 'All I can say is it's as well my Bob's busy elsewhere and not about to have a rummage once we get to bed, for it'll make it worse.'

The girls laughed. The Factory Girls' song 'All or Nothing at All' was now playing over the tannoy. Perhaps it would be too much for Viola to play the saxophone, even for a little bit, at Stevie's? What date was it? Beth couldn't remember. As she wrapped the pellet she asked the others.

'It's the fourteenth,' replied Fran, 'which is a Saturday.'

'Aye,' Sarah agreed. 'By, I hope Stan's not on shift. I want him to come.'

Beth wished Bob could be there and hated that he'd had to leave last night. They had stood together by the telephone box, and he'd wanted her to go back to the hall while he waited for Tommy, but she wouldn't. 'Every moment I can be with you, I will,' she'd said.

He'd touched her cheek in the cold. 'Look, Beth, war is difficult. I—' He'd sounded so serious.

She'd kissed him, stopping his words, wanting his arms around her. She'd said against his mouth, 'Aye, I know, you keep saying that, but 'tis the same for everyone. That's why, when we can, I want us to be together.' He'd held her away, looking at her in the darkness. She'd smelled the beer on his breath and the cigarettes.

He'd given her a bit of a shake. 'We'll always do what we can for one another, though, won't we? Everything we've had counts for something, eh?'

'Aye, of course,' she'd said. She could feel the strength of his grasp even now, and tears threatened. She went to wipe her eyes.

Fran shouted: 'Beth. No.'

Gaines was by her side then, his lips thinned, his voice tight. 'Well trained, are you? Wiping your eyes is a classic beginner's mistake. So much for safety procedures.'

Beth knew he was right. 'But Fran warned me,' she said. 'So the safety procedures work. We look after one another, see.' She resumed pasting, feeling the warmth of his breath on the back of her neck because he was standing too close. His nose whistled as he breathed. She hated that and placed the wrapped pellet on the stand, then moved the stand on the conveyor belt. She began a new box of pellets and ignored him, continuing to paste, wishing she'd seen him enter. He moved on. She and Fran looked at one another.

'So, who won in Bolton's office?' murmured Fran.

They looked around. Patrick was walking along Valerie's row, and Gaines was heading to the door. He turned, standing with his back to it, his eyes darting everywhere, but there was no sign of Mr Swinton or Miss Ellington.

'Surely they haven't been sacked?' Fran whispered. Mrs Oborne was looking along the workbench at them, frowning. Fran shook her head, then shrugged. Mrs Oborne nodded, and went back to pasting.

Even at the dinner break it was Mr Gaines strutting up and down the canteen, his white coat glistening and stiff as a packet of starch. Somehow it withstood the steamy, cabbage-smelling atmosphere 'How . . . ?' said Viola as she ate the watery grey rabbit stew. 'How is it so white when he's been all over the place today, familiarising himself, or so he's said?'

It was only when the break was over that they saw Mr Swinton and Miss Ellington enter. From their frowns it looked as though their headaches were still throbbing, or maybe they'd had bad news? Perhaps both? A flurry of worry went around the canteen as all the girls filed out into the corridor to be back at their posts for one o'clock. Ahead, the detonator fillers in their soundless felt shoes turned off to their workshop while Fran, Beth and Sarah continued on to the pellet workshop. Beth heard hurrying footsteps catching them up. It was Miss Ellington. 'Well?'

Miss Ellington moved alongside, sighing. 'Gaines is kingpin, it seems. Sent by London to sharpen up security after the break-in and establish some proper regard to safety – Bolton's words, though he looked sick as a parrot.'

The women walked on, but Beth had been thinking. 'If he's kingpin, Cyn, surely he can't be spending all his time in one sector? What about the underground shell-filling?'

Miss Ellington grimaced. 'He's to give everyone the once-over in turn. We have the privilege of being first, while clearly he still has a build-up of energy. He has the power to transfer or sack anyone, and Mr Bolton has just informed us that, thanks to Gaines, Mr Swinton and I are on a warning.'

Beth's headache worsened. Fran and Sarah cursed.

'What about Mrs Oborne?' asked Fran.

'I'm to have a quiet but firm word,' said Miss Ellington. 'I will also warn everyone to stay sharp, no mistakes if possible, and to curb tongues or risk their jobs.'

'Good luck,' Fran called after Miss Ellington. The only reply was a wave.

'The man's mad,' muttered Beth. 'He must see that the war needs every trained person.' She stopped. 'Well, I suppose I didn't help, nearly wiping my eye.'

Sarah sighed. 'Every factory has incidents, ours fewer than most, or that's what the foreman told us in Scotland. He also told us that we were the best-trained girls he'd had.'

Fran nodded, thinking it was true, for she was the only one who had almost seen the grip in time. There, Ralph, she thought. What about that for a change of attitude, eh? Fran linked arms with Beth as they approached the door to the pellet workshop. 'Aye, you can say that again.' Sarah did, but it was automatic, and no one even smiled.

The end of the shift couldn't come quickly enough, and at two, when the aft shift took their places, the women hurried to the changing rooms, gulping water from their bottles, picking up all their belongings, desperate to be away from the Factory. They were checked for contraband as they left the changing rooms by Miss Ellington and Mrs Raydon, who'd come back from the shell-filling sector, just for today. Then hurried into the cold fresh air and approached the gate.

Fran said, gripping Sarah's arm, 'Oh no.' There stood Gaines, alongside the guards, the wind tugging at his overalls, which were still untouched by dirt.

'He looks as though he's a sail,' muttered Sarah. 'Perhaps he'll take off.'

He was rechecking the fore-shift and Barry's face told a story. The girls reached the guard post behind Valerie, Sandra and Mrs Seaton, and waited as Maisie's bag was searched by Gaines, and Marjorie's by Barry. They heard Barry say, 'You telling us we're not doing our jobs, Mr Gaines?'

Gaines continued to poke around Maisie's bag. 'You might have noticed I'm not saying anything. So, best just do what you're paid to do, and get on with your job.'

Barry checked Valerie, Sandra and Mrs Seaton's bags and pockets while Harry lifted the red and white pole. Fran was next. She opened her bag for Barry, who was swearing under his breath. He checked her pockets. She moved on, but Mr Gaines called her back.

'I've just been checked leaving the changing room and again by Barry, and I have no pellets,' said Fran. 'Why would I take them?'

'Lavatory rolls get taken too.' He was looking at her as though he was about to catch her red-handed.

'Oh dear,' whispered Mrs Oborne, who had come up behind Beth.

Fran looked at him and said, slowly and clearly, 'I wipe my bum with my own toilet paper in my own netty, thank you, as I expect you do, Mr Gaines.'

She pulled her bag on to her shoulder and barged past him. He started to shout, 'Just—'

Beth had been checked by Barry and slid out after Fran, calling back to Gaines, 'Morale-building is as important as checking for toilet paper, Mr Gaines. Did they not teach you that at "I'm a little Hitler" school?'

'Oh dear,' Mrs Oborne said again, as she joined the queue of women intent on shoving past him. All the girls destined for Bert's bus heard Gaines's cry of pain as Tilly Oborne's immodest weight found his right foot.

They heard her call, 'Boots with hard toecaps are good for safety, Mr Gaines. You might do well to consider that. Not steel, of course. Don't want you going up in a blaze of glory, eh?'

As they headed for home, the bus was full of chatter, outrage and worry over Miss Ellington and Mr Swinton.

'Gaines can't last,' decided Sarah finally.

'Why not?' answered Viola. 'His sort somehow have a way of hanging about.'

'Aye,' Maisie said. 'Like a bad smell.'

After a while the bus quietened and the women sat back, some almost asleep, as the girls on the back seat whispered that it was bad enough having to fight a bliddy war, without having a bliddy overzealous official. What's more, one who made a virtue of rudeness. They wondered if perhaps shaking them up was all part of the investigation, or did Gaines think one of them was in cahoots with those who'd tried to break in?

'He might think it'll panic us,' called Maisie, 'make us confess to breaking down the fence when it were the wind that took it down, for heaven's sake.'

Fran murmured, between sips of her water, 'Who knows? He's staying at the Rising Sun, believe it or not. Bet Mildred

61

is right put out having such a ray of sunshine, but it's a bit of money in the till. Maybe Stevie will take his photograph and ask him to smile?'

Mrs Oborne called, 'Well, he'll have to wait a bliddy long time before he gets one out of the miserable old beggar, and when he does it'll crack the lens.' She called down to Bert then. 'You hear that, Bert? Another misery guts has landed, but one who's worse than you, believe it or not. And why're you crawling along? We want to get home sometime this week.'

The bus fell quiet as they waited for Bert's reply. It took a while coming, which wasn't like him. Finally, he said, steering steadily round a bend in the road, 'You be quiet, our Tilly. This bliddy tyre is getting worse, so I'm taking it real slow, lass. Don't want to have to walk home, do you? The depot are fitting a new one when I get back.'

The bus chatter was muted now, and everyone seemed conscious of how slowly they really were going, noticing how the bus seemed to be slipping a little as Bert steered around corners.

'Bliddy hell,' groaned Maisie, 'the bairn'll be home from school and Mam's alone in the shop. Still, the lad can help her weigh up something or other. Be good for his arithmetic . . .' She stopped and looked out of the window.

Fran followed her gaze and saw that snowdrops could be seen where the drifts had been. It would be daffodils, then bluebells soon. Next to her, Viola muttered, 'So, we've Gaines who's a beggar, and Swinton who isn't any more, and Ralph isn't either, you say. So, what was the lad like before he improved?'

Beth called across Fran to Viola, 'If he's improved. He was horrid, now he's nice. He'll stay nice, or he won't, so divint fret yourself, lass.'

Viola grinned. 'Maybe he and Gaines went to the same school.'

'Aye,' called Maisie. 'Could be the school of bad manners, eh?' But she sounded preoccupied, her eyes now fixed on Bert.

Fran suddenly sat bolt upright. She could feel the bus had slipped, and now it was drifting across the road, swaying from one side to the other, and the back was sliding. Silence had fallen. Fran shouted, 'Bert, Bert, what's happening?'

Some of the women were standing craning over those still sitting down, staring out of the windows, then to the front.

'What the—' shouted Bert. A deer bounded over a wall, straight in front of the bus. There was a squeal of brakes, and Bert struggled with the steering wheel. The deer bounded on. Fran saw its face, uncaring, unaware. It was soon gone, over the far hedge. Its rear leg caught on a branch, but was then released. The bus juddered, lurched forward, the front dipping on the right, and there was a screech of metal on tarmac, sparks flying up from the road. The bus seemed to tip, before righting itself. Beth was thrown to the floor as the back of the bus whipped round, and they heard Bert's panicked voice.

'Tyre bliddy burst – I can't hold her. Hang on, pets. Hang on.'

Above the shouts and screams a horn sounded, just once. Bert shouted, 'Oh bliddy hell, no. Hang on, hang on.' There was a screeching, the bus was twisting, it almost rose at the front, then there was a thud, and finally a crash. The bus seemed to tip again, then sank back. Women were thrown over the seats in front and those who had been standing went down like skittles. Sarah and Fran landed face down in the aisle, a weight on top of them, squashing Fran's ribs. There was silence for a moment, and then the sound of a

63

horn again, one which went on and on. Fran lifted her head. Bert was slumped over the steering wheel.

Mrs Oborne rose from the aisle, scrabbling up on all fours, her headscarf askew. She started to stagger along to Bert, clambering over the other passengers. Maisie was slumped over the seat in front, but trying to stand. Her face was pale, her nose pumping blood.

Someone was crying. Fran tried to push herself up from the floor, watching Sarah trying to do the same next to her, but there was still something too heavy stopping them. Fran craned round, feeling sick. Something wet ran into her mouth, and she tasted blood. Viola lay on top of them. Still there was the sound of a horn. Why didn't it stop?

'Get him off the bliddy horn, Tilly,' Fran yelled. 'I'm on my way to help.'

'There's a car an' all,' Tilly replied. ''Tis on the verge, smashed into a tree, crumpled and smoking. Bert's hurt. Someone help me, please. And someone else get to the car. Oh God.'

Chapter Four

Earlier that morning

Waiting in the study, Ralph watched the clock hands tick slowly round. His father had telephoned the mine to excuse Ralph from the fore shift, explaining that he needed to sort out some business with his son. He also confirmed that Ralph would be there for the fore shift tomorrow, on the coal sorting screens until he was completely recovered from his illness.

Ralph stared out of the window, paced to the desk and back to the window, wondering if Professor Smythe was on his way. Well, of course he was, but would he be here at twelve as he had said? Did it matter? He pressed his head against the cool pane. Nothing mattered, as long as he came. They had discussed little on the telephone for Smythe had deflected Ralph firmly. 'Best to meet for a chat. *Copperfield*'s such a good book for a thesis,' Smythe had said, his voice sharp and no-nonsense.

Ralph looked towards the top of the drive and, as though by an act of sheer will, Smythe came sweeping round towards the house – or was it Smythe? It wasn't his car. The Bentley crossed in front of the house, the gravel flicking from the wheels, stopping so suddenly it skidded. The passenger door opened and out Smythe slid, smoothly, crisply, which gave further lie to the doddery old fool act. He pulled his coat around him as it billowed up in the wind. Ralph glanced again at the clock on the mantelpiece. Midday. So, on time, absolutely on the dot.

Smythe's driver slammed his own door shut and sauntered round the front of the car, wearing a tweed coat, his matching tweed cap set at an angle. Together they headed up the two steps to the front door. Ralph hurried across the hall to let them in, glad that the children were at school. They'd be back for lunch at two. Later than usual because it was the nature ramble, or some such. Ralph's parents were elsewhere, on a shopping spree. They were due back at the same time as the children.

The school had to be mornings or afternoons only, such was the volume of children now that there were so many evacuees in the vicinity. This month it was mornings for the incomers, while the village children had the aft shift, or so Abraham had informed him. That would never have been the term before the war, but now everything seemed to be a shift.

Ralph opened the door before the bell rang. Smythe nodded, whipped off his hat, slapped it against his leg, and entered, waving one hand behind him. 'Yeland, this is Ralph Massingham, who is a bit of a toerag but has the potential to be "other", or so we all hope.'

Yeland merely smiled, removed his cap and carefully put it in his coat pocket. He held out his hand. Ralph shook it.

'Pleasure to meet you.'

Yeland nodded. 'Let's see if I can return the favour when our little chat is over, eh?'

Smythe headed for the study. 'I gather your father is elsewhere, with the enchanting Mrs Massingham. So, we have the stage to ourselves?'

Feeling as though they were ducklings paddling in the wake of a bossy mother, Ralph nodded as he and Yeland followed Smythe. The professor strode to Ralph's father's desk and sat in his chair. Ralph closed the study door behind him, his mind racing. Who was Yeland? Into the silence he said, 'May I take your coats, gentlemen, or fetch you a cup of tea? Fresh leaves today as it's Monday.'

Smythe looked at him. 'No need for pleasantries. We have things to discuss, final decisions to make.' He gestured to one of the two chairs that Yeland was busy placing before the desk. 'Sit.'

Ralph obeyed the order. Yeland did not, leaving the second chair empty. Instead, he strolled to the window and, as Ralph had done earlier, rested his head against the cold glass.

Into the silence Smythe said, 'So, Ralph, you have been complicit in two acts of sabotage in this grubby war – that's all, as far as we know.'

Suddenly, Yeland's voice came from behind Ralph. 'Yes, as far as we know. Tell us how you communicate.'

On the telephone the previous evening, Ralph had thought about telling Smythe of his days as a Fascist, but the professor had cut him short. Suddenly, Ralph thought of Smythe tapping the Massinghams' telephone in order to understand exactly what Ralph was up to; perhaps if Smythe could do it, so could someone else?

Ralph looked at Smythe, then behind at Yeland, but the man was no longer there. He was now standing by the bookcase. If this was meant to unsettle him, it was bloody well working. Ralph started by explaining that he had been a fool, had tried the Communist meetings and the Fascist ones.

Yeland was behind him again. 'We know all of that. Tell us how you communicate. That is what we have asked for, so that is what you will deliver. Anything and everything about it, no matter how trivial.'

Smythe sat quite still, his face expressionless.

Ralph began again. 'I have to telephone Tim Swinton at his home as though we are friends. I say, "I will speak to you another time, when you are less busy." This warns him to go to a particular call box. There is a different one for each day of the week. My calling time is nine o'clock in the evening.'

Smythe was writing it down in a leather-covered notepad. Ralph could hear the scratching of his fountain pen. The professor looked up. 'Carry on.'

'If he needs to phone me, he merely telephones here, or sometimes catches me as I'm passing the public phone box in Main Street, as he did yesterday evening, wanting me back on the job, eyes and ears on alert. His ability to catch me like this makes me feel as if someone is watching me. Someone who then contacts Swinton, no doubt using the same call box a few minutes ahead of me.' He told them of yesterday's call in detail, the shadow he had seen disappearing down the lane, and the old woman who appeared.

Smythe looked over Ralph's head and nodded at Yeland. 'Tell us about how you came to be up in the north again.'

Ralph explained that he had been instructed to return from university to work in the pit and halt production as and when he could.

Yeland gripped his shoulder. 'On to Bell Seam.' His grip tightened, digging in so hard it was only just this side of pain.

'I rang him. I received instructions to block Bell Seam to prevent it being reopened just in case the safety survey deemed it possible. The survey was scheduled for the night shift. To facilitate my act of sabotage there was a long length of fuse and a stick of dynamite left in the right-hand corner of the bike store. These were to be secreted under my shirt once I'd arrived early for the foreshift and I was to set the dynamite in place behind a prop marked with a "V".'

'Marked how?' Smythe snapped.

'A chisel, I expect. It was gouged.'

Smythe nodded. Ralph was cold and wished he'd lit the fire. No wonder the two men had kept their coats on. Yeland released his grip and began pacing to the window. Ralph didn't turn, but could see him out of the corner of his eye.

'Where was it gouged?' Yeland asked, his breath steaming up the glass.

'I was told it would be two feet from the ground. I just went along the seam, feeling the props at that height. I could have used my lamp, but I didn't want to be discovered. It was about eighty feet into the seam.'

Yeland turned and sat on the seat next to Ralph. He took a silver cigarette case from his breast pocket, offered it to Smythe and then Ralph. Both shook their heads, Ralph because his hands were shaking.

He explained how he had set everything in place and run out the length of fuse, knowing that after he'd worked at the face he would return to the main seam, bringing a tub of coal to hitch to the horse train. It was then that he would return to Bell Seam and light the fuse. His pretext would be that he was doing his 'business'.

'Business?' queried Yeland.

'A . . . a number two.'

Yeland blinked. 'A what?'

'A bowel movement.' Ralph knew he had gone scarlet.

Smythe waved Yeland along. 'Don't be obtuse, Yeland. Have some compassion.'

Yeland stared at the tip of his cigarette. 'Continue.'

Ralph did, explaining he had done as ordered, without realising there were surveyors further down the seam. He himself had made it out before the whole lot came down.

Smythe leaned forward. 'Let us be clear on this. One stick of dynamite, eighty feet in. Only one stick, not two? Not another charge further in?'

Ralph was confused. 'No, I did exactly as I had been told. I ran the fuse wire along the base of the wall, slipping it round, or behind the props if I could. I killed two good men.'

Smythe and Yeland were nodding. 'And the aftermath. Anything at all?'

'I telephoned Swinton. He was unmoved by the deaths, beyond, of course, that they made me a murderer. This he added to my list of reportable sins, should I decide to back out. If I did so, Tim made it clear, as he had from the start, he would hurt my parents.'

Smythe merely nodded. 'What else, however trivial?'

Ralph tried to think. How trivial was trivial? He went back over that dreadful day, that week. Then he remembered that Mr Swinton had called into the church later, wanting to speak to the vicar because he'd heard someone say they'd seen his son on that very day, on his motorbike, and the lad hadn't been to see his father, who had no idea where he was living or anything about him. Ralph told them this, adding, 'Lord, do you think Mr Swinton suspects Tim? Tim was jealous, you see, of Davey and Stan because they bested him in the Massingham scholarship. It was their fathers who died, or rather, I killed.'

He stared at Smythe, who was still writing. Yeland said, 'Maybe, maybe not, but carry on.'

'With the break-in,' snapped Smythe.

Ralph told them how he'd learned about the fence being down from Amelia, who worked in the office. She was a silly girl, gossiped too much, let things slip. They had been out together a few times, as Tim had urged him to get to know the Factory girls, especially those who would drink too much and give away information. He addressed Yeland now, who was still sitting beside him and was on to a second cigarette.

'The fence was blown down in the storm, a storm which raged for a few days. It was a gift for me, because I carried out the task knowing I could make it fail, but it would appear to Tim I'd tried. I got into the grounds, but a dog and guard intercepted me. I retreated in the storm. I cut myself on the fence. It went septic, and I was out of commission, thank God. I was pleased because I wanted to die. The trouble was the co-op wouldn't let me.'

Now Smythe smiled and it was one that reached his eyes.

They took him back over both incidents, and the timing of Tim's post-wedding-tea phone call to the box. Then there was silence, the only sound the ticking clock. Ralph saw that it was two. The children would be home any minute, brought back by Farmer Thompkins.

Both men rose. Yeland shook his hand. 'That'll do, for now at least. We have further investigations to make, of course. We will be reviewing the original investigative report on the Bell Seam incident, and initiating our own. There is already an investigation launched into the break-in. So, if you need to rectify anything that might be construed as misleading . . .'

'It's what happened,' Ralph insisted.

Smythe came around the desk and headed for the door. 'Show us out then, Ralph.'

He did so, opening the front door and accompanying them to the car. Yeland opened the driver's door, leaving Smythe and Ralph together. Smythe pressed a piece of paper into his hand. 'Phone numbers – learn them, destroy the paper. Call regarding anything of interest, however trivial it may seem. Anything whatsoever to do with Tim Swinton, the pit, the Factory. Gently, for eyes will be upon you. And not just ours. You remain a good little member of the cell. Call from a telephone box. Clear?'

Ralph nodded. 'I asked Tim a question about who else would be interested if he wasn't. He didn't like it.'

'Don't do that again,' said Smythe. 'Just listen and see what mistakes he makes. If you are rumbled, rest assured your parents and this tidy sum of children will be safe. Tim

71

is not the only one capable of having eyes everywhere.' He opened the passenger door, slamming it shut after him. Yeland revved the engine, turning in a tight circle, and off they drove, with no acknowledgement, just the crunching of gravel beneath the wheels.

Ralph sighed, exhausted, but relieved, oh, Lord above, so relieved. He could make amends or he could die trying and his parents and the children would be protected by these two men. He heard the tractor then, coming up the drive with the evacuees. He waited and saw his parents following.

He realised he couldn't bear to talk, to listen; he must absorb all that had been said, all that he had said. He spun round and ran to the roadster in the garage.

Alfie was there. 'Visitors, Ralph?'

Ralph grinned. 'Entertaining my father's friends is quite a chore, and one was my professor. I was chatting about continuing my degree once the war ends. And about a few business affairs with my father prior to that.'

Alfie shrugged. 'Continuing your degree, eh? We'll all be in our bath chairs by the time the war ends.'

They both laughed and Ralph agreed. 'Most likely, but now I'm making good my escape, just for half an hour – blow away some cobwebs, not to mention my hangover. How's yours by the way?'

Alfie grimaced. 'Best ignored, for only time will tell whether I'll live or not.'

Ralph was still laughing as he backed out the roadster, letting his father drive through the arch before waving and then lowering his window. 'Just taking her for a spin. Smythe came, with a friend. Sorry they missed you. I will report on my return.'

Farmer Thompkins was taking the children along the other side of the house where he could turn in the stable yard, now so sadly empty of horses. As Ralph drove off, he wondered if a pony would be a good idea for the children. He could teach them to ride, since Stan, Sid and Norm left him standing where football was concerned – but only because his own game had been rugby.

He reached the bottom of the drive, turned left and headed out of Massingham, driving between hedges and drystone walls, whistling, feeling the tension peeling away from him, because he wasn't trapped, wasn't powerless. He was on the way to doing his bit. Yes, he could die, but so what? At least his guilt would be at an end.

As he drove round Hanging Tree corner, he thought of Fran and her guilt. Should he have spoken to her as he had? Would she wonder where his thoughts had come from? He drove on and on, and perhaps that's all he could do. Just go on, as he had advised Fran.

He didn't drive fast, for there could be a pheasant on the road, or deer; besides, what was the point? He was in no hurry. He had a day off, for heaven's sake. He rounded a bend, but—What the hell—He braked and skidded as the back of a bus slewed towards him, blocking him; huge, dark, it took the sun away. It was tilting, coming straight towards him. He pressed down hard on the horn. It was the Factory bus. Women on board. Fran, Sarah—Closer, closer. He spun the wheel. He mustn't—No, don't hit it. No, not them. Mustn't hurt them. He spun the wheel. He was broadside on, but the bus kept coming, so he drove for the ditch, hard and fast, leaving the road clear for the spin of the bus. He saw the grassy verge, the wall, the tree, but what could he do? He roared forward, out of their way, into the tree. He felt the pain, the steering wheel against his chest, the agony of his leg; he tasted his own blood, then nothing as his head crashed through the windscreen.

Chapter Five

Fran shouted over the groans: 'Viola, shift your arse, lass, we need to get up. Go on, Viola. Beth, give her a hand. Let's get her on the back seat, lay her out.'

'I'm not bliddy dead, I divint need laying out.' Viola's voice sounded weak.

'Then get off us,' grunted Sarah. 'We're not a mattress. We've got to get up, lass. See if you can first, eh?'

Beth listened but couldn't smile. Her lips were split, and she was hanging over the seat in front like a rag doll. Her head hurt, but the bridge of her nose was worse. She murmured to herself, 'Get up, get up, you great dollop.'

She braced herself, putting a hand on the window. It slipped in some blood. The side of her face throbbed and now she remembered slamming into the glass. She looked down at Mrs Seaton, half on a seat, half kneeling on the floor. Their eyes met. Mrs Seaton said, 'I'm not a big dollop, I'll have you know,' and they both tried to smile. This time Beth heaved herself upright, reached down and pulled up Mrs Seaton, who sagged onto her seat. Beth then moved along to Viola.

'Anything hurt, pet?'

Viola turned to look as Beth hauled her onto the seat. The girl's eye was swollen. 'Bliddy hell,' she said. 'I can't lose an eye an' all. It'll be me nose next, and I'll be even more of a sight.'

Beth nodded, blood dripping onto Viola's mac. The girl's headscarf lay on Fran, but it slipped to the floor as Fran scrambled to her feet. Sarah forced herself upright too, just as Fran called, 'No time for napping, Mrs Hall. Tilly needs us.'

Just then Tilly yelled above the sound of the horn, 'Will someone give me a bliddy hand? The old bugger's out of it.'

Fran threaded her way down the bus, careful to avoid those still trying to sort themselves out, and still the horn went on. Beth wiped the window, and looked for the car. Mrs Seaton winked at her. 'Aye, you're a mucky pup, you are, bonny lass.'

Beth didn't understand. She didn't understand anything. Mrs Seaton dug in her mac pocket and pulled out a hand-kerchief, passing it over. 'The side of yer face. Bit of a bash you've had on the windowpane, I reckon. Split the skin, and your nose got a bash and all – dribbling down, it is.'

Ah yes, that was right. She hit her head. And her nose. It was then that Beth saw the car. A roadster. Ralph's? Yes, surely it was Ralph's. But he was on the fore shift. What the hell was the time? 'Stay there,' she ordered Viola. 'Stay there, divint move. You canna see anyway.'

Edging along the aisle, Beth followed Sarah and Fran. Behind came those who could walk. Fran and Sarah pressed against the cab waiting, as instructed by Mrs Oborne who was leaning over Bert, with Sandra helping. Mrs Oborne looked up, and shouted to Beth. 'Lead 'em out, there are enough people here.'

Beth did, hanging on to the rail and stepping gingerly down the steps and into the cold air, tasting the blood from her nose and feeling the stinging of the wind on her split lips. Behind her Mrs Oborne said, 'That's right, bonny lad. Let's have you off that horn, eh?'

'It might bring Farmer Thompkins down, though,' Beth yelled back. 'We need help. Got to get the bus off the bliddy road, and Ralph out of his car.'

At that, silence fell, silence except for the horn. Tilly

Oborne turned to look down at Beth as she stood on the road. 'Ralph, you say?'

'Aye, 'tis his car, I'm sure of it. Smashed into that tree. He tried not to hit us, I reckon. You can see – no brake marks on the road.'

Bert was groaning as Tilly and Sandra moved him gently. The horn finally stopped. He said, his voice feeble, 'Aye, you're right,. That Ralph did all he could to miss us. He put his foot down and drove hard at the bliddy tree instead. He'd have had us all over the bliddy place if he'd hit, so he drove at the bliddy tree. He drove . . .'

'Hush now,' said Tilly.

Bert fell forward onto the steering wheel again, and the horn resumed its noise. Tilly said, 'Leave it – we need a bliddy tractor,' then bellowed down the bus: 'We need three women back down the road, and another three up round the bliddy bend.'

'That'll be me,' Maisie yelled, already on the road, 'because I'm already on me way round the bliddy bend.' She hurried off, clutching her handkerchief, already sodden with blood, to her nose.

Within seconds those able to move were off the bus, some to wave any oncoming traffic to a stop and some heading along to Farmer Thompkins' house, in case he hadn't heard the horn. Tilly and Sandra tended to Bert, while Fran, Beth and Sarah and a few more headed round the back of the bus to the roadster, then wished they hadn't.

It was his head, smashed through the windscreen, that horrified them all. They hesitated, then Beth went forward, past the others, her nose hurting, but her head just thudding a bit. Sarah ran after her, grabbing her arm. 'Look, is it steam or smoke from the bonnet? Will it explode?'

Beth turned to Fran, and saw Viola too. 'You should be laying down, lass.'

Viola shook her head. 'Divint be ridiculous. If I should, so should you and most of the bus, and there's not time. We need to be careful – pulling him back through the glass could hurt him more.'

Valerie came forward. 'Is he alive?'

Ralph's face was badly cut, his head too, and blood was dripping down onto the bonnet. Fran moved, and Beth smiled slightly, because it was always Fran who was the leader. Wonderful Fran who was leaning out across the bonnet to Ralph. Beth watched as Fran touched his face, gently. 'We're here, bonny lad,' she said, her voice loud enough to reach him above the sound of the horn. 'We're here, and we'll keep you safe, and get you out.'

Ralph was deep in a world of pain, somewhere dark and cold, but where there were no thoughts, no fear, no whirling torment, just pain, waves of it, like the surf, rolling in, washing out, dragging, scratching on the sand, on rocks, tumbling him, tearing him. He breathed, but why? It was too hard, and the waves were dragging him against the rocks. Rocks that tore and hurt. But there was something soft now, something holding him steady . . . Seaweed? He was floating, out of the surf, and he could rest his face against the softness.

He floated, resting, breathing in the gentle, soft breeze so like a voice, a gentle voice, one that rose over the roar of the surf. He was floating away from the harsh sand, the rocks, leaving it behind. The breeze kept repeating, 'We'll keep you safe.'

Safe. He rested his head against the warmth and gentleness, but the pain was here, again. The waves surged, he moved, and screamed because there were daggers in his cheeks, his ears, his head, his neck. In his leg, his body. The breeze sighed, 'Howay, bonny lad, you stay still. Remember, we'll keep you safe. Just wait.'

He felt the softness, heard voices. He was safe, like he'd been with the co-op. Like he'd been with his daddy. He could smell the cigar smoke.

So, he waited, because they'd told him that was what he must do.

Fran was still straining over the bonnet, keeping her hand against his face, and the effort hurt her strapped arm and damaged shoulder, but that was of no importance. After a while, Beth took her place, talking as Fran had, and when it stretched her arm too much, and her own cuts and bruised head hurt too badly, Viola took her turn, with her half a hand. So, on it went, just as the sound of the horn went on and on, until finally those left around the bus came and took their turn, and no one looked away at the sight of this young man dying, for they were Massingham girls, and they would do what had to be done.

Fran sat on the verge, in the cold grass, her head resting on her knees. So, this was the whelp, but it wasn't, it was the nicer Ralph, and they didn't know what to do, other than be here, and she wanted her da, Stan, Davey, someone who could tell them, help them, help him.

She looked up, and at last heard the tractor. She rose, stumbled and straightened. 'It's Farmer Thompkins.'

'Right, Bert, up you come, lad,' yelled Mrs Oborne. 'No, just sit up straight, no need to try and get out. We'll sort that.'

'Oh, aye, I bet you bliddy will. Drop me on me head an' all, I reckon.' It wasn't his usual shout, but it was something.

Beth stood, her nose no longer bleeding. 'Thank God Thompkins is here. Thank God Bert's being himself.' She pushed Fran. 'You go, fill in Thompkins, then come on back here. He's still alive, our Ralph is. He's fighting, I reckon,

78

but then he's a sort of pitman.' Her laugh was strained, but it was a laugh.

Fran tore across to Thompkins, who was clambering down from the tractor, yelling, 'Doc's on his way, ambulance too. Should be here any minute now. The lasses caught me on the road after I took the bairns home from school, so I nipped to the farmhouse to get the missus to telephone 'em all, including the Massinghams. First off, best clear the bus off the road, eh? Don't want a collision.'

He was already fixing a chain to the bumper and then to the tractor, shouting at Mrs Oborne, 'Keep him in the cab. Let me shift the bus, eh.'

'Tilly told Bert if he didn't come round she'd ram that horn where it would hurt, good and proper,' Valerie called out. Mrs Seaton and a few others were laughing, but it was high and hysterical, and exhausted.

'When I've pulled the bus round,' Thompkins shouted, 'I'll have a look at who's hurt the worst, so I can direct the doc, then at least I can say I've done me best, as the bishop said to the actress.'

Thompkins straightened the bus by dragging the rear round to the side of the road, his tractor roaring, the huge wheels spinning, all the while calling down to the women. 'I left two of the lasses further along the road to direct the medics and with Mr Massingham along an' all it'll be a bliddy shambles, like a ruddy wedding tea. I heard yours went well, our Sarah? Sorry I couldn't be there – a beast with bad feet.'

Mrs Seaton was now on the verge, watching with her arms folded. 'Poor beggar, I know how it feels, mine are a right trial, I'll tell you that for nothing.'

Thompkins switched off the engine. 'Who's worse, do you reckon?'

Fran gripped his arm and dragged him towards the

roadster. The farmer took one look, scratched his head beneath his cap and said quietly, his weathered face serious, 'Best we do nowt 'cept what you're doing till we've got the doc. Poor little bugger.'

'Is it going to catch fire?' called Sarah.

Thompkins was already wrenching open the damaged driver's door and though the engine had stalled, he switched it off, throwing the keys to Beth. 'Hang on to those. I canna smell petrol, so I reckon 'tis just steam from the radiator. Let's face it, it'd have gone up by now if it were summat worse. What I will tell you is that he's a bliddy mess.' He pointed through the door to Ralph's leg. 'Nasty gash, and God knows what else. I divint want to move him back through that windscreen. That's when most damage is done.'

'That's what our Viola said,' said Beth.

Thompkins moved back to the road, took out his Players and offered them round. Sarah didn't take one, but instead took her turn with Ralph, quietly talking to him while the others walked with the farmer towards the bus, standing well clear just in case of fuel spillage, lighting up the cigarettes he'd tossed them, then waited for the doc. He finally stubbed out his own and headed towards the steps, calling up to Mrs Oborne, 'Stand aside, lass.' He clambered on board. 'Aye, you'll live to be a bliddy nuisance, our lad, but the doc's on his way. Reckon he'll give you an enema to liven you up.'

'Bugger that,' said Bert, his voice sounding stronger.

Thompkins climbed off the bus to join the girls, and nodded across to the roadster. 'I divint like to see this, even though 'tis the whelp.'

Fran spun round, in tears. 'I'll not have you saying that. He steered away from us, so's not to hit us. That's why he's got his bliddy head stuck through the bliddy screen.'

'Aye,' Beth said, 'so you divint call him the whelp, not again, never again, d'you hear. No one's to do that.'

As Thompkins looked from one to another, all of them standing hunched against the cold, their arms crossed, bloodied and bruised, he nodded. 'Then I won't. You finish your cigarettes, stub 'em out proper with two vehicles a bit battered, then nip across the road and take over from Sarah looking after Ralph. He's done good work today, as you say.'

Fran saw that his hands were trembling. He looked up, winked at her, then made his way back onto the bus. It was then that they heard the ambulance bell, and Fran wept with relief, but still took her turn to cup Ralph's face . She called out against the noise of the bell, 'They're coming, Ralph. They'll get you out. Hang on, bonny lad.'

It was four o'clock and the gloom wasn't far away as the ambulance braked and four ambulance men piled out of the back, whilst the driver stayed at the wheel.

Thompkins called, 'Reckon Ralph's the worst.' The men nodded, and two made for Bert and the other two for Ralph. The women were waved aside, and once the men saw what had happened with Ralph, the driver was called over. Dr Dunster arrived in his old Morris, then, closely followed by Mr Massingham.

The Factory girls all returned to the bus once Bert was safely in the back of the ambulance. They picked up their bags, which had been thrown into disarray, and waited for another bus, which was on its way from the depot. They were sore, tired and shocked. Even Tilly Oborne just sat in her seat, lost in her own thoughts. Fran dabbed at Beth's lips, while Sarah licked her handkerchief and wiped away the drying blood from Fran's chin.

Viola laughed. 'That's disgusting. I hated it when me mam did that to me.' She fell silent, before saying, 'Mark you, I'd give me right arm for her to do it to me now.'

'Aye, well, you've given half your left hand, lass,' called Maisie, 'so let's not have you giving anything else to anyone else, for she's up there, on her cloud, looking after you, else you wouldn't be here now. You'd be in Scotland in bits.'

Viola sat quietly. 'I reckon you're right, Maisie,' she said finally, 'and it warms my heart, so it does.'

Mr Massingham clambered up the steps. 'The other bus is here, ladies. But before you go, I want you to know that I believe you have kept my son alive, for he and Bert are both in the ambulance, on their way any minute. Bert is bruised and shaken up, and I believe will be kept in overnight, but it depends what they decide at the hospital, of course. My son has a cut leg, and not unsurprisingly . . .' He stopped, his voice breaking. He swallowed, coughed, then continued. 'Not unsurprisingly, a head injury. I suspect that when he recovers he will not be an oil painting, as there could well be scarring. But again—' He shook his head, and the tears were rolling down his face. He whispered, 'Again, I thank you from the bottom of my heart, because Thompkins tells me that there was always someone with him.'

He turned to go. Fran called from the back of the bus, 'Mr Massingham, Ralph steered away from us deliberately, into the tree. Bert told us that had he hit us it would have been so much worse for all us women. So we thank him, and you make sure you tell him we know what he did. You hear me?'

He didn't look up, but he did say, 'I hear you, Fran. I always hear you, always listen, my dear. After all, you shout so loudly and so well, and remarkably often.' It was said with such fondness that it raised a laugh.

The ambulance left. Dr Dunster, grey-haired, with a limp from a riding accident, waited for Mr Massingham to make his way to his car, and then came onto the bus, checking everyone over. 'Bumps, bangs, cuts, right. I'll swab and stitch them, how about that.' It wasn't a question. He stitched Maisie's head, dabbing it with antiseptic, and she bellowed, 'That bliddy hurts.'

'Man up,' he muttered. He stitched a few more, including Beth's head, on the side, just three stitches. Eventually he slapped his bag shut and nodded. 'Go home, sink into your tin baths if you've the energy. Keep the cuts clean. You'll ache, you'll heal. You'll probably have another headache tomorrow, this one not caused by elderberry wine, eh, Mrs Sarah Hall?'

He headed back down the bus, yelling over his shoulder just before he disappeared down the steps, 'I want to say have the day off work tomorrow, but it's like talking to a brick wall, eh. I'll say it anyway. Stay off work – you in particular, Viola, for I checked that hand and you need a different type of job. I'll tell the Labour Exchange that, if you'll let me.' He was off again, waving. 'Off to a lass giving birth.' He drove away.

They looked at one another, and Mrs Oborne shouted, 'Can you imagine what a fuss Gaines'll make if we don't turn up? I for one am not having that.'

Fran, Sarah, Viola and Beth grinned, then Beth wished she hadn't as her split lips hurt. They all left it to Fran to say, 'We'll be there.'

Chapter Six

Davey had travelled south on the night train, feeling as though his heart was being torn out of his body, leaving Fran and everyone. He bussed straight from the station to Bletchley Park, near Milton Keynes, in order to work a full shift, though his eyes were almost out on organ stops. There were, however, codes to break and he was already half an hour late. He tore up the drive, having been checked at the gate by the guards, and slipped into the hut.

He shouldn't have had all those special beers of Stevie's, though, because as he took his place at his machine, the nearby clacking of those already hard at work increased his hangover more than a notch. He sighed, stretched and looked around. Next to him, his fellow lodger, Daniel, raised his eyebrows and pointed at the clock.

Davey grinned, whispering, 'Aye, well, it's a long way, lad, so be glad I'm here at all.'

Daniel laughed and went back to work. As his headache thudded, Davey was grateful there was no sunlight streaming in through the windows since, as usual, they were shrouded by blackout blinds day and night. Overhead, the dim lights shifted in the infernal draughts, just as the blinds were doing.

Why the hell no one taped over the edges of the windows to exclude the draughts, he had no idea. Davey shook his head, then wished he hadn't. All he wanted to do was lie down and die. He muttered, 'Bliddy Stevie.'

'You're an infernal grouch,' said Daniel, 'and who is bliddy Stevie?'

'The publican of the Rising Sun. He provided the beer and will be at my wedding, so you have been warned. You have booked time off, haven't you?'

Daniel nodded. 'Beer, my lad, which you tipped down your own throat. Or did Stan and the others drag you screaming to the bottles, eh? Just get to work, shirker.'

Davey adjusted the settings on his decoding machine, which was a replica of the German Enigma, the machine that put the messages into code in the first place. The settings they had been given for the day had been worked out by others, using the huge Bombe machine that their brilliant minds had created. He punched in the first of the intercepted messages, forwarded to Bletchley by couriers from listening stations all over the country. He stared at the pile to the left of his machine, brought in by a Wren. Thousands more to come, he thought, but all in a day's work.

Norah, the supervisor, had been walking along the rows of decoders and he could hear her stop right behind him. She leaned over, flicking his hair. 'Good of you to spare us some of your time, Davey Bedley. Only half an hour late. See that clock over there? You should be here at eight. Good wedding, eh? Hasn't put you off your own next month?'

'Oh aye, and oh no, lovely Norah, not put me off my own, since you won't have me. Sad to say, I'll just have to make do with my Franny.'

Norah slapped his shoulder and laughed, moving on and calling, 'If I was thirty years younger, maybe I'd consider it.'

'Nah, you wouldn't, Norah,' Daniel muttered. 'He's a right beggar, you know. Leaves crumbs all over the breakfast table, and probably in the bed.'

Everyone laughed, but no one stopped work, for there

was no time. Click-clack they all went, punching the keys, converting the code to something that supposedly made sense, but as it was in German, it was the translators in their hut who would note that and make sure the relevant people saw it. Davey's German was good enough to work most of it out, and he had a quick eye for recognising an operator's hand. It meant he could report troop manoeuvres simply by noting what one particular operator was transmitting.

At last, Norah called the shift for their lunch break. Davey sighed with relief. Perhaps food would help. Still, before he and Daniel hightailed it out of the hut for the canteen, Davey offered to work through the break. Norah waved him aside. 'Eat. I recognise a hangover when I see one and I want no vomit on my watch. You've caught up anyway, so bugger off.'

He and Daniel walked across the gravel in front of the red-brick mansion and bet on grey mince or grey rabbit? They entered the steamy canteen and queued, Davey staring down at the mince that was slopped onto his plate by the elderly woman in the hairnet. He picked up a knife and fork from the end table, his stomach lurching. Food? Perhaps not, but someone would want it, so he followed Daniel to a table where there were a few spaces, and sat down next to him on the bench. He took a mouthful and found that in fact he was ravenous.

He began to eat, his hangover and tiredness lifting, and he told Daniel of the pheasant sandwiches, and of Stevie's old boy who brewed the special beer and had somehow managed to get hold of yeast. 'We were right pigs,' Davey said, scraping up the last of the potatoes, and then drubbing his bread in the remaining gravy. He pointed at the plate. 'Aye, you know what, I reckon it doesn't need washing.'

From just behind them they heard Daisy say, 'You're disgusting.' Davey sighed. Daisy had caused such trouble, accusing both of them of having their way with her when drunk. Though at least she hadn't said it publicly.

It was only later that she had confessed she was pregnant. She had been looking for someone who could be tricked into believing he was the father, for it transpired that her RAF boyfriend had been killed in action, and her parents didn't want to know. Daniel and Davey had promised to help, and so she clung to them like a limpet. Thankfully, Daniel's father, a vicar, was trying to find a mother-and-baby home for her.

Davey thought again, as he had done a lot recently, that the old boy had better get on with it, because Daisy reckoned she was about eight months along. She also reckoned the layers of clothing and corset made her look fat, not pregnant. Was it only because he knew she was that he thought that was rubbish?

Daniel was whispering to her, and she nodded. He raised his voice just a little, so that Davey could hear as well. 'We'll see you off from your landlady's and pay for the taxi to the station. Dad's booked the trains for you. I've got the tickets safe. The home will look after you. Got your bags packed?'

She nodded. 'They're ready in the hall of my lodgings.' Davey was so relieved at what he'd heard his headache lifted further. God bless Daniel's father, because now she'd get sorted, and what's more, they'd be free of her.

'Come on,' Daniel called past her to Davey, 'back to work.'

Davey took his plate to the trolley, but diverted back to the table, squeezing Daisy's shoulder. 'Seems we'll see you later, lass.'

Once they were outside, they dawdled, looking towards the lake where in the winter some of the Bletchley workers had skated, and Daniel explained: 'One of Dad's congregation heard of a place for unmarried mothers that has a vacancy. It's attached to the parish, so he can keep an eye on her and help find somewhere for the baby at six weeks. It's the least we can do for the pilot. He was no more than twenty, she said yesterday. She's nineteen. It's a bloody pig's ear.'

They headed towards the hut, their scarves blowing in the wind. 'Aye, for the babe an' all,' Davey muttered. 'Won't she try her parents again? Then she could keep it, perhaps?'

'I tried to persuade her when I got Dad's telegram yesterday,' Daniel said. 'She was still adamant. She knows her father wouldn't countenance it. Whether she'll come back here, who knows? I know it's unchristian, but I hope not – we know how tricky she can be.'

They stopped and stared back at the lake. It seemed so calm against the turmoil of Daisy's life. Daniel said, 'All that nonsense about sleeping with her. Mark you, lad, here I am, a nice, God-fearing lad, and there you are an unreformed pitman, and she went for you first. Still trying to get my head round that.' He slapped Davey on the back.

They watched a flight of geese take off from the water, honking and circling overhead. Both men watched until they disappeared and by then Norah was heading towards them, her long woollen cardigan flapping, the scarf she always wore following suit. The wind snatched the smoke from the cigarette in the corner of her mouth. She tapped her watch. 'Five minutes, lads. If you want a quick Woodbine, get on with it.'

Davey called after her, 'Is that an offer, Norah?'

'Now would I break the habit of a lifetime? Buy your own, lad. I'm just a poor old woman.'

Daniel was pulling out his Player's. 'Have one, Davey. Keep yourself calm for your wedding day.'

Davey produced the matches. Daniel laughed. 'Your contribution, eh? Yes, that just about sums us up?'

'Howay, stop your mithering. You know right well we take turns.'

'Ah, but it's good to spark you up from time to time.' Daniel paused. 'How old do you think our Norah is?'

They set off towards the hut as they tried to find a number, and ended up at fifty-six. There was no reason, Davey thought; it was just that she looked it.

The afternoon passed as it always did, hectically, with new intercepts arriving just when they'd cleared a pile. Finally, it was the end of the shift, and Davey's headache was worse again, but it would be, poring over the machine, listening to the click-clacking, thinking of Fran. Darling Fran, soon to be his wife. What would she wear? Did it matter? She'd look utterly wonderful in rags. He picked up the last intercept, decoded it and handed the pile to the Wren who stood behind him and was already beginning to reach over his shoulder.

'Thanks,' she said. A posh voice, but then many were, just as most decoders were graduates, not pitmen; but could they set cryptic crosswords, as he could, and get them placed in a magazine? It was this expertise that had brought him to Professor Smythe's notice, via Stan and a contact of the old boy's, and to a position here. As Davey straightened, easing his shoulders, he cringed inwardly as he thought of bounding up to Smythe at Sarah's reception and yacking about his son. Thank God for Fran saying the right thing. But whether she said the right thing or not, thank God for her, full stop.

Daniel stretched. 'I recognise that soppy smile. Fran on your mind, eh?'

Davey was about to reply when Norah clapped her hands. 'Off you go, fore shift. Leave those nice warm seats for the aft shift. No need for overtime today, you'll be pleased to hear, especially Davey hungover Bedley. And you'd better hope it's a steady day here when it's your turn to wait by the altar. We can't let you go if there's a rush on, lad.'

Davey, who was rising, sat down again with a thump, his mouth dry. 'But . . . but . . .'

'There speaks a woman with no heart,' groaned Daniel. 'Don't believe her, lad. She knows very well Marigold on the aft shift's got a few friends on call to cover for you and me if this lot can't handle the traffic.'

Davey rose and pulled a face at Norah, who shook her head. He grabbed his mac off the back of his chair.

'Sorry, lad,' she called, 'it weren't a nice thing to do, but I wanted you to know just how others are putting themselves out for you. But it's fair because you've done your share of taking the load for them. So, everyone, this is my way of saying you've grown into a team, and I'm proud of you. Teamwork is what will get us through. Off to the bus now, if you can get your big heads through the door.'

As they left, the next shift hurried to take their places, while Davey nodded to himself. Aye, they were a team, though not quite like Auld Hilda, where their lives depended on their marrers.

Once outside, Daniel slung an arm over Davey's shoulders. 'Come on, Mrs Siddely might have some sugarless scones for tea, she said, if we're on time. If not, the gannets will have them, which I believe means the children, though Colin and Martin aren't backward in coming forward.'

They crunched down the gravel and on to the concrete, heading for the entrance. The trees overhanging the drive were ahead of those in the North; the buds were burgeoning, and there was a magnolia just this side of the guardhouse that threatened to have a wonderful display. They showed their passes, waiting for the pole to lift, and then loitered with the others waiting for the bus.

Colin and Martin, who months back had taken Morris's place, were already there, Colin with his face in a book as usual, and Martin whistling. A few of the girls were smoking and chatting. As Davey and Daniel drew nearer, they heard one of the girls say, 'I think she's pregnant. Take a good look at her when she comes for the bus, because if that's fat, I'm the Queen of Sheba. So good riddance. It's not right. I mean, where's her sense of decency and respectability, is what I'd like to know.'

'Whose by-blow is it, more to the point?' a mousy girl in a WRNS uniform almost spat. She saw Davey and Daniel watching.

'Our Daisy's going not a moment too soon,' Daniel whispered to Davey. 'The trouble is, she hasn't made many friends.'

Colin looked up from his Ngaio Marsh novel and muttered, 'Change that to *any* friends. She's been too silly, too damaging. She was bad enough accusing you two lads, though we kept that between ourselves, as far as we know, but I hate to guess how many others have had the same thing thrown at them?'

Martin interrupted his whistling. 'Though to be fair, she seems all right now. She was in the midst of grief, remember.'

'Worthy of a writer, that was,' Daniel whispered. '"In the midst of grief", indeed, and the thing is, you're probably right. But as you know, it's sorted. However, in all honesty, and Dad would clip my ear to hear me say this, I feel for the mother-and-baby home. She's a bag of tricks, is our Daisy.' Davey saw the Wren whispering to the others, nodding towards the four of them, and then raising her eyebrows knowingly.

Daniel had seen her too. 'You do realise, Davey, when you and I get off at Daisy's stop and walk with her to her landlady's to wait for a taxi, fingers will be pointed.'

Martin looked enquiringly at Colin, who nodded. 'Well, let's make that the four of us, eh? Then they can each point a finger at whichever one of us they choose. They should have more to think about, don't they know there's a bliddy war on. Damnable little cows.'

Before he could stop himself, Davey wagged his finger at him. 'Language, our Colin.'

Their laughter carried across to the girls, whose looks said, *There you are, choose which one is the father, for they're all alike.* The men just shrugged; and they didn't care a jot.

As the bus drew up, Daisy came waddling down the drive as fast as she could, and the lads made a point of meeting her, waiting as the bar was lifted for her. All five of them pitched up at the bus, arm in arm, with Colin helping her on. They followed her up the aisle, staring fixedly at the four girls, who blushed and turned to stare out of the window.

When Daisy's stop was called, the men helped her off the bus and again linked arms on the pavement before setting off. Colin chatted, as only he could, about absolutely nothing as they sauntered along past the 1930s houses with their hedged gardens until they reached The Haven. They stood back while Daisy knocked on the door. She turned and looked at them, her face expressionless, her small eyes set deep and her thin lips turned downwards as usual.

Daisy's landlady opened the door, gesturing to two cases without saying a word. Davey reached in and picked them up before retreating to the pavement as the landlady slammed the door, saying, 'Can't say it's been a pleasure.'

The five of them waited as the wind grew chilly and Daniel checked his watch. 'I said five thirty, so any minute . . .' And sure enough, a taxi drew up. Colin opened the boot, shoving in the two cases.

Martin spoke to the cab driver. 'Help her out with them at the station, there's a good bloke. Here, I'll pay you for it.'

The driver waved the money away, saying, 'No need. She's about to drop any minute, so best we get there quick, eh?'

Daisy stood by the rear door, which Daniel held open. She reached out. 'I have your home address to write and thank your father, Daniel, and your lodgings here. And I will, and Davey too.' They shook hands. She turned to Colin and Martin, shaking their hands too. She drew out a pad and pencil, asking Davey to write down Fran's so she could apologise to her for the trouble she'd caused.

'There's no need.'

'But there is.' Daisy's eyes filled. 'It must have been horrid to think the man she loved had been with someone else.'

He scribbled *14 Leadenhall Terrace, Massingham, Northumberland*, and handed it to her.

She looked at them all. 'You've been so kind to me, and I was ridiculous, quite lost my head. Forgive me. Peter would have been ashamed of me.'

She eased onto the back seat and Daniel shut the door. The taxi drew away, and all four of them sighed with relief. 'I shouldn't say it,' murmured Daniel, 'but I'm glad that's the last we'll see of her.'

It was what Davey, and probably the other two, were thinking as they set off to walk back to Mrs Siddely's, but then Davey muttered, 'How would anyone behave in Daisy's situation? If I died, would Fran cause so much harm and upset?' No one replied, and he shook his head, knowing she would not, because there would be the family, and Massingham, to keep her straight. That sort of a family was something Daisy seemed not to have. Oh, bliddy shut up, he told himself, it's not our problem any more.

At the main road they waited for a truck to pass and Colin said, 'Hearing his name, Peter, makes it much sadder. But I agree, I'm glad she's gone. Not sure how she'll pan out after the baby, though? If she was bad as this with her boy in blue being shot out of the sky, what will she be like if she has to give up the baby?'

'Trust you to make us uneasy all over again, you beggar,' said Martin.

They crossed. It would take them almost an hour by Shanks's pony, but as Colin said, 'There might, in spite of the lateness of the hour, be some scones left, and suddenly I'm hungry again.'

Davey handed round his Woodbines, concentrating on the thought of scones, and as they walked their moods lightened. It was Daniel who said, 'I don't think I'll open her letter if she does write. Dad will deal with everything, it's what he does, and what the home does. We've helped when we had every right to turn away. Let's just wish her well, and the bairn, and forget it ever happened. And will someone give us a light? My cigarette's waiting to reach my mouth, and my fingers are sick of holding it.'

They laughed, and Colin lit their cigarettes as they huddled round him, shielding the flame. Davey inhaled and they set off again, chatting, and he realised Norah was right, the hut *was* a team, and the four of them were marrers. Though they might not save one another's lives, they had joined together to support someone else. And if that wasn't what marrers did, he was a bliddy Dutchman.

Chapter Seven

That evening, Davey called Fran at their usual time. The phone rang and rang and he was about to give up when she answered, sounding . . . Well, not right.

'Fran?'

'It's been a beggar of a day, Davey,' she said. 'For a start there's a pig called Gaines here to sort us all out.'

'Gaines?' he queried.

Fran rushed on. 'Aye, the investigating security officer, or some such, determined to find things wrong. Cyn and Mr Swinton are on a warning.' She was crying.

The world stopped for Davey. Franny crying? He looked down the road, the scones lying heavy in his stomach now. 'Fran? Franny?'

She told him the rest now, ending with the message from the Massinghams. Ralph was in a coma, with a head injury, a gashed leg and bruised ribs, but alive.

It mattered – Ralph mattered to him, he realised with surprise. 'Bliddy hell. Oh Franny . . . But you, how are *you*?'

'I ache. I'll have black eyes, but my arm's no worse, nor my shoulder, and I don't need stitches in my bonce, Dr Dunster says.'

He stared out at the queue forming in the main street of the village, at the houses that edged the road, just dark shadows in the unlit street, and could have kicked the phone box to bits. He breathed deeply. 'You'll take the day off.'

She just laughed. He repeated, 'You'll take the day off.

Let Gaines sweat. You've to take care of yourself, let the bliddy war take a back seat.'

'Maybe, Davey,' she said, 'but you'll come back for our wedding? You have to – you must promise – because everything else is such a damned mess.'

A woman tapped on the door, pointing to the church tower where there was the pale gleam of the clock. He nodded, wanting to tell her to bugger off. Instead he said, 'I told you, I'd crawl, bliddy crawl to be there, but we'll talk again when I telephone tomorrow, as usual.'

'Oh, Davey,' she said. 'I love you, bonny lad.'

He said, 'I love you more' but they were out of time, and he was speaking to an empty line.

That afternoon, Fran had arrived home late, with Viola. Her mam was up at Massingham Hall with the co-op, helping with the bairns, while Sophia was at the hospital with Reginald. Ben was in the kitchen, their mam's medicinal enamel bowl at the ready. 'We heard the news. Alfie told us before rushing off with Sophia to the hospital.'

The two of them had bathed Viola's cuts and bruises, and then her hand. Ben had ordered the lass to bed in Fran's truckle. 'Mam's said you must, and Fran'll be up there and all, once she's spoken to Davey. I'm to keep an eye on the two of you, while Stan takes care of Sarah.'

Knowing she was beaten, Viola had headed up to bed, and Ben had then bathed Fran's cuts, drying them as gently as he had Viola's, and then pasting on the lavender grease his mam had left out.

As Ben was finishing, Stan had burst into the kitchen and hunkered down by his da's armchair, gripping Fran's hand. They looked at one another. 'You all right, lass?' he asked.

'Oh aye, nowt that a good night's sleep won't cure. Viola's in my bedroom so I can keep an eye on her—'

'No,' Ben interrupted, 'I'm to keep an eye on you both, Mam said.'

Stan and Fran grinned at one another. Stan nodded. 'Course you are, lad, and they'll be glad of it too.'

Ben slumped in the armchair opposite Fran. 'Mrs Smith will be back for Beth, so that's all right. When Fran goes to the phone box for Davey's call, I'm matron, in case Viola needs anything.'

Stan had left, calling that he and Sarah would collect Beth and meet Fran at the phone box at nine, but first he was off to check on Beth. Fran and Ben heard him running across the yard, but there was no slam of the back gate. Instead, there was the sound of Stan returning and poking his head round the door.

'Sarah told me Ralph steered away and into the tree so's he'd miss the bus. I owe him.'

At nine thirty, Sarah and Stan, Fran and Beth walked back home. They'd waited for Bob's call, but it hadn't come. Fran, Sarah and Stan had watched as Beth paced back and forth until finally she'd sighed, 'He'll have gone back to sea. Aye, that's what's happened. I'll get a letter in a day or two.' Her voice was little more than a whisper.

Stan nodded. 'Aye, well, that's the navy for you, but come on, time for bed. We'll walk you back.'

Viola and Fran were woken at three thirty by Annie Hall calling, 'It's time for work, if you're up to it, lasses. If you are, I'll have eggs ready.'

Fran groaned, her face sore, her body aching, especially her shoulder from reaching for Ralph. 'Aye, Mam,' she called back, 'down in a tick.' Viola was already getting dressed, groaning as she pushed her arms into her blouse. 'Were it too uncomfortable on the truckle?' Fran asked, pulling on her skirt, then brushing her hair, which though she'd washed out the blood was still a mite sticky.

'I were so tired I wouldn't have noticed if the sky had fallen in, Fran.'

Fran smiled, then regretted it, because Beth wasn't the only one with a split lip. 'You have first run at the netty,' she said.

'Very kind of Your Majesty.'

'There's a torch on the hook to the left of the back door.'

Down they went, into the kitchen, where the blackout blind was still down. Annie Hall came out of the scullery, and paled. 'Holy Mother of God,' she whispered.

Viola scooted to the back door, unhitched the torch and headed for the netty. Fran sat at the table, wishing she could just lie in bed all day, but said to her mam, ' 'Tis fine, looks worse than it is. You should see the other bloke.' Her lip hurt too much to laugh, her nose too, and she didn't even want to think of her right eye.

Her mam came to her and held her gently. Fran breathed in the familiar smell of soapsuds. 'Oh Franny, you look like a panda – black eyes and white as a sheet. Maybe we should put you in a zoo. It'd be safer, even in with the tigers, I reckon.'

Fran nodded rather than smiled as her mam stroked her hair. 'I kept Viola with me, Mam, because it left Sarah and Stan in peace, and besides, we both needed company, though at least I talked to Davey. But Bob didn't ring Beth, Mam, just when she could do to hear his voice, poor lass, so he must be at sea. More to worry about. Do you know, I hate this bliddy war.'

Her mam stroked her hair. 'Hush, hush, I know. Now, will you go back up the wooden hill to bed?'

Fran shook her head. 'I'm off to the scullery to wash,

then out to the netty. I reckon Viola could do to be clasped to your pinny and told she's a bit of a panda too.'

Her mam laughed. 'Lord knows what our Ben'll say when he sees you at the end of the day. The lad did us proud, even washed up the bowl. How about that for progress, eh?'

As Viola came back into the kitchen, Fran asked her mam what she'd been longing to ask since she got up. 'Any news of Ralph before you left the Hall last night?'

Her mam shook her head. 'We stayed until they returned. But you saw him get into the ambulance, and there's nowt different. He's cut and banged about, with a nasty gash in his leg, and they're worried about septicaemia as he's just got over it. But there's more concern about his brain. Sister Newsome said maybe 'tis a bit bruised, as it were a right old bang. So, we wait and see, though there're no promises he'll wake.'

As Fran opened the back door, taking the torch from Viola, she said, 'So it's an if.'

Her mam just nodded. Fran couldn't bear it.

After the scrambled egg that hurt their lips too much to enjoy, they lugged their bags with their water and day shoes, not to mention their gas masks, to the bus stop, past the pitmen going the opposite way. 'Be safe,' the girls called.

The pitmen stared through the gloom. 'Bliddy hell. Be safe, lasses.' 'Heard our Ralph were a belter – missed you on purpose, and him once a bliddy Fascist, too.'

'Aye, but there were others who went to the Commie meetings.'

'Aye, right enough, man. So maybe we were wrong about the whelp.'

On and on it went, and with every footstep, every jolt, the girls answered, 'Be safe.' 'How do.' 'Right enough. Don't call him a whelp.'

They turned right down Main Street. The bus was

already there, the women climbing on board carefully. Was Bert driving? They hurried as much as they could, for Stan and Sarah were waiting. Sid and Norm were with them, their caps slanted to one side, Woodbines in their mouths, as usual. But, thought Fran, it was not quite as usual, for Ralph had put them first, and they all knew it.

When they arrived, Stan pushed back a strand of Fran's hair and tucked it up under her woollen hat, then cupped her cheek as she had cupped Ralph's. ''Tis the boss man from the depot driving. Bert'll be back soon.'

Viola said, 'I remember at the wedding Bob said pretend could be reality, or something like that, and here we all are, pretending we're all right. And so we are.'

'Aye, we are. We're breathing, aren't we?' Fran gave a careful smile.

They heard Beth calling now, 'Howay, wait for me.' They turned, and Sid and Norm hurried to meet her, escorting her to the bus while Beth refused to let them carry her bag. Stan murmured, 'I bliddy hope Bob's letter arrives soon, or he phones tonight, for I bet she'll be there for nine. Howay, anyone else think he seemed a bit strange at the wedding?'

'Shh,' Fran said, for Beth was close, and besides, she *had* noticed and didn't want to think what it might mean. It was enough to get into work, paste the pellets and get home again in one piece.

Beth reached them. 'Right, on we get.' Her words were barely audible, for she couldn't move her lips, both of which were very swollen, just as the bridge of her nose was. Her eyes too, and half closed. There was a stitched cut on her hairline, and a bruise was beginning to appear.

Sarah kissed Stan and clambered onto the bus. Today there was no Bert to yell, 'Get your arses up them steps, or I'll leave you.' The others followed, setting off down the aisle, then Sarah stopped. 'Back seat? It's where we—'

'Back seat,' insisted Fran.

Beth agreed. 'Aye, we'll not be thinking of sitting else-where, for what were it you said Ralph told you, Fran? Face what you're worrying about and move on. So, we were on the back seat when we suddenly found ourselves on the floor or over the seat in front, and here we are again. So we'll sit on the bliddy seat, and that's bliddy that.'

Fran began laughing, and soon the other three were as well. As they moved along the aisle, they checked to see who was missing. Everyone was here. They reached the back seat, sat, and held hands. Together they faced it, like everyone else.

'Now we move on,' said Fran.

Viola muttered, 'Well, if the driver gets a move on, that is'.

The depot boss shouted, 'Right, off we go. Let's get this charabanc on the road. I'm Mr Harris. And you are the most remarkable women I have met.'

'Aye, well, flattery will get you most places, Harris,' Mrs Oborne shouted back, 'but putting a good tyre on that bus'll get you everywhere, including into me good books.'

'You divint want to be in her bad ones, Mr Harris,' yelled Maisie.

'Fate worse than death, that is,' added Sandra.

Mr Harris laughed, then drove off, finally picking up from Sledgeford. None of the Sledgeford women said any-thing about the incident. They took their places quietly, until Amelia clambered on board and set off down the aisle. She stopped, looked and said, 'Good heavens, I knew you'd look bad, but those lips, those eyes . . . Even a bit of slap wouldn't help.'

'And you can sit down and keep your own bliddy lips shut,' bawled Mr Harris, 'or someone will feel like shutting them for you, you daft cow. Slap, I'll give you a bliddy slap.'

Everyone was laughing now, really laughing, and things

were better, almost all right. They watched as Amelia sat down with a thump in the first available seat.

Viola looked along the back row. 'There, we're laughing. I reckon that first we pretended and now it's real. Perhaps that's what Bob meant?'

'I didn't understand him,' said Beth. 'Never heard him say it before. But aye, that's what he could mean. I'll ask if he telephones the box tonight, for I were thinking as I lay in my bed, while me servants scattered rose petals over me to help me sleep . . .' They were laughing again. She waited, then continued '. . . I was thinking he might be at sea trying out the refit, and not had time to scribble a note, and would be back in tonight.'

The others thought about it and nodded. 'That makes sense,' Sarah mumbled, her lip bleeding again. She pressed the handkerchief Beth handed her against the split, and they were quieter as they carried on to the Factory. In fact, everyone was until Mr Harris pulled into the siding.

'Anyone left on board after five minutes is a cissy,' he called.

They waited for Mrs Oborne's retort. And waited. Finally, to everyone's relief, they heard her say, 'I reckon the sooner our Bert gets his great big arse back on that driver's seat the better, for you'll get to see for yourself that you're in the company of a bliddy army, Mr Harris, who divint take kindly to being called cissies. By, you'll likely find yourself bunged in the luggage hold contemplating your misdeeds and wondering why you've your trousers tied round your throat.'

It wasn't her usual bellow, but it was good enough, and they all clambered from the bus and made their way to the gates, their passes at the ready. Even Maisie had hers in her hand. 'That's a flaming miracle,' muttered Beth. 'Our lives are complete.'

Everyone laughed again.

As they reached the gates, Harry and Barry were checking the last of the girls off an earlier bus. They waited. The wind blew. They pulled their woollen hats further down. Finally, Harry reached for Mrs Oborne's pass, then looked up. 'Bliddy hell.'

'Language, man,' said Mrs Oborne. 'You should see the other bloke.'

Harry looked down, checked the pass and said quietly, 'We heard a tyre had blown, we just didn't—'

'Aye, well, now you do,' said Maisie, holding out her pass, 'and this wind is chasing up me skirt and whirling round me unmentionables, so get a move on, for today I've got me pass in me hand.'

Barry beckoned her over. 'Canna have the wind being cheeky, can we now.' He looked in her bag and patted her on the shoulder. 'You be safe, you hear.'

This was what both guards said to every one of them, and it reminded them that they were the daughters of pitmen, and they straightened their hunched shoulders, regardless of their aches and pains, and began striding towards the Factory. In front of them, others were keeping to the main thoroughfare, before heading along to one section or another. It was like a city of flat-roofed brick buildings, thought Beth, not for the first time. She'd never walked to the end.

She looked up at the sky, which was lightening now dawn was on the way. See, Da, she thought. I'm a pitman's lass and I have the sort of bruises you had after most shifts, and that's all, and I'm striding along with the rest. And tonight my man will call the telephone box, and I'll tell him as though 'tis nothing. That's how we'll see this bliddy war through, and there's nowt complicated about it, just like you'd say.

They marched in through the doors of their section and into the changing room, hanging up their macs, shaking themselves out of their boots, pulling on overalls and stepping into their day shoes. Those who would be in detonators stepped into their spark-free felt shoes. They took out the scarves from their pockets, ready to create turbans, and in their place put several clean handkerchiefs in case their cuts opened. They put their rings, hairpins, kirby grips, anything contraband, in their boxes, checking one another for anything forgotten. And then they waited, quietly, Amelia's words still ringing in their heads.

The door opened, Miss Ellington and Mr Swinton entered. They scanned the room, but nothing showed on their faces.

'They must have expected to see a zoo full of pandas,' muttered Mrs Oborne.

Mr Swinton went through the safety and security procedures while Miss Ellington started to check them.

'No Gaines?' called Fran.

Mr Swinton stopped. 'I do hope you're listening, Miss Hall?' It wasn't really a chastisement, for his voice was gentle.

'Oh, indeed I am. I did just hope, as it is security and safety, that we would have a second security officer checking us.'

Mr Swinton winked. Everyone gasped with delight.

'He'll be here any minute,' called Miss Ellington. 'He left his clipboard in the SO's changing rooms. Quite forgot it, it seems.'

The door opened and in came Mr Gaines, checking his clipboard. Without looking up he snapped, 'Resume the safety and security rules, if you will, Mr Swinton.'

Beth watched Swinton as he resumed; it was much like a times table chant, there was a rhythm to it that she hadn't noticed before. She began to nod, Fran joined her and soon everyone was doing it, and the laughter began, faint but there. Gaines finally looked up, his face screwed in complaint. But then he saw them and froze, looking from one woman to another.

Mr Swinton stopped and turned to him. 'Is there a problem, Mr Gaines?'

Gaines looked at Miss Ellington, who said to Mr Swinton from the far side of the room, where she was still checking the girls, 'Only that I need Mr Gaines to help with the checking, which he seems to have quite forgotten about. Time is ticking, Mr Gaines.'

Gaines rose on his toes and held up his hand. 'Forget the time. These women, they're . . . Well, they're not fit for work, surely.'

Mr Swinton stuck his hands in his overall pockets and rose on *his* toes. 'Ask them.'

Gaines did, settling back on his heels, his clipboard tucked underneath his arm. In reply, Mrs Oborne moved in front of the women, and not to be outdone, rose on *her* toes, put her hands in her pockets, then settled back on her heels too. 'We're quite fit. Just a few bumps and bruises, split lips, black eyes, scalp cuts, some stitches, but nowt to make a fuss about. We need checking for contraband, though, so you'd best get a scamper on or the night shift'll be late off, and they'll not be too pleased. Neither will we, will we, ladies?'

She turned, a hand to her ear. A resounding 'No' was bellowed by the women.

Mrs Oborne returned to her place. Miss Ellington pointed to the clock. 'Five minutes.'

Mr Swinton rattled through the rules as Gaines rushed around the women, checking for silk, nylons and hairpins, but these were old-timers, and he'd find nothing that shouldn't be there, thought Beth.

Gaines returned to the front, and Mr Swinton reiterated their roles, which were the same as yesterday. They filed out behind him, and this time Gaines stood to one side as they left the changing rooms. 'Be safe,' he murmured to each of them, his voice different.

As Beth walked along with the other girls every bit of her body wanted to slump, but not today, or tomorrow, or ever.

Chapter Eight

Earlier that day, Tuesday, 3 March

Annie gathered a few extra chairs around the table. The co-op women still had rugs to finish for the Briddlestone's order, for if there was no order fulfilled, there was no payment, and their girls would have no help with bills or with saving for the headstones, even little Betty's.

She checked the kettle. They'd had fresh tea leaves yesterday, so these would be a bit pale and wan, but they were used to that now. She heard the others coming through the backyard and smiled. Little would be said about their lasses' bangs and bruises. It would be just another day.

She brought a plate out from the scullery and cups, chipped, but whose weren't. Would Mrs Adams bring broken biscuits from her corner shop? By, that'd be nice, but if not, it wouldn't matter for they had work to do, and would be together. Just as their girls had, and were.

She placed the milk jug on the table and some honey, but not much, for they had mostly forgotten the taste of sweet tea and kept it just for emergencies. Annie stopped then, her hand to her mouth. Should she have put some in Fran and Viola's tea this morning? But then they'd have thought she was worried, which would be a burden for them. Of course she was worried, she was their mam.

She shook her head again, thinking her head would go flying one of these days with all this shaking, for she wasn't Viola's mam, for heaven's sake. But someone had to be now the lass had no one. Well, she supposed they all were, she, Maud Bedley and Audrey Smith, though it did seem best to keep Viola here, in one place, to give Sarah and Stan space. Even when Fran were wed to Davey he'd be back down south straight away, so aye, best she stay here.

She could hear Madge saying that she was down for the ARP evening shift. 'Which is plain bliddy daft, for we've had no bombs over this way yet and I canna see any on their way.' The door opened, and in they came, bringing the chill with them. Boots were kicked off and glory be, Mrs Adams put a brown paper bag on the table.

'A few broken ones, and if anyone tells the ration man, I'll have to whack her over the head with my broom.'

'Nonsense, for you'll need it to fly around the night sky with your pointed black hat on,' Madge laughed, adjusting her eyepatch, which was deep blue today.

Maud Bedley settled herself in a chair, her proggy frame on her lap. 'She'll get the air raid sirens going, Madge, then you'll have cause to blow your whistle right enough.'

Annie made the tea and let it mash while they settled themselves. Audrey Smith, Beth's mam, muttered, 'I'll swing for Bob. No call last night, no letter this morning.' She sighed. 'But it's the war. They never know where they'll be, and the women at home knowing nowt.'

Maud nodded. 'Will she keep going to the telephone box?'

'Broken biscuits on the plate,' Mrs Adams interrupted. 'Are you ready with the tea, our Annie?'

Annie poured while Madge passed round the biscuits, saying, 'Briddlestone's want us to get the rugs to them by the end of the month, don't they? We need to get a bit of steam up, for we've Fran's wedding dress to sort out as well, Annie.'

Maud stuffed half a biscuit in her mouth, dusted off her hands and hooked a quarter-inch-wide red cotton length through the hessian and adjusted the frame to a more comfortable position. She preferred the smooth look of a hooky to a proggy rug. She thought the short lengths knotted through the hessian looked ragged, whereas the hooky was a smooth, looped finish. She looked at Annie.

'I reckon we need material a bit different to our Sarah's. The lasses wondered if there's a bit of spare curtain or material on a shelf somewhere at Massingham Hall? Does it seem heartless to mention it, with the lad in hospital? Poor wee thing. Just got him better from the sepsis, and now this. Never thought the little wretch he were would turn out to be a good 'un. Missing the bus, hitting the tree.'

Maud sipped her tea. 'I phoned Sophia first thing to find out the news on both Ralph and Bert. No improvement for Ralph, but Bert will be home tomorrow and back in the cab soon as wink.'

Audrey nodded. 'That'll please our Tilly. She'll have someone to be rude to again.'

'Tilly always finds someone to be rude to,' said Annie, 'but she'd rather it were Bert, for he's rude back.'

'Aye, and I reckon he's the one who starts it, more often than not.'

But the women were only going through the motions, for their thoughts were with Ralph.

Putting down her proggy prod, Annie said, 'I can't bear to think of him with his head through the windscreen, and I fear his body hasn't the strength to fight after being so poorly.'

Audrey nodded again. 'I want to be there, tending him, with all of the co-op, and maybe the girls, on shifts, like we were with the septicaemia.'

Looking deep in thought, Madge sorted out a series of short blue lengths and prodded them through her hessian. Finally, she said, 'Reginald must sort it with Sister Newsome so we can visit, regular like, take turns with the girls and the marrers, and owt else who wants to help. We need to talk to that bruised brain of his and tell it to shift its arse, and let the lad heal quick.'

Mrs Adams adjusted her frame and straightened her back before setting to work again, hooking through a long length of softer red. 'Aye,' she muttered, ' 'tis important he knows he's not alone and that his effort was appreciated, and that there's a place for him in our lives. Then I reckon he'll fight.'

Annie got down a pencil and notepad from the mantelpiece. 'Right, good idea, I'll draw up a rota, and when we're in Newcastle on our shift, we can take the rugs that we've finished to Briddlestone's. I reckon they should pay more for rush orders, so we can talk to that Mr Whatever-his-name-is.'

There was a tap on the door. It opened and in came Sandra Young's mam, Meryl, from the top end of Leadenhall Terrace, wiping her feet, looking at the spare chair, then at the kettle Annie had put back to simmer on the slow plate. 'Shall I sort out another cup all round? I've brought a twist of new tea leaves.'

The others looked at one another and Madge said, 'If it's the first time of use, you can wear the bliddy kettle, Meryl. On you go.'

Meryl laughed, placing her frame by the chair and putting the kettle on the hot plate.

'By lass, bit of a dry throat, eh,' said Madge.

The others laughed. Meryl muttered, 'Yes, I've a powerful thirst, Madge. I've been ironing for Reverend Walters and his sister all morning, and me basket's still full of Dr Dunster's wash, so will have to leave when you go up to the Hall, but enough of that – what's to do about this wedding frock? Time's a-wasting. At least we're doing the same food as at Sarah's tea, aren't we?'

The women nodded, though Maud said, 'Not so sure about the pheasant, but I've a mind for one of us to ask, since it wouldn't be fair if me lass were given that treat and Fran not. But then the Massinghams have enough on their minds, and what if the lad—'

'He won't die,' snapped Madge. 'We'll not have it, the girls won't either, and I reckon the lads'll haul him back out of the fiery furnace by his ears, so that's that.'

The others nodded, and waited. Maud continued. 'So, anyone going to step forward to ask about the pheasant?'

There was another wait as they looked at one another. Madge grinned. 'If worst comes to worst, I'll find me best eyepatch, the one with bells on. Reckon that'd charm the birds from the trees, and pheasant from the Massinghams.'

They were all laughing, because Madge hadn't gone quite that far with her taste in patches, but it wouldn't surprise them if she did. Maud nodded. 'Done. That's a problem sorted. If they can't, and the pheasant aren't willing to be sacrificed, we'll think of something else.'

As Meryl made the tea, Maud went on: 'But as well as the wedding frock and tea, we need to sort the rota, for there'll be no merriment in Massingham if the lad dies.'

Madge protested, 'I were joking about going to talk about the bird.'

'Too late,' the others said, as though with one voice. 'You might bring it up this afternoon. We should leave about ten past two.'

'And if the wind changes, our Madge,' added Maud, 'that face you're pulling will get set in stone.'

Again, there was laughter, but now it was Audrey Smith's turn. 'So, you'll do the rota and put the word around, eh, Annie, so we can tick that off. Now, the dress: Cyn Ellington said that Mr Swinton would let us use one of the Factory sewing machines, and with Viola still in that workshop it makes it easier. But there's a new bloke, Gaines or something like that. A bit of a tartar, or so I heard the girls saying.'

'Where's that cuppa, Meryl?' Mrs Adams called as Meryl came over with fresh tea.

Beatrice Adams sipped thoughtfully, looking over her cup at them all. 'When we're helping out Sophia with the evacuees, we'll talk with her, though this afternoon might be too soon to bring it up. Let's see how she is. It'll maybe take her mind off Ralph, and ours off our poor lasses. We can have a ferret about in the attic. I doubt she'll think it's pushy, for a wedding canna be changed and we've only a month.'

The women worked on and talk became desultory, moving on from hoping the girls were feeling more or less all right, but knowing they weren't, to hoping they were safe at the Factory and their itches not worsening, although they knew they would be. They changed tack and spoke of Stan and Sarah's happiness, and Ben's relief at his sister arriving back safe from Scotland, if not quite in one piece, and then, again, of his care for them yesterday.

'Aye, and he's to give Fran away, or so Stan's decided because he needs to be Davey's best man.' But all the time they were worrying about the girls, and Ralph, and Bert.

As it passed two o'clock, Maud Bedley put down her hook. 'There, another one finished. They said they wanted ten wall hangings and ten rugs for the floor. What do you reckon on this one? Wall or floor?'

The women crowded round.

'As you've a swathe of red, and some pink,' said Madge, 'I'd say wall hanging or it'll show the dirt. But 'tis time those who can were pedalling up to the Hall, or we'll be late. Two thirty we said.'

The others agreed, returning to the table just as they heard boots clomping across the backyard and Stan shouting, 'Mam, Mam.' He was panting as though he was running.

'What now?' muttered Annie. 'Not more trouble. An accident in the pit?'

Madge shook her head, in the middle of packing up her frame. 'The hooter's not gone, so no. Besides, there daren't be more bad news. I won't have it.'

They stared as Stan burst in. 'Albright got a call from Mrs Massingham in the pit office. She thought you said midday. She's worried you've had bad news. We ran once fore shift were ended. Are the girls all right?'

'Oh Lord, but we agreed two thirty, ' said Audrey. The others were nodding as they finished packing up their frames. Audrey continued, 'Oh poor lass, if she's forgotten the time it means she's in a right flummox and who can blame her.'

The women were dragging on their macs. 'Stan,' Annie said, 'go and telephone the Hall. Say we are sorry, and will be there by two thirty. Don't let Sophia think she got it wrong. I'll leave a note to remind Ben and he can keep Fran and Viola in line. You keep an eye on Sarah and Beth.'

Madge was at the door. 'Aye, we'll say we got caught up in the wedding. One way to bring in the pheasant, eh? Meet you on Main Street, Annie. Out of the way, Stan. We should have thought . . . The bairns, the worry, and Sophia so pale and tired.' She was off. They heard her call, 'Howay, Sid and Norm. No panic. On your way. Our lad's forgot all about you.'

The two pitmen laughed. Sid said, 'As long as all is well.' They heard them run up the back lane, calling to one another, then guffawing.

Beatrice Adams was putting on her mac too, and her boots. 'Remember, I canna come. My new girl, Emily, is still learning, just a bairn really. I'll be with you in spirit.'

'No more can I,' said Meryl.

Within twenty minutes, Madge, Annie, Maud and Audrey were cycling into the wind, finally turning up the long drive to Massingham Hall, where snowdrops nestled at the foot of the drystone walls. They were supposed to be a sign of hope, Annie thought. Aye, well, that was sorely needed today, one way or another. Well, when wasn't it, because there always seemed to be something.

They pedalled hard, their wheels digging into the gravel at the front of the house and pinging off their ankles, and then they whirled under the arch and into the yard. The Rolls wasn't there. They dismounted, not looking at the gap where the roadster would usually be.

'At least we're not towing the cart with the frames,' panted Audrey. 'That makes it a bit easier.'

'*We?*' blurted out Madge. 'Did the woman say *we*? I reckon it should be me, for the cart seems to find its way to my bike as if by magic, pet.'

They were laughing as Madge, rubbing her leg, which was mottled from the cold, continued: 'Remind me, when I'm rich and famous from making eyepatches for the gentry, to have a concrete forecourt in front of me mansion, eh? Or at least a million pairs of silk stocking to keep me gorgeous pins safe and, above all, warm.'

They hurried across and down the steps towards the basement kitchen. It was dead on two thirty. They knocked on the kitchen door, which was opened by Sophia.

'Oh, thank God, and I'm such a fool. I didn't even look at the calendar, I just had it in my head—' Sophia shuddered with harsh sobs. 'So I phoned the pit. What will they think of me?'

With the help of the others, Annie guided her to the huge pine table where milk and home-baked biscuits lay ready for the children. Mrs Phillips came in from the scullery, wiping her hands, looking relieved as she hung the towel on the brass rail of the range. A stew was simmering on the hot plate, the lid rattling.

Mrs Phillips turned and said in a voice barely above a whisper, 'Eleven children is too much for any soul, especially when Mr Ralph is in hospital with no one knowing nowt about owt, and Mr Masssingham sitting by the bed when he could be here, or at least cut himself in half or something useful like that. They need a nanny, another pair of hands.' The cook looked upset. 'Mrs Massingham's as pale as a ghost, she is,' she continued. 'Worn out if I know owt about owt, but more'n more I reckon I know nowt about nowt.'

Annie held Sophia as her sobs continued, watching Maud Bedley go to Mrs Phillips, hold her close and say, 'You go on home, Lily, lass. We'll be staying for however long we're needed.'

'Aye,' said Mrs Phillips, 'I will if you can manage, pet. Me old bugger canna be trusted to clean out the tin bath right and proper after the shift, and besides, he needs his back scrubbed. The vegetables are chopped to go with the rabbit stew for the bairns' tea, and I've tidied two of the bedrooms and done some ironing . . .' She petered to a stop. 'Aye, well, best I get off, eh, pet?'

'So, no news?' Audrey said, helping her into her mac. The older woman shook her head. 'Nowt. Nary a word's come through on the phone, but it's early days.' She was whispering now. 'I have to say, had it happened a while ago I'd not have been so sad, but he were becoming a right gentleman that Mr Ralph were – well, is.' She drew breath, upset, then headed for the door, and they heard her shout back as she mounted the steps to the yard, 'Aye, he were a gentleman at last. Yer could talk to him, and he understood yer sadnesses.'

Oh, of course, Annie thought. Lily's brother, Bill, had been killed fighting in North Africa last year.

Sophia, quiet now, pulled away from Annie. 'Oh, poor

Mrs Phillips.' She ran to the back door and up the steps, calling, 'Thank you for staying. And making biscuits. I've made a fool of myself ... so selfish ... But he was my charge, then my son, and I knew he could be the man he's become. I always knew ... And now, who knows ...'

The women heard all this, but it was Madge who went after her, bringing her back while Audrey pulled out a stool at the head of the huge kitchen table, tapping it. 'Sit yourself down, eh. I reckon a nice cuppa won't do any harm while we wait for the tribe. Out playing at the back, I reckon, the lasses as well?'

Maud was boiling the kettle and spooning used tea leaves into the teapot, saying, 'Now, how will the bairns know to come back from the field for biscuits?'

Sophia was pacing backwards and forwards. 'They're not here. Farmer Thompkins brought them back from school on the trailer and when you didn't come he took them to the farm for Mrs Thompkins to take them on a nature trail.' Sophia laughed, wiping her face. 'They must think nature trails are all country folk do. The school did one just the ... Oh, dear, I just seem so up and down these days, and I know Ralph's in good hands, and Bert is improving, but when you didn't come I thought the girls might have taken a turn for the worse ...'

Annie shook her. 'You, my girl, are tired.'

Audrey patted the stool. 'Come and sit. Let's have a cuppa before the invasion of the monsters, because we are setting up a rota for visiting and talking to Ralph, so that daft brain of his knows he's not alone and gets down to sorting itself out, eh?'

'Aye,' added Annie, 'and until then, we'll remember Farmer Thompkins, and if there's any nonsense out of the bairns, we'll get him up here to skelp their behinds, just like his da did ours. Do you remember when he found us in the orchard?' The co-op laughed. 'And Thompkins did the same to our girls, and the lads. Tea, then let's plan to lighten your load.' Annie checked the clock.

Sophia smiled at them all. 'Yes, a plan. You're very good with those.' Her voice broke again and she banged the table. 'Damn and blast, I might be his stepmother, but I love him as though he were mine.'

Annie jerked her head at Maud: in other words, hurry with the tea. Maud did so, and they were supping it when they heard the tractor, and then the shouts of thanks before the sound of feet on the steps.

Annie stood. 'You be strong, our Sophia. They don't need you falling about the place, they need gumption. Have you told them about Ralph?' Sophia shook her head.

The children almost fell into the kitchen, grinning at the co-op. Eva hurled herself at Sophia, who had moved towards the children, saying, 'Did you hooligans have a good day? How did the nature trail go?'

She was hugging Eva, and the others clustered round, wanting their pats, strokes and hugs, then scrambling onto the high bench at the table, squabbling for a space. When none was left, they hoisted themselves on the remaining stools.

'Biscuits,' crooned Tommy.

Stanley held one up. 'One each, eh?'

'There are eleven, Stanley,' said Audrey, 'and how many are there round the table, including the grown-ups?'

He dropped the biscuit back on the plate. 'Oh, not one each, eh?'

Audrey laughed. 'Well, let's see. Ladies of the co-op and Sophia, can we possibly deprive these starving children of Mrs Phillips' divine oat biscuits?'

'Yes, we can,' roared Madge. 'None for the bairns.' They all laughed as Madge continued, 'Of course we can't. So, eat up.'

While they did the women congregated by the back door, trying to decide whether they should take them for a game of footie, all of them on the back field, or tell them about the accident – or was it best to wait for definite news? In the end, Sophia whispered, 'Let's wait to see what's what, and instead of being outside, away from the telephone, let's think of good things, like Fran's wedding. We'll go to the attic, see what we can find in the way of curtains and material. She can't have the same as Sarah, it simply won't do.'

Annie said, 'If we used the other curtain that matches the one Sarah's dress is made of and covered it with net, it would look different. If there are any such curtains tucked away, rather than being greedy . . .'

Sophia nodded. 'You lifesavers can be as greedy as you like. Let's at least look. I haven't been up there for years, so who knows what's in the trunks. There might be toys or bikes or something scattered around that could be useful for the children. I do remember a rocking horse that belonged to Ralph. Why on earth didn't I think of it before?'

Only when there were crumbs left on the plate, hands being wiped across mouths, and glasses of milk finished, did Sophia groan, 'The flannels are in the scullery. Let's remember another time.' Then she beckoned to the children. 'Come on, we're off on a voyage of discovery.'

Five minutes later, Sophia was leading the way up the back stairs to the fourth floor and the empty staff bedrooms. Empty, because the girls had all decamped for war work, and so too had the housekeeper. Eva, walking along the corridor with Annie Hall, said, 'Howay, Mrs Hall, I reckon we could each have a room when we're really old and in the pit or the Factory, and might not want to sleep with our friends.'

Annie pulled her plaits. 'Oh, my wee bairn, you'll be

back at home by then, for the war will be finished in a few years, you mark my words.'

Eva stopped in her tracks, suddenly quiet and still as a statue. The other children had halted and were looking at one another. Abraham said, 'But we will still come to stay with Mrs Massingham? Mr Ralph will still help us with homework, and hear our times tables? He's started to make us learn them, you know. Says it's how we'll get good jobs.' Then he looked towards Sophia, whose mouth was set in a grim line. 'Where *is* Mr Ralph?' he asked. 'He said he'd hear our six times table, didn't he, Eva, when he were off shift?'

'Aye, and I've learned it an' all,' Dora nodded.

Enid was shaking her head. 'Oh, he's probably all bathed and clean, and out doing business with Mr Massingham. He did some yesterday, didn't he? You said he was away working when he divint come in for tea. You did too, Mrs Hall. You said that.'

Abraham looked at Sophia again. 'You were out doing business an' all, so Mrs Phillips and the co-op put us to bed. So I reckon business is good, or that's what me da used to say, when he were out all hours.'

'Aye,' Marty piped up, 'so Sophia must have learned her tables, so she could do business, which means Mr Ralph is right. The co-op and all, for they do business with Briddle-stone's, so they learned them—'

Eva hadn't said a word, when she was usually first off the starting block, but perhaps she didn't want to go home, thought Annie, looking more closely at the child. Then she shook her head free of thoughts. There were enough questions already, and what they needed were answers, in the form of news of Ralph. Then the Massinghams *should* tell the bairns, because they mustn't hear from someone else.

Sophia clapped her hands and set off again along the corridor. There were photographs of the staff on the walls, some with the Massingham family as they enjoyed the Summer Fayre they put on every year, or had done before the war. Annie wondered if it would still be held when the war was over? Besides, why couldn't it be held during the blessed thing? It'd perk everyone up no end.

'Come on, onward to the attic,' called Madge. 'Let's find the trunks – and toys.'

'Just up the stairs at the end,' said Sophia.

Annie had a sudden thought. 'Perhaps one of us should be downstairs to hear the telephone, Sophia?'

Madge nodded. 'You're right. I'll go.'

'There's a telephone on each floor, including the house-keeper's room,' said Sophia. 'The one with the "Blue Bedroom" sign, Madge, if you have the patience to linger.' She walked on as Madge slipped away from them, hurrying back along the corridor.

Eva seemed to have come to herself and looked from Sophia back to Annie. 'Is Sophia all right, Mrs Hall? Why does she have to hear the telephone? And she's a bit strange today. Howay, but she's sick and pale a lot these days, come to think of it. But ladies are like that, me mam said. Something to do with time of the month, but—'

'What happens at a time of the month?' asked Abraham.

Annie grabbed Eva's hand and then Abraham's, hushing him and half running. 'Come on, let's catch Sophia.' The bairns looked at one another and raced along the patterned runner. No need for the maids to get cold feet rushing to the bathroom in the dead of winter, thought Annie. Mark you, the retired housekeeper had said there were fires in every room, and proper beds, not the narrow ones she'd had at her old job. Eva panted, looking up at Annie.

'Well, is she all right, because that time in the month is dragging on, in't it? Seems to be all month, and today's worse than ever.'

120

'Of course she's all right, but it is tiring being a mam to so many, and it's a big house to look after. But look at her go now, because she's excited to be opening trunks and finding toys. It's like Christmas, isn't it?'

At the end of the corridor they climbed the steep staircase, following Sophia, who took the heavy old key hanging beside the door and turned the lock. The door creaked and the children shrieked as they walked through clinging cobwebs into the roof space, lit only by a few skylights translucent from the dust. There were many trunks, metal and leather, and also wardrobes and shelves of linen, ornaments and books. Through the gloom, Annie could see a huge rocking horse in the corner, hidden below the eaves. The bairns had seen it too and tore across, clustering around it, pulling the bridle, rocking it; then Eva clambered on, trying to find the stirrups.

'I want a turn,' called Enid.

Sophia was peering at the labels on the trunks, but glanced round. 'I believe the word is *please*, Enid.' She straightened, smiling at the co-op ladies. 'If I police the rocker, ladies, do work your way through these. See what's here. Why not find something for the bridesmaids too?' She gestured to the trunks. 'There might be some summer dresses you can alter, or bolts of cotton fabrics.'

They each took a trunk, checking the labels, although most were indecipherable, the ink long since faded. Lifting the lids, they disturbed the dust of ages. It billowed up and motes played in the beams from the skylight. In Annie's trunk there was a melange of men's clothes smelling of mothballs. Lying on top was a tweed hacking jacket, size 34 – ah, so for a youngster, she supposed – with tissue paper in the creases of the folded sleeves. Ralph – well, a younger Ralph. She thought of him now in a hospital bed, his head bandaged. Yes, they must definitely have a rota for visiting, for surely voices would help, and the touch of a hand on his, a stroke of his face as the girls had done while he was in the car.

She found she was stroking the rough, hairy tweed. It would itch, but – oh, another sleeve seemed to be hugging it, from a black suit, smoother.

She was about to shut the lid, but thought it best to refold the suit. She pulled at the sleeve, and out tumbled a British Union of Fascists uniform jacket that had been hidden beneath. She stared, then dropped it as though it burned her fingers, seeing the faded but legible name, *Ralph Massingham*, written inside the collar. Her mouth went dry and sour. It was true. All the stories of the Massingham whelp as a Fascist were true. This uniform showed he had been more than someone who went to Commie and Fascist meetings alike. It meant he really had been, or still was, one.

She stared around, seeing and hearing nothing – for Fascists were traitors, Nazis, hateful beings – until Eva's shout broke through.

'Mrs Hall, Mrs Hall, look at me.'

Annie slammed the lid shut and stood up. She stared at Eva, who smiled down from the horse, but she didn't really see her, her mind racing. So, was he *still* a Fascist, or a Nazi? Were they one and the same? She realised her hands had clenched into fists. Oh God. What would it do to Sophia, and to Reginald? But of course he wasn't, not still. This was a boy's uniform. But why had he kept it? He'd probably just forgotten he had it. That was it, yes.

She stood straight. For that uniform, the personification of that wickedness, surely did not represent the lad she'd nursed, nor the lad that her husband Joe had begun to admire for working in the pit. Moreover, this was not a family that would house a traitor. She sat down on the trunk. But what if there was another uniform, for a man?

Or perhaps not a uniform, but a man who was still a believer in what that uniform represented: a belief that was wicked, cruel, merciless. A belief that was the enemy of everything Britain held dear; a belief they were all fighting against. Whom should she tell?

Eva called again, as she scrambled off the horse, 'Howay, Mrs Hall. Come and see what the boys have found.'

Annie rose, forcing a smile but not daring to leave the trunk, because somehow she had to protect this family until ... Well, what? Until somehow she knew the truth. She made a show of looking to where Eva was pointing. The boys were clustered around an old pedal motor car. Abraham was saying to Sophia, as she heaved Enid onto the rocking horse, 'Please, Sophia, can we play with it down in t'yard? Maybe Mr Ralph will take it down when he's heard our tables – if you say yes?'

Sophia was trying to smile, looking from the rocker to the car, but finding no words. It was Maud Bedley who said, 'Well, maybe Stan, Sid and Norm would take both down if we get Alfie involved too, Sophia? What do you think?'

Just then Audrey cried out, 'Howay, look, look. Silk, a whole bundle of it. It's new, wrapped in tissue paper. Aye, it's parachute silk. Come here, our Annie. It's so delicate. Sophia, you come too, for you might not want it cut?'

Sophia left the girls around the rocker and joined Annie by Audrey's trunk. Sophia examined it. 'What do you think, Annie? You're the mother of the bride.'

Even the children crowded round now, though Eva had gone quiet again, looking from one adult to another. Sophia lifted it. The children gasped at the parachute silk billowing in all its glory. Everyone gasped. Eva said, 'Fran'd look like a bliddy princess, so she would.'

'Language,' said Madge, wagging a finger. Annie tried

123

to concentrate, tried to think of Fran dressed in such finery, but all she could see was the black uniform.

'How odd,' said Sophia. 'Whose parachute could it be? I must ask Reginald. Oh, no, I remember, he had a cousin in the air force. He stayed once, left stuff behind. Heavens, he's jolly high up now. We will assume he's forgotten.' Her look of innocence fooled no one, for Sophia was clearly on a mission. 'Oh indeed, finders keepers, eh?'

The women laughed while the children looked bemused and Marty sighed. 'Can we get back to the rocking horse and car?'

Audrey nodded. 'Off you go, and leave us to the important work, bonny lad.'

Madge was examining it. 'Oh look, a tear, several, in fact – the seams have split. Faulty. That's why we have it. Yes, finders keepers.' She folded it up again.

Annie nodded. 'If that's all right with you, Sophia?'

'More than all right. Fold it up and wrap the tissue paper round,' said Sophia. 'Let's turn it into something else, just in case anyone comes back for it, then it'll be too late. Any luck with summer dresses?'

Maud had found some material hidden in another trunk and showed them: blue, pink and pale green. 'Job done,' muttered Sophia. 'Time for another cuppa, weak though it will be, and for the children to have fresh air.' She looked closely at Annie. 'Fresh air wouldn't go amiss for you too, Annie. You look quite out of sorts.'

As the others began to leave the attic, Annie searched in her pocket for anything that would tie that damned trunk shut. Nothing. She cast round. There on the window ledge was a ball of string and a knife. She rushed across, cut a length and tied down the sneck of the trunk, cutting the ends short. She hid the knife behind a trunk tight up against the south wall, then hurried after them. Sophia had been right about turning the silk into something unrecognisable and the same must apply to the uniform, for no matter the truth, it must be turned into ashes.

Sophia waited at the foot of the attic ladder. 'Lock it, would you, Annie?' She pointed to the old key on the wall. Annie did, pocketing the key. There, no one was getting in until she was able to get back here and burn the bliddy uniform.

Once in the kitchen, the children tore outside, but then Eva came hurtling down the steps again and stood in the kitchen doorway, arms akimbo. 'Why did you say Stan were to bring down the horse and the car? Why canna our Ralph, eh? What's going on?'

No one spoke. Instead, they all looked at Annie, who, they thought, so often had the answers. She swallowed, because today she had too many questions of her own.

Eva spoke again. 'You all look like they did when they were trying to tell me Mam and Da were not coming out of the rubble cos they were dead. He canna be dead, not Mr Ralph, for there hasn't been a bomb and he were on business with his da, or . . .'

Annie saw the fear on the bairn's face, the lips that started to tremble, and pulled herself together, holding out her arms to the lass. Eva didn't move, just looked, and what in heaven's name was a daft lad's old uniform, discarded but not hidden, to do with anything? A real Fascist would have made sure it couldn't be found in case it would raise questions. Aye, that was right. As Eva continued to look at her, Annie called, 'Come here, our Eva.' It was a command, one that the child obeyed.

Annie waited until the child reached her, then crouched down. Annie looked at Sophia, who nodded, biting her lip, her eyes full. Annie's voice was quiet. She brushed aside Eva's blonde fringe. 'Ralph has had a car accident. He is in

Newcastle Royal Victoria Infirmary. Mr Massingham is with him, to find out what's what. Ralph is asleep, you see. His brain is tired. We didn't tell you because we have no real news yet. But we are all praying he'll recover, and you know, I feel he will.'

She realised then that she didn't quite feel that, but she hoped. Eva was staring, her blue eyes steady, as though she was looking right into Annie's mind. A mind, Annie realised, that was still mulling over Ralph, because she'd seen the feeling in him, they all had, when he'd been ill. There'd been kindness, appreciation, courage; the biting of his lip as they'd poked, prodded and dressed the wound.

Aye, he had a heart, and traitors couldn't have hearts, they could only pretend, and if you were sick with fever and pain, then that mask would slip. She smiled broadly, back with Eva, and kissed the child's forehead, holding her close, whispering, 'We'll go and see him when I've made up my rota, talked to Fran, Sarah, Viola and Beth to see when they can go, and the lads, and he can listen to you bairns reciting your times tables.'

'Rota?'

'Our plan, Eva. We always like a plan.'

She stood as Eva nodded and said, 'By, Mrs Hall. Our Ralph said you were straight and true, he did, so I know I can trust you.' Then Eva turned to Sophia. 'Will you promise, not just feel, that he'll be all right? For I divint want to lose another someone I love.'

Sophia shook her head, holding Eva's hands. 'No, none of us can make that promise. I say, as Mrs Hall has just said, that I feel he will recover, and what's more, we hope, oh how we hope, that he will. We will just have to send him our love on the wind and wait, and while we're waiting we'll just go on as before.' One of Eva's plaits had loosened and Sophia absent-mindedly redid it while Maud fetched another ribbon from the pot in the scullery.

The phone rang at that moment, and Eva spun round as Sophia dashed to answer. They listened as Sophia said, 'Oh, darling. No worse? Sister Newsome said what?' They were all holding their breath. Then Sophia laughed, a real laugh. 'Well, of course, but you're way behind, though don't tell Sister Newsome or she'll whack your hand. You see, the co-op are drawing up a rota, and the children can chant their times tables when it's their turn. Fine, we'll sort it out. Come home soon, darling.'

That evening, as usual, Fran was by the telephone box on the corner of Main Street when the phone rang. She pulled open the door, snatching up the receiver. 'Is that you, Davey?' It was, and to hear his voice made the day so much better. 'Oh Davey, I have silk. Mam brought it back from the attic at the Hall. It's a parachute, probably an unused reject we think, for there are rents and a note saying "Not fit for purpose", but there's more than enough for a dress. Oh, Davey, I'll be as smart as a pin going down that aisle, and I've never worn silk before, but it's so smooth, and if you didn't already love me, you'd fall for me like a ton o' bricks. I'm so pleased, bonny lad. I was thinking I'd look just like Sarah and there we'd be, framed on the mantelpiece while our bairns wonder why she and I look like two peas in a pod. There's enough cotton material for bridesmaids' dresses an' all.'

Davey was laughing, and she shook her head. 'It might be funny to you, but girls are different.'

'You can say that again,' said Davey.

Fran did. He laughed even more, then said, 'I've got news. Daisy's settled in the home. All seems well. So that's the end of that, and I canna tell yer how relieved I feel she's gone. But I gave her your address, as she wants to apologise, though I doubt she'll write.'

Fran grimaced. 'Well, I suppose if it makes her feel better—'

'Oh, Franny' he interrupted, ' I love you so much. You're a kind lass.'

They talked on and on, and all she wanted was for him to be here, for ever, with no need for these calls. He'd go to the pit, she'd run his crossword magazine, and once he was on his feet, he'd give up the pit.

It was only when Beth tapped on the door, pointing at her watch, for it was almost Bob's time, that it was Davey's turn to interrupt. 'How is Ralph doing?'

She sighed. 'Sister Newsome thinks regular visits might well stimulate his brain, help to bring him back. Too late, though. Mam was already drawing up a rota. Those two, Sister Newsome and me mam, are a terrifying force, they really are.'

Chapter Nine

Wednesday, 4 March

The next morning, as Bert edged away from the bus shelter on Main Street, grumbling as usual, Tilly Oborne was yelling, 'Don't you be dawdling along just because you've had a night in hospital and think you're a wounded hero, lad. Lounging about all yesterday, and only back at work today. Keep your hands on the wheel, your eyes on the road, and your gob shut. It's been a slice of heaven having your boss treat us with some respect.'

Bert hooted his horn. 'Still got a gob on you, you old besom. I thought you might have learned some manners with me poorly, but miracles are hard to come by.'

The women laughed fit to burst, and then started talking about the visiting rota, for the co-op had been calling on people and adding names to it. The visitors had to be slotted in according to shifts and school, but could start in two days, according to Sister Newsome. Alfie would drive people to and from the station, and the Massinghams would pay for the train fares.

'Aye, me mam and I are on the list,' said Sandra.

Fran nodded. 'So I saw, and all the co-op ladies are too, but most women in and around have their own bairns and canna leave them, they've pitmen that need looking after—'

'Others, like us, are doing war work,' Beth chimed in. 'But we're going on Saturday, or so the co-op have ordered,

129

and as always they must be obeyed, God bless every last one of them. Come with us, Sandra.'

Mrs Oborne stood up and came towards the back seat, swaying and shouting to Bert, 'You go steady now, you daft auld fool. Have a look in your mirror and see that I'm standing up, eh.' She dared to lift one hand from the back of Mrs Talbot's slatted seat and pointed at Fran, who was talking with Beth about Bob, and where he could be, for he hadn't phoned last night either, and still no letter.

'D'yer reckon I could miss that great big behind of yours in me mirror?' yelled Bert. 'I'm driving as careful as I can, so get back in your seat. I divint want another sore head and nose, and neither do you. Your black eyes are worse today and would scare the wits out of any Nazi squaddie you came up against.'

'I'm not standing here, putting me life at risk, for the good of me health,' Mrs Oborne yelled back. 'And you're no picture either, while we're on about looks. Two black eyes, and a squishy nose.'

The whole bus was laughing. Mrs Oborne, her grey hair tinged green by the Factory chemicals, her lip swollen, her eyes black, snapped: 'Frances Hall, I am standing here looking down at a bride-to-be who looks a real fright – and her bridesmaids look just as bad. I need to take measurements, and what's more, we need to get some leeches on them eyes. I'll speak to your mam, for you're to sing on the fourteenth.'

Beth, who'd been writing a note to Bob, looked up. 'I'd forgotten about the booking with everything that's going on.'

Mrs Oborne sighed, raised her eyebrows and gestured for Fran to stand up. 'You'll not be seeing the dress till you have your fitting, but let me tell you, pet, I reckon you're going to look a picture. Or once the leeches have had a good suck, anyways.'

'Me mam knows all about leeches, Mrs Oborne,' called Sandra. 'She's talking to your mam today, Franny.'

Fran was standing up, waiting. Mrs Oborne shouted to everyone on the bus, 'You're all to keep your mouths tight shut once we get to Sledgeford, for the outfits'll be made in the sewing room at lunchtimes, just as Sarah's were, and I don't want that Amelia shouting about it while we've got that Gaines marching about the place.'

'He were quiet enough yesterday,' said Maisie, 'though he kept a bliddy close eye on us all. Mr Swinton did his best to keep him moving, but . . .'

Mrs Oborne was dragging a tape measure out of her mac pocket. 'Steady as you go, Bert.'

'I heard Cyn Ellington say that Head Office want Gaines to keep an eye on Swinton and Bolton for any sagging in safety and efficiency after the break-in,' said Beth, folding up her letter and putting it in her bag.

Mrs Oborne spun round, yelling to Bert, 'And before you say a word, our Bert, that's nowt for yer to comment on. I'll not have you cast aspersions about me sagging places.'

Fran braced her legs against the seats on either side of the aisle, excitement soaring, for this was her wedding dress they were discussing. Soon she would be Mrs Bedley, and Davey would hold her in his arms, and they would lie together, and . . . She stopped, her arms wide while Beth and Viola steadied her and Mrs Oborne pulled the tape measure around her back, bringing it to the front. She repeated this around Fran's waist, hips and down her leg.

'That'll do. Sit yourself down.'

Fran did while Tilly Oborne made her way back to her seat.

'Aren't you going to write it down, Mrs Oborne?' called Viola.

'No need, lass,' answered Maisie. 'She's a brain like a

calculator. She can remember numbers like nobody's business. It's the cutters she'll have to write it down for.'

As they turned into the main street in Sledgeford, Bert called back, 'Amelia Cartwright's there, again. So, nothing about the fourteenth at the Rising Sun, and nowt about the frock. And cos I said that, I reckon I'm invited to the wedding, and let it be remembered I'm partial to a pint of beer.'

He hooted, braked and stopped. The women of Sledgeford climbed on, with Amelia, Brenda and Rosie the last up the steps. Amelia made her way to the spare seat in front of the four girls. 'You won't mind if I sit here,' Amelia muttered to the baker's wife, Mrs Elson. It wasn't a question. She plonked herself down, swinging her legs round, her arm along the top of the seat, and smiled at them. 'Wedding not far off then, eh, Fran? All ready? Dress made, or are you wearing Sarah's cast-off? Hope your face sorts itself out. Quite a picture. Well, you all are.'

Fran gritted her teeth. How the hell had Ralph gone out with her?

Next to Fran, Sarah shook her head and answered, 'All under control, Amelia, and what's more, I wouldn't call me frock a cast-off. Worn just once and the finest curtain used—'

Beth interrupted: 'But as you weren't asked because you're such an arro—'

Fran took over. 'Yes, as Sarah said, all under control, thanks, Amelia.'

Amelia continued: 'I heard that young Ben did his little best with the gramophone for the dancing, Sarah. But our trio could always entertain your guests, Fran. We would do a friend's price.'

Sarah and Beth gasped and gently pressed their elbows into Fran's ribs. Fran drew in a sharp breath and not just because her ribs still ached, but because she wanted to strangle Amelia. 'We've sorted all that, Amelia,' she said, 'and if we took Ben's role off him, he'd never forgive us. He does it really well too.'

Viola leaned forward. 'I'll be playing the saxophone when he's had enough, but I, of course, won't charge.'

Amelia flushed. 'But how could you charge, when they've rescued you like a stray and given you a place to lay your head?' She swung round to face the front.

There was a long pause, then Beth muttered, 'Oh dear,' as Fran half stood, only to be pulled down by Viola, who shook her head at her, saying, 'I wonder where you'll be working today, you three? You seem to be Mr Swinton's head girls. I heard him tell Miss Ellington yesterday that he could put you in any department and you'd just get on with it, no fuss. Must be a good feeling to be so well thought of, in spite of those eyes, lips and not to mention noses. Howay, best we wear brown paper bags over our heads, or we'll give Amelia nightmares.'

'Best we don't,' muttered Beth, 'then something good'll come out of it.'

Sarah said quietly, as Amelia buried her head in a book, 'Swinton's trained us well, all of us.' She was scratching the rash that covered her arms. 'It's these bliddy chemicals, though. They make me itch and look at yours, Franny. We'll be even more prickly, not to mention yellow, for your wedding. Yellow skin, black eyes and split lips, what—'

Amelia turned. 'Goodness me, talking about chemicals. What would Mr Gaines say, eh, if he got to hear of it?'

Overhearing the exchange, Mrs Oborne yelled, 'He only would if someone on the bus talked out of turn, so we'll know where to point the finger, madam. Besides, it were chemicals they mentioned, Miss Amelia Cartwright. You have chemicals in your lodgings with Valerie, don't you? So shut your noise. We don't want sore ears from your blatherings, and you don't want them neither from having yours boxed.'

'Oh aye,' Valerie called down the bus, 'bleach, or vinegar we have. And a mop. I'll teach you how to use them one day, Amelia. And howay, surely you're not so short of bookings that you have to get shirty because Ben's playing the gramophone. As for being a stray, you'd know all about that – after all, me mam took *you* in.'

Fran leaned forward and whispered, 'Amelia, just give us a chance. Let everyone be your friend, for it must be lonely coming up from the South. We're sore today, our faces are throbbing, our patience is long gone, and though we understand you feel lonely . . .' But she couldn't be bothered. It was true they were sore, but she didn't mind because last night she'd slept and had been dream-free, and all she wanted was for Ralph to recover and to thank him. When they visited, would he be able to hear her? For there had been no improvement, apparently. But it was only a couple of days, so what could they expect?

Amelia pulled her felt hat further down, turned a page in her book and ignored everyone. Fran sat back as Beth said, 'I meant to bring a cushion. These bliddy slats are driving me mad. I think me arse was bruised when the bus swung round.'

'Divint you be telling your Bob,' yelled Valerie, 'or he'll be back here in a jiffy to pat it better.'

They settled back, like the rest of the passengers, and waited for dawn.

At last they approached the Factory, and as Bert pulled into the siding they all rose, gathering up their bags. Aye, thought Fran, just as it always was. As Amelia stood, Fran felt guilty, but knew to look it in the face and push it to one side.

The four of them waited while the bus emptied from the

front. As Amelia stepped out into the aisle they followed her, saying goodbye to Bert when they reached the cab, able to see his black eyes now.

'Leeches,' Beth instructed. 'If we're to suffer, so should the rest of the world.'

'Our Tilly's bringing some round,' he grumped. 'Trust her. Anything to make me suffer.'

Beth leaned closer. 'Anything to make you better. She's missing her sparring partner because she has to be gentle with you.'

'That's being gentle? Lord above,' Bert cackled.

They set off to the gate and were searched as usual. 'Best get rid of those black eyes, girls. You look as though you've done ten rounds in the ring with a heavyweight,' Harry said. 'As for you, Fran Hall, the Bedley boy will do a runner.'

They kept walking, turning left along the narrow path to the entrance of their section building. Mr Gaines was standing just inside, counting them in. His nose was red, with a drip on the end that wobbled as he breathed. They gave him a wide berth and hurried along into the changing rooms. He arrived moments later, and just stood until Cyn Ellington advised him, crisply, to make himself scarce while the women changed and divested themselves of contraband, adding, 'For goodness' sake.'

They slipped into their overalls before Fran checked her hair, throwing a kirby grip into her box. It glinted in the overhead light, and there she was, back in Scotland. Her heart raced, her breathing quickened, she couldn't hear the room, all she could see was the Scottish workshop. She stopped, really seeing it, looking it square in the face, hearing Ralph: *Frances Hall, the dead don't want your sorrow, your guilt. They want you to live – for them. You tried to stop it. That's what's important. So face it, look back at it, see the truth, then give yourself permission to move forward.*

With the fading of his voice, she breathed in deeply, seeing the kirby grip lying in the box, the light still glinting, but she felt the ground beneath her feet, heard the chatter around her and felt quite calm. She stood up straight. Yes, it would come back, but then she'd make it go. Yes, she was sure. She closed her eyes and tried to send these thoughts across to the hospital, into the ward, along to Ralph. Could he hear them?

Sarah nudged her. 'Wake up.'

Gaines entered again, the drip gone. Fran wondered where it had dropped. He cleared his throat, presumably preparatory to spouting the rules, for where was Swinton? Around her, women were sighing. But instead of listing the rules, Gaines folded his arms.

'Now, let's see just how much you *really* know. We'll start this end and you can each provide a nugget, in any order. It'll show me just how well you've really been trained, eh?' He pointed to Valerie. 'You first.'

She began chanting as though it was a times table. 'One. Never speak of work in or out of the Factory.'

Sylvia took up the same chant. 'Two. No matches or lighters to be taken into the workshops.'

Mrs Oborne. 'Three. No eating with fingers which have touched chemicals unless carefully washed first.'

Maisie. 'Four. Wedding rings to be removed or covered. Jewellery, matches, cigarettes in our boxes.'

Sandra. 'Five. No going to the lavatory without an escort.'

Angela. 'Six. No coughing at the workbench—'

Gaines interrupted. 'What happens if you want to cough?'

Geraldine. 'You step away.'

Fran. 'Seven. You wear cotton, no nylon or silk.' She held up her hand and conducted Maisie, who said, 'If only.' Because it was always what she whispered. The others sniggered. Mr Gaines looked round. They looked back.

Sarah said, 'Eight. We wear protective footwear when necessary.'

Beth. 'Nine. We don't have the tannoy on when in the detonator workshop.'

'Why?' Gaines shot back.

Mrs Oborne and Maisie looked at one another and Maisie yelled, 'Because we could singalong with *Workers' Playtime* and blow our bliddy heads off, and yours as well.'

More laughter. Someone said, 'Well, there's a thought.'

On and on they went as the clock ticked. Finally, as though Fran's conducting was catching, Gaines used his hand as a baton, slicing downwards. 'Enough.'

But not for Mrs Oborne, who asked, 'Where's our Mr Swinton, sir? Because he is ours, you know? Wouldn't care to think anything had happened to take him away. He'd miss our panda eyes and our swollen lips.'

There was silence, and everyone looked from Mrs Oborne to Fran to Gaines. Were they expecting Fran to say something too?

Gaines ignored Mrs Oborne as though she was an irritating mosquito and began designating roles for the day. Fran heard herself speaking over him. 'We'd like you to answer Mrs Oborne, Mr Gaines. 'Tis only courteous, and after all, we're his trainees and if he's ill we'd like to know, for we're a team and he's our leader.'

Other women started to add their pennyworth, led by Sarah, who said, 'Aye, would you like us to work through the rules backwards, for we could, we're that well trained. Or you could just tell us where Mr Swinton is.'

'Yes, wouldn't feel comfortable without his beady eye on us.'

'Sick of hearing them rules we were, and having him check our work, but the thing is, we know our jobs inside out, thanks to the old bugger.'

'Hated the whole bliddy nagging till we came to realise it saved our lives.'

Mr Gaines peered around the changing room. 'Mr Swinton is keeping an eye on the workshops, and now, if you don't very much mind, I will continue with today's placements.' His voice was icy.

Miss Ellington had not said anything, she just stood listening, and so they could tell that she agreed with their every word. The door opened and yet another new security officer entered, then stood beside her.

Fran smiled a little, for they'd be checked properly for contraband before they left the room. It was then that she drew back her shoulders and lifted her head, accepting that it was, indeed, the SOs who were the final checkers – not Fran Hall. So, you were right, Ralph Massingham, she thought.

As the time drew near to six, the start of the shift, Gaines's voice penetrated Fran's thoughts about Ralph. 'Young, Jones, Hall and Hall on detonators.'

Hall and Hall, Fran thought, smiling at Mrs Stanhope Hall, while Beth muttered, 'Detonators, of course we bliddy are.'

'Better than the pellets,' said Sarah. 'With the wedding coming up we don't want a group of rash-covered daffodils gliding up the aisle.'

'But no music while we work,' Fran mused. 'That's a shame.'

'Aye,' Sarah agreed. 'My Stan and me were talking of "All or Nothing at All" before we got up, reckoning we should sing it at the pub and then have it at the wedding, and you, Franny, could dance—'

Gaines was approaching. 'Did I say you could talk?'

Quickly, Fran replied, 'We thought you were done, Mr Gaines. Just on our way, Mr Gaines. Won't be no trouble, Mr Gaines.'

Beth moved her along. 'Shut up,' she whispered as he

said to Viola, 'Miss Viola Ross? If you can sew, you can fill detonators.'

At that, everyone stopped dead, turned and looked at him. Miss Ellington forced her way through. She took hold of Viola's wrist, showing Gaines the half-amputated hand, still bandaged. 'You know perfectly well, because Mr Swinton and I told you, and even Mr Bolton had it on the list he gave you, that this young woman has already paid the price for working with explosives, and therefore she is not suited for anything but the sewing workshop. Just as I can no longer work as an operative.' She waggled her handless arm in his face. 'It was blown off in a detonator shop. This lass cannot afford to lose another.'

Mr Gaines held steady, gimlet-eyed, his voice grim. 'That's as maybe, but we're short, and targets—'

From the doorway came Mr Bolton's voice. 'I do believe I'm correct, am I not, Mr Gaines, that Viola is for the moment incapacitated. I admire zeal, but only in its place.'

Viola spoke up. 'But mebbe Mr Gaines is right, if I can sew—'

'You can't work with detonators,' Fran insisted, unable to bear the thought of her friend at risk and she, Fran Hall, doing and saying nothing. 'Not yet, it's too soon, you know perfectly well it hurts. You will shake, you will wince, something will go wrong, and I'm not bliddy having another—' Fran stopped dead. 'I just think it's too soon.'

Mr Gaines coughed; it was an ineffectual noise, and his colour was high as he nodded. 'Perhaps I can find someone else for the detonators. Off you go, all of you, and to the sewing workshop with you, Miss Ross.'

His capitulation was so sudden, Fran thought. Was he embarrassed? Couldn't admit it? But then they were all hustled along to their workstations, the four girls wearing non-spark felt shoes.

Chapter Ten

As they headed down the corridor, Beth patted the wall and the posters that were stuck all along it, and whispered, 'You behave, wall. No bulging. Not that it were your fault. Explosions do that to walls.'

Sarah laughed. 'Give it a pat for me and all, pet.'

Fran nudged her. 'And one for me and Sandra.'

Beth slapped each poster four times. Valerie joined them as she was for the detonator workshop too, with Mrs Oborne some way behind.

'By,' said Sarah, 'I can still picture that wall bulging, then returning. Like a bliddy wave coming in and going out.'

'And the floor lifting, tossing us about. How many other workers will be hurt before the war is over? How many will suffer from breathing in the chemicals?' whispered Valerie.

Who knew, Beth thought. Best not to think about it.

'I hate the rash from the fulminate of mercury especially,' Sarah said suddenly.

Beth smiled. 'At least you've got your Stan to scratch your back these days.'

Sarah flushed. 'Oh Beth . . .'

'And so far,' murmured Valerie, 'we're not mad like hatters from the mercury.'

Fran grinned. 'Ah, that's what you think, but how would we know, for we'll all go daft together.'

Beth listened, but didn't respond, because she was thinking of Stan, scratching Sarah's back, and why, oh why hadn't

Bob been in touch? She missed him terribly, and felt a fool waiting in the cold for a whole hour last night before traipsing home, trying to pretend it didn't matter, shaking her head at her mam, who had said, 'He'll have written, pet, saying he's been sent to sea. You know what the post's like.'

She sighed, hating the detonators: the tiny copper caps used to initiate a weapon's triggering process. Well, it wasn't so much the copper tiddlers she hated as the disgusting, highly sensitive lead azide, which looked so like sugar, and the fulminate of mercury that was so sensitive it was like Amelia. She laughed to herself. Oh aye, that lass was sensitive, but happy to put the boot in whenever she pleased. Beth smiled again. Well, that really was mercury to a T.

They entered the silent room to take the place of the night shift. The women who were leaving had tiredness writ large on their faces, scratching themselves through their clothes because they must not touch their skin. It was so quiet. No footfall, only the soft swish of felt shoes. No talking, only whispering. No music, just danger. As they passed, everyone ignored the girls' bumps and bruises just as they had done yesterday, knowing sympathy was not needed. They waited for Swinton to reach them, never before thinking they'd be pleased and relieved to see him. Beth tried to concentrate on him, not the fulminate of mercury that could break down and leak into their skin or be breathed into their lungs . . . She could feel the itching increase at the very thought.

She felt her split lips, touched her sore nose and half-closed eyes, for she must not touch them again while in here. It was this she would think about, her safety here and Bob's at sea, for that must be where he was, and she must stop being so bliddy selfish and mithering about a letter and a phone call.

'Maintenance repaired everything so quickly after the explosion. It just took a few days to get it all back up and running again,' whispered Fran.

Sarah nudged her. 'Aye, well, we have targets, just as the pitmen have. Look how quick they cleared Bell Seam, eh. Stan—'

'Oh, here we go, back to Stan,' Fran whispered, winking at Beth. Then she grew serious, her voice little more than a breath. 'You have to concentrate, our Sarah. No mooning over me brother. You too, Beth. No worrying about Bob.'

Swinton had reached them. He held up a finger, his voice so quiet they had to lean in towards him. 'No more talking, not even whispering. Remember, it has been outlawed in detonators since the accident.'

They followed him to the workbench and stood by the stainless-steel barriers with the Perspex windows. Beth loathed the masks they had to wear, because the cotton-wool wadding grew hot and itched.

'On you go, lasses,' Swinton whispered, 'and be safe.'

The pitman's prayer, eh, thought Beth, from the mouth of Swinton who had never been ... She stopped. Or had he once been a pitman? She looked closely and there, just showing above the collar of his overalls, was the blue scar she was seeking.

'Oh, I never thought ...' she whispered. 'You were one of us?'

'Oh aye, till I hurt me back too bad, so then I went into the chemical factory. That's why I'm here. Now, you know the drill, but I will tell you again: concentrate, concentrate, concentrate. I'll be here. Patrick's in pellets.' Beth watched as he moved on to the rest of the shift, giving the same instructions.

The girl who stood next to Fran breathed quietly, 'Come on, no loitering, we've targets, you know.'

'Uh-oh,' Sarah whispered.

Fran merely pulled down her mask and whispered to the girl, 'Teaching your grandma to suck eggs, eh.' With a snap she returned the mask to its rightful position. The girl began to work, realising any more comments would not be a good idea. Sandra, further along, nodded and her black eyes crinkled. By, that must have hurt, thought Beth.

They collected their small containers of fulminate of mercury from the hatch and carried them back to the workbench; at first the containers had been carried in through the external door, but that had proved too dangerous. The belt brought along the first tray of copper caps and Beth lifted it onto the side and sprinkled mercury into them one by one, using the spoon thingy, as they called it. As always, Beth's head began to ache but it didn't stop her working quickly, far quicker than the bossyboots next to Fran, for they were the cream of Swinton's workers.

She smiled, for she was the cream of women in Bob's eyes too, and he loved her as much as she loved him. She stopped, the spoon full of chemicals held above the detonator caps, the copper glinting, her breath uneven, for she realised that Bob had not said at the wedding tea that he loved her. He'd just said that he knew she loved him. Or was she wrong? She tried to think.

'Beth,' whispered Fran, 'don't stop, we've targets.'

She nodded and worked on, and in spite of the mask could almost feel the powder seeping into her split lips, into her lungs. And from her lungs to the rest of her organs, not to mention into her skin. She'd itch tonight worse than ever, but as long as she didn't make a mistake, as long as there wasn't an explosion, she'd be alive enough to scratch. If Bob was here, he could scratch for her, or rub in lavender grease. If. If. Where was he? At sea? On shore, as he'd said? Where? Why no word? Why no words of love at the wedding, for she truly couldn't remember a single one.

As she placed the copper cap in its stand, she decided she would go again to the telephone box at nine, and the next night, and the next. He'd said he was in refit. He hadn't said he loved her, but his eyes had, hadn't they? She shook her head. Work. Concentrate.

She sprinkled more powder on more copper caps as the hours passed, then returned each tray to the hatch. She finished another tray, took another from the belt as it trundled along. Was Fran right? she wondered. Did the hatters really know they were going mad, or was it just everyone around them who saw?

Be quiet. Concentrate. She sprinkled the powder. Was her headache improving? She felt a cough coming. She lay down the powder container and spoon and stepped back, coughing. Sarah worked on, as did Fran, who turned briefly to check her. Beth nodded. Fran's eyes crinkled.

She was a good one was Fran, always there for you, but Sarah had a lot of gumption too, for she'd held Fran and the others together in the explosion at the Scottish factory. Or so Fran had said. Aye, she'd kept them saying their times tables as they lay under the bricks that took Viola's hand. But no, it was the machine that had done that, sliced right through.

Sarah stepped back from the bench now, coughing alongside Beth, whispering, 'I always think it's the bliddy powder, but I expect it's because my throat's dry and I need a drink. If I start swinging from the ceiling lights, you'll know I've gone mad.'

They laughed so quietly it was little more than silence, and then stepped back to the bench. On they worked until their break was called. The girl who had told them to 'Come on, no loitering,' looked at Fran as they walked to the door. 'I need to learn to keep me mouth shut. You're all much quicker, cleaner, sharper than me.'

Fran shook her head as they left the workshop. 'Howay, lass, you will be grand.' It was enough, for the lass was part of the team and they needed to stick together.

At lunchtime they joined Mrs Oborne, Valerie, Maisie and Viola in the queue for shepherd's pie, having first washed their hands. Clean hands, clean everything, Beth thought. She looked down at the shepherd's pie, which seemed to be mostly carrots and potatoes, but hot, though the plates were cold. They sat at their usual table as they wolfed it down, their turbans dusty with chemicals, their overalls too, but they'd shake them out, hang them up, and they would be washed. As they ate it was good to hear music being played over the tannoy. Mrs Oborne wondered aloud if there was more news of Ralph. Who knew? Beth thought, and shrugged along with the others.

Valerie asked if there was news of Bob. There wasn't. 'Perhaps he's gone to sea,' Beth said. 'He went in such a rush we didn't have time to say much except what a bugger the war is. 'Tis all so complicated, or something like that, he said.'

Maisie laughed and her eyes sparkled, her freckles seemed to dance. 'Aye, that's true enough. Here we are, working where we could get blown up, and itching like a cloud of midges have got at us, but on the other hand we're taking home enough to pay the rent and not worry about where the next penny's coming from, so 'tis good in a way.'

'Aye, till we get blown up, or lose a hand or . . .' Sandra

stopped and looked at Viola, avoiding staring at her damaged hand. 'Strange old world,' she ended up, embarrassed.

Mrs Oborne stepped into the breach. 'But enough of that. What are you Factory Girls singing at the Rising Sun?'

Cyn Ellington came along at that moment. 'Hush up, Tilly. If I heard that, so did others, and Bert said to keep it quiet in case Amelia, Brenda and Rosie get wind of it and muscle in on the booking.'

Sarah shook her head. 'My Stan said that wouldn't happen. Stevie and Mildred are wise to her now and would elbow her back where she came from, but I reckon we should rehearse. We've done nowt. Can we use the storeroom, Miss Ellington?'

'No sign of Gaines,' said Miss Ellington, 'so why not skedaddle there while you have the chance. If he appears, or Miss high-heels Amelia clippity-clops along, we'll give you a knock.'

The three girls looked at Viola. Fran said, 'You'll sing, or play too, of course, so up you get. You're one of The Factory Girls now, so no slouching. Aye, and the fee will go four ways.'

Beth scraped her pudding bowl, then pushed back her chair as Fran headed for the storeroom, disappearing inside. Beth held back the others. 'We need to spring a surprise song on her and Davey at the wedding, so keep an eye on which one is her favourite, eh.'

'Aye, that'll please 'em,' Sarah agreed.

They hurried after Fran, with Beth saying, 'Bob's favourite is "Ten Cents a Dance". Who knows, he might come if it turns out he *is* in refit. It needs a saxophone too, Viola, if your hand's up to it.'

They entered the storeroom, its shelves full of cleaning materials, mops and buckets resting against the grubby whitewashed walls. Fran conducted them into the two they liked best: 'Embraceable You' and 'Putting on the Ritz', both of which they had prepared for New Year's Eve at the Rising Sun. Viola followed them, picking up the words. They ran through them a second time, and grinned at one another. Beth nodded. 'Aye, I reckon we've got those nailed, eh?'

There was a knock on the storeroom door. 'Time's up, girls.' It was Tilly Oborne. 'Make sure you sing "My Baby Just Cares For Me". My old bugger likes it, and I have to give him a treat from time to time. Not enough to spoil him, mind.'

They were laughing as they rejoined the clatter of cutlery and the chatter that drowned out the tannoy. There was the scrape of chairs as women saw the time and rushed to place their dirty plates on the trolley. The girls hurried back to their table and drank up their glasses of water. For a moment, as they headed for the door, Sarah linked arms with Fran. 'Any other favourites?'

'I love "It Had to Be You",' said Fran. 'It's what I think of Davey, you see. I've thought it since we were wee bairns, and now I'm the most beautiful woman . . .'

The nearest tables heard and clapped. Fran curtsied. Someone else called out, 'What about "On the Sunny Side of the Street"?'

Miss Ellington had locked the storeroom door and joined them, saying quietly, ' "My Baby Just Cares for Me" is a favourite of someone I know.' She raised her eyebrows and her pale skin flushed, her face alive with fun.

'That wouldn't be a certain Mr Parrot, would it? He who lets you give his canaries some chickweed from time to time if you're very good? That certain Simon Parrot who runs the Canary Club now Beth, Sarah and Fran's fathers are on their cloud?' It was Viola who said this.

Miss Ellington winked at Beth. 'Aye, this Viola's turned

into one of you, no doubt about that. But why not, when she's living with Fran. You have moved in, haven't you? Makes sense, for otherwise there's too many women bossing our Stan around.'

They were all sniggering, but Miss Ellington looked at the clock above the door and became serious. 'Back to work now. All of you, concentrate, eh? And Viola, make sure Mrs Oborne's written her measurements for the wedding dresses and 'tis kept safe, for we'll need them for the cutouts. Best to bring in the material soon, while Barry and Harry are on the fore shift.'

Viola set off across the canteen to the sewing room, waving, and it was only then that the others saw the bloodstained bandage around her hand.

'I'll just go and fix that,' muttered Miss Ellington, 'but she's not really right. It's the repetitive work on the sewing machines that does it, and we mustn't have it going septic. It gets no time to heal, you see.'

Fran shook her head, saying as they headed to the detonators, 'She insists on working, says she needs to pay her way at the house, but Mam says we can manage. Too bliddy proud, that's what she is.'

'No, we'd all feel the same,' said Sarah, 'but we need to keep that hand properly bandaged.'

Maisie was whistling as she came along the corridor behind them and Beth asked, 'Does your mam need help in the shop, Maisie?'

Maisie shook her head. 'This Emily seems to be working out well. Why, are you thinking of moving jobs, our Beth?' She was laughing.

Beth just shrugged. 'We're worried about Viola working with that hand.' They walked on, Beth touching the posters, muttering each time, 'You behave, wall.'

Fran looked thoughtful. 'Mam was saying that eleven

bairns are too many for Sophia to manage, and the co-op are all on the lookout for someone to help out. I wonder about Viola. What d'you all think?'

'Good idea,' Beth muttered. 'They'll pay well too, I reckon, and she'd be good with bairns.'

'I'll give Viola a nudge when I get home, on the quiet,' said Fran.

Beth pulled a face. 'As long as she doesn't think you're trying to get rid of her, for divint forget she'll have to live at Massingham Hall.'

'Ah, aye, you're right.'

They all fell silent.

'We'll box clever then,' suggested Sarah. 'Just say poor Sophia is looking for someone, and maybe she'll take the bait.'

As they neared the workshop they heard Mrs Oborne panting up behind them. She tapped Sarah on the shoulder. 'I heard all that, and don't you worry. You work on Viola, and the co-op will set to work on Sophia.' Mrs Oborne's laugh was hearty.

All four were standing in the corridor as the workers returned, because they could tell Mrs Oborne hadn't finished. 'Mark you,' she continued, 'they'll get to work on Viola too, make her feel sorry for Sophia. Aye, we can start that on the bus, all of us. Poor wee thing, we can say, with all them bairns and the worry of Ralph, and there's Mr Massingham right busy, and how can she manage when the nanny went months ago after making a fuss about a few wet beds? I mean to say, what if Sophia breaks in half, eh? What happens to the bairns then? It would be our faults for not doing more . . .'

The girls shook their heads, their mouths hanging open. Finally, Fran said, 'You're wicked, and so is the co-op. Mere mortals don't stand a chance.'

Sarah was walking backwards towards the door. 'That's more than enough to make anyone feel sorry for someone, but you know, I reckon it's close to the truth for Sophia's been looking right pale, and that were before Ralph . . . I do so wonder how the lad is. I really want to see him on Saturday.'

Mr Swinton was holding the door open, his green overalls not as pristine as Gaines's, but pretty close. He was thinner than before, Beth thought. And older, his grey hair tinged yellow. But of course, why wouldn't he be, he was around the chemicals too. 'In you get, you lot,' he said quietly. 'Time's a-wasting.'

'You were all nearly late,' Mr Gaines shouted from behind them, 'chatting and laughing. That's no way to win a war.'

Still holding the door, Mr Swinton called softly, 'No shouting, if you please, Mr Gaines, this is a silent area and they were not late. I hope you put that in your little black book to report to Head Office, for Mr Bolton runs a good section and you have yet to visit the others, or so I hear. Any timetable for moving on to them?'

Mr Gaines swished back along the corridor and Mr Swinton looked after him, not at the girls as they passed by into the workshop.

'Well,' whispered Fran. 'That were telling him.'

Chapter Eleven

Friday, 6 March

After the fore shift, Fran, Viola, Sarah and Beth congregated at Beth's house, sitting around Audrey Smith's kitchen table, the range clicking as the fire belted out the heat. It was four o'clock and they were waiting for the arrival of their mams, who were bringing back the leeches from a local woman, Mrs Merryweather. The girls wished it was a normal day and that the women were up at the Hall instead, but this afternoon it was Madge and Susie, from Allotment Terrace, who were helping not just Sophia, but Mrs Phillips' niece, Joy, who had been taken on as nanny.

It had put them all in a worse mood, but they had to be careful what they said, for Viola wasn't aware of their proposed plan for her to give up the Factory.

Beth hoped the girl wouldn't last, because what had Mrs Phillips said? Oh, yes: 'Maybe a miracle will happen and we can make a silk purse out of a sow's ear.' And then there was Sandra. How on earth could that accident have happened?

As though reading her mind, Sarah said, 'I wonder how Sandra is?'

'I know,' Fran said, leaning forward and tracing the pattern on the oilskin tablecloth. 'I keep thinking of her. Her mam is at the hospital with her, but it was such a freak thing. How could a dropped lunch plate chuck up a splinter like that, right into her eye? Caught the table, they say, and bang, bit like shrapnel. By, I can hardly bear to think of the pain. And we four laughing away in the sewing room, fitting the paper pattern, never realising until she wasn't at the workbench. Made me feel real bad, still does. She was making me laugh on the bus on the way in.'

Sarah was nodding. 'Poor lass. Not working at the Factory long. But you know, her mam told the co-op before she shot off for the hospital that she were glad, for a bad eye'll keep her out of the bliddy danger zone for a while. We'll know more tomorrow when we go in to see Ralph, for we can nip into the women's ward and visit her too.' She put her hand over one eye, and tried to work out how much anyone could see.

'Well, she might not lose her sight, remember,' muttered Beth. 'Maybe they can hoick the splinter out. If not, she'll get comfort from Madge – look how she gets about, and she'd take the lass under her wing. At least Gaines canna have a go. That could have happened in her own home.'

The kettle had begun to boil, so Beth hurried over to the range and moved it to the simmer plate. The rattling of the lid ceased but she stayed watching it, all the time listening for footsteps in the yard. Nothing. She tidied the brass rail, folded the tea towels and looked up at the clock on the mantelpiece and her da's clay pipe, her mam's wedding photo, and her own. She reached up to touch the image of Bob, so smart in his bridegroom's suit.

Yet again, she'd found no letter waiting when she'd rushed home today, but she'd be at the telephone box as usual this evening. And tomorrow she'd touch the posters as they headed for the detonator workshop, and again the next day, for luck, theirs and his, for if he was at sea, he must be safe. She thought again of Sandra. Poor wee lass, but she'd have some time off for it to heal, for she mustn't get chemicals in it, or would she wear an eyepatch and come in? No, they hadn't let Madge work there. Oh shut up, she told herself. The lass would be fine, surely.

She sat with a thump in her da's armchair, running her hands over the threadbare arms, leaning back as once he had, watching Viola easing her poor hand, trying to find a way to rest it comfortably on the kitchen table. 'Howay, Viola, come and sit in me da's chair. I've got it warmed up for you.'

Viola shook her head. 'I'm all right, Beth, really I am. I was just thinking of Sandra, of leeches, of poor Ralph.' She dropped her hands to her lap.

No, you're far from all right, bonny lass, thought Beth, knowing from Fran's glance that she felt the same. 'Has Sandra's accident, and Ralph's, brought back bad memories?' she asked. 'You know, with your hand?'

Viola looked surprised. 'Oh no, not my hand. It's these leeches, as well as poor Ralph and Sandra.' She grimaced and fell silent.

Sarah rose and paced backwards and forwards, digging her hands in her cardigan pockets. 'I canna quite like the thought of them leeches either latching on to me face and sucking out the blood. Bad enough on the moor when we went there to collect the moss with the mams – do you remember, Beth?'

Beth nodded for she certainly did, and how sometimes when they were up to their ankles in the peat bog the little buggers would latch on to any bare flesh, then have to be burned off with the end of a Woodbine.

It was Fran who said, 'Stan were muttering that he and the lads would stand guard in your backyard, Beth, and dash in to burn 'em off when they'd sucked out the dead blood. And Sarah, it was your mam who said she'd clip his ear, for the leeches had to go back to Mrs Merryweather since she'll need 'em again.'

Viola held up her hand. They heard the sneck on the back gate being lifted. In the silence that fell in the kitchen the clatter of footsteps drew closer. The back door opened, and the girls sprang to their feet. Beth stared at the jam jars the mams carried, which contained the long black leeches. 'Thank heavens the lids are on,' murmured Viola, sitting down again with a thump, then standing and slipping from the table towards the door. 'You know, I reckon . . .'

Mrs Hall blocked Viola's escape route. 'I reckon, Viola, that you are going to sit down and be administered to, pet.'

Viola backed towards the chair and sat. 'Whatever was I thinking?' she muttered.

'Indeed,' Fran whispered.

Beth laughed, and Annie Hall turned to her. 'Since you are already hogging an armchair, sit down, put your head back and do as you're told, bonny lass.' She nodded to Audrey Smith. 'She's your problem, Audrey, best get to work. There's a wedding in four weeks or so. They're performing at the Rising Sun in little more than a week, and tomorrow they're on the rota for a visit to Ralph. Canna have them scaring the vicar at the wedding, the customers at the Rising Sun or the patients at the hospital, not to mention if Ralph came round and there they were, a crowd of pandas. He'd think he'd died and gone to Noah's ark or something.'

Fran took it upon herself to crosstalk her mam. 'I'd think more kindly of you all if you weren't enjoying it, but you're dribbling with the very thought of getting them . . .'

Her mam turned on her heel and followed Mrs Bedley and Mrs Smith into the scullery. The girls exchanged looks. Beth gripped the arms of her da's chair and waited. It didn't take long for her mam to emerge. Then it registered with Beth that her mam's headscarf was still tied beneath her chin, and she still wore her mac and boots. Boots in the kitchen? Was her mam as nervous as she was, then? She saw that her mam's hands were freshly washed as she brandished some tweezers, and that the jam jar's lid had been removed.

'I'd like to register a complaint,' Beth said.

'Ignored,' muttered her mam, concentrating on using the tweezers to lift a leech from the jar without hurting it. 'Little beggars they are now, slim as you like. But not for long, soon plump up when they're doing their job.'

Beth felt her innards contracting with horror. Her mam snapped, 'Lie back, close your eyes, and think of England.' When her mam used that tone, Beth knew obedience was the only course. She lay back but before she closed her eyes she looked at the other three, who sat frozen, watching her. The other two mams were about to approach when Madge came in from the yard wearing a silver eyepatch.

'I've me own tweezers. And a pot of little fellows.'

'You should be up at the Hall, helping Sophia,' Fran shouted.

'D'you think I'd miss this? I've left Susie and Mr Massingham helping that Joy, but if ever a name was misplaced that's it. She has a mouth which turns down so far it touches her chin. Young Eva said if it were a bag, everything would fall out.'

Her mam loomed over Beth, smiling. 'It won't hurt, lass, and soon you'll be back to being a bit yellow and just as beautiful as you were the day you married your Bob.'

As the tweezers approached, and her mother's forehead crinkled in a frown of concentration, Beth shut her eyes.

'Divint open your peepers, whatever you do,' her mam murmured. 'Or they'll have a munch.'

'Mam,' wailed Beth. 'Don't say that.'

Beth felt the leech touch her skin, a cool length of something living that contracted, moved, clung. Then another, and another, and instead of trying to imagine what was happening, she thought of Bob, of the music they'd danced to at the wedding, of the bairns they would have. Would they be dark like him, or pale-skinned with auburn hair like her? Would they play with Fran and Davey's bairns, and Sarah and Stan's? Who would Viola marry? Norm? Or perhaps Sid? Would poor Ralph recover? Would Sandra be all right? When would the war end? Would Bob go back to the Minton pit? But she didn't want to leave Massingham. Perhaps he'd join Auld Hilda? Perhaps, but first they all had to survive.

The next day, after the shift and once they'd bathed, Alfie met them at the top of Sarah's back lane. The girls were nervous because they didn't know how Ralph would look, or how Sandra was, and they wanted to turn around and go home. Alfie tossed his cigarette into the gutter as the four girls clambered into the car, but as he began to drive away, Stan, Sid and Norm came running out of the back lane, flagging him down.

'Room for three little ones?'

Alfie opened his window. 'Hooligans, the lot of you. Get in, one next to me, the girls on your laps in the back. Out you get, girls – let the louts in.'

After the kerfuffle they set off again, with Viola in the front, to preserve her hand, Fran on Norm's lap, Beth on Sid's, and Stan with his arms around Sarah.

'Yer'll pick us up, will yer, Alfie?' yelled Stan. 'If not, Ben and his new marrer William said they'd cycle the bikes to the station. It'll take several trips for them, though, and they have homework . . . They said they'd phone the Hall to find out, unless you drop into 14 Leadenhall to let him know on your way back.'

Alfie looked at Stan in the mirror. 'Course I'll bring you

back. I'm not having you lot cluttering up the roads, and besides, the boss'd have me guts for garters.'

'Any news?' asked Viola.

Alfie was serious now. 'Nary a bit. I divint know he were capable of doing such a thing – heading straight into the bliddy tree instead of making it worse for you lasses. How did you like the leeches? Worked their magic, though. I reckon you won't scare Thompkins' horses now.'

Fran reached forward and snatched off his cap. 'One more word about the worst experience of my life and this goes out of the window.' She tossed the cap to Viola. 'See he behaves.'

She sat back against Norm, who whispered, 'Were it right bad?'

Fran shuddered. 'Not so much the sucking, though it did sting, but it was seeing the little beggars turn into big beggars. Anyway, the bruise has almost gone, and it's just a deeper yellow.'

They were in good time for the train, and as their tickets had already been arranged by the Massinghams all they had to do was collect them and wait on the platform. The lads huddled together over their Woodbines, while the girls shared the lippy that Sophia had given their mams to pass on.

It was then Fran asked the question of Beth: 'Any letter?'

Beth shook her head. Viola slipped her good hand through Beth's arm. 'He must have been rushed on board?'

Beth just nodded. She had written each night to his lodgings, just in case the refit was still going on. If he had been sent to sea, the letters would be there for him on his return. If he hadn't . . . Well, it might be that they were too busy. 'Howay, wherever he is, he'll be safe, for I touch the posters,' she murmured.

Viola pulled a face. Beth laughed quietly. 'We say to the

pitmen "be safe" and have to believe it works – and it does, sometimes. So I touch me posters.'

The train took half an hour, then they caught a bus, reaching the Royal Victoria Infirmary in time for visiting hours. They stomped up the stairs in their boots, and along the gleaming corridors, heading for the ward where Stan and Davey had lain, which was now where Ralph 'existed'. For that was the word they'd arrived at. Suddenly, Stan stopped, his hand up like a traffic policeman.

'Stand by, enemy approaching.'

They all laughed, for it was Sister Newsome, her beautiful thin face alert with humour. She stopped in front of them. 'Ah, your turn on the rota, eh? Only two at a time, the rules say, though I have left a probationer nurse in charge and she might not know them.' She winked. They grinned, and she looked at Viola. 'Hold up that hand.'

Viola did, for no one ever disobeyed Sister Newsome, not even her husband, Dr Wilson, they suspected.

Sister Newsome shook her head. 'Aye, as I thought, and as the co-op told me on their visit to Ralph. So, we need to find you a different job, my girl. You need do nothing to facilitate that, for the co-op is on the prowl. However, until such time as they find something appropriate, you will take the utmost care. I do not want you returning to receive my tender care, for if you are readmitted I will make it my task to take over the women's ward again just to punish you. Is that quite clear?' She was talking to them all, and they nodded.

Sister Newsome stood to one side. 'In you go, then. Talk quietly about normal life, though what the hell that is these days, who knows. Try nature, the evacuees. Touch him, gently. Sing to him, quietly. Not you, Stan, I beg you, for you have a voice like a foghorn.'

Sid and Norm sniggered, but stopped when Sister

Newsome's gaze swept over them. 'Yours, my lads, are absolutely no better. I seem to remember you were here one Christmas with broken arms after a pit accident and quite upset Father Christmas on his rounds. Such rude words to a carol, indeed, and not even in tune. Carry on. Don't forget Sandra is just along the other end of the corridor.'

She marched off, and now they laughed to one another, for Sister Newsome was the best of the best. She never, ever forgot a patient, and would go to the ends of the earth for each and every one.

They entered the ward through the double doors, leaving them swinging in their wake. Visiting hours had already begun and there was a low murmur in the ward. A young nurse sat at her table in the middle. She looked up as they all tiptoed to her, their boots making as little noise as possible. 'Ah,' she said, her dark hair tucked in a bun, with just a few strands escaping the starched white cap. Fran thought she looked about twelve. 'Sister Newsome mentioned that four pandas would be visiting Ralph, and possibly some pitmen. But I see no pandas with my little eyes?'

'Indeed not, pet,' murmured Sarah. 'Our mams obtained leeches.'

The probationer nurse merely nodded. 'Oh yes, Sister Newsome's suggestion when they telephoned from Massingham Hall about the rota. Leeches work a treat. Ralph is in bed four. We tried moving him to a quieter room, but he became distressed. Sister Newsome was delighted, for it showed he was responding to something, but what? That is the mystery, and where is he in his mind? So, he is back in the ward. When his brain has rested, we hope for his full recovery.'

'When, not if?' Stan asked.

The nurse, whose badge proclaimed her to be Nurse

Williams, nodded. 'I like to say when, and deal with if only if I have to.'

'Lord,' Fran whispered as they walked away, 'sitting at that table is another Sister Newsome in the making.'

'I'll be first in the lifeboat,' murmured Sid.

They ranged themselves around the bed, and there Ralph was, washed free of blood and as white as the bandage around his head. He breathed lightly, quietly. Almost not at all. They took turns to sit and hold his hand, so warm, but of course, because he was alive, and anyway, the ward was too hot. Viola felt overwhelmed when it was her turn to reach out to hold his hand, for her heart had twisted at the sight of him. Why? She barely knew him. His hand was heavy, non-responsive, his palm slightly damp.

She talked of the Factory, for that was all they could call it, of the wedding dress that must be made, of the buds that would be breaking when he came home, and of the songs they would sing at Fran's wedding tea.

'You mustn't miss the wedding, Ralph. What would Eva say, eh? She has a new nanny whose mouth turns down. Eva says if it was a bag everything would fall out, crash, bang.' She paused, for it brought memories of the car crash, and the broken plate, the splinter darting up.

She gripped his hand. Poor Ralph, poor Sandra. She examined his face – he seemed peaceful. The top of his ear had gone; his bandage was pristine. She looked at her hand resting in her lap. The blood was seeping through her bandage and how she wished it was she, not Joy, who had the job, for then she would get better and easily able to look after Sophia, the bairns, and perhaps Ralph would be home and in need.

As the others talked quietly amongst themselves, she

whispered to Ralph, 'I haven't been able to admit that a different job is the only thing that will help the healing, and the pain. But who knows, perhaps Joy might turn into a silk purse and be better than me. Besides, how could I leave the Halls, after all they've done?'

Viola stopped, then went on, her voice louder now, 'But enough of that. Alfie drove us to the station. Our Ben is doing his homework, but finding time with William to work on crosswords. You remember him doing that, like Davey, eh, but with George? George has moved to Devon with his family to be nearer his mam's family.'

She heard Sid's whisper in her ear: 'See Ralph's ear? By, pet, you make two bookends, you do. Must have been the windscreen glass.'

'Aye, I did see it,' she murmured. 'You drove off the road to keep us safe. You poor, poor lad.'

As Viola fell silent, she heard Fran, Beth and Sarah begin to sing, very quietly, on the other side of the bed:

> There's a long, long trail a-winding
> Into the land of my dreams . . .

Viola joined in, singing as softly as they were. The lads almost whispered the words, but contrary to Sister Newsome's accusations their voices were deep and true.

The singing grew louder, for the other visitors were joining in, as were the patients, and they moved on to 'Keep the Home Fires Burning'. While they sang, Viola leaned close to Ralph. 'This is for you, Ralph. All for you, bonny lad. You rest now, and wake when you're ready. There'll be some of us Massingham folk here every day, so you won't be alone, and believe me, we won't let you go, d'you hear? Because we claim you. Do you understand – we *claim* you.'

He didn't respond, or stir, but words didn't just disappear, she thought. They would reach him, just as her breath had swept his face.

Ten minutes before the end of visiting, the girls sped along the corridor, leaving the lads chatting to the unresponsive Ralph, not holding his hand, but patting his arm in a way that made the girls laugh. They entered the ward to see Meryl standing beside Sandra's bed, straightening the sheets. The lass was sitting up against a pile of pillows, and waved. She had a pad over her left eye, secured by bandages wound around her head.

The girls clustered round, Fran telling Sandra she and Ralph should share a room and gossip about Massingham. The thrill might help them both. Viola smiled, but again there was that twist in her heart. What the hell was the matter with her? She could still feel the weight of Ralph's hand, its warmth, and again the twist. He had watched her as she played the saxophone at Sarah's wedding, his smile so kind, and there he was, lying in the bed, so vulnerable.

Meryl settled back on her chair, and they asked how Sandra was until the girl laughed. 'I am here, you should ask *me* how I feel.'

Viola came to her senses. 'Well,' she said. 'How do you feel? What does the doctor say?'

Her mam laughed, a deep and throaty laugh. 'She's feeling nowt for she's on painkillers, and the doctors say nowt for they can't tell yet, beyond they've got the little beggar out.'

'Little? *Little*?' queried Sandra. 'It were a bliddy great lump. But how's the lad?'

'Same as everyone says,' answered Sarah. 'Existing. I wonder what he's thinking, *if* he's thinking? If his brain was outside his skull, we'd slap a few leeches on it and suck the bruise out.'

They grimaced. Fran said, 'But we canna do that, that's the problem.' Viola could see that she was upset.

'It's not fair,' said Beth, 'septicaemia and then this. And I felt I were looking at his dead body . . .' Her voice broke.

Suddenly even Sandra was biting her lip. 'Aye, I slipped along this morning. It broke me heart.' She pointed at her eye. 'This is nothing. If I lose me sight in this eye, I can compete with Madge for the best eyepatch. But that lad . . . What if he doesn't wake? Well, he saved us all that day.'

As they left the hospital, they saw Professor Smythe approach with a younger man in tow.

'Visiting Ralph, sir?' Stan called out. 'Not sure you'll be allowed into the ward.'

Professor Smythe reached them, lifting his homburg to them all. 'Ah well, I might be allowed to slip past the redoubtable Sister Newsome without too many bites taken out of me. Indeed, Yeland could be my wingman, and suffer the worst of it.'

They looked after them as the two men swept on. Fran muttered, 'He must be right fond of Ralph after all.'

Smythe and Yeland stood either side of Ralph's bed for the five minutes that Sister Newsome had allowed. Smythe touched Ralph's hand. 'You rest easy, lad. Get yourself fit and well, eh? We need you, but you know that.'

Yeland, on the other side of the bed, gripped Ralph's hand. 'Pleasure to shake your hand, lad. Smythe has a point. Up and at 'em, eh.' He gave Ralph's hand a shake. 'Listen now. Up and at 'em. We'll be in to see you again.'

As Sister Newsome flapped them out of the ward, Smythe said, 'You'll take care of the silly sod.'

'I take care of all my silly sods, Professor,' Sister Newsome called after them. 'You behave yourself now.'

The sound of Yeland's laughter echoed along the quiet corridor.

Chapter Twelve

Tuesday, 10 March

Mr Gaines found his way to the telephone box outside his lodgings at the Rising Sun in Minton. He rammed in the coins as though he and the telephone were at war.

Plomer at Head Office answered. Gerald Gaines pressed button A. He'd known the bureaucrat would be there, working late, if only to appear indispensable. Well, it wasn't that idiot who was indispensable, it was the management and workers of this particular munitions site – or any munitions factory – that held that honour. What's more, he didn't have time to bloody well waste like this. There was a bloody war on.

He drew in a breath, trying to sound polite. 'Mr Plomer, it's Gaines. I've been through the whole site, investigating the break-in, the explosion, any and all mishaps, misadventures, concerns in all sectors. I've checked the progress of the erection of the double fence, the patrols, the dogs and—'

Plomer's voice was terse as he interrupted. 'I don't need to listen to a novel. What's the verdict?'

'Clean as a whistle, exemplary management all round. In particular, I found Swinton's supervision and training without fault. The explosion in his sector was bad luck. It has been, quite honestly, a complete waste of my time and energy.'

Plomer's voice, when he finally replied, sounded as though he was hanging on to his temper with difficulty. 'Your tone doesn't become you, Gaines.'

'Well, let me say, *sir*, there are places that I do need to be investigating instead of fiddling about here. It was the storm that tore down the fence, and the intrusion was thwarted by the guards and their dogs. I interviewed each guard thoroughly. They reckon, as do the police and the military police, that there were signs of a car but the tracks were covered by the snow. So, there's nothing further to report on that except they are on alert for another attempt, but as the manager of the whole site told me in no uncertain terms, this is their permanent default position.'

Plomer seemed to be rustling papers. 'And the detonator explosion? The accident ratio in comparison to others?'

'The incident ratio at this site is less than the national average. The figures will be in my report. Swinton in particular has safety down to the nth degree and as I've just said, the explosion was an accident, as is factored into this type of factory. The workers understand safety like no others, especially in Bolton's sector, led by the example set by Swinton. The other sectors are also above par. You asked me to check for loose talk. I must point out that this is something I do as a matter of course. I have witnessed nothing out of turn. Nothing. I did, however, pick out hearsay faults within the administration building and personnel – one person in particular, a low-grade worker. This I will also put in my report as needing some further investigation.'

There was silence. Finally, Mr Plomer said, 'If you've nothing more to add, Gaines, I will now insist, demand, require – whichever appeals to you – that you remain in post with eyes and ears open, and report here on the sixteenth, Monday, first thing, for your next assignment. Do not forget that there is such a thing as the wool being pulled over one's eyes. Pay attention to the buildings you mentioned.'

Gaines wasn't sure if his grip would break the receiver or his fingers first. 'With respect, sir, I repeat, there are other factories. And the security officers here are perfectly capable of following through on the administrative staff. Neither do I allow the wool to be pulled over my eyes,' he shouted. 'I am a man of experience.'

But Plomer had already hung up. Gaines slammed down the receiver. 'Bloody imbecile,' he said aloud. 'There's a bloody war on, we can't waste—'

Someone tapped on one of the panes. A woman called out, 'There's a queue.'

He nodded, pushed open the door and held it for her. She smiled. 'Got to phone me mam. She expects it on a Tuesday at seven thirty.'

Gaines smiled, and it was a relief to be pleasant. He didn't agree with Plomer's directives to shake 'em up, shock 'em. He set off across the road in the gloom of the blacked-out village and pushed open the back door of the Rising Sun, knowing he'd be sitting alone at the bar because he was the big bad wolf. Well, of course – he was an outsider poking his nose into people's working directives, their performance, their dignity. He was sick of it. He'd underline the wasted time until the sixteenth in his bloody report, and they could damn well put up with it, or shove it where the sun didn't shine.

The bar was quiet. Mildred Pertwee, the landlady, asked, 'Pint before your tea, Mr Gaines?' He nodded, resting his elbows on the bar. She drew down a tankard from the shelf and began pulling the pint. 'Then another early night, is it, so you're up with the birds? Or are you slipping off to keep an eye on the night shift?'

Gaines just sighed. 'Yes, might as well, no sleep for the wicked, eh? All right with you if I come in about two, to be up again for the fore shift? A nice line in domestic utensils they make, eh?'

Mildred nodded. 'Aye. Just be sure not to lose the key.

Canna have people slipping in to get at the booze and then we find 'tis the investigator at the bottom of it all, can we?'

Though she smiled, her eyes were cold. Well, Gaines thought, sipping his pint, it was the nature of the job to be hated, and he couldn't tell the landlady that so far he'd found nothing but good at the Factory, more or less. There was still that silly girl from the South who ... Well, there was just something loose, and the antipathy between her and the other workers ...

'I'll be leaving Sunday,' he said.

'Aye, you're booked in till then, so you'll get to hear The Factory Girls sing on Saturday. We take a bit of a collection for the widows and the families of them who don't come back from wherever 'tis they work. We just see their yellow skin, the rashes, the lost limbs, the graves, for them lot making ... domestic utensils.'

There was a pause heavy with resentment before she added, 'So, you can dig deep in them pockets of yours, eh?'

He finished his pint, holding her stare, then nodded. 'Pleased to, Mrs Pertwee.'

Mildred flushed. 'Right then, good of you.' She lifted her head, rallying. 'Mind, I'll be keeping me eyes on you when the jug goes round.'

Gaines made a promise to himself to put in ten bob. 'I'll be having spam fritters, if that's all right with you. Then I must be off.'

After wiping down the bar, Mildred plunged the cloth into the sink beneath it, shaking her head and smiling. 'I 'spect you met Mr Swinton. Them workers have done him proud, 'tis said, wherever it is they work, and that's softened him. They're right fond of the old bugger, and he of them.' She laughed to herself. 'Bliddy miracles happen, eh?'

She looked up, and obviously remembered who she was talking to as the smile disappeared. 'I'll get your tea.'

Mildred swept through the door into the kitchen and came back with a tray holding his spam fritters, a baked potato and sprouts. Gaines placed his half-finished pint on the tray and carried it to a table by the window. He looked down at his meal, sick of the war, of the dark streets, of the stress and tiredness all around, and most of all – of spam. He picked up his knife and fork. Gone were the days when he had a dab of dripping on his spud.

He cut right through the potato, eating the skin too. Some didn't, but his mother had said the goodness was in the skin. He smiled. She was dead now, after the First War. Killed herself when his old man didn't come back. And now there was another war. Suddenly, he wasn't hungry, for she'd be ashamed of him kowtowing to the bosses and not leaving this lot in peace.

He poked at the final piece of spam, not wanting it, but no one wasted food these days, so he finished it. He put his knife and fork together and picked up his tankard, hearing the door open. Men entered, laughing. They stopped when they saw him. He finished his beer, deciding that after this night shift and the fore shift tomorrow, he'd only cover one shift each day, and just keep his eyes open. That was enough for him, and the Factory.

Chapter Thirteen

Saturday, 14 March

On Saturday morning, just as they had done for the last few days, the co-op set off to Massingham Hall with their proggy frames in Madge's cart, leaving those listed on the hospital visiting rota to fulfil their appointed shifts. As they cycled along Main Street, Annie Hall was leading the charge, as Madge liked to put it.

'I know I'm slow,' Madge called after her, 'but it's pulling this cart.'

Maud Bedley, cycling behind Annie, shouted back, 'I don't mind doing a turn next week. We canna have your eyepatch getting splattered with flies now the rain's finally stopped. By, I thought we'd need to build a bliddy ark.'

The sun was out, the wind behind them, and at last it was dry enough to burn things, thought Annie, but she put the BUF uniform out of her mind and instead wondered just how much longer Joy would last, because she was hopeless and Reginald must get rid of her, for Sophia was too gentle. What's more, Viola badly needed to get out of that bliddy Factory and would be wonderful with the bairns, so would slot in right nicely.

Talking of slotting in, she thought, each day they'd come she'd brought the attic key in her mac pocket, just as she had today, but Reginald Massingham had never been home. She urged herself on, willing him to be there, for she must talk to him, see the truth in his face. It would then be his duty to burn this symbol of all that they were fighting against, or so she'd decided.

Behind her, Maud Bedley nodded towards Audrey. 'I know I ask every day, but has she heard from Bob yet?'

Audrey shook her head. 'Daft to worry as she does, for these days who knows where any of 'em are, but she's decided he weren't himself. I could strangle the beggar, really I could. She's such dark circles under her eyes, and she's skin and bones for being off her food, what there is of it, and her itch is right bad, with the yellow making headway.'

'Aye,' called Annie, 'Fran's said much the same, poor lass.'

'At least they're at the Rising Sun tonight,' replied Audrey, 'so that'll take Beth's mind off it, and the rehearsals have helped an' all. How's the wedding dress coming along? And the bridesmaids' frocks too?'

'Tilly Oborne's on the case,' said Beatrice Adams. 'Nips in there at meal break, so the silk's cut out, slippery beggar though it is, and the cotton for the bridesmaids, and she's going to see if Mr Swinton will let them have a quick fitting behind Gaines's back. They feel they owe their foreman that much respect. They did wonder whether to clear it with Gaines himself, for he has calmed down, but didn't dare in case it caused trouble.'

They were struggling up an incline now, and Beatrice, hunched over the handlebars, panted, 'Oh Lordy, I wish our Emily weren't such a good worker, for if she weren't I wouldn't have been on this bliddy bike, getting a sore bum and worn out into the bargain. Instead, I'd be stuck behind the counter sorting out customers and their ration books.'

Annie laughed, then found herself watching a seagull who was joining its kin on the ploughed field to the right of them. Above, sparrows chattered on the overhanging syca-more branches festooned with buds. On they went, past more fields, until they reached the boundary of the Massingham land. 'But when you think on it,' she murmured, ' 'tis all Massingham land. Reginald just rents them other fields to Thompkins.'

'Thinking aloud, Annie?' Audrey laughed. 'Thompkins treats them well. Good farmer, and a good walloper. Remember how his da used to whack our bums for scrumping his apples?'

They were all laughing, even Madge, who had been brought up elsewhere and only came to live in Massingham just before her husband cleared off. A bugger he was, Annie thought; hurt her, he did. Took an evil bully to hit someone hard enough to take their eye. It made her think of Sandra, whose eye had been saved, but whose sight was compromised. She couldn't work in the danger zone, so had opted for the sewing workshop when she was well enough. If only Viola would give up. But she was too stubborn.

Thinking of Sandra led her to Ralph, whom the girls had visited yesterday. They thought they had felt a tremor in his hands, but was it their imagination? They didn't know and had come home elated at Sandra's news, but upset about Ralph, though it was progress of a sort. The thing was, they had hoped for more. Perhaps Smythe had too, because he and Reginald had been chatting in the corridor, slipping out while the Massingham girls had twenty minutes.

They turned through the gates of the drive at last and pedalled the final stretch, Annie remembering Ralph as having more colour when the co-op had visited on Tuesday, and again on Thursday. She had not felt a tremor in his hands then, though she had told the lad to get a grip, come home and stop worrying everyone. But the thought of worry brought the problem of the uniform to the fore again. What did it mean? If she found she couldn't trust Reginald, then could she trust his son? Who would she go to if that was the case? Perhaps Professor Smythe, for he seemed to know everything.

She swallowed, then set her mouth in a grim line as they cycled along in front of the house, the bliddy gravel flicking as always. Whatever she had to do, she would do it, and that's what Joe would have said too. They turned into the garage yard, and there it was, the Rolls-Royce. For a minute she wished it wasn't there, but then told herself to stop being so bliddy wet.

She bumped along the cobbles with Audrey beside her and the others following, leaving the bikes near the Rolls. As they did so, Alfie slipped down the ladder from his rooms.

'Howay, ladies. The bairns are waiting for their rug lesson, and the lads'll be ready for their footie later. That's if the boys are eager after their shift.'

Maud Bedley muttered, 'They'd better be, they've had their orders. And the lasses said they might be up an' all, though they're singing at the Rising Sun this evening. You'll be helping with the footie, will you, Alfie?'

'I'll do anything for a cuppa, ladies.'

'Howay with you,' grunted Madge, 'you'll be playing footie, cuppa or not, or I'll need to know the reason why, lad.'

They set off towards the kitchen just as the door opened and the bairns tumbled out, rushing towards them, the boys grabbing the frames, and the girls the bags of old felted sweaters, coats and materials that they knew would be their task to cut into different lengths. Eva waited, the bag she had taken from Maud Bedley clutched to her.

'We've nowt to tell yer about Mr Ralph. Nowt, Mr Massingham still says, 'cept he's improving a bit, but you know that, for you've visited. We did too, but he just lay there. We held his hand, we said our tables. Sister Newsome said that he quite likely heard, but was still too tired. That's good, you co-op ladies, in't it, for him to hear? And this morning

Sophia had a funny turn she did. Went all white and sweaty. The sweat made drops on her forehead. She's sitting down with the rest of the bairns.'

The women looked from Eva to one another. Mrs Adams sniffed. 'Where was that Joy? Why wasn't she helping?'

Marty called from the top of the basement steps, 'Oh, she's gone – said she were fed up with wiping noses, having her sleep disturbed and making bliddy scones.'

'Language,' called Annie.

'Aye, that's what we said, but she told us to bugger off,' said Abraham, coming to take Annie's bag of materials.

Melanie was skipping ahead of them now as they made for the steps. 'Her auntie, Mrs Phillips, skelped her legs, she did, with the spoon this morning. She didn't half yelp, and took off with her bags, shaking her fist.'

Annie stopped and turned to look at the others, who were all smiling with relief. Maud Bedley turned to Eva. 'Did poor Sophia have to get up in the night—'

'Has Mr Massingham found anyone to fill her place?' interrupted Madge.

Eva shook her head. 'I don't know, Missus Madge, and no, we didn't wake Sophia, or that Joy, for she'd skelp our backsides if we did. We divint like to tell our Sophia what she were doing. We'd told the lads they must keep their mouths shut, even if they had a bad dream, so when Marty woke he said nowt, you know, the one like me and Melanie have after we had to lie in the rubble with our dead families.'

No one could speak, not at that moment, but when Eva raced ahead of them, Maud Bedley whispered, 'Something must be done. Fretting bairns, and one worn-out woman.'

Madge agreed. 'Aye, and we know exactly who – Viola.' They crossed the yard, trying to decide how they could manage to have someone here if Mr Massingham was away, because even if Viola agreed, she'd have to give her notice at the Labour Exchange.

'Well, till it's sorted,' said Madge, 'Alfie can do it. Time he learned how to grow up.'

Audrey sniffed. 'That'd be a first. They're always three and a half.'

They hurried to the kitchen, though Eva's words still resonated, and Annie thought she'd rather sit for a moment and have a bliddy good cry. She saw Sophia sitting on a stool at the end of the scrubbed pine table, overseeing two bairns rubbing lard into flour. Sophia looked up.

'Guess what's for lunch?'

'Onion and carrot pie,' shouted Eva, 'with a few bits of rabbit. Sophia will tell Mr Massingham it's juicy, but we know it isn't, not really.'

Sophia raised her eyebrows and murmured, 'Out of the mouths of babes and sucklings . . .'

As the others sorted frames and material to be cut at the other end of the kitchen table, Annie slid out of the room.

'Howay, Annie,' called Maud, 'not doing a runner, are you?'

Annie stopped momentarily. 'Of course not, just need to visit the toilet and then run up to the attic to pick up me hanky. I reckon it might have dropped in the trunk, which is no way for it to end its days.'

Annie started to close the door, then stopped again. 'I'll look for old blankets too. I reckon the bairns could cut them up after they've done these.' She pointed to the material they'd brought from Massingham. 'They might manage a rug for Briddlestone's between them, eh? Then there's pocket money to share. Will that be all right with you, Sophia?'

Melanie looked up from an exercise book. 'I'll help carry it, Mrs Hall.'

Sophia shook her head. 'I think you need to work on

those times tables Mr Ralph gave you before he hurt himself, so you have them ready when he comes home. And yes, Annie – a perfect idea.'

Annie set off up the stairs, marched across the entrance hall, her heels clicking on the tiles, and knocked on the study door, for this was where Reginald normally was. She waited.

'Enter.'

He didn't look up as she went in, but continued writing. She closed the door behind her.

'Just a moment, my darling.'

Annie coughed. ' 'Tisn't your darling, Mr Massingham. It's the ogre from Leadenhall Terrace.'

He looked up in surprise. 'Why, Annie, this is a pleasant surprise. Ogre indeed? You look cold, have you cycled up? Alfie will always fetch you, so telephone from the box, eh? I'm just thankful that you are all so helpful to dearest Sophia, especially now Joy has decided to wave us goodbye. Now, how can I help you? Oh, do sit down.'

Annie waited by the door. 'We have no time, Reginald.'

He half rose. 'Is Sophia unwell? She's been—'

'Come with me. I have something to show you in the attic.' She turned on her heel, not giving him a chance to reply. She led the way towards the stairs, her heart thumping, fearful her courage would desert her, so she quickened her pace, listening for his footsteps. Was he following? Then she heard his heels on the tiles and the creak of the stairs as he gained on her until they were walking alongside.

'You're being most mysterious, Annie.'

She merely said, 'I don't want to speak of it, Reginald. Not here.'

On they walked, side by side, and gradually her heart slowed, but still her shoulders were braced as though to receive a blow. Up another flight, until they reached the empty servants' quarters. She waved towards the rooms as they passed. 'These would serve well as bedrooms for the children, and there are more than enough rooms to have just two in each.'

He was panting now.

'You should get more exercise, Reginald.'

'Indeed,' he muttered, 'and have you thought of dropping the co-op in favour of the parade ground? I've often thought you and Fran would make superb sergeant majors.'

She laughed suddenly because he was chuckling, and her nervousness lessened as they headed for the attic door, which stood locked at the top of the stairs. This was Reginald Massingham, kindly Reginald. But behind the door lay *that* uniform.

Once at the door, she took the key from her pocket. He merely raised his eyebrows.

'Let me.'

She handed it over. 'I wanted to keep anyone else from entering the attic until we had decided what to do.'

Reginald looked confused as he unlocked the door.

He placed the key on the hook and gestured for her to enter first. Annie stepped into the dimness, and again the cobwebs clung. She muttered, as she headed for the end of the attic and the trunks, 'At least they're not the thick beggars you get in the unused seams of Auld Hilda.'

Stooping below a beam, he was next to her now. 'I hated them, especially if they caught my mouth. And the blacklocks . . . ghastly beggars.'

She turned, surprised that he should know, and then remembered that his father had sent him into the pit when he was in his last year of school. The pitmen had been against it, but the lad had shown his mettle, and it had influenced his management of his pits from then on.

'Aye, my Joe hated them an' all, but it'd be a strange pit-man who didn't.'

She had stopped by the trunk that contained the clothes. She turned to check that the door was closed, worried because they should have locked it from the inside, but it was too late now. She laid her hand on Massingham's arm. 'You need to see this, Reginald. Then you need to dispose of it so it never sees the light of day again, for your lad has moved on, I'm sure he has. If you don't, I will, for I cannot let it survive a moment longer.'

She held him back, looking up at him. 'You have to remember that most of the young 'uns went from one meeting to another, curious, or just for something different to do. They stopped all that nonsense when war were declared. It weren't right, most reckoned, to dabble in owt once Hitler and Stalin showed themselves up for what they were.'

At her words she saw shocked understanding dawn. He murmured, 'Oh dear God.'

Ah, so he didn't approve? She remembered then Bob going on at the wedding tea about pretending until something became real. Or did he say until it *looked* real? Was this what Reginald was doing, pretending?

She released his arm, stooped, drew out the rug-making scissors she had tucked away in her pocket and cut through the knotted string. She stepped back. 'Aye, well, best you see for yourself, and then we need a plan.'

Reginald knelt beside the trunk, unhooked the metal clasp and in the dim light from the skylights lifted the lid. There sat the hacking jacket, undisturbed. He stroked it. 'This was Ralph's when he was at school. It seems so small.'

She touched his shoulder. 'Aye, and I'm right sorry to mither you with all this when we don't know what the outcome is for the lad's health, but we divint want him bothered by it, or if worst comes to worst, we divint want it found and his memory besmirched.' She watched Massingham's hands grip the jacket, scrunching up the tweed till his knuckles showed white. She patted his shoulder. 'Aye, I know your heart is tearing apart with the thought of him . . .'

There, she was pretending too, for while she spoke these words part of her was examining this man she had come to admire.

He swung round and looked up at her, and the torment she saw matched how she had felt when Fran was hurt in the accident, and Stan, too, in the pit a few years back. Then there was Joe, and sweet Betty who'd barely drawn breath. That look could not be false. But he had not seen the uniform yet.

'Oh, Annie, if only you knew . . .' He trailed off, swallowed, his eyes on her. 'If only I could tell you, but I swear . . .'

She tightened her grip on his shoulder.

His hand covered hers. 'You are a remarkable woman, Annie Hall. I do hope we are, or can, if, at all possible, be friends?' It was a real question, his grey eyes intent on hers, his grip tightening. She had accepted friendship from her marrers and the Massingham people without question, but this was different. This was the squire, the pit owner, who, she only now realised, had steadily become a human being to her. One with all the vulnerabilities of any other person, a man who was the husband of her friend Sophia and the father of Ralph. And here was this uniform that could change everything.

She pointed to the trunk, unable to answer him. 'Look.'

Mr Massingham drew in a breath and lifted the hacking jacket, holding it to his face. It smelled of mothballs, but Annie could see he was thinking of the young Ralph. He laid it to one side, and there it was again, in all its black vileness. The uniform. Again she watched him closely.

In a whisper Reginald said, 'He got in with that damnable fool Tim Swinton. There we were, Mr Swinton and
I, two fathers unable to acknowledge to one another that
they had lost control as their boys flirted with the unmentionable. Unmentionable to me at least, and I'm sure to Mr
Swinton. I suppose it was a time when our lads were wondering what Communism was all about, and Fascism.
Perhaps they thought one or the other was an easy solution
to our economic woes?'

Annie shook her head, certain and determined. 'We
can't be mithering about why and who, but about what it
means now.'

Still on his knees, Massingham whispered, 'He has confessed his past. Please trust me that this has changed, for I
could not tolerate anything "other". He cannot bear the person he was. He is working for restitution, and much of that
is due to you and the co-op, your reluctance to give up
when you nursed him, your care, your goodness. I can tell
you nothing more, but I say again, please trust us.'

They stayed almost locked together in a bubble. Finally,
Annie nodded. 'I reckon the best thing will be to find something to put it in, and you must take it out secretly, perhaps
to the bottom of the garden where the gardener has his
compost and leaf burner, or so I believe. The bairns were
talking of it because he'd said he'd tan their arses if they
dived in the leaves once more.'

Mr Massingham lifted the uniform from the trunk, letting Annie replace the hacking jacket. He stood up, the
uniform over his arm. Annie let the lid drop, then hurried
from one trunk to another, looking for material. Finally, she
found some curtains, threadbare and faded. She pulled out
one, and a blue blanket for the bairns' proggy rug, and
spread the curtain on the floor.

'Wrap it up in this.' Her tone was brisk.

'Yes,' he obeyed, as though he couldn't wait to get rid of it.

' 'Tis time I was back in the kitchen, so it's up to you to get that –' Annie pointed to the uniform '– out of the house. Perhaps you have petrol in the garage?'

They smiled briefly at one another. There was misery in his eyes, understanding in hers.

They hurried to the door. He locked it behind them and they set off down the steps, along the corridors and down more stairs until they were at the top of those leading to the entrance hall. 'Just a minute,' she whispered as she heard Eva calling at the top of the kitchen stairs.

'No, Sophia – she's not down yet.'

'Go out through the front door,' Annie whispered. 'You've a lighter?'

Reginald nodded. 'I'll have to avoid Alfie somehow.'

'Give me ten minutes,' Annie muttered, 'and I'll call him in for a cuppa. Then out you go. The bairns are all inside, or were.'

She began to hurry down the final flight into the hall and Reginald hissed after her, 'How can I thank you?'

'Friends,' she hissed, stopping halfway down, 'don't need thanks. Just burn the bliddy thing.' And she hurried down the stairs to the kitchen, brandishing the blanket.

'Got a right nice blanket and me hanky.' No one was to know it had been in her pocket all the time.

Massingham waited ten minutes, then slipped down the stairs and out of the front door, almost tiptoeing across the gravel. He peered into the yard and saw Alfie was heading down the steps to the kitchen. Reginald hurried into the garage, grabbed the can of petrol and almost ran through the walled garden and along to the rear of the gardens. He made for the piles of sodden leaves beside Old Ted's shed.

God bless the woman, for there was the incinerator,

scorched and blackened, but perfect. Old Ted was only here two days a week now, because his rheumatics played havoc with his joints.

Massingham lifted the incinerator lid and peered in. A thick layer of ash, quite dry, lay at the bottom. He dropped in the uniform poured over some of the precious petrol, lit one of his business cards and, readying himself, let it float down onto the material. Slamming on the lid, he waited. Almost immediately smoke rose from the funnel.

'Burn, damn you,' he muttered. He would tell Ralph when he next went to the hospital that the uniform was gone. He would not mention Annie Hall because he didn't want her involved in what was to come should Ralph survive. As the heat grew, and the smoke, he stood back and whispered to himself, as he often seemed to find himself doing these days. 'How has it come to this? What will Annie think if you end up before a court, once the war is ended?'

As he stared at the leaves piled high, some of them took flight in the wind. He envied their escape for he so often longed to be elsewhere, to leave it all behind – the secrecy of his work for Smythe, his factories, the war, the worry about his son, his grief for his actions.

He stepped forward, his hands up, feeling the warmth as the heat rose from the flue creating a shimmering image of the trees that grew at the end of the side lawn and wondering how he'd had the gall to ask the woman his son had widowed to be his friend. How could he? But how could he not, for they *were* friends and he would do all he could to help the Halls, and the Bedleys, and the whole lot of these people of his, even though the world was going to hell in a handcart and nothing was normal.

As he watched, the fire slowly died. He lifted the incinerator lid, wincing at the heat of it through his folded handkerchief, and peered in. Only ash.

Reginald picked up the can and returned to the yard, seeing Annie and Alfie at the top of the kitchen steps. She was facing the garden, Alfie the house. On seeing Reginald, she grabbed Alfie's arm, pointing up to the house martin's nest that was being built in the eaves of the old cold store. As Reginald slipped into the garage with the can, he could hear her saying, 'I think they're a sign of good luck.'

'Maybe, but they're also bliddy messy, with their pooh everywhere.'

'It'll be new life chattering up there.' Annie folded her arms as Reginald slipped from the garage to the yard. He was so fond of this woman who was barely older than him, but was so like his mother in the way she always stood her ground.

Alfie wiped his hands on an oily rag. 'For you, then, but clear it with the boss – Sophia, I mean.'

Reginald smiled to himself. He was surrounded by women who were bosses. He came to them. 'We'll ask her, shall we, Annie?'

Annie smiled as Alfie stepped back, grimacing. 'Oh, I didn't hear you, Mr Massingham. I didn't mean nowt disrespectful, I just—'

Reginald waved him down. 'It's true, lad, Sophia is the boss, and we mustn't forget it.'

Alfie sniffed. 'Can anyone else smell petrol?' They both denied they could.

They went in for tea, but not until Annie had told Reginald that Viola should take Joy's job, as a matter of urgency. He agreed that she would be perfect.

Chapter Fourteen

It was the meal break at the Factory and the excitement around the table was tangible, for it was the night of the concert at the Rising Sun. Beth wished she could feel at least a little of it, but she just couldn't. She poked at the grey meat, wondering what it was but not caring, because here they were, two weeks on, and still no word from Bob. She didn't even go up to the telephone box any more, relying instead on Fran to come running if he called.

Yesterday, Fran had told the table they had finalised the details of the wedding tea: the pheasant promised by Ralph had been confirmed by Mr Massingham, the ingredients for the cake were slowly being collected, and the order for the home-made elderberry wine, and beer, which Ralph had placed with the Rising Sun immediately after Sarah's wedding, had also been confirmed by Mr Massingham.

She tried a piece of meat and felt sick. Was Bob at the bottom of the sea? Was his letter lost along the way? Had he fallen out of love? She stopped, thinking instead of the next visit to the hospital, but she couldn't remember when it would be. At least Sister Newsome had told them that there was a difference in Ralph's colour, and his breathing, but they could tell that themselves. In spite of the occasional tremor, though, he had still not responded when they squeezed his hand. It seemed to have really upset Viola.

Beth sat back on her chair, looking from left to right as the chatter whirled around her, a bit like the thoughts in her head. She saw that Viola, sitting next to her, had finished her meal, and as always had placed her knife and fork tidily together. Everything Viola did was tidy, except for the blood that was seeping from her bandage. That wasn't tidy.

She looked at Viola's hand again, and thought of Ralph bleeding in his car, the top of his ear missing, his cuts, his gashed leg, but at least they were still not septic. Sister Newsome had used sphagnum moss. She hadn't dared not, she'd said, mentioning the co-op by name. Sandra was improving as well, though still in hospital. Viola was still working in the Factory.

Bob *must* be on patrol, and she wouldn't listen to this voice that was saying *but . . . but . . .* For he hadn't said he loved her. He had said that war was complicated. He had said he was in refit. He'd talked about pretence. And he hadn't written for two weeks. Nor had he phoned.

Beth forced herself to find some words as Viola folded both hands in her lap, trying to hide the seeping wound. 'Viola, you should rest up, you know. Fran's mam has said you shouldn't be working, not at something like the sewing bench which rubs it so bad. She says it to you every morning, me mam says, as she pours your cuppa.'

Viola looked down. There was a smear of blood on her blue overalls. Beth noticed. 'Oh pet, let's take you to the toilet. We can go without an escort here, because it opens off the canteen. Come on now, eh.' The pair of them pushed back their chairs. The tannoy was playing 'Ten Cents a Dance'. It was Beth's main solo for this evening, and Bob's favourite song. She sang along as they walked together.

Beth sponged Viola's overalls until only a wet patch remained. She checked Viola's hand, taking out her handkerchief. It was Bob's. He'd left it, and she carried it with her because it brought him closer. For a moment she hesitated, wanting to hold it to her face, to smell it, because she was sure that the scent of him remained.

Viola stretched out her hand. 'I know it's Bob's. Don't use it on me.'

'Howay.' Beth smiled. 'Let's make another bandage of it on top of that one, for if Gaines sticks his beaky nose into the sewing room, he might create merry hell if there's blood on the material. Wouldn't put it past him to make you pay for it, even though it's his last day.'

Viola shook her head. 'He seems to have accepted we're all right, and just goes through the motions.'

Opening up the handkerchief, Beth folded it and bound it round Viola's hand. 'Aye, but not enough to know we're working on the wedding dress. I reckon he'd have a fit and charge us with misuse of Factory machinery.' She should tear the handkerchief, knot it to secure the dressing, but again she hesitated.

'Tuck it in,' Viola whispered. 'It's too fine a weave to tear, eh?'

Beth smiled and said, 'Or you could go to the nurse right now and she'd do it proper, but . . .'

Viola nodded, and they looked at one another in the mirror. 'But,' Viola finished for her, 'she'd sign me off till it's healed proper, and I've to pay me way at the Halls'. I just have to—'

'You don't,' Beth interrupted. 'It were a terrible injury and no one expects—'

'I do. I'm on my own, and I must make me way, cos there's no one to fall back on. I canna take charity.'

'With friends it's not charity, and you'll make some money this evening.'

Shaking her head, her shoulders rigid, Viola looked anxiously at her hand. Then she relaxed. 'It isn't oozing through,' she said, just as Fran stuck her head round the door.

'Come on, we're to have a wedding-frock fitting in the

sewing room. We've just time. Not just me, bridesmaids an' all. Mrs Oborne says it's safe because Gaines hasn't been sticking his beak in our sector, not for days.'

She disappeared, and the two girls smiled at one another. Beth pulled Viola through the door. 'Aye, and we'll see if there's some offcuts from the cotton bridesmaids' dresses, and those can go around the handkerchief as well. I reckon some more of Mrs Hall's goose grease and lavender would help. But—'

'Oh, hush. Besides, I have the lavender before bed, and Fran has her sphagnum-moss mix on her rash. It's like our very own hospital, so it is.'

They hurried back to their table, but their plates had been taken to the trolley for them, and Valerie merely pointed to the door that led to the corridor. 'Miss Ellington is in the corridor, waiting to escort you to the sewing room. Mrs Oborne says time's going on and she's worried the measurements might have changed, especially for you, Beth, for you've gone thin as a rake. Be quiet about it, since Swinton doesn't want to give Gaines a swansong to warble to Head Office.'

The two girls set off towards the door, weaving round tables and then following Miss Ellington down the corridors. Beth touched each poster until Cyn pushed open the sewing-room door. The new supervisor, Mrs Iris, was helping to pin one of the bridesmaids' cut-outs on Sarah, but there was no sign of Fran. Mrs Iris nodded towards the storeroom. 'Mrs Oborne and Fran are squashed in there while Tilly fits the dress. A dress no one is to see, of course.' She raised her voice slightly as she added, 'Though with Tilly's bum in there, how they're managing I can't imagine.'

'I'm not bliddy deaf,' shouted Mrs Oborne, 'so you watch it, Doris Iris.'

They were all laughing as Mrs Iris stepped back, looking

at Sarah, who was wearing cut-outs that had been pinned together. 'Turn around, let me see.' She stared, tilting her head to one side. 'Aye, you'll do. I'll unpin you at the back, so ease out of the rest, or you'll be pricked. Next, please.'

Beth pushed Viola forward. 'Here you go, lass.'

Viola worked her way round the benches, most of which bore sewing machines, whilst others were heaped with material.

'Viola,' said Mrs Iris, 'you could have taken off your overalls while you waited, for heaven's sake. You, Beth, start getting out of yours, for you're in them trouser ones. You'll have to show your knickers for you've no underslip, so don't be a violet.'

Beth grinned as she started to unbutton herself, but then came a sharp rap at the door, and before anyone could speak, it opened. Mr Gaines stood there, eyes darting. As Viola spun round in her underslip and blouse, he said, 'What's this, then?'

Beth pulled her overalls closed, her breath quite gone, while Viola hid behind Mrs Iris.

Miss Ellington, who had been sitting at a workbench, stood, blanching. 'Mr Gaines, a month or so ago we were allowed to fit our Sarah's wedding dress. We don't use the Factory's materials, and they are cut and sewn during the meal breaks, admittedly using these sewing machines and thread. We know it's not procedure, and it's my fault, no one else's.'

Still framed by the doorway, Mr Gaines said, 'Carry on, then. Can't stand in the way of romance, eh? Best to say nowt to Bolton. So I haven't been here, I haven't seen this. I don't like paperwork any better than the next man. After all, this is hardly going to affect the running of the war.' He half saluted as they stood there, stunned. He turned, then swung back. Was he expecting them to have moved? Well, he'd be disappointed, Beth thought, for they were frozen in place.

'And break a leg this evening. That's what they say in the acting world, isn't it? It's my last day, so I fancy a bit of a sing-song. Miss Ellington, you should know that this is a factory like no other. And you'd best tell Swinton, in case I don't get time. If I do, then there's nothing wrong with telling a body twice, eh? Ladies, it's been a pleasure, but I dare say you can't say the same.' He left.

They listened to his footsteps, which stopped after a few yards. They heard him returning. Still no one moved. He re-entered and said, 'My report will be going in. But tell Swinton I was too hard at the start. You look after him, his training's kept you safer than many others would have done. You can tell him that as well, if you would be so kind.'

He left again, and they didn't stir, not until his footsteps had faded completely, then they looked at one another. 'Bliddy hell,' muttered Mrs Oborne, peering out of the storeroom. 'I thought nowt could surprise me. Best get on.' She slammed the door behind her. They heard a screech from Fran and Mrs Oborne saying, 'Stop mithering. It were only a pin, and the good thing is your blood hasn't gone on the silk.'

They waited for Fran's reply. It came: 'Oh, so that's all right then.'

'The lass daren't say more,' muttered Mrs Iris. 'Mrs Oborne is too big, the storeroom too small and Fran wouldn't stand a chance.'

Still amazed at Gaines, they sprang into action, with Mrs Iris pinning the cut-outs on the other two bridesmaids, adjusting here and there, pins in her mouth. At last, with five minutes to spare, they were out, all except for Viola and Mrs Iris, who would tidy up before the shift returned. The women hurried down the corridor and Beth's heart was suddenly much lighter – Gaines was being nice, Swinton had kept them safe, and with all this good news some must shake off on her and Bob. Still, though, she touched the posters. Mrs Iris had said she must eat properly, and not mither about things that hadn't happened.

Besides, Mrs Iris had said, removing the pins from her mouth, she didn't want to have to take her dress in again, and what would Bob think of her looking like a skeleton clanking along behind the bride, casting a pall over the proceedings? Beth had smiled. 'You're right.' That was all. She didn't have the energy to say more.

Now they followed Miss Ellington back to the canteen, then down the detonator and pellets corridor, all the while talking of the upcoming wedding, the excitement, and this evening's songs. Mrs Oborne peeled off for the pellets. Beth made for the detonator workbench, and pictured them all standing for the photographs outside St Oswald's, with the April lambs in the fields and the daffodils along the verges, and she'd look at Sarah and Fran, and their wedding rings and husbands, and know that their bairns would play together, a new gang would form, and their husbands would be friends, and it would all go on and on. If Bob came back for the wedding, of course.

Fran and Viola hurried home from the bus stop, leaving Beth to head for the corner shop to run an errand for her mam. The girls dashed past the hens, though Fran had second thoughts and stopped, for her da had always spoken to them whenever he entered or left. She lifted the feed lid. Her mam had cut up the outer cabbage leaves and placed them in the old bowl on top of the grain. Fran tore them up and fed them through the chicken wire. 'There, my precious feathered beings,' she crooned. 'Let's be having a good lot of eggs, and you, Mr Cockerel, you keep 'em in order, eh?

And tell 'em how grand Miss Franny Hall looks in her silk wedding dress, eh? Or will when 'tis finished. Oh, it's a sight, Mr Cockerel. Such a grand sight.'

She only realised Viola was beside her when the girl said, 'Aye, and you should ask your ladies to lay a lot of good eggs for the sandwiches at the wedding tea.'

Fran nudged her, dusting off her hands. 'Aye, you listen to our Viola, or it's no more feed.'

'Stan were in earlier, giving them a handful,' her mam called from the back doorstep, 'and Ben when he got in from school, and now you. So they should lay like never before.'

Fran patted the wire. 'You are bad, bad birds, for you divint tell us you'd already had your tea, and now we're ready for ours.'

She grabbed Viola and pulled her towards the back door. They left their boots outside, under the seat of the chair her da had always used. After his death, Stan's boots had filled the empty space, but now he had an old chair at Sarah's. For a moment Fran felt that her world was changing too fast, but then her mam called, 'Howay in, Fran. 'Tis as well you spoke kindly to the hens.'

Fran shut the door behind them. It was then she saw egg cups on the table and stiffened. Boiled eggs for tea meant news. Good or bad? Which? There was no one to ask, for Viola was already washing in the scullery, alongside her mam, who was holding the towel. Fran joined them, forcing a laugh. 'Have we been good wee girls, our mam, to have an egg?'

Her mam shook her head. 'You're always good bairns, and don't let anyone tell you different, and so is our Ben. He's sold another crossword and is upstairs finishing his homework so he can start "setting" another.'

Fran sagged with relief and pleasure. Davey would be so

proud of the lad, for it was his teaching that had made it possible, and his introduction to the editor of the magazine that took so many of Davey's crosswords. Stan had told the lads about Ralph saying at the wedding that he'd help find a publisher for the puzzle book Ben and William wanted to produce when they were older. Their next hospital visit was the coming week, and they'd try and sneak in an extra one, so they could take Ben, though he'd already been with their mam.

She washed, and she and Viola made their way back to the table. Her mam checked that the water was boiling in the pan, then one by one, as though they were the most fragile objects in the world, she lowered the spoon, sliding the eggs into the water. It was the only thing her mam ever timed. 'Three minutes, lass. Keep your eye on the clock, and, Viola, give our Ben a call. I want you two settled down for a bit of peace and quiet, for you've the sing-song tonight and you'll be tired. I tell you, I'm right glad you're not heading up to the Hall, and that you have Sunday off.'

Viola went into the hall to call Ben, who hurtled down the stairs at a run. She held the door wide open, flagging him to slow down. He was wearing socks and slid to a stop at the table, arms outstretched. 'Did Mam tell you?' He sat on his chair, receiving a tap on his head with a spoon from his mam.

'Into the scullery and get them clever hands washed.'

He shot there, full of the energy of success, as Viola and Fran grinned at one another.

'Mam, it's not me hands that's clever—' he called.

'—it's your brain,' Fran and Viola shouted in unison, for it was what he had said last time.

He tore back in again and sat. Fran checked the clock. 'Three minutes, Mam.' She loved this, her family all together. Things as they'd always been, even though some were missing. Out came the eggs, the shells drying on the spoon as if by magic. They'd be just soft enough, they always were.

As they dunked soldiers in the yolks, Ben said, 'I reckon I should come to the Rising Sun tonight with everyone else cos I've done well.'

Annie, sitting at the head of the table, merely looked at him. 'Howay, our Ben, getting a crossword taken doesn't mean you've added a few years to your age. Sorry, lad, you'll stay here with me, and that's that. I've wool that needs winding.'

'Oh Mam—'

One look from his mam was enough, and Fran hid a grin as he subsided into muttering under his breath about a prophet having no honour in his own home.

Viola surprised them all. 'John 4:44. If you're going to mutter quotes, lad, then best to know where they're from.'

Ben stuffed a soldier into his mouth and pushed the spoon around the inside of the shell until the white curled round and came out in one piece. It sat glistening on his spoon while he said, 'Who's to say I didn't know?'

He opened his mouth and spooned in the egg, chewing, looking around as though he'd won the argument. He shoved in his remaining soldier too.

Fran and her mam were looking at Viola. 'By, lass,' said Fran, 'that's quite summat to know your quotes like that. Worthy of a crossword setter, eh, Ben?'

Viola was watching Ben as he continued to chew, his cheek bulging. She hid a grin. 'It's common sense to know, young Ben. Then you won't get clever clogs like me picking you up when you think you've been a smarty-pants.'

Annie rose from the table, collecting the plates and waving them all down. 'Wait, I've something for afters.'

Ben watched her go. 'Afters? But we never have afters these days.'

From the scullery, his mam called, 'Well, today, we have, so tra la.' Fran wondered what on earth her mam was up to.

Annie stood at the doorway holding a plate of four scones, one each. 'The bairns made them.'

'Scones?' Ben spluttered, crumbs falling from his mouth.

His mam held the plate out of range and clipped his ear. 'That's disgusting. Not sure you should have one with all this showing off.'

Ben swallowed, again and again, until finally his mouth was empty. He dragged the back of his hand across his lips and almost earned another clip, but he dodged his mam's hand and said, 'I reckon our Viola should be a teacher. She's clever, knowing the Bible, and she'd teach bairns a lot. And they'd like her an' all, for she wouldn't keep clipping 'em.' He rubbed his ear and grimaced.

The women laughed. 'Good try at changing the subject,' said Viola.

Ben watched his mam carefully slice open the scones, then fetch butter and honey from the scullery. 'What?' he said. 'Where . . . ?'

'Farmer Thompkins brought the bairns back from school in his trailer in the week and had some butter and honey to spare for Sophia and the co-op. He said that Mrs Massingham looked fair wore out, and time we found her a helper, especially with Joy gone. Someone good with bairns, who'd put up with no nonsense. But where'll we find such a one?'

Annie buttered the scones, then added honey, closed them up again and handed the plate to the girls first. 'Savour these, pets, they'll keep you going this evening.'

Only then did she pass it to Ben, who placed his scone on his own plate and just stared down at the priceless object.

'Oy,' Fran called, watching him closely. 'Where's that noddle taking you now?'

Ben looked at her, then at Viola, then at his mam. He

looked again at his scone, then up at Viola. 'Can you make scones, our lass?'

She laughed. 'Of course I can. Why? Have you come up with a crossword clue or something?'

Fran was cutting her scone into quarters, watching Ben because he so reminded her of her da, and it wasn't just the dark hair and eyes. She smiled, for she'd guessed where this was going and it was in absolutely the right direction. Oh, clever Mam, clever lad.

'Well, I've come up with something,' said Ben, 'but it isn't a clue. Viola, I can see how carefully you washed your fingers before you sat to eat, but, lass, you've more than one bandage on that sore hand and it seems to me the top one's a man's handkerchief, and see how it's oozed right through. I reckon 'tis time to give the Factory a miss and help out Sophia, for you know a lot, and it would be different work and more kindly to your hand. What'd you think, Mam, for she'd have a bigger bedroom, I bet? Then you wouldn't have to squash in with Fran and sleep on that hard truckle.'

There was a heavy silence. Fran murmured, ' "Out of the mouth of babes and sucklings" – that's Psalm 8. See, I know me quotes too, Viola.'

Viola looked from one to the other, then down at her half-eaten scone. 'Psalm 8, verse 2, it is. But Ben, Mrs Hall, Fran, you've been so kind and made this my home. How can I go up there, to a bigger bedroom? It would be so ungrateful.'

Fran reached across and grabbed her good hand. 'Don't be—'

Her mam came around and rested her hands on the lass's shoulders. 'Aye, this is your home, you know it is. We're your family, and the same can be said on behalf of Sarah and Beth – that's how things work round here. But we're not blind, we see you need to rest your hand. We also see Sophia's need. I've already spoken to Mr Massingham, and he likes the idea. It'd be like being a governess and a big sister to the bairns – and a cleaner, a knee-washer, an ear-skelper.' They were all laughing now. Viola looked again from one to the other, really looked, her auburn fringe falling over her eyes, her smile broad. Annie continued. 'The Massinghams and the bairns will also make you feel like family.'

Annie kept her hands on Viola's shoulders as the girl tried again to rise. After a minute Fran could see that slowly Viola was relaxing. Ben spoke again. 'Besides, them bairns need someone who sounds like them, cos though that Mrs Massingham is all right, she's a bit above, if you know me meaning, and you're Geordie, like the bairns, and us. Some of them have lost a mam or a da or a sister in the war, or all their family, and so have you. They're 'vacuees and them that have mams and das could be at the Hall for years before they go home. Them that divint have mams? Well, I'm not sure. They could be there for ever, and how would Sophia manage? Not sure what would happen if the bliddy Nazis win, mind, and I divint think I'm sure of much, when I hear myself bliddy speak.'

'Language,' shouted Fran and Annie automatically, laughing as Ben crossed his arms and scowled.

'As I were saying . . .' he lifted his voice above the noise, '. . . they need someone like them. They said that, when I were up with Stan, Sid and Norm playing footie this afternoon, cos it were more than the footie with us they liked. It was the way we said things.'

He scowled even more, then slumped. 'Oh, I divint know how to put it.'

Fran leaned across and kissed Viola on the cheek as Annie returned to her chair. 'Stop mithering, Viola,' Fran said. 'If you don't want to go, or do want to go but find you don't like it, then come back. By then I'll be in the front room with Davey, when he's here, and I might as well stay there, so me little bedroom is yours.' She stopped, turning to her mother. 'Oh Mam, we were fitted today. Me dress is like a dream, and the girls' dresses are too, and Gaines—'

Viola was leaning forward. 'Aye, Gaines found us, but said nowt, beyond he were pleased with the Factory, right pleased. He's moving on, probably to investigate other factories.'

'Poor buggers,' Ben muttered, grinning as all three repeated, 'Language.'

Once the scones were finished and they'd washed the pots, Annie put lavender paste on Viola's hand, then a fresh dressing and bandage, kissing the bairn on her cheek. 'There, now have a sit-down, for you'll need to set off for the Rising Sun in time to get there without a fluster. Taking your saxophone an' all?'

'Oh aye. I'm playing for Beth singing "Ten Cents a Dance". It's such a sad, beautiful song about a woman being rented per dance by roughnecks, sailors and all sorts, and sometimes she thinks they really like her, but no, they're just paying for a dance, using her. It's one Bob likes, and the music is grand.'

Fran agreed. 'I know Bob's her husband, but I could skelp him for just disappearing. How difficult is it to write a letter even if he had to rush off?'

'She'll find comfort in the three of you being married,' said Viola, 'and like her, you'll be without your husband, Fran, which will help, for I reckon she's got a bit agitated with Sarah having Stan to hand, if you get my meaning. Meanwhile, and get your violins out, I haven't even got a boyfriend.'

'Oh, not soppy stuff,' moaned Ben.

'For now, Viola, forget about boyfriends,' said Annie.

'Think of your hand. Let me know what you decide about a job.'

'But if I do go,' whispered Viola, 'who'd put me paste on? How could I pay to keep me room here, for being in service is never good pay.'

Fran just shook her head. 'I reckon your hand'll be better in no time if you're not overtaxing it, and won't need paste. What d'you think, Mam?'

Her mam nodded. 'Aye, of course it will. And the money will be enough, and you are family, so you won't pay to keep your room – whatever next. Just don't make it too long before you decide, eh.'

Fran watched Viola relax, moving her fingers in time to a tune in her head, probably one they were singing this evening, and then looked at Ben, growing up so well, and so kindly. She heard her mam singing as she moved about the scullery, the scrape of Viola's chair as she went to join Annie.

She leaned back and closed her eyes, thinking that once Viola chose to take the job, for she would, Fran could see it in her eyes, there would be time enough to sort out a lad for her. Then they'd be *four* married women, and their bairns would be marrers, and their mams would be grandmothers. The only things that would make her mam happier would be to have her husband as a grandfather, but not just that, her babe, Betty, growing up to have a family too. She sighed, and in her head she took a step forward, out of thoughts of the past, to stay in the present.

Chapter Fifteen

Beth headed for Mrs Adams' shop once Bert had dropped them all back in Massingham after work. She'd promised her mam that she'd pick up some bacon. The bell jangled. Inside, the shop was dark, as usual, because the windows were not only criss-crossed by blast strips, but pasted with war posters. Mrs Adams waved from the counter. Behind her the jars of sweets were almost empty. There were a few tins on the shelves and in front of the counter was a large sack of potatoes.

Beth handed over her ration book, and Mrs Adams weighed and wrapped the two rashers in greaseproof paper.

'That'll make the veggie pie more exciting, eh?'

'Aye, thank you, Mrs Adams.' She put her hand in her mac pocket. All she had was a few pence for the bacon – was it enough? Like a child, she held out her hand.

Mrs Adams took the coins. 'Thank you kindly, pet.'

Beth turned, but Mrs Adams called her back. 'Howay, pet, some broken biscuits never go amiss, eh, for your cuppa?'

'I've no more money on me, Mrs Adams. Will you put it on the slate?'

'No need. My treat. 'Tis a long time to wait for you lasses between letters, eh? You imagine all sorts. My Maisie did an' all.'

Beth just smiled, because Maisie's husband Derek hadn't come back from Dunkirk, so how did that help?

'Hurry on home now, pet,' Mrs Adams continued. 'You must be weary, and you have a busy evening at the pub.'

The bell jangled as the door closed and Beth headed away from Brady Square, turning left down their back alley. She dodged through the ten-year-old footie players, who groaned as she caught the kicked ball and threw it to the wrong team.

'Howay, Beth. You should have thrown it to me.' It was Aiden Martins from next door. 'You've a letter waiting, me mam said.'

'What?' Beth turned, her heart leaping. 'From me Bob?'

'Ah, me to know and you to fi—'

He stuck out his tongue and caught up with his marrers, who were scrabbling round near the goal chalked on the opposite wall. Young Timmy from number 4 yelled, 'Come on, Aiden, kick the ball.'

She ran on. He must have been at sea and had written the minute he got back, poor beggar, and what had she been doing? Mithering, that's what. She was bliddy daft, oh yes she was. She could eat now, and that'd make Mrs Iris happy, and Mrs Oborne too, for she'd said on the bus, 'You've gone skinny, like a wee rabbit.'

She reached the gate, opened it and tore across the yard and into the kitchen. Her mam swung round, pointing to the newspaper on the floor by the door. 'Boots.' It was a command.

Beth laughed, dropping the bacon and biscuits on the table before backing to the newspaper, tearing at her laces, rushing so fast she knotted them. 'Bliddy hell,' she shouted.

'Language,' her mam called from the scullery.

'Oh Mam,' she wailed. 'Let me see the letter.'

She slipped off her boots and tiptoed on the cold flagstones towards her mam, who stood in the doorway, waving an envelope.

'Who told you? I wanted it to be my surprise.'

'Aiden.' Beth made a dart for the letter.

Her mam dodged, laughing, then handed it to her. 'Here it is, pet. See, it says "Mrs Beth Jones" in his royal blue ink, so maybe you'll eat your pie, not poke at it, especially as it's got bac—'

Beth wasn't listening, devouring the sight of Bob's handwriting and the ink he used. She had been ink monitor at school, mixing up the powder and filling the inkwells that were lined up on the teacher's table. Bob had laughed when she'd told him as they lay in the meadow together years later, saying she must have been a beautiful monitor.

She drifted into the hall, hearing his voice in his head. Perhaps he was going to be at the Rising Sun tonight. Perhaps they'd arrived back in port yesterday or the day before, and it was his turn for leave. Perhaps, if it were more than one day, they'd lie together in their bedroom tonight? But if not, maybe he'd be back for Fran's wedding, all the married girls together, and the husbands too, just like she'd been hoping.

Her mam called after her, 'I'll have a cup of tea waiting for you, when you've come down from that fluffy white cloud, eh?'

Beth nodded, walking along the hall, hearing her mam say, 'You must eat before you leave for the pub, and I'll put the bacon on top of the veggie pie – not much for a singing star, but there you are.'

They both laughed.

'You'll already know the others are calling for you at seven, or so Maud Bedley said. That'll get you there by eight if you pedal fast. I'm working on me rug with Annie and Maud as we thought the last ones you want watching when you have to put on a show are your mams. Ben'll be with us, winding some wool, though he's gagging to go.

Him and his marrer William think they're older than they are, daft bairns.'

Beth laughed again, and holding the letter to her breast slipped into the front room, her bedroom, her and Bob's bedroom. Soon Fran would be in her own front room with Davey, when he was at home. Lucky Sarah, to have Stan with her, lying with him every night, knowing she was loved. Well, of course, now she had Bob's letter she knew she was too, but to have that person lying next to you, his arms around you, his mouth on yours. She shook her head and walked to his side of the bed.

'Aye, lad,' she murmured, sitting where he had lain. She held the letter in her hand, reluctant to open it in case his love tore at her too much. 'Don't be so bliddy wet,' she told herself. 'First you miss him, then you worry, and when he's here, in this writing, in this envelope, you still make a fuss.'

She opened it.

Howay, Beth. A letter from me at last, lass. I have been trying to write this for a while.

Beth smiled. So, he had been thrashing about on the waves. Who could write when nowt was steady? She was surprised there weren't salt-water stains on it. She read on:

I am imagining you sitting on your da's chair, opposite your mam, and right glad I am that you are safe and with your friends close by. Friends, family and marrers are real important, lass, you just remember that. And if this arrives on the day of your Rising Sun sing-song, then I hope with all my heart it goes well. For I'm sure it will, with the four of you. I'm glad there are four of you and that you are all there together, when I won't be.

She smiled, stroking the bed. Not here, not yet, but soon, she thought – soon. It didn't matter that he wasn't coming tonight, for he'd thought of her, remembered, and so she'd sing for him and only him. Aye, Mrs Jones would sing for Mr Jones. She kissed the letter. 'I can put this in my pocket, my lovely lad, and feel you close. Just as long as you are alive. As long as you keep writing, and come when you can, eh? For we've a war to win, and sometimes I forget that.' She read on.

As I just said, I've been trying to write this for a while, but I couldn't find the words, but now I've got to . . .

Her mam called from the hallway. 'You keep an eye on the time, lass. You need a bit of a wash and brush-up, so make sure you stop dreaming about your man by six thirty. That's not long.'

Beth heard her mam, of course she did, outside the door, in a world that seemed a long way from her. A world that began to fade as she read on and couldn't understand what he was mithering about.

. . . because it isn't fair not to. War is so complicated, like I said to you at Sarah's wedding. And it was a grand wedding. Just think on it, lass. There was Stan, glowing with happiness, he was, when once he thought his heart were breaking because you'd left him for me. But it wasn't broke, was it? He found love with Sarah, you see. And love that is so big it spills out for everyone to see.

War's a bugger, for everyone, for it takes us to places we didn't know existed, and to people. You see, well, you see I can say that for I've come away from Minton pit, been on a minesweeper and been blown out of it, wallowing in the bliddy water, cold and hurt, and been rescued. I've been helped by nurses. Well, one nurse in particular. A nurse – d'you see what I'm saying? D'you see why I say it's all so complicated?

Beth looked up from the letter, her mouth dry, her eyes stinging, her mind utterly and completely numb, for she

203

didn't *see*, wouldn't *see*. Instead, she listened to her mam singing 'Ten Cents a Dance' in the kitchen. It was one of the songs she, Beth Jones – yes, Jones – would sing. 'Yes, Jones, for I'm your wife, *I'm* your wife, and who hasn't faced death, Bob? We do every day, sorting out your ammunition. Our Stan faces a dirty death, me da died. *Your* da died. So, what's a bit of water, a bit of pain and fear that makes your life more complicated than mine?'

It was a whisper. Her throat was too tight for anything else. And she wouldn't read his words, his complicated, stupid bliddy words. Of course, she wouldn't.

She rose, walked to the window, looking at the darkening March evening. No one used the front road of the terraces unless they were the postman or had cars, and no one had cars. Or rather, few had cars. Yes, just a few, like the Massinghams, who were married, so they shared a car. Married people shared with one another. Aye, they did. She rested her head against the cool glass. Made herself breathe in for four, out for four, as Mr Hall had told them all. She recited the two times table, as Sarah had taught those caught under the rubble in Scotland.

'See, that's what is complicated. I don't want to read what your sort of complicated is, Bob Jones. You have a nurse, and I'm just a factory girl – is that your "complicated"?'

She looked down at the letter in her hand, stared at the royal blue ink – not the words, just the colour – scrunched it up and threw it across the bed, *their* bed, until it hit the wall and bounced back to lie on the rug. She stared at it, then out of the window, breathing, reciting the three times table now, but still her throat was tight, and though her words floated on the top of her mind, beneath it was numb.

But then she turned again and walked across the threadbare rug to the ball of paper. She opened it up. Had the evening become so much darker in just a few minutes?

Because she couldn't see even the colour, and it couldn't just be because her eyes were full of unshed tears. She blinked. Her eyes cleared as the tears ran down her face, off her chin and onto the paper. Smudging the ink like she had thought the seawater might. She had to read on. She could be wrong. Aye, that was it. She was wrong.

You see, bonny lass, it's like when you left Stan for me. You see, I am leaving you for someone. I wrote, so you'll understand. You can see how Stan picked himself up, and with your marrers you can do the same. By, lass, it doesn't mean I didn't love you once, it just means my world is bigger now, with more people to choose from, different sorts, interesting sorts, and it's here I've found love. Nowt wrong with you, lass, it's me that's changed.

Don't you go fretting about what to do with any of my things I might have left at your mam's. You keep them, or sell them for what little they're worth. I'll be here for a while, ashore, refitting, but I don't need them.

'Oh, aye, that means I chuck away that wedding photo on the mantelpiece, does it? Or I can keep that for meself, can I, Bob Jones? All to myself to look at, and it'll keep me warm of a night?'

She slumped onto the bed, aware that she was shaking her head. He'd gone into the wide world and seen her and Massingham for what they were – shabby, sad, stupid – worth nothing more than a letter in royal blue ink. For she wasn't a nurse, different, interesting.

The light was fading, and she realised he hadn't even signed it. The letter lay on her lap and she stared at nothing. And thought of nothing. She made herself breathe, concentrating only on that, for she had a concert tonight. Her throat must open enough to sing. She must stand upright.

She must smile. For it's what Fran would do, and Sarah, and Viola. She straightened, but the effort was fit to break her in half.

Her mam knocked on the door, then opened it. 'Just look at you, sitting in the gloom, dreaming. Draw the blackout and put the light on, lass, for you've to change into your smart clothes. That frock you wore last time, eh? Or would have worn if Miss fancy-pants Amelia hadn't butted in and taken your booking.'

Be quiet, Mam, she wanted to scream. Just be quiet, for I am trying to breathe. Her mam pulled the curtains and put the light on. 'There you go. Smarten yourself up, even though you'll be on cloud nine now you've heard from him. Quick, quick, for you'll want to eat.' She closed the door.

In the light Beth breathed in for four, out for four. Again and again. She saw then that there was a PTO in the bottom right-hand corner. She turned over the paper.

I know it seems cruel, abrupt, but I tried to warn you at Sarah's wedding, though for a moment I were conflicted. I was there, with you, the smell of the pit, the familiar faces, and I tried to pretend, to make the pretence real. But it weren't enough, for I didn't fit no more. So, bonny lass, I need that we divorce. 'Tis the right thing to do, you know, bring it to a tidy end. And you see, I want to marry me nurse. Write to me at this address, me digs, it is. Let me know you are all right, and will sign the papers when I sort out what's needed by the court.

Bob

Chapter Sixteen

The girls' cycle lamps were mere slits, the moon bright enough to remind them of the road to Minton, but not bright enough for them to see one another. Beth hadn't eaten her meal, which she had put in the bin when her mam wasn't looking. She felt bad about the bacon, and had slipped it back into the remains of the pie. Beth had drunk her tea, though, for it was warm and she was so cold. Deep down cold, and she'd shivered. Her mam had seen and brought down her own best cardigan. 'Put this on under your mac, pet. Spring evenings are a mite chilly.'

Beth had wanted to lean her head on her mother's shoulder and feel her strong arms come around her while she wept. 'Hush, pet, my wee one,' her mam'd say. 'I'll go and see him, sort it out for you. You leave it to your mam, or if your da was alive he'd go and see him. Daft beggar. I'll send that nurse on her way. Who does she think she is?'

As the owl hooted, Beth lifted her head to the moon. Aye, that's what her mam would say. But Beth had said nothing to her mam, for she had to sing for her money, and would use it to go to Grimsby first thing and see him at his digs. Why else had he written his address? He would just send the papers, so it meant he wanted her to come. She'd show him that her love was big enough for his world, and that she was a singer as well as a factory girl, and could be as complicated as he liked. Of course she could.

As she cycled she thought of the co-op, who always said, 'Once you have a plan, everything's better.'

'Well, it bliddy isn't,' she whispered as they cycled round the bend.

Fran laughed. 'Isn't what?'

Beth shook her head. 'Never mind. Let's go through the songs, eh?'

They did, and were word-perfect. Stan, Sid and Norm brought up the rear, clapping, cycling along 'no hands'. The girls laughed, Beth too, or so she pretended. Bob was interested in pretending. For a moment the bitterness almost choked her. She sensed Fran drawing alongside, and then Viola, and they cycled three abreast while Sarah slipped back and rode with Stan. For once, Norm and Sid were not smoking, for their Woodbines had burned through so fast in the night air that they ceased to bother.

When a van tooted behind them, they slipped into single file so that it could pass, and Beth thought of Mrs Bedley, whom she had helped to stop drinking while Sarah and Fran were in Scotland. Remembrance of Mrs Bedley's battle forced her to breathe more easily, for a moment, for surely that mammoth effort cancelled out her hurting Stan, for that's where her mind had been taking her. She had left Stan for Bob, she had hurt the lad, but as Bob said, Stan was happy. So, she could tell Bob that she didn't deserve to be dropped in her turn. Would it help? She doubted it, but she must try.

She bowed her head, hearing the swish of their bike tyres, just as she had heard it over the years as they'd cycled here, there and everywhere. Who in the whole of England was better than these people? 'Who?' she said aloud. 'Not a nurse who's a stranger.'

Fran and Viola dropped back to cycle with her again and Viola asked, 'Who? What? Where?'

Beth didn't know what she was talking about and just shook her head, for she was reciting her times tables silently.

She laughed aloud, but it sounded harsh, even to her. So far, she hadn't been under rubble, but if it happened it would be a relief. She could die then. Fran looked at her and muttered, 'Nerves, we're all feeling them.'

Beth was glad no one had heard that she'd had a letter, not yet. It was only the neighbour who knew. But news would carry on the wind, she was sure. Not tonight, though. Please, not tonight.

Viola started singing 'I Get a Kick Out of You.' They all joined in, even the lads, and Viola's saxophone, perched in her basket, was rattling so loudly in its case, that she reached forward and patted it.

They moved on to 'All or Nothing At All', panting as they pushed harder on the pedals. On they sang through their repertoire, and finally came to 'Ten Cents a Dance'. Beth let the others sing, hardly able to listen when they reached 'sailors . . . can pay for their tickets, and rent me.'

Are you listening in your digs, bonny lad? she thought. Is that what you did, paid for a ticket and rented me? You might just as well have been those rough guys in the lyrics who 'tear my gown'. But not my gown, just my bliddy heart.

Finally, they rode into Minton, in good time for their eight o'clock start.

They scrambled from their bicycles, propped them up against the rear wall, and felt their way in the darkness to the rear entrance and through the outer door. Stan led the way, knowing where the sneck on the bar door was, as Sid muttered, 'Fiddling about, he was, when the snow were on the ground and it were cold enough to freeze the whatnots off brass monkeys.' He called over the girls' heads, 'Aye, howay, lad, remember 'tis high up, for the love of Mike.'

Stan had already found it. 'Hush yerself, you daft ha'p'orth.'

They laughed as they half fell into the bar, and no one noticed that every sound Beth made was false.

The bar was already full to bursting, and there were Mr and Mrs Oborne, waving madly at them, and Mildred, Stevie's missus, pointing to glasses of elderberry wine set out on a tray, waiting for the girls. The air was full of smoke from the fireplace, the clay pipes and cigarettes. There was the scent of beer, a drink that Beth's da had told her, when she was a bitty bairn, burned out tonsils. Stevie was pulling pints, though only of the regular kind, not the special brew.

Fran led the way to him. 'Are we all right for the special on April second, Stevie?'

Stevie shrugged, his tea towel over his shoulder. 'What's important about the second?'

As the chorus of protests rose, he conducted it, grinning. 'Ah, that'd be the wedding then, eh? Would I let you and Davey down, lass? 'Tis all ready. Mr Massingham paid the bill. And no, Ralph's not recovered consciousness, but Mr Massingham was just making good on the lad's promise.'

Stevie nodded at Beth. 'It's a shame you and Bob were wed before Ralph changed his spots, eh, Beth.'

Beth nodded. Viola was making her way to the 'stage' in the corner, and lifting her saxophone from the case. Stan passed the wine to the girls, and tankards of beer to Sid and Norm. Norm put up a hand, surveyed the room, and looked at Sid.

'Three, two, one,' Sid muttered. He and Norm put their fingers in their mouths, and their combined whistles silenced the room. Sid grinned. 'The girls are here and will sing in ten minutes, so hush your noise when you see them reach that corner, eh?'

'You hush your own noise, young Sid,' shouted Tilly Oborne. 'Course we will, or I'll want to know the reason why.'

'Oy, oy,' Stevie said, wiping the bar. 'I'll have no fisticuffs in here, our Tilly, you hear?'

Beth heard it all, and somehow it was as if she was clinging to all these friends, all these voices, to the taste of the
elderberry wine. All these fragments of memories. Aye,
Bob, this is my shabby world, and once it were good enough
for you, she thought. There was a draught as the door
opened, and Stevie forced a smile as a quietness descended.

'Howay there, Mr Gaines. Just in time for the show. Did
you manage to make your phone call?'

Fran stepped forward into the quietness, for Mr Gaines
had come good, eventually.

'Let me buy you a drink, Mr Gaines, to thank you for
telling us that the Factory was one of the best you'd ever
investigated. A factory that makes domestic utensils, I
might add.' There was a general rustling of interest amongst
the drinkers.

Sarah and Beth dug into their pockets and brought out
coins. 'Make that the three of us buying you a drink,'
Sarah said.

But then Mr Swinton rose from the settle at the back.
'Howay, it's my turn. I reckon I owe you a thank-you, too,
Mr Gaines.' He drew close and in an undertone said, 'Mr
Bolton had a quiet word with me and I'm much obliged for
your kind remarks on me training and running of the sector.' He was holding out his hand, and Gaines shook it, the
two men smiling at one another.

Miss Ellington, who had been chatting quietly to Simon
Parrot by the fireplace, came across. 'Much as I like this
bonhomie, you should be on, lasses.' She pointed to the
clock. 'And I'd like you to sing "My Baby Just Cares for Me".'

'Oh, would you indeed?' called Stevie.

Mildred flicked him with her tea towel and said, 'Mind
your own business, you meddlesome old fool.'

Stevie grinned, his gold tooth glinting. Fran stared. Glinting just like—She stopped the thought. No, she'd faced up to

the glint of the kirby grip. This thought no longer belonged in her head.

Stevie raised his voice over the quietening drinkers. 'Note, if you will, the jug on the counter for the widows, the injured and all what . . .'

The girls made their way to the 'stage'. The wine hadn't touched Beth's core. The three of them stood together, with Viola off to the left. Above the clapping they heard Tilly Oborne boom, as only she could, ' "Blue Moon" would be grand, lasses.'

Fran laughed. 'You'll have what you're given, Mrs Oborne.'

Sarah nudged Beth, who forced a laugh, for these were her people, her marrers, but the floor wasn't firm, the air seemed to whirl. She shivered. Sarah's arm slid around her.

'Makes you nervous, doesn't it, bonny lass? But they're our friends, our world, and they just want to listen. Howay, maybe your Bob'll be here next time, and in two weeks it's Fran's wedding, and he'll no doubt stay longer than just a few hours. You just think on that.'

Fran was tapping her foot to the saxophone introduction of 'Putting on the Ritz', and then they were into the song, and Beth knew the words, knew the steps they had decided to include and the smile that must match the smiles of the others.

As the song ended, a man brought over more glasses of elderberry wine on a tray for them. She thought she knew him. Viola played the first few bars of 'On the Sunny Side of the Street'. Beth took a glass. Sarah nudged her and frowned, whispering, 'No, not from that beggar Norris Suffolk. Don't you remember, he sold me mam the drink night after night, racking up a load of interest.'

Beth stared at the wine, then at Norris, the black marketeer. He winked at them. Beth replaced the glass on the tray.

'No,' she said. 'I helped Mrs Bedley to stop drinking your

stuff. Stan saw you off. I came out with the rolling pin to whack you, but I wasn't needed.'

He shrugged and walked away. There, Bob, she thought. I've helped see him off twice now, so I'll see off the nurse, you see if I don't. She stood straighter as Sarah whispered, 'I'm surprised Stevie's let him in.'

Her words were as wispy as the wind and floated up and away. They sang 'My Baby Just Cares for Me', then straight into 'Blue Moon' to cheers from Mrs Oborne, and this time it was Norm who brought wine, which they took and sipped during Viola's saxophone solo. Beth looked out at the audience, not at her friends, for they mustn't see her face, not really see it. She sipped, felt her body loosening, and it didn't matter that it seemed a cloud of lights was whirling around her head.

They clapped Viola; Beth gulped her wine. They sang 'Embraceable You' and she moved with the three girls, for now Viola was singing too, and they kept on the notes even though there was no instrument to help them. They sang on and on, and the room was getting warmer. Sweat trickled down Beth's back, but inside she was still so cold.

As they sang 'Night and Day' she saw Norris being shown the door, and Valerie passing him on her way in. Valerie waved. Another tray of drinks arrived, this time from Amelia. How odd. Beth was swaying to the music, but smiled her thanks, though Sarah shook her head, so Beth took hers, too, and put it behind her on the table that stood to one side.

Fran said, 'We'll need water, it's so bliddy hot.'

Beth nodded. 'So hot . . . too hot to breathe. Yes, breathing is hard, but we have to try, or we'll die. We shouldn't die, should we?'

Fran eased herself to Beth's side. 'Howay, sweet lass,' she murmured. 'What's to do?'

Beth felt Fran's arm around her shoulders now, and her head lying against hers as Sarah sang 'Love is the Sweetest Thing'. She wanted to tell Fran, wonderful Fran, that love wasn't sweet, it cut and sliced into every part of you till all you could do was keep breathing. But why? 'Why breathe?'

Fran tightened her grip. 'Beth, what's happened? We breathe to live.'

Beth sighed. Fran, upright, strong, about to be married to her Davey, so in love, so happy. Who was Beth to complicate it? Aye, complicate. She shook her head. 'I miss Bob summat terrible sometimes, that's all. Daft.'

'Come on,' said Fran, 'do our steps, eh? One step forward, one to the side and one back, and just think, you'll see your sailor soon, eh. You've had a letter, we've just heard from Mrs Oborne. No need of telephones while the co-op has ears like bats. That's so wonderful, but no wonder it's made the missing worse – for tonight.'

Beth reached back for the wine that Sarah didn't want and drank it. It was sour, warm, but she was so thirsty, and her head were banging fit to burst. She looked at her friends, who were her strength, especially Fran. 'Aye, but I will see him soon. And you will be married and we'll be the three married girls, eh.'

To the soaring sound of the saxophone, they started to sing 'Blue Moon' again as people had asked. She'd be paid tonight, and tomorrow she'd catch a train to Grimsby. Once he saw her, he'd know she was enough, because she could sing, she could dance, and she had made him happy before, so she would again.

Fran squeezed her hand. 'That's better, a grand smile, in time for your song. Give it a good belt, my sweet lass. Bob might not be here, but neither is Davey. Look around and see who is – our friends, our people, our marrers, and out there are the pits, the smell of sulphur, the smouldering of the slag, the whistle of the winding gear. Aye, we're here, where we belong, lass, so sing "Ten Cents a Dance" and make them cry, eh?'

She and Sarah stepped back and to the side, going to stand with Sid, Norm and Stan, who wrapped his arms around Sarah, his wife, as Bob used to do with Beth. Aye, his wife.

Viola was playing 'Ten Cents a Dance', and Beth sang the words, and thought that Bob might well not have ripped and torn her gown but . . .

She swayed and sang with her eyes closed. She stepped forward, paused, breathed. But . . . he had indeed torn her apart. Viola's saxophone was sweet and true while Beth hummed and danced as she had rehearsed. Stevie turned off half the lights as they had instructed. Then, in the gloom, Beth took back the stage, all the time thinking of her husband . . . And now her voice was growing in power, one she had not known she had. She stepped forward again. Would he also rent the nurse, too?

Viola followed with her saxophone as Beth sang, swayed, singing low, then high, wondering all the time how she could go on living. Aye, that was complicated. But no you couldn't pay enough to rent me Bob. There was Eddie Corbitt studying her intently. There was Josephine from the sewing shop, and Mrs Iris, Valerie from Sledgeford, and tears ran down their cheeks.

But there were no tears from Beth, because she was a star, *she* was Bob Jones's wife and she had to be tough and strong she told herself. Again the two of them stepped back, and to the side and to the front. Yes, she was a star and not a hostess for rent.

Viola was beside her now and her saxophone was rasping, then soaring. Together they swayed and stepped, and

Beth's voice was so pure that no one moved, no one drank, as the two girls held the stage. On she sang. On played Viola, her saxophone glinting. Can you hear my thoughts Bob as I tell you I own myself? Beth conducted. They stopped together, panting.

They stood still in the silence. For a moment no one moved. The two girls held hands. Mrs Oborne had her hand to her mouth as Fran and Sarah stepped forward, but it was Sid who came to wipe Beth's tears. It was then that the applause burst across the room, and Cyn Ellington forced her way through to Beth and Viola. She hugged both of them and whispered, 'You should sing when the war is over, you two, and Fran and Sarah too, just as you have done this evening. But if you sing that song again, our Beth, and you play for her, Viola, I'll have to bang your heads together, for 'tis too haunting, too true, and so strong.'

Now others were clamouring around them, but it was Fran leading them towards the queue at the bar. 'I reckon a glass of water and then wine, eh, girls?'

She held Beth close, saying into her hair, 'I divint know what's going on, but you were the queen tonight, and Viola the princess. It was grand. Sarah and I don't know where to put ourselves, because we love you both so much. The lads have a table. You go and sit.'

'No, you go,' said Viola, 'we're too happy, so we'll get the drinks and bring them over.'

Beth and Viola looked at one another and the world steadied for Beth, because Bob weren't going to set her aside like a rented, ten-cents-a-dance hostess. She'd not let him.

Stevie was serving those in front, but saw them and called, 'Let the stars through, and don't you two dare sing and play like that again, for me tea towel's wet and it's not seemly for a man to have something in his eyes that makes 'em run.'

216

Mr Gaines stood to one side, gesturing them past, saying, 'That was very grand. Something to remember.'

Viola finally reached the bar as Eddie Corbitt turned to them, a glass of wine in each hand. He thrust one at Beth, one at Viola. 'Get it down you, lasses. You deserve it. Your Bob'll be proud when he hears about tonight, Beth. And your da would have been right moved.'

At that moment, right behind her, Beth heard Amelia Cartwright's harsh whisper, felt the moist heat of her breath on her neck.

'Well, Beth, fancy you throwing back the wine as you're doing when you're the one who ticked me off in this very pub and warned me the drink was giving me a loose tongue.'

Beth swung round, keeping her voice equally low. 'Ah, Amelia. Aye, I did, but it wasn't good to be speaking about the fence and making clear where you were really working, was it? You could have got yourself in a lot of trouble, and who's to say someone weren't listening, for divint forget, there were an attempt to break in not long after.'

Amelia flushed and raised her voice. 'At least I didn't stand on a stage and make a fool of myself, caterwauling to all and sundry. What's happened to you, anyway?'

Viola turned round and caught Beth's hand, which was about to come up and slap Amelia. 'Beth was good to you,' she whispered, 'and tried to keep you out of trouble. You and everyone in the pub knows it.'

Amelia thrust her head forward. 'You weren't there, and besides, all I said back then was that the fence round the Factory was down. How was I to know someone would break in? It's not as though they blew up the ruddy detonator block or anything. Besides, that was then, this is now.'

'Just be quiet,' Viola continued in a whisper. 'You've done it again, you idiot.'

'D'yer want this tray of drinks or not, girls?' Stevie called.

Then, more loudly, 'Thanks everyone, nice lot of money in the jug, but room for more.'

Mr Gaines nodded. 'I'll take the lasses' drinks to the table, Stevie. Pop them on my bill, and a pound for the jug, if you will.'

Stevie grinned and passed the tray over Eddie's head to Gaines, who forced his way ahead of the girls. Beth followed, worried that Gaines had heard. How could he not? Would she and Amelia get the sack? Behind her, Beth felt a tug on her arm. It was Amelia.

'Did Mr Gaines hear?' The girl was pale, anxious.

'I hope not,' muttered Beth. 'Besides, his report is in and he's away from here tomorrow.'

Leaning towards Beth, Amelia nodded. 'Anyway, I'm administration and it's absurd to link me in any way to the break-in, and I'll thank you to remember that. What's more I suggest you don't even think of taking to the stage when all you're suited for is the factory floor.'

Amelia's voice might have been low, but Viola heard. 'You're a horrid piece of work, Amelia.'

Amelia stormed off, and Beth just shook her head, because of course Amelia was right; she was in administration, and Beth *was* on the factory floor. Was it any wonder Bob loved a nurse?

She was cold again as they followed Mr Gaines through the swathes of people who were patting them on the back and calling, 'Grand you were, lasses.' 'Divint know you had it in you, our Beth.'

When they reached the fireside table, Stan offered round his Woodbines, while Mr Gaines deposited the drinks, moving off to talk to Cyn Ellington and Simon Parrot. Beth sipped her drink while the conversation ebbed and flowed around her, but nothing seemed real, not even when Stevie made his way over to them as the clock struck ten.

'Any chance of an encore, girls? After which I'll call time, and I'm right sorry Norris Suffolk were bothering you earlier. He's banned because we don't want to be tarred with his black-market brush. It were Josie that served him, knowing no better. Sorry to you, Sarah, most of all, since he sold your mam all that back-of-a-lorry booze.'

He was sweating with embarrassment. Sarah just smiled. 'Don't be daft, he was no trouble. Besides, we're big enough to give him a good bop on the nose if needed.'

They made their way to the stage, and the clapping of the audience somehow stirred Beth, who straightened up, smiled, and then found the strength to whisper to Viola, 'Is your hand all right to play, or will you just sing?'

Viola eased her saxophone strap and patted the instrument. 'All right for now, but if it hurts, I'll sing. It's like your song made me feel like I own myself, so 'tis up to me to decide what I do and what I allow others to do to me. That was so clever and strong, but so sad.'

Beth let the words sink in. Clever? She wanted to believe it. They sang their encore songs, and as Viola played the introduction to the favourite "Blue Moon", Beth felt Sarah's arm slip around her waist.

'Beth, bonny lass, we all think you're not feeling yourself, pet.'

Beth forced a smile. 'That's because I'm not – it's you with your arm round my waist feeling me, daft girl.'

'Probably exhausted with the relief of hearing from Bob, eh?' murmured Sarah.

They sang.

The audience joined in, and Fran saw Amelia standing to one side and beckoned her to join in, along with Brenda and Rosie. Amelia shook her head and wove her way through the audience, taking her coat from the hook by the front door and slipping out.

Sarah waved the other two girls to the stage, and they came. The five of them rolled straight into 'The Very Thought of You', and as the girls swayed to the saxophone, Beth sang it for Bob, and saw Fran's face, and knew she was sending it to Davey. There was Sarah, reaching out to Stan and joining him on the floor, dancing. Sid leapt forward and grabbed Beth, and Norm took Fran's hand for a dance, leaving Rosie and Brenda to sing on. Just the two of them, for Viola was dancing with Eddie Corbitt. Beth closed her eyes and let Sid hold her, for he was her friend, part of the gang. On they danced, and in that moment she felt safe, protected, and as though she couldn't possibly fail tomorrow.

Fran grabbed her and they were back on stage for 'A-Tisket, A-Tasket', and on they sang through their encore repertoire, but they weren't singing alone. No, the whole pub joined in, and Beth felt the comfort of it, of them, and couldn't believe that Bob could not see the value of this world, no matter how many others he experienced. She knew then that her task was to make him see the privilege of being here, in Massingham, with her.

Back in his bedroom at the Rising Sun, Gaines wrote an addendum on the copy of his report. He noted that he had witnessed Amelia Cartwright being indiscreet when she'd had a drink or two, as well as deeply unpleasant. He noted down her exact words and advised a warning, or dismissal. One copy of the report, an updated one, would be left with the Factory. Another, also updated, he would deliver to Plomer at Head Office. A third would be delivered to Professor Smythe, for whom he also worked, though no one had any inkling of that.

Chapter Seventeen

Sunday, 15 March

Well before dawn, Beth rose, dressed and counted her share of the money earned last night. It should be sufficient. She crept from her bedroom – *their* bedroom – into the kitchen, where the range was only slightly warm, but to riddle the ash would alert her mam. She crept out in the dark to the netty, then back to the scullery to wash. She cut a few slices of bread, spreading a thin layer of dripping on each, filled a bottle with water, and put them all in her bag. She wasn't going to work today, for it was Sunday and they weren't often required. Even if they had been, she had something else to do. Something more important.

There were very few miners clomping along the lane as she crept from the house into the yard. Those that were would probably be the maintenance crew. She squeezed her bike's tyres. Yes, full enough. She placed her bag in the handlebar basket. Gently, she lifted the sneck, pulled the gate open and slipped through. The wind slammed it shut. She froze, listening. No, nothing. Her mam slept on.

Her woollen hat pulled well down over her head, she rode towards Main Street, her lamp giving a slit of light on the cobbles. Bob's letter, *her husband's* letter, was in her bag. She had not telegraphed him, it would be a surprise, and if his landlady said he wasn't in she would wait. Before she arrived, she would go into the lavatory on the train and put on the little bit of rouge she had left; she would also mark seam lines down her calves with her eyebrow pencil. She had a vestige of lippy, dry and cracked, but better than nothing. She would beg, plead, show him how much she loved him.

She cycled over the cobbles, clenching her jaw as the jogging splintered her headache into jagged bits. She reached Main Street, and wondered how Mrs Bedley, Sarah's mam, could have woken with a hangover every day when she'd been in her lost state. She turned right along Main Street, unsure what time the train really went, but Stevie Pertwee had said there was one about six thirty. It was only five now, maybe a little later, but she wanted to get there just in case Stevie was wrong and the train came earlier.

Did she have to change trains? She didn't know, but would ask when she bought her ticket. On she cycled, passing the bus stop. She'd be back for the bus tomorrow, happy because Bob would have held her, said he'd been daft, that seeing her was all he needed and it wasn't complicated after all. Suddenly she was sobbing, her nose running. She had read books but never known what it meant to be blinded by tears. She squeezed the brakes and juddered to a stop, her hand to her mouth. 'Shut up. Be quiet,' she whispered, her voice hoarse, her throat sore. 'I said no tears. It must be all right, for I canna be alone, I canna have me Bob not wanting me. I canna—'

She heard boots on the road, someone was running, a man's shout: 'Beth, bonny lass. Oh, bliddy hell, Beth, what's amiss, pet?'

She gulped, rubbing her face with her hands, then pulling her hat further down, gripping the handlebars and finding the pedals, for she must escape. But it was Sid, still shouting, and now he was gripping her arm, stopping her and the bike.

'Lass? What's amiss?'

'Leave me be, it's just the bliddy coal dust in my eyes, Sid. Let me alone.' The sky was lightening, dawn threatening, so it must be past five, nearer five thirty or later, and she must get to the station. She must go and she mustn't look at him, or he'd see what she had hidden all last evening and throughout the long night in bed, alone, trying not to allow the tears. But they *had* come, here on the road, and she felt so sick, so scared, and now she felt her throat thickening, her eyes filling again.

She mustn't. No. Sid's arm was round her now. She pressed her lips together, swallowed, cleared her throat and forced a sort of laugh. 'Leave me alone, Sid. I have to go.'

Sid, his cap slipped to the left as always, ignored her. He held her more firmly. She wrenched free and shouted, 'I can't miss the train.'

He still stood firm. 'Stop being such a bliddy fool and tell me, for you're going nowhere like this. What train? Why the tears? Why the "Ten Cents a Dance" with its awful sadness, so . . .' He stopped, but still didn't release her. 'It's Bob, isn't it? Is he hurt? Why didn't you tell us? We're yer marrers. I'll get me bike. You're not going nowhere alone.' He stopped. 'Where is he, anyway?'

'I'll miss me train,' she whispered. 'I have to tell him he can't . . .'

Sid stepped in front of her now, his hands covering hers, his legs either side of the wheel. A pitman was hurrying past, his bait tin rattling. ' 'Ow do,' he called.

The pithead gear was singing. Above, a crow cawed.

Beth stared after it. Sid had said she mustn't go alone. He cared, they all cared, but the girls were happy, and Viola were in pain with her hand. Ralph was right poorly and there was the rota, so she *mustn't* heap more on anyone. Sid leaned forward now, so close she could feel his breath on her face.

He whispered, 'Bob's not hurt, is he.' It wasn't a question. 'But he's hurt you. What's he done? Tell me, for I'll not let you go, bonny lass, till you do, whether you miss your train or not. Then I'll come with you.'

They stared at one another, and she hadn't realised that his eyes were so kind and his lashes were so long they should be a girl's.

'No,' she whispered. 'I don't reckon it'll help to have a lad along when I talk to him. You see, he thinks he doesn't love me. He thinks he wants a divorce because war is complicated . . . He says war shows you different worlds, different people. I reckon he's seen and liked clever people – nurses who made him better. He's found a special one.'

She stopped, her voice breaking. 'I 'spect what he means is his world divint just have to be factory girls with yellow skin, rashes and streaky hair.' She could hear her voice; it was like a thin, torn proggy length. It didn't sound like hers at all. 'But the war won't last for ever,' she went on. 'I could get another job, be more interesting. I worked in an office before the war, but he's probably forgotten—'

Suddenly, Sid let her go and stood to one side. 'You haven't told yer marrers?'

'They're happy making plans for the wedding, they have their men. There's the worry about Ralph, and about Sandra. Viola's hand won't heal. Best to leave them be.'

Sid tapped her on the arm. 'You're right, you don't need me. You best get going, lass. Off you go now and may your God go with you. Be safe.'

He had already begun to run, and she looked after him. Aye, even Sid had things to do in his own world, like the rest of the gang. Well, even if she were just a factory girl, she could still cycle, still catch the train, still try. She set off again, hearing Sid's footsteps fading, and felt even more alone.

*

Fran was riddling the grate and chatting to her mam about the feel of the silk on her body and Mrs Oborne saying it'd be such a beggar to sew that she was going to tack it with good, close stiches to hold it in place, else it would slip when it was machined. Fran felt tired and had wanted to sleep in, but her body couldn't forget the habit of early mornings any more than her mam's could. She muttered, 'By, I'll be glad when I'm back to office work when this bliddy war is done.'

Annie Hall laughed. 'I reckon you and your Davey'll have a brood by then, and that'll put paid to lie-ins till they leave home, if they ever do. And divint forget, you'll be working on his crossword magazine, or maybe he, Ben and William will work together.'

They both spun round at the crash as the gate banged back against the wall and boots pounded across the yard. Fran leapt for the door, but as she did so it opened and Sid stepped in. 'Glad you're up, or I'd have had to dig you out. Get your coat, our Franny, and get biking to the station. Have you money?'

Fran just stared and Sid snapped, 'Get your bliddy self to the station. Our Beth's on her way to that bastard husband of hers, who's written for a divorce because war is complicated or some such rubbish. I'll give the beggar bliddy complicated. He were never one of us, and he was right off-kilter at Sarah's wedding. She's off to see him. She's been weeping, I could bliddy—' He stopped himself and just stared at the two women, who were trying to absorb all that he was saying.

'I'm not the one to go with her,' he almost shouted. 'It would make her look weak, or as though she had a lover, something he'd use to get back at her. Besides, I'd bliddy rip his throat right out with me teeth. Best 'tis her marrers. I'm away to get Sarah sorted. She'll meet you there, at the station, I 'spect. So, have you money, or shall I give you some?'

Fran shook her head. 'We were paid last night. Go for Sarah.'

The door slammed in his wake. Annie disappeared into the scullery to cut bread and dripping and fill a water bottle. 'At least you've had a cuppa, our Fran.'

Viola burst into the kitchen in her nightdress, her hair awry. 'What's up? I heard Sid.'

'Nowt to worry you, lass,' Annie said.

Viola put her hands on her hips. 'Oh aye, then why is Fran rushing around like a blue-arsed fly?'

Fran was stuffing the bottle of water and the bread wrapped in greaseproof paper into her bag, and then her arm in the sleeve of her mac.

Annie went to take the bag from Fran as she struggled. 'It's Beth. Something's amiss. Fran'll tell us when she gets back, whenever that is.'

'It'll be this evening, Mam, has to be, we've work tomorrow.'

'I should be there helping with whatever it is,' Viola shouted.

Annie held up her hands. 'Hush. You and I, Viola, have to chat about whether you've decided to help at the Hall, so you're not going anywhere.' Annie turned to Fran, who was opening the back door. 'I've cash in the tin.' She pointed to the old biscuit tin on the mantelpiece.

Fran shook her head, already halfway out. 'No, I've the money from the Rising Sun in me mac pocket.' She hurried into the yard, but her mam had already taken the lid off the tin.

'You don't know how much you'll need,' Annie shouted. 'Stay where you are.'

Fran knew better than to move as her mam sent Viola

out after her. Viola put the money in Fran's pocket. 'I'll feed the hens. Take care – and of Beth.'

She held open the gate. Fran pushed her bike into the back lane, then pedalled as though the hounds of hell were snapping at her heels, bumping over the cobbles, her mind full of Bob, and divorce, and Beth, the song last night, the drinking, and she knew she should have asked more questions. 'Oh, Beth.'

She tore up to Main Street, snatched a look either way and crossed, knowing that last night her mind had been too full of wedding arrangements, dresses, love and Davey.

Davey. Her Davey, who had received a letter from Amelia telling him that Fran was having a 'do' with Ralph. To begin with he had believed the letter. Then Fran in turn had thought he was involved with Daisy. It was a time of hell for them both, and the memory of it still dried her mouth. Oh, poor Beth. Bob was her husband, for heaven's sake, they had made promises. Please, she thought as she raced along, let it be something and nothing. Ahead of her, she saw Sarah pedal out of *her* back lane without looking, cross the road and tear off towards the station.

Fran caught up and Sarah snatched a look at her. 'I'll bliddy kill the beggar,' she seethed. 'Bliddy Bob. Why the hell didn't she tell us? Why didn't I notice? Sid thinks she didn't want to say as we were so happy, and Viola still so hurt.' They were cycling at a speed they had not achieved since they were bairns, but it didn't seem fast enough.

'Did Sid say what time the train was?'

'No. But who knows these days anyway? Bliddy war. Complicated, our Bob thinks. Well, I'll bliddy complicate *him*.'

'Where are we going, anyway?' Fran asked.

'Oh, I divint know,' said Sarah. 'Grimsby?'

'Sid never said. Just to get there, be with her.'

'Aye, when haven't we been together, eh?'

Beth had her ticket. The train *was* about six thirty, but the stationmaster had said, ' 'Tis difficult to say these days, with troop trains, and freight . . .' He'd paused, tapping his nose. Beth had tried to smile, for the freight was probably the ammunition they were filling. She made her way onto the platform, bracing herself.

'See, Bob, I might be a factory girl, right enough, but it's war work, and where would you lads be without us, eh?'

She moved down the platform keeping her eye on the stationmaster, who'd said he'd make sure she got on the right train. He'd also said she might or might not have to change trains: 'Who knows—'

'—these days,' she'd finished for him. He'd laughed. She'd smiled, though her head was still splintering into different degrees of headache, and her courage was ebbing.

She sat on the platform bench, not wanting to be in the waiting room. Slowly breathing in and out, she recited, one times two is two. Breathe. Two times two is four. Breathe.

She wouldn't think of Bob, she wouldn't worry about him not being there, she wouldn't worry about him turning from her. She felt in her bag for her eyebrow pencil. She must remember to draw the line down her legs. She had written the note to her mam with it. The pencil had felt so heavy in her hand: *Back tonight. I have somewhere to be. I am all right. I love you, Mam.*

As the sky lightened and the birds sang, Beth huddled into her mac. The breeze brought the sulphur, the smell of coal, and the horizon looked like a series of giant molehills, though molehills didn't smoulder. These moles were her people and she realised she was scared to leave them. She shut her eyes. Ten times two is two. She shook her head. Stupid girl, ten times two is twenty. Eleven times two is twenty—

'Beth,' someone called. Beth turned, not believing the voice. But it *was* Sarah, and beside her – Fran. They were running, but their footsteps were drowned by the whistle of an incoming train as it rounded the long bend, its wheels screeching and sparks flying, the engine roaring and wheezing, its stack billowing smoke. Fran was shouting, her hands cupping her mouth, her bag and gas mask bumping against her hip.

'Grimsby, all aboard for Grimsby,' yelled the stationmaster.

'We asked where you were going and bought tickets,' Fran shouted. 'The guard said we might have to change trains, but who knows—'

'—these days,' interrupted Beth.

She waited for them. The train came to a stop and doors swung open, passengers alighted while others came streaming from the waiting room. The girls reached her, Fran hugged her so tightly that she could barely breathe. But she must breathe.

'Oh Beth, how could he? How could you go without us? Oh, bonny lass, sweet, bonny lass.'

They were jostled as people with cases clambered on, and Sarah pulled both of them towards the door. 'We must get on, try to get a seat, and don't you dare think you are to sort this on your own. Don't you bliddy dare, Beth Jones, or Smith, or whatever the bliddy hell you choose to be.'

Beth was on to the three times table as Sarah pushed first Beth, then Fran into the crowded corridor. They looked through into the nearest compartment, but there were no spare seats so they stayed where they were, squeezed between two sailors leaning back against the compartment wall. Fran raised her eyebrows at the other two, but Sarah merely shrugged. 'No point in looking for a seat. It's enough we're on the train, eh.'

Standing in the corridor with them were soldiers and airmen, as well as the sailors, whose tallies around the base of their caps were missing the names of their ships – for all was secret in war, Beth thought. So many secrets. Bob had his secret – he thought he had stopped loving her – but now it wasn't a secret, was it? It was out in the open. A divorce requested.

The servicemen passed cigarettes between them. The sailor next to Beth asked, 'How about you, lass?'

Before she could answer, Sarah said, 'Oh aye, but if you give a cigarette to one, you must give it to all, for we come in a package, don't we, Beth?'

Beth nodded, but one was married and another soon to be, and she might be divorced. She closed her eyes, the shame of it engulfing her. No one she knew had ever been divorced. Her poor mam, that she should have to bear the stigma.

Sarah nudged her. 'Here you are, sweet lass. Our new friend has given us each a cigarette and now he's going to light them.'

The lad grinned. 'Your wish is my command.' He struck the match, and the girls inhaled, smiling their thanks. 'No need to ask where you work,' he murmured. 'My mam's in one o' them factories an' all. The itch drives her mad, and her hair's all colours.'

'Tell her to try a sphagnum-moss dressing,' Fran whispered, 'or mebbe lavender goose grease.'

He nodded, drawing on his own cigarette, turning side on and leaning with his elbow on the window rail, blocking the corridor. 'The stemming's the worse, she tells me,' he whispered. 'All that yellow powder gushing from the machine into the rubber containers. Gets into her skin, then onto the sheets. She has to have one set of sheets special like for her stemming shifts. I take me 'at off to you girls. 'Tisn't easy, not at all.'

An airman struggling along was blocked by the sailor. 'Move aside, old boy. Nature calls.'

'Fly over him,' yelled a squaddie.

'Such a good idea. I might have a bomb on board as well.' Everyone laughed as the airman squeezed through, nodding to the girls. 'You headed for Grimsby?'

Fran nodded back. 'Will it go straight there – have you heard?'

The sailor answered, leaning back now, as they were. 'Who knows—'

'—these days,' apparently everyone in the corridor yelled.

On they travelled, hour after hour, as they pulled into sidings and waited for goods trains to pass. And while they stood, they whispered together and finally Beth passed them Bob's letter. Sarah read it first, as Fran simply slipped her arm around Beth and held her tightly talking of the countryside they were passing, the dresses they would be trying on tomorrow in their lunch hour, and how wonderfully she, Beth, had sung at the Rising Sun.

Fran paused, accepting another cigarette from the sailor, though Beth shook her head. Fran inhaled, then said, 'Stan heard someone from the Haywain pub getting our details from Stevie to sort out another booking.'

Beth tried to listen, but had worked her way through the four times table by the time Sarah handed Fran the letter. She read it and handed it back. Beth returned it to her mac pocket. None of the girls spoke, but Sarah pulled out a packet of Player's. 'By,' Fran muttered. 'You going up in the world, lass? Woodbines and roll-ups not good enough?'

Sarah laughed. 'Shut up and have one, or not.' She passed the packet to Beth. 'Sid gave them to me. Felt all the marrers, the lads as well, should have come, but we could have his Player's instead, because I said there was no need for a fistful of pitmen. I said they'd be better placed sorting out the digging and raking of our das' allotments. Time the potatoes were in, for heaven's sake. Our das'll be shouting down their orders else.'

Fran shook her head. 'They should be planted on Good Friday.'

Sarah laughed again. 'The day after yer wedding, then. But I bet we're in work, so we'll have to plant the chittings after shift – or before.'

Fran took a Players, once her Woodbine was finished, as Sarah offered the sailor a cigarette. He refused. 'Keep them. You're off to see your husband, are you?' He pointed to Sarah's wedding ring.

Beth spoke up. 'To see mine. He's on a . . . well, on a ship.'

He nodded and smiled. 'That's the way of it.'

He returned to talking to his mate, and the girls huddled together. 'Fine, Beth,' Fran murmured, 'we've read the letter, and I were so angry, then when I turned it over I were more angry.'

'So you're going to find him to talk it out?' Sarah asked. 'Find out if he's gone off his bliddy head, or if it's really what he feels, is that it?'

After a pause, Beth whispered, 'I wanted him to see me, to see the girl he married, made promises to. I reckon he's forgotten, got swept away by this new world, and by complications, and every other bliddy stupid thing he's said.' She finished on a shout, but no one turned. Aye, well, it's best, Beth thought, for if anyone said anything, I don't know whether I'd burst out crying, or beat them over the head.

The other two were quiet, their faces grim. Fran said, 'I hate this war.'

Beth looked down at her hands. 'I hate this yellow, I hate the itch, and no bliddy rouge is going to make a halfpenny difference. I'll still look like a grubby daffodil.'

At that, the sailor turned. 'I heard you, and don't ever say that. 'Tis a badge of honour, that colour is, and so too any hurt the work causes. They should give you lasses a bliddy medal, I reckon. And me mam an' all.'

He turned back to his mate, and the girls looked at one another and smiled, but it didn't reach Beth's eyes. How could it, for what if Bob looked at her and didn't see what this young matelot saw? Well, if that happened, she must be strong, for it was her marrers' happy time just as it had once been hers.

Chapter Eighteen

They had to change trains, and then again as they finally neared Grimsby, which the sailor recognised. At this point Fran dragged Beth along to the toilet to put on make-up, treading on feet and apologising with a smile. Sarah waited until they were out of earshot, then explained to the sailor why Beth was to be in Grimsby. 'I want whistles, I want praise for her when she comes back, but I don't want a word to be said about "Hope it works out."'

The lad looked offended. 'Give us a bit of credit. Though I'd like to deck the bastard. It's no way to behave.'

The whisper went down the corridor to the right and to the left. The train was slowing and Sarah saw that the sky was lighter towards the sea, or that's what Clive, the sailor, had said. The sunlight was glistening on the roofs of the town and the gulls were circling as Beth, followed by Fran, edged along, past the men, to the accompaniment of whistles. She was scarlet when she reached Sarah and whispered, 'Do I really look all right?'

Clive leaned forward. 'By, someone's going to be right pleased to see you, I'll tell you that for nothing. Or if you're not meeting anyone, I'm free.'

'Stand aside, sailor boy,' called the airman, 'let the grown-ups get in first.'

'Give the pongos a chance, lad.' This from a red-haired soldier. 'We match, you and I, miss. So, look no further.'

Beth was smiling as they pulled into the station and joined the rush to leave the train, queuing to hand in their tickets. The ticket collector tipped his cap and gave them directions to the street where Bob had his lodgings. Clive wasn't far behind, his kitbag over his shoulder. 'Be safe,' Sarah called after him.

He swung round. 'You an' all, lasses. Be safe, be lucky.' He flicked a salute and his eyes were on Sarah, who mouthed, 'Thank you.' He grinned in response and hurried off.

Beth watched him go. 'He's only a lad.'

Fran shook her head. 'Oh no, he's a man, an ordinary man doing extraordinary things, so he's a hero. Now, come on, fancy pants, let's try and remember the directions.'

There was a harsh sea breeze tugging as they neared Bob's lodgings and Beth shivered, pulling her hat down. She read out the address to a man who was waiting at a bus stop. He reaffirmed the directions they had been given. They kept on walking, and though they passed no bomb damage on this route, they knew there had been raids, of course there had, it was a busy port, and what's more, served trawlers converted into minesweepers. It was on these that Bob served. Her Bob.

On they hurried, taking the second road on the left, then the first on the right into a street of terraced houses, and now they merely had to find number 12. They past windows taped against bomb blast, the same tape on the panes of a telephone box. Was this the one that Bob used to telephone her ? Or was that nearer the port?

Fran stopped, and pointed ahead. 'There's number twelve.'

Sarah gripped Beth's arm. 'We'll hang back. This is between the two of you, but we will be within hearing distance. You are *not* alone, lass, and are quite the bonniest of girls.'

She kissed her, while Fran squeezed her hand, whispering, 'He's your husband. He's just got muddled. On you go.'

They waited by a lamp post on which a rope swung. They pulled their macs tightly around them, turning up the collars. 'This wind's bliddy freezing,' muttered Sarah.

'Breathe in the sea air, dodge the gulls' droppings and stop your mithering,' grunted Fran.

They were watching Beth all the time, and she was drawing closer, now passing number 10. They edged out to the kerb so they had a clear view, ready to rush over if they were needed. Eventually, Sarah replied, 'Bird droppings are good luck.'

'Don't be daft,' Fran muttered.

Beth turned, checking to see that they were there. 'I canna bear it for her,' Sarah said.

Fran swallowed, seeing Beth's hand lift as she sought the doorbell to number 12. When she was in control of her voice, she said, 'Aye, no more can I, but you're right, we canna bear it for her, we can only help her to carry it, and we'll all do that, the lads and us.'

Beth saw no doorbell. She snatched off her woollen hat and put it in her pocket, fluffing her hair, feeling its dryness, knowing that the auburn was streaked almost green in places.

She looked sideways to the girls, who nodded. She knocked, waited. No one came. She had braced her shoulders, but now she let them slump and almost walked away.

'Give it a bliddy whack with your knuckles, pet,' called Fran. 'Think of Amelia, eh?'

Beth felt the laughter then, and heard it, high-pitched, almost hysterical, and it was from deep inside her. She pursed her lips. It stopped.

She beat on the door with her knuckles, and again she waited. She heard footsteps, but they weren't Bob's. His landlady's, then, but the woman would know where he was.

The door opened. A young pregnant woman stood there, frowning. She looked tired. 'Yes?'

Beth said, 'I'm right sorry to disturb you, but I wondered if Bob Jones was in? I know he lodges with you and . . .'

The woman stared at Beth, looking from her hair to her face. 'You're yellow. You're Beth.'

Beth smiled with relief, for Bob had talked of her. 'Oh aye,' she said. 'But it'll be gone when the war's over. It's just—'

'Why are you here?' the woman interrupted.

Beth saw movement from the left; it was Fran and Sarah edging just a bit closer. She shook her head, annoyed, for what business was it of Bob's landlady? 'I need to see me husband, that's all,' she snapped. 'But it's no business of yours, really.'

The woman sighed. 'Oh, I think you'll find it is.' She turned and called, 'Bob, you said you'd sorted it and here's Beth on the doorstep, and how the hell she got our address, heaven only knows.'

Our address . . . ? Beth felt the pavement tilt, just for a second. She reached out, and there was Fran, moving like lightning, gripping her hand, and Sarah, skirting round, linking her arm through hers.

'She knows because Bob wrote to her,' said Fran, 'saying he wanted a divorce, something about—'

Beth interrupted. 'Thanks, Fran, but I will speak. My husband said something about war being complicated, about meeting others, about wanting a divorce. Something about a nurse. *Nothing* about a baby. He hadn't the courage to come and say it to my yellow factory face. No, he wrote it in his royal blue ink.'

The woman stepped back, flushing, and shouted again. 'Bob, get down here and sort this out.'

Bob almost tumbled down the stairs, looking as though

he'd just woken up. 'What's the noise about? You know I'm on duty again tonight.'

He stared at the three girls. Patting her belly, the woman turned back to Beth. '*We* need a divorce because *we* need the allotment from his pay. The allotment that you receive at the moment. I need to be his wife, see.'

She turned on her heel and pushed past Bob, muttering, 'This isn't fair on her, or me. You said you'd sort it properly.'

Bob stood in the doorway, his feet bare. He just nodded.

What the hell does a nod mean? Beth wondered. She said quietly, 'You need to shave, bonny lad, if you're to keep up with your nurse, who sounds as though she's practising to be a matron. You look a right mess.'

He reached out. 'I'm sorry, lass. It's wartime, things happen. I didn't mean to hurt you.'

Beth was ice-cold, but clear in her mind. She kept her voice level. 'Now, I have to decide whether to divorce you or not, and I'll take me time. And I'll put your clothes into the Salvation Army, and anything else I find that is yours, for you've nowt I want.'

Bob looked from her to the other two. 'Reason with her, Fran. I wouldn't have let this happen for the world, but war's—'

'—complicated,' Fran finished for him. 'Aye, you're right, it is, lad, for factory girls an' all, especially when they're sorting out your weapons for you. They get steeped in the yellow, you see, they itch, they lose hands, feet, lives even, if things go wrong. You might remember Viola, who played at our Sarah's wedding. *Our* Sarah, not yours, not any more. You might remember Ralph, who's just driven into a tree rather than hit us or hurt us more'n we were when the bus lost a tyre. He's in a coma. You might remember Sandra dancing at Sarah's wedding. She's in hospital now. There will be more of us hurt.'

Sarah spoke. 'So don't you talk to us of complicated, and not your nurse, neither, as mentioned in the letter—'

Bob exploded at Beth. 'You showed them?'

Sarah let go of Beth's arm and stepped forward, but it was Beth who said, 'Howay, you daft lad, tuck your outrage in your pocket and take these few minutes like a man, for 'tis the last time you'll be seeing us. I thought I'd sort it by coming, I thought you'd see what you were throwing away. I thought you'd just lost yourself for a bit. Aye, well, maybe you have, but I see you standing there, hiding behind "complicated", when what it is, is that you couldn't keep your willy in your drawers. Nowt complicated about that, eh? So here we are. You stuck with a bairn on the way, and her with no wedding ring, so no allotment. Aye, that's complicated. As for me? I'm seeing you as you are. 'Tis not a pretty sight, lad. And trust me, I'll keep that allotment for now at least. You should have thought of such consequences earlier.'

She looked at the other two. 'Let's go home, to *our* people, who cope with complications, eh? Who dig the coal, and fight the war too.' She began to walk away, her head held high, hearing Fran and Sarah clattering along behind her.

Fran stopped and called back, 'You're a fool, Bob.'

'I'll not give up,' he called. 'That allotment money's mine by rights.'

The woman shouted then. 'Just give us the divorce. Is that too much to ask?'

The three of them walked on, heads up, striding, laughing as though they hadn't a care in the world, and it was only when they turned the corner that Sarah and Fran linked arms and let Beth cry.

'Oh Beth,' whispered Fran, 'you were grand. I'm so sorry.'

When the train finally reached Massingham at eleven that night, they almost staggered down onto the platform, sick with tiredness, following their fellow passengers as they headed towards the ticket collector. She was home, Beth thought, but they were empty words, for she would never again be here with him, never bear his bairn, never . . .

They walked past the bench beneath the waiting-room overhang. Men sat there, their cigarettes glowing. What train were they waiting for?

'Howay,' one of them said, 'we thought you'd run off to Australia.' It was Sid. He stood and joined them, and so too did Stan and Norm.

'It's been a long day,' said Fran, 'and you should be in your beds, lads.'

They all walked towards the queue. 'And let you three run amok on your bikes?' said Sid. 'Oh, I reckon not.'

The ticket collector took their tickets. 'Cycle safely. You take care, our Beth, for the lads have shared your news.'

Beth thought she would cry again, but she must not. Instead, she said, 'Aye, you take care an' all.'

As they headed for the bikes she heard Stan tell Sarah that they'd waited from six o'clock, for there was no way the lasses were cycling back alone. 'We're a gang, and we won't ever let that stop.'

Beth nodded slightly. Aye, a gang would wait, and it touched her heart, for she had hurt Stan when Bob had started to call and they'd played about behind his back, yet still they protected her. Still they were here for her. She cycled with Sid alongside as they all shepherded her to her house.

Her mam was up. She took her into the warm kitchen, sat her in Beth's da's armchair, and then waved her marrers on their way. But all Beth wanted was something to stop the pain, for she had acted as though she was strong for hours and didn't know how she could continue for a second longer.

Chapter Nineteen

Monday, 16 March

Fran woke the following day and groaned at the thought of work. Bleary-eyed, she rolled out of bed as her mam banged on the bedroom door, calling, 'Get yerself up and downstairs or you'll miss your bus, and if there's a dress fitting, you'll miss that an' all. I've Viola standing by the back door, holding your bag at the ready. Bert'll be raging. When are you due on the aft shift? You should be on that soon, surely?'

Fran dressed quickly and ran down the stairs, past Viola, who called, 'I've let the hens out, and fed them.' Fran slammed the netty door behind her.

Once she'd washed in the scullery, the pair of them ran towards Main Street, for it was four in the morning and Bert would be revving. She shouted to Viola as they turned towards the bus stop, 'Not sure if Beth'll be here, for how she'll get herself out of bed I canna imagine.'

There was no queue at the bus stop. Bert was pulling away, changing gear and leaning on the horn. Sid, Norm and Stan were clipping along ahead of the bus. Stan saw them and waved Bert down, shouting at the pair of them, 'By, here come the weaklings. T'other two are on board.'

'Beth deserves a bliddy medal,' panted Viola. 'Not sure I'd be up and at it.'

Bert jerked to a stop, calling through the cab window, 'Get yourselves on this bus right now, and if it were anyone else I'd have gone, so I want no spam sandwiches at your wedding tea, our Franny, just piles of pheasant, and afters would be good an' all.'

As Fran and Viola hurried up the aisle, Mrs Oborne yelled, 'Howay, you old beggar, stop your mithering and get your foot down. You'll be lucky to get anything other than a thick ear at the tea, if you go on like this.'

Fran and Viola sank onto the back seat with the other two. Sarah looked half asleep still, and said, 'I haven't even had a cup of tea, and my throat's as rough as the bottom of one of the Canary Club's cages.'

Fran was sitting next to Beth. 'Aye, I overslept and didn't have time to eat either. What about you, Beth?'

Beth smiled slightly. 'I were fine. It's my fault you didn't.'

Mrs Oborne swung round. 'Nowt's your fault, our Beth. Nowt, you hear, none of it. Bob's behaviour is his own, and if Fran had wanted some toast, t'was up to her to get up.'

Fran rolled her eyes. 'How do you know what's happened?'

Viola grinned. 'I bet it's something to do with those three pitmen heading for the pit right this minute. One's your brother, married to our Sarah, and they've all got big gobs and were on the platform to meet you.' She reached across Fran and squeezed Beth's leg.

Beth just smiled. It was all she could summon because her courage had seeped from her, and the loneliness, pain and shame had begun. For of course she must agree to a divorce – how could a baby be born illegitimate? Her mam would post Beth's letter to Bob today.

The guards raised the red and white pole when the girls arrived at the Factory, and once they'd been checked, they walked along the wide roadway, which as always seemed to go on for miles, then turned left into their sector. Ahead, they saw Swinton at the double doors. He was smiling. Beth smiled back as Fran said, 'Cheerful, eh. I reckon it's because Gaines has given him a tick in the report.'

He ushered them in, and once everyone was there, he followed them to the changing rooms, his clipboard at the ready.

He called, 'Before we begin,' he called, ' 'tis the sewing room for you today, Beth, with Viola Ross. Fran and Sarah will be in the stemming room, I'm afraid. I'm right sorry, but you're my clever lasses and able to be moved about.' He put up his hand. 'Aye, I know, I'll try to move you tomorrow. Can't have you bright yellow and clashing with your dresses.' He read out the week's allocations for the rest of the women. Then he read through the safety and security regulations, and all the time Miss Ellington stood beside him, with yet another new security officer.

Beth just kept thinking, with a sinking heart, that she was in the sewing room when all she wanted was to die, but just her, no one else. With detonators she could have done it – perhaps.

The hands on the clock were ticking away the seconds, the minutes, and were nearing six o'clock. She needed to sit down, to lie down, for her legs were weak and her body too heavy to be supported. At last Mr Swinton rose on his toes, nodded, smiling fit to burst, then swept out, calling, 'Best hurry and change. Fittings in the sewing room at lunchtime, Fran and Sarah. Beth and Viola will already be there, of course. Best have a wash, for you don't want to be putting powder on your finery. Indeed not.'

The door closed on him. Miss Ellington gestured to the new security officer. 'Miss Jenkins from Cardiff.'

The two security officers moved amongst them as the girls donned their overalls. Beth put on her trousers, hiding the backs of her legs, which still had seam lines. How stupid she felt now, for why would an expectant father be interested in lippy, rouge and pencilled seams?

Miss Ellington stopped next to her. 'Turn around for me, lass, though no grips will matter today. Mr Swinton wants to give you a rest till your mind's on its feet, if you see what he means. You're all – every one of you – too important to put in danger.'

'Too important?' Beth whispered.

'Oh aye, you're all the salt of the earth, and don't you forget it, not for a moment.'

'Salt, eh?' Beth whispered again, sounding like an echo. But there were no spare words, no real words, and her legs ached, and she was too heavy for them. She put out a hand. Miss Ellington held it.

'Your life isn't over,' Miss Ellington said quietly. 'It's just beginning. Now you're to find out just who you are, like I had to.' She held up her handless arm, whispering, 'I lost my hand, and you think you've lost your heart. We both lost our men and are not the only ones. Look at our Maisie, making a life for herself.'

'I divint know you'd lost your man.'

'Aye, he didn't like me hand being gone, so he went too.'

Beth closed her eyes. Oh, poor Cyn, but she hadn't shamed her family. 'Ah, but I've lost my reputation,' she said. 'A widow's summat different to one who is divorced. There's shame with it, you see. A family's shame.'

Miss Ellington looked shocked and could find no words, but then Mrs Oborne, having wound her way through the girls, joined them. 'Why's the auld devil so chipper, our Miss Ellington?'

'He's been congratulated by Bolton because Gaines said nice things in his report.'

Mrs Oborne crossed her arms and said, 'Oh, and about everyone?'

Miss Ellington nodded. 'Aye, we all did well, or so Bolton said. There were one or two problems, but he didn't say what, and he wasn't about to, either.'

'By the way,' called Fran, 'Mam asked me when I returned last night to remind everyone to keep checking their hospital visiting time on the rota. There's still not the improvement we'd all like to see, so we have to keep trying. We're off on Wednesday.'

'Right you are,' called Maisie. 'I'm going with Valerie and Susie tomorrow.'

After one final check, Miss Ellington flapped them out of the changing room and sent them on their way.

Fran and Sarah headed off to the stemming workshop, pulling down the turbans they had made with their scarves to try to cover their hair, for any strands that escaped would suck up the yellow and stain. Once they'd taken the place of the night shift, they resumed where those girls had left off, first adjusting their masks, then tipping the powder from a big box into the top of a machine, pulling the handle, shutting their eyes as the powder whooshed out of the funnel into the rubbery container beneath, which they all called the 'thingummybob'.

As it whooshed, clouds of the chemicals puffed into the air. When the rubber containers were full, they were moved along the belt to who knew where, to be mixed with who knew what, for they were never told, and knew better than to ask. The powder wasn't explosive in itself, but became so once added to something else. Or so it was said.

Fran tried not to think about it, or of the stemming sheets they'd need on their beds tonight. Or the worsening rash. By, she hoped it really was just one day, for imagine the wedding night, the yellow seeping into the sheets. What romance was there in that? To stop herself thinking of it, she said, 'I wonder if we'll ever be told what the powder is, and what it does to us.'

Sarah shook her head, the yellow dusting her eyelashes and eyebrows. 'Probably not, and do we want to know, for it must come from our innards through our skin onto the sheets?'

Fran looked at her. They smiled beneath their masks, pulled their handles and out whooshed the powder. Mindless work, but that was the problem, for it couldn't be mindless. You had to think, to concentrate. Sarah's hair was showing below her turban. Fran called a warning across the music that was playing over the tannoy. Sarah pulled the turban down rather than push up her hair, for she mustn't touch her skin.

Fran tried to think of Clive, the sailor on the train, and not the powder that made them feel sick and dizzy by the end of the shift because some filtered through their masks, and was breathed in. Where was he going? Would he survive? Then her mind strayed to Bob. Aye, lad, she thought, this is the powder that helps your shells explode and makes your wife yellow, while your nurse stays pale and unblemished. She thought of Ralph. Would he have more colour when they went to visit on Wednesday? Would he react? Oh Lord, she hoped so.

'I can feel me rash spreading,' muttered Sarah. 'It's not yet, but I feel as though it is.'

'Aye,' replied Fran.

They might chat, but they never stopped working, hour after hour, and it was only when they were told it was the meal break that they stretched, eased their backs, went to the washroom and could finally scratch their scalps, their arms and their hands, and then wash again, for their fingers came away from their scalps covered in powder. They hung their heads over the basins and scratched until the loose powder lined the ceramic bowls. They ran water, sluicing the powder down the plughole, hating it.

Lunch was the familiar grey meat, but at least it was hot. They queued and barely smiled as it was slopped onto their plates and they headed for their usual table. Beth was already there, clean, tired and smiling a smile that didn't reach her eyes, but why would it? It would be a while yet, and Fran thought of how she'd felt when she thought she'd lost Davey. She sat down next to Beth and stared at the mince.

'Why the bliddy hell can't it be brown, with thick gravy, or is that too bliddy much to ask?'

They all fell silent. Mrs Oborne looked up from the head of the table. She smiled. 'They do the best they can, and it's—'

'—warm and wet,' everyone around the table shouted, then laughed.

Mrs Oborne looked at Fran. 'It's a bliddy awful world, isn't it, sometimes, and our Beth knows that more'n most. We'll say no more, our Beth, but just know we love you, and we have your back.'

Beth stared at her and pressed her lips together. She nodded, pushed her plate away and finally said, 'I haven't touched it, Franny, so stuff your face with more grey mince, and that'll really give you something to mither about.'

It wasn't actually funny, but somehow it was, and they couldn't stop laughing. Beth sat back and nodded. 'Looking at the clock, we need to get bride and bridesmaids into the sewing shop to make sure everything really is right, especially for the silk, for we canna have any re-sewing, or so Mrs Iris said.'

Viola rose with the other two. 'Come along, for I fear Fran might be getting fat with all this lovely meat. Hurry.'

The laughter followed them out of the canteen, and once

back in the sewing shop Mrs Iris came to meet them, a bandage in her hand. 'Hand out, then, Viola. We need to change that bandage. The Factory nurse said that something more than sticking a finger in the dyke needs to be done, and you're to go to the doctor and be signed off, for 'tis not healing.'

Fran looked at Mrs Iris. 'It's not septic?'

'Oh no, but we don't want it to be, do we?' The supervisor's frown was concerned, not cross. 'What about this job I hear you might do for the Massinghams?'

'Bliddy hell, is nothing sacred?' muttered Mrs Oborne.

'Not when I'm about,' said Miss Ellington, entering on the tail end of Mrs Oborne's mutterings. 'So, you, Viola Ross, are to go up to Massingham Hall later today with the other three girls for support, because even yesterday when you and Mrs Hall had your talk, you were dithering about letting everyone down, or so I heard when Annie came to the allotment in the afternoon. But the nurse has shared with me that being signed off means you're out of here. Mr Swinton knows you are giving in your notice. When you have the doc's certificate, you just need to tell the Labour Exchange that your war work is ended.'

Viola was looking from Miss Ellington to Mrs Iris, who was nodding. 'Dr Dunster knows you're on your way to him after today's shift.'

'I told Mrs Hall yesterday that I had decided I should be here. It seems like running away from the danger. Why should you all be undergoing this life while I sit on the sidelines?'

Mrs Iris just looked at her. 'Take a look at your hand, you've done your bit. The co-op is always up at the Hall, and your marrers will find their way up, so you won't feel alone. So, that's all sorted.'

Beth glanced at Viola and realised the lass was relieved.

She nudged her, whispering, 'Ah, I see. You didn't want to confess it was too much, Viola, and that's brave, but you have to give in sometimes to improve things. Or these women will do it for you. Besides, there's a desperate need up at the Hall, you must be able to see that.'

Viola slipped her good arm around Beth. 'How wise you are, how wise you be, I see dear Beth's too wise for me.'

Mrs Iris was shepherding Fran into the storeroom where the materials were kept, and so too the dresses.

'Fran first,' called Miss Ellington, 'for no one must see her dress. In with you, Mrs Oborne, with the pins. Sarah, you're next.' She picked up the pincushion from the table, handing it to Mrs Oborne.

Sarah laughed. 'By, Miss Ellington, you've been learning bossiness from Mrs Oborne. Not sure I can cope. What do you think, Beth?'

Beth was listening to Viola as she said, 'Be wise, too, Beth. Listen to your own words. Sometimes we have to improve things when it all goes wrong. My mam and da were killed, and I lost a bit of me hand and ear, but I came here with Fran and Sarah, and look . . .' she nodded towards Miss Ellington, Mrs Iris and Mrs Oborne's retreating back '. . . we don't even have to say what we want, because they already know. We have to let them help, eh?'

Beth nodded, because it was expected of her, but Viola didn't know that she, Beth Jones, deserved what was happening, for she had fallen for Bob when she and Stan were together, boyfriend and girlfriend. She had hurt Stan. And now she was being hurt. It was right that shame and hurt were to be hers. It was how the world worked, so she would bear it. But it wasn't fair that her mam should suffer. She just didn't know what to do about that, and it was hurting her mind as she tried to sort it.

Chapter Twenty

At six thirty that evening, Viola, Fran and Annie Hall met Sarah and Maud Bedley in the back lane, and together they all cycled towards Main Street and then on to Massingham Hall. Annie led the way and beckoned Viola forward, leaving the other three to cycle behind in single file, their slit lamps juddering their meagre light onto the road. Viola could barely hold the handlebars, such was the pain of her hand, and now that her decision was made she hoped with all her heart that the Massinghams would like her – the bairns, too – and they would offer her the job.

Annie turned her head briefly. 'You have to understand, our lass, and I've said it before and will go on and on saying it, that our house will still be your home, our family always yours. You'll be in Fran's bedroom on your days off. Fran'll be downstairs with Davey. Well, not with him, for he won't be here much, but you get the picture. So, let's move on to this evening. You've brought your saxophone with you, that's good, for I said to the bairns that we would be having a sing-song and that seems as good a way as any to see if you like them and they like you, eh?'

Viola nodded. 'I played at Sarah's wedding, so they might be sick of seeing and hearing me.'

'Never,' Annie laughed. 'Trust me, they'll fall at your feet. Just get rid of this gormless look you're wearing on your face now, like those rabbits staring up at Farmer Thompkins' gun.'

Viola roared with laughter and said, 'I pity any German invaders that come up against you, Mrs Hall.'

'Howay, lass, drop back now, as I can see Mrs Bedley roaring up on the outside to talk about her proggy rug which'll hang on someone's wall once 'tis delivered to Briddlestone's. They were mightily pleased with the ones we delivered when we visited Ralph the first time, and want a few more.'

Viola did as she was told, for these women were the rulers of the universe. She laughed again at the thought as Fran caught up and asked, 'What?'

'Aye, what?' Sarah puffed and panted.

'I reckon the co-op women wouldn't need an army to beat back the Germans, or the Japanese. Just themselves and their proggy frames.'

They were laughing as they finally turned into Massingham Hall. 'Mind,' Fran muttered, 'I wish they weren't so bliddy independent, or we'd have had young Alfie collecting and returning us.'

'Weakling,' her mam called back.

'Aye,' shouted Mrs Bedley as the sheep beyond the drystone walls either side baaed. 'Cycling 'tis good for yer ankles, so think on that.'

'Oh, what do they matter when we're to go up the aisle looking like bliddy daffodils?' Sarah said to her mam, panting. 'And why isn't Ben here? Wasn't he supposed to come?'

'He's head down puzzling out another crossword, and William's doing one too. Got the bit between their teeth, they have. By, if the war goes on much longer they'll be snaffled up by Davey's—'

'Mam,' yelled Fran. 'Walls have ears.'

Her mam laughed, saying to Mrs Bedley, 'I don't reckon that drystone has, or that the sheep are listening. I said nowt out of place anyway, did I, bossyboots? I was only going to say "place".'

They had reached the house and Viola grinned as the gravel crunched beneath them on their way to the yard. Not even a chink showed between the curtains, but the grandeur of the place could be seen in the moonlight. Would the Massinghams treat her like a servant? Mrs Bedley had said no, and so too had Beth, who was staying at home with her mam, trying to sort her head out, she'd said. Her heart more like, thought Viola.

They were about to enter the yard and she looked at Alfie's flat above the garage. Would she be put somewhere like that too, on her own? She swallowed, scared, wanting to be part of 14 Leadenhall Terrace after all. Besides, her mam had always been dead against Viola going into service. 'But I'm more a governess, Mam, and Mrs Sophia isn't your usual nob,' she whispered to the memory of her mam. 'And I won't stay unless I'm sleeping in the Hall, and that's that.' She sounded braver than she felt.

'I don't know,' Fran murmured as they bumped over the garage-yard cobbles, 'talking to yourself when you're to be in charge of hooligans.'

At that moment the basement door opened and Eva yelled, 'They're here, Sophia, they're here.'

The women were forced to brake as the children hared up the steps, Eva in the lead. They clamoured around them until Eva shouted so loud that the bairns stopped their frenzy.

''Tis no way to show we're good bairns to Miss Viola. Especially as she's the one who played in the church like a bleedin' angel, even though she has a poorly hand.'

'Language, Eva,' called Sophia.

'Sorry, Sophia. A bliddy angel.'

Viola ducked her head, loving this child instantly and wanting to laugh herself silly, and she could see that all the women were having the same problem. Annie Hall dismounted, propped her bike up against the garage doors and the others followed suit. By now, Sophia was shepherding the bairns down into the kitchen and Viola joined the others as they followed.

The children were sitting down, warm milk in beakers in front of them, along with biscuits, home-baked. Eva clambered down from her high stool and led the women to the spare ones. 'You're to sit here, but you're to have tea instead and a biscuit too. They're still warm, and we didn't pick our noses, so there's nowt in them that shouldn't be.'

Viola stared, her face rigid, but it was no good, she couldn't stop the laughter that forced itself up and out just as Mr Massingham entered from the corridor, rubbing his hands.

'Well, and here we all are, and I do hope everyone has been on their best behaviour.'

'I've tried to be, Mr Massingham,' Viola said, before she could stop herself.

She saw the mouths of the children drop open, and Sophia turn away, her shoulders shaking. Mr Massingham stared at Viola, who feared she had gone too far. She so hoped not, for the co-op and the girls had been right all along, and she knew already she should be here, with these bairns who bubbled with life.

Mr Massingham was grinning at his wife, who lifted her head at last, wiping her eyes, which were alive with laughter. He raised his eyebrows, she nodded, and he laughed, a booming laugh. 'Oh, you'll do, if you'll have us? That's the big question, isn't it, children? Will Miss Viola Ross come and help Sophia with you horrors? Let's hope she can bear to leave the Halls for the bosom of a new family when she has as many days off as she likes, if only she'll be here the rest of the time? We have a nice bedroom for her at the end of your floor, with a soft bed, and no pea under twenty mattresses, so she won't be black and blue. What do you think? Can we persuade her?'

The children were nodding, their faces eager. Eva said, 'Aye, can she bear it, for just a few days a week would be grand, and we know she'll go one day, for people do when it's war. They go and don't come back, for they might have died or found something better, so she mustn't feel badly if she wants to leave. But it would be kindly of her if she'd give us some of her life, wouldn't it?'

She really was asking the others, who were following her every word. When Eva finished, they huddled together, then separated again. Finally, they nodded, solemnly. Viola was thinking how these bairns were like her, for whether they were orphans or not, their parents were still missing from their lives.

So, yes, indeed, she'd give these bairns as much of her life as they needed. She lifted her head and Mr Massingham came over and handed her his handkerchief. 'Wipe your eyes, my dear, then I must have it back to do the same. The little horrors get you every time. But say no, if it is your wish to do so.'

Fran sidled up. 'I reckon we should send that Eva into battle alongside the co-op, but her weapon will be words. The enemy would run home just to be with their families.'

She linked arms with Viola as Mr Massingham moved away. Viola looked around the children, making eye contact one by one. 'I reckon it's an aye, don't you, my bairns?'

That was it then, thought Fran, watching as Viola took her saxophone from its case and started to play, though her hand was oozing again through its bandage. The children began to sing, 'One man went to mow, went to mow a meadow . . .'

Fran felt her mam's arm slip around her waist. 'There, our Franny. This'll work well for all under the Massinghams' roof, eh. We just need Mr Ralph to come home, restored to health, and who knows ... Viola will be here, sweet Viola, and just what our Mr Ralph needs to keep him on the straight and narrow.'

Fran turned, astonished. 'Oh, Mam,' she whispered. 'Do you reckon? Really, I would never have thought—'

'Hush, and listen,' her mam commanded. Fran couldn't, for that thought had never occurred to her, but her mam was so seldom wrong ... Not that she'd ever tell her that, for they'd never hear the end of it.

Her mam whispered as the saxophone soared, 'Remember you're to visit on Wednesday, so says the rota.'

Chapter Twenty-One

Tuesday, 17 March

Viola had an appointment to see the doctor at four fifteen because he'd been called out on an emergency the previous afternoon. She and the girls walked through Massingham after their return from the fore shift and sat in the waiting room, looking at the war posters. Spuds and Spam – Eating for Victory. Make Do and Mend. Doctor Carrot, the Children's Best Friend. Finally, Mrs Dunster called from her desk, 'The doctor will see you now, Viola. You girls wait here.'

Fran and Sarah did as they were told. The clock ticked on to four thirty. They paced, sat, then paced some more before Fran said, 'Surely he'll sign her off?'

Mrs Dunster, who always wore her hair in a bun and had steel-rimmed glasses, snapped, 'For heaven's sake, sit still and stop fretting, it's scaring the horses.'

Fran looked around the room, where the only other person waiting was Mr Salmon. He winked and muttered, 'Me days of going over the jumps be long gone, lass, but I still fancy a bit of a roll in t'hay from time to time.'

Mrs Dunster sighed as the girls laughed. 'That's quite enough of that, Mr Salmon. We'll be hearing all about your oats next.'

Viola emerged at four forty five as the girls were giggling. She was waving a letter. 'Right, I've to go to the Labour Exchange right now.'

Mr Salmon headed towards the surgery, then, with his hand on the sneck, spun on his heel. 'As for me oats—'

'Enough,' roared Mrs Dunster.

Mr Salmon was laughing as he shut the surgery door behind him. They began to explain to Viola as they left, only to find Alfie waiting in the Rolls-Royce. 'Your mam said you'd be here, Fran. Viola's to give me the letter and I'll get it to the Exchange, and then she's to get on and pack, since Eva insists you are needed tomorrow. Though I heard tell that the Canary Club has some elderberry wine waiting come six o'clock, after your tea. A sort of celebration and farewell for our Viola, and a perk-up for our Beth.'

He snatched the letter, ducked into the car and set off as the others looked at their watches.

Beth linked her arm through Viola's. 'The die is cast, bonny lass.' Her smile still didn't meet her eyes, though at least it was a smile, Fran thought. But aye, Mrs Iris was right, she was as thin as a rake and would soon disappear. There'd just be a green frock walking along the aisle behind her and a bunch of daffs wobbling about in the air. Fran knew she was being daft, but it hid the worry over Beth, and the fury at Bob.

She came back to the present as they stood in the sun, at the end of the doctor's drive, looking across the posher end of Main Street while Sarah said, 'Right, tea first, and then, Viola, you must pack, since I can't see you objecting at the first fence.'

Viola looked confused, so Beth explained about scaring the horses. When she'd finished, they set off arm in arm, keeping to the sunny side of the road. As the detached houses became streets of terraces, Sarah asked, 'Your first job at the Hall tomorrow is . . . ?'

Viola was clearly puzzled, then, as Sarah pretended to

throw something up in the air, her face cleared. 'Ah, confetti . . . Of prime importance, eh?'

'Stop causing mischief, Sarah,' Fran said, 'for you know it vexes the vicar. Try and put them off, Viola, eh?'

'I'll do my best,' Viola replied,' but what about my brides-maid's frock? It's still in the sewing workshop and not finally fitted yet.'

Fran shook her head. 'Beth was in there again today. Any news . . . ?'

Beth said, her voice tired and thready even to her own ears, 'Unless you eat your head off and get fat, it'll fit, and Mrs Iris and Mrs Oborne are just starting on the sewing. They've been so busy working on overalls for other factories they've had to put the more important work aside . . .' She paused for the laugh she knew would come. It did. 'But they promise they'll be ready for the big day, or Mrs Oborne will want to know why. So, we're safe, for who'd dare cross her?'

Fran took over. 'We'll miss you, bonny lass, but you'll not escape us, so never think you will. But you'll come to the hospital tomorrow, our Viola? For if you don't, then it's my mam who'll want to know why. Four of us, or none of us, eh, Beth? Because we stay together as marrers, divint we?'

'Aye, together,' said Beth, 'that's right. And I 'spect Mrs Hall's already set it up with Sophia.'

The next day the girls rushed home from the bus, washed, changed, had a cuppa and ran out of the house. At five o'clock Alfie was there in the Rolls-Royce, waiting near the bus stop in Main Street for the girls, as well as Stan, Sid and Norm. As they clambered in, they saw that Viola was already there, on the back seat, grinning. She held up her hand and the bandage was clear of blood. 'See, just one day without rubbing it again and again on the sewing-machine table and 'tis already getting better.'

Alfie was puffing on a Player's, but wouldn't let them smoke. 'I have me window open so can flick me ash out there, but knowing you lot, you'd flick yours here and there.'

He ignored the protests, just put his foot down to get them to the train station. As originally arranged, the Massinghams had paid for the tickets and they merely had to collect them. They arrived at the hospital for visiting hours just as Sister Newsome opened the double doors to the ward.

When she saw them she held up her hand. Stan, who was leading them like goslings stopped. 'Turn, keep going. First door on the right.'

Stan looked at Sister Newsome, then the others. 'Why?' He stepped to one side to let a clutch of visitors into the ward.

Sister Newsome shook her head. ' "Why?" asked the lad. Because I say so, I reply, but also because we had a bit of success yesterday. Young probationer Emily Stott thought to ask Mr Massingham if there was anything that had made our lad feel particularly safe as a child. He thought of cigar smoke.'

Sister Newsome raised her eyebrows. 'Well, we can't have cigar smoke in the ward, so the porter trolleyed Ralph into a side room where Reginald was instructed to have a good puff of the blighters he always carries. Very soon those infrequent tremors of the hands became actual movements. Follow me.'

She led the way, then paused outside a door 'Here we are,' she said. 'Your task today is to talk to him of Fran's wedding, because Reginald told him when he nipped in briefly this morning, of the bairns' plans they made with Viola over their breakfast today to cut and colour confetti. Viola, you should remind him of the card young Eva drew and left for him when she came. You'll find it propped up behind his water jug on the bedside table. Stan, you might like to talk of the pit; Sid and Norm, perhaps the Canary Club, as Simon Parrot and Cyn Ellington were in earlier in the week. Beth, talk to him of Bob – swear if you wish. Sarah, not too much sweet talk about Stan. Fran, talk of the dresses. And while this is ongoing, one, or all of you, will keep up smoking that cigar. No need to blow it in his face, just sit by the bed.'

A visitor was hovering, clearly needing to speak to Sister Newsome. She reached out and held the elderly woman's arm. 'Good to see you, Mrs Ashington. Now, you youngsters, off you go.'

They entered the room, where the curtains were drawn and the blackout blind pulled down. A low light glowed overhead. The bed had been set up between two windows. Chairs were stacked at the side. The boys spread them around the bed. On the bedside table was a wooden box containing the cigars.

'Where the hell does Massingham get them these days?' Norm grunted, taking one and rolling it between his fingers, holding it to his ear. 'Ah, 'tis a bit dry. Probably from before the war, then. Who's to have the first puff? Careful, it might flare up.'

While the lads sorted that out, Fran and Sarah sat on one side of the bed and Viola and Beth on the other. This was their third visit and it didn't bother them as much as it had to see someone they knew lying so pale and still.

Beth said, once the boys had joined them, 'Howay, Ralph. Not up and dancing yet, I see, but it won't be long, bonny lad. Then you can have a bit of a waltz with me. You'll have heard me mam tell you of Bob. He's a right idiot, throwing me over when I look like a daffodil, and what's nicer in the spring than a touch of yellow, eh?'

Surprised, the others laughed, even Norm, who was

coughing as he took his first puff. Was it only Fran who saw the white of Beth's knuckles as she balled her hands?

Sid snatched the cigar from Norm. 'Like this, bonny lad.'

Stan stared. 'How do you know? Smoke 'em under the bedcovers, hey?'

Sid shook his head. 'My grandda used to save his pennies and have one every Christmas. We had to sit on his knee while he showed us how to light it without the flame touching the cigar, so it were just the heat that got it going, and then how to sort of sip at it, not take a bliddy drag. That's right, isn't it, Ralph?' He looked at the lad in the bed and murmured, 'Aye, I haven't thought of it for a bit, but it's a good 'un. I can remember the smell, the feel of his arm around me. I liked me grandda, right enough.'

On they chatted, taking turns to hold his hand or pat his arm. Viola spoke of her plans for confetti cutting and colouring with the children, and perhaps teaching them the saxophone. 'But your Da will have told you this.'

Ralph lay motionless, a smaller bandage around his head and his bandaged leg under a raised cage that kept the weight off the gashed calf. Fran reached out, and held his hand, and there it was, rather more than a tremor, almost a flicker. She squeezed, saying quietly, 'I'm grateful to you, Ralph, for your words to me at Sarah's wedding tea, because my dreams are improving. We're all grateful to you for sacrificing yourself instead of hitting the bus, but, lad, it's time to stop laying about like Cleopatra and get yourself back to Auld Hilda, eh. And 'tis as well you know I have a bone to pick with Viola, for she knows the confetti making will annoy the vicar.'

Viola laughed, and took over again, talking about Eva's card and holding his hand, feeling at home by his side, his hand lying in hers. 'Ah, and Fran's right, I reckon the confetti will be Reverend Walters' worst nightmare, for he'll have to clear the churchyard of it. But Eva wants a pile, so a pile there will be. But whether we throw it is another matter.' She was watching his face and Fran laughed again, as Viola noticed how much his hair had grown.

'By, our Ralph,' she went on, 'wait till I tell the bairns that you need a haircut. You see, I work and live in the Hall now, so never fear, I will make sure they're not hiding scissors and a pudding bowl when I bring them Friday.' She laughed quietly, then felt him squeezing her hand.

Had she imagined it? She squeezed back, and checked his face, – his eyelids were trembling. 'Hush,' she called. 'Can you see his eyes? Quick, someone get Sister Newsome.'

Stan came to stand by the pillow, peering down, and then Ralph opened his eyes and looked into Stan's. Viola stood. He looked at her. She still held his hand. He squeezed. His eyes closed.

Sister Newsome hurried in. Viola said what had happened. Stan confirmed it. They were shooed from the room, and Sister Newsome pressed a button. They heard a bell sound along the corridor. They waited outside, Sid still holding the cigar. Dr Wilson hurried past. 'Smoke it, or ditch it,' he rasped, his stethoscope swinging as he whirled into the side room.

The door shut behind him. They all sat, and only Sid smoked. After five minutes, Sister Newsome and Dr Wilson came out, deep in conversation. Dr Wilson smiled when he saw they were all still there. 'Go in again. He's back in the world he's been inhabiting, but now we feel he's on his way home. Highly satisfactory. I wasn't looking forward to confessing to the co-op, or you lot, that there would be no progress, ever. I think I would have been rousted fairly comprehensively, but you might want to tell your mother, Fran, the good news. I will telephone the family.'

Viola was first back in the room, wanting to see Ralph's

eyes open again, and for him to look into hers. But he lay as before. She didn't mind, for he had smiled, or his eyes had, his grip had been firm, his hand warm, and he had woken, for her. For that's what she believed and her heart twisted, just as it had done on their first visit. She watched him and listened to Stan talking to Ralph now, telling him that Albright had him down for sorting the coal on the surface screens when he chose to shift his arse, and there it was again, that sort of pang, a twist.

She sat with her hands in her lap, realising only now what her mam had meant when she said that the first time she met Viola's father, her heart had flipped over. They shook hands and something had passed between them, even before they knew one another's names. It was love.

Sarah was describing the dresses, ending with, '. . . though why you'd be interested in dresses, Lord knows, but Sister Newsome's word is law.'

Stan passed the cigar to her. 'You've made the end wet,' Sarah complained, waving the smoke away.

Beth leaned over, looking at Ralph, holding his hand again. 'Why does the smell of cigars make you feel safe, bonny lad? For me it is the smell of me mam's baking, and everything about her.'

Sid nodded, taking his turn with the cigar, then passing it on to Norm. 'What makes me feel safe is spending an hour or two at the Canary Club with me marrers, where there is the smell of the seed. Makes me think of my da and his canaries. Howay, just talking about it brings to mind sitting on the upturned barrels, and all of us being there. And there were my grandpa, of course, but I've told you this already. Aye, I miss the old devil.'

Viola reached forward again and gripped Ralph's arm. 'For me, it's music, singing, the saxophone, oh aye, and the smell of a roast chicken in the range, and people round the table. I reckon Mrs Hall cooks the best chicken, but that's just for specials. Mrs Hall does a lot, doesn't she? Nursed you when you were poorly, and now she's set up the rota, but she divint make us sign up. We all want to come. Massingham people want to.'

It was Beth's turn for a 'sip' of the cigar, as Norm called it. She sipped, coughed and passed it on, pulling a face. Fran grimaced, but took it. 'Must I?'

Viola insisted. 'It's for Ralph, so stop being picky and take a sip.'

Fran did, and thought she'd burned her mouth. She passed it over the bed, the ash falling on Ralph's blankets. Beth brushed it off. As she did so, they saw his good leg move. Or did it?

They all fell silent, then Sarah said, 'The thing is, Ralph, if you're not at the wedding, Eva will have a word or two to say, so best you stop slouching and come back to us, eh? You think of the smell of the cigar, think of why you like it, for that safety is still here.'

They all stared at his leg. Perhaps it hadn't moved? Perhaps it was their imaginations? Viola left to find Sister Newsome, who popped her head back in and took his pulse, looking round at them all, her grin wide. 'We're on the way. If he opens his eyes again, come for me.' She checked the watch pinned to her uniform. 'Best you be on your way. Nip and see Sandra first. The news is confirmed that she'll have limited sight in that eye, but she's remarkably stoic. But then, you lot are.'

Sister Newsome raised her voice. 'Your marrers are off, bonny lad. You'll be seeing them at home any day now.'

She beckoned them all out, snatching the cigar from Norm's hand. 'I'll have that. Dr Wilson is partial to a puff.'

Sid was the last to leave, herding Beth out before him. 'You're a hard woman, Sister Newsome.' He raised his voice. 'Don't you let her get the better of you, Ralph, lad. We need you home in one piece for the wedding, and this woman bites. So, make your escape, eh.'

They headed towards the women's ward, but Meryl and Sandra's Auntie Gertie were by her bed. They saw the girls and waved them in, while the lads stayed in the corridor. Sandra was buoyant because she'd thought she'd lose the eye completely. She gripped Beth's hand. 'Trust me, losing Bob won't be as bad as you think. Things aren't. Don't know why, they just aren't. There's always a way through, lass. Besides, I'd rather be in sewing, saves me getting that bliddy rash.'

Chapter Twenty-Two

The days in the lead-up to Thursday, 2 April, sped by. It was the day before Good Friday, and the only one Davey and Daniel's loss could be covered by two extra decoders, so the Factory had followed suit, with the stipulation that Easter Sunday would be a working day. As for the stemming, Mr Swinton was true to his word and made sure the girls were no longer in that workshop.

Instead, they swung between the detonators and pellets. Each day, it seemed, the yellow subsided a little, the itching too, but not enough, never enough, and on the bus to and from the Factory, they scratched, laughed, talked about the wedding tea, the decorations for the Miners' Club hall, Ralph and Sandra, and prayed, absolutely prayed, that there'd be no bombing of Davey's train line, or an emergency at his 'place'.

It seemed to Fran and Sarah that Beth was slowly accepting the loss of Bob. And the quietness of their friend became something they accepted as the excitement mounted. On 24 March, Ralph was moved to a rehabilitation unit to regain the use of his muscles, and improve his co-ordination and general awareness. His telephone calls to Massingham Hall were less hesitant, his understanding more complete, and Viola found herself rushing to answer the phone just in case it was him, and they would talk of the children, of his exercises, of the calf muscle that had been sewn back together and was healing, though it was still weak and stiff, and then she'd pass him to Sophia, who was still very tired, or Reginald, who was still busy and seemed to have endless meetings, some with Professor Smythe.

She told Ralph this, and Ralph said, 'Poor old boy, he's had a bad chest.'

'Who?' Viola said, puzzled, because Reginald had been really well.

There was a pause, and then Ralph muttered, 'Oh, Professor Smythe. He popped in, you know how he does. Always seems to be here, there and everywhere.'

All this Viola told the girls when she met them at Fran's house to be fitted for her bridesmaid's dress. For the girls and the co-op, it seemed a period of calm, even with the increasing but happy pressure of the wedding.

On Tuesday, 31 March, Fran expected to be able to bring her dress home on the bus, but Mrs Oborne shook her head when Fran hurried to the sewing room during the meal break. 'Not today, but tomorrow, Fran. I want to re-sew your hem, for the stitching's snagged.'

The next day, Fran and the girls hurried along to the sewing room at the end of the shift, and then rushed to the bus with their dresses carefully folded in hessian bags. As they carried them above their heads along the aisle, the other Factory girls clamoured to see them, making Fran laugh and shake her head. 'No, not a chance.'

At that point Maisie stepped into the aisle. 'Hush your noise, daft things. You take one step towards those bags and you'll have me to deal with.'

They set off, the dresses safely stored in the rack above the seats. As they drove away, Bert yelled, 'Aye, you leave the biggest bag alone. What's Tilly Oborne ever done to you? It's my life she makes a bliddy misery.'

Everyone laughed, Beth too, but it was that same thready, strained sound they had come to accept as normal. Or almost. Fran smiled at her, whispering, 'I so want to show you, but I canna or me mam'll go mad. Bad luck, she says. The marriage won't last, she says.' Fran stopped, closed her eyes. 'Oh Beth, I didn't—'

Beth laughed loudly, far too loudly this time. 'Aye, well, I reckon our Bob must have had a peek at mine, eh, and it doesn't matter, not a bit, Fran. I never think of him, 'tis not worth the effort, eh? But I think of your big day, and it brightens my world.'

Sarah leaned forward. 'It does, Franny. As for you, Beth, you're a trouper, a bliddy trouper, and we love you. You just go from day to day, step by step, and sometimes we forget how brave you are, but we don't, not really, not deep down.'

The three of them sat back, looking down the bus, their arms linked, and Fran couldn't bear it for Beth and wanted to beat Bob around his lugs, for Beth had heard nothing from him and didn't know what was happening. The good thing was the allotment of Bob's pay was still coming through to her, though Beth felt the bairn should have it when things were sorted. Sorted? Beth always stopped at that point, tailing off. Perhaps she still hoped that the silence meant Bob was rethinking, but, thought Fran as they left Sledgeford, the child would always be there, in the background, and so too the nurse. What a mess it was.

The thought of the bairn made Fran think of Daisy and her bairn. According to Davey, who had heard from Daniel, who had heard from his father, the girl had contacted no one, written no letters, and certainly not to Fran, but it was better that way. For, much like Amelia, Daisy had caused too much trouble. However, it appeared that Amelia had had her comeuppance, for at the start of the week, Miss Ellington had shared with them that Amelia had received a warning about loose talk, following on from Gaines's report. Any repetition would result in her dismissal.

Fran sighed, wishing the girl had been sacked straight away, but at least she didn't take their bus now, she simply worked her nine-to-five shift and had stopped strutting about on those high heels as though she was Queen of the Nile.

The bus trundled on, and the further they went from the Factory the greater her excitement grew, for tomorrow she would become Mrs Bedley and this evening Davey would be here, though of course she wouldn't see him. Everyone was singing 'Night and Day' and she joined in, and then they went into 'A-Tisket, A-Tasket'. The girls linked arms, and now Beth was singing too. They sang and sang until they reached Massingham, and then collected their dresses and carried them along the aisle again.

As they headed down the steps, Bert called, 'I'll be there to take you all to the wedding, or the guests anyway, and bring you back, as well as eat my sandwiches you'll have put to one side, our Franny.'

His laughter followed them down the pavement, the women's good-luck calls also carrying to them, and they walked together from the bus talking of Davey's call yesterday evening, so full of excitement and longing to see her. They left Fran at the back gate and she almost ran across the yard, then double-backed to say hello to the hens, before running again into the kitchen.

'Mam, I've got it.'

'Got what? As though I don't know,' her mam called from the scullery, drying her hands as she came into the kitchen.

Fran held up the bag, waving it. 'Me dress, Mam, what else? What if it doesn't fit? There was no time to try it on today. What if the hem's come down again? What if it's too creased?'

Her mam laughed and took the bag. 'Howay, take your

boots off and shut the door to the hall. Stan, Sid and Norm are moving me bed down into the front room for you, and I don't want them nosing.' She was drawing the dress from the bag, laying it on the back of Fran's da's armchair.

'By, our Tilly's done a crackin' job, God bless her soul.' Annie folded the bag. 'Of course it'll fit. It did a week ago. It's our Beth's that'll hang like a coat hanger, though Mrs Iris took it in a bit, on the quiet. I'll keep the hessian, for it'll make good backing for a proggy, I reckon. Make do and mend, eh? Now, into the scullery. Have a wash. Canna have your grubbiness on it.'

Fran rushed into the scullery as her mam said, 'Sophia was down today. By, she's looking a lot better, more rested, but still tired. It'll take time, though. Exhaustion picks at your core, so it does. Reginald thought Ralph might be back from the rehabilitation unit today, but he's not quite ready. Just wants one more day of the exercises, and there's a chance he'll be at the wedding, if he can get transport from the Carlyle unit.'

Fran had stripped and was washing and drying herself, not listening, not really. She peered out into the kitchen. 'They lads won't come in, will they, Mam?'

Her mother shook her head. 'They know it's women's work in here.'

Annie clambered onto her armchair, holding up the silk wedding dress. 'Get over here, lass. Arms up, little Franny.' She dropped the dress over her daughter's head; the silk was cool as it slid over her body. Her mam looked. 'You'll do,' she said.

Fran stood there, looking down at herself, smoothing the dress, so light, so smooth. She turned, and looked over her shoulder. She, Franny Hall, was to be a married woman, she was going to walk down the aisle without her da, she was to sleep with Davey, in her mam's bed that the lads were bringing down now. At that thought she paused, then suddenly wanted to rip the dress off, wanted to forget all about tomorrow, for she didn't feel like Fran Hall, she felt strange, lonely, frightened, for she wasn't a bairn any more, but was to be a wife.

She looked up at her mam, opened her mouth, but then there was an almighty bang from the stairs and Stan shouted, 'For the love of God, why does the thing have to be so bliddy heavy? Lift your end, Sid, get it over the newel, eh, and stop fannying about.'

Her mam started laughing, and between the bangs, the shouts and the laughter it was all right again, all normal: she was Fran, this was her mam, and her brother was helping set up the bedroom, and she'd still be here, like Sarah was still with her mam. Aye, it was almost all right. Mother and daughter looked at one another, and smiled.

'Aye you'll do, pet,' her mam repeated, 'you'll do fine, our Franny. But let's get it off you now, for I don't want you seeing it in the mirror until tomorrow, eh? It's then I want you to feel like a right princess and not before, because I can't have you prancing about, showing off, when we've sandwiches to cut. But trust me, it fits like a glove.'

She came down from the chair, unzipped Fran and eased the silk wedding dress from her, folding it up again in the bag. 'When the lads have gone, I'll hang Tilly's masterpiece up in my wardrobe so it's all tickety-boo for you.'

She left it on the back of the armchair again and straightened the old sheet on the end of the kitchen table, picked up the iron from the hot plate with a tea towel, and began pressing her own lilac outfit for the wedding. Fran sat at the other end of the table and ate the sandwiches her mam had cut before washing her plate in the scullery. She carried the makings of some of the sandwiches for the wedding tea back to the table, and had started spreading margarine and adding a light dusting of grated cheese when Sid came in from the hall, rubbing his hands.

'By,' he said, 'I reckon we'll be moving them all back again when our Davey goes down South and Clark Gable realises you're on your own, Mrs Franny Bedley, and swims the Atlantic to get to you.'

Fran laughed as her mam upended the iron on the table, and used the tea towel from the handle to beat him towards the back door. 'Don't you be giving the lass ideas, our Sid.'

He came to sit down while her mam poured boiling water into the teapot, finished off her pressing and hung her outfit over the airer. Fran finished the sandwiches, wrapped them in greaseproof paper and Sid took them to the meat safe hanging outside on the back door.

By this time Norm and Stan were at the table, and they all gulped down tea, eyeing the biscuits, which were a precious batch her mam had baked for tomorrow. She allowed them one each. Fran looked at her brother. 'What time is my lad due into Massingham?'

Stan winked, wiping his mouth free of crumbs. 'He's here, train were early. We wouldn't let him meet you off the bus, so instead he's gone off to dance the night away in Newcastle with his lady of the night. We're to make sure he staggers back before tomorrow, wiping the lippy off, in time to make an honest woman of you.'

Her mam flicked him with a tea towel while Fran called, 'Mam, you could have told me he was here.'

Annie nodded. 'Aye, I could, but I wanted you to try on your dress, not go roaring around to see him, as I feared you would, and the bride should not—'

Fran shook her finger at Stan and the other two. 'Listen, lads, I know you'll take him out, but don't you get him that drunk so he's good for nothing tomorrow. I couldn't bear to see him being propped up at the altar while I glide down the nave towards him. And you're *not* going into town, surely.'

Norm tapped the side of his nose with his finger. 'Ours to know and yours not to find out, lass. 'Tis his last night as a free man, so have some sympathy for him, for the love of God.'

It was Norm who received the flick that time, and with his arm over his head, he yelled, 'It's April Fool's, so don't take on so, Mrs Hall.'

Stan was looking at the clock. 'By, lads, time we were off, eh?'

They shoved back their chairs and Fran, who followed them to the door, called, 'Thanks, you three. You take care of me daft lad, you hear, or you'll have me to reckon with.'

Sid and Norm headed into the yard, but Stan stepped back into the kitchen and hugged her. 'You have a good life with your lad, our Franny. He loves you so, and wanted to come on round when he arrived, but 'tis bad luck and we've had enough of that, though Sandra and Ralph are on the mend. Talking of luck, how is our Beth?'

'She's carrying on, lad, step by step, being bliddy brave. But not right, though who would be? Too quiet, too tired, too thin. I could strangle him.'

'You and a dozen others.'

He spun on his heel and set off across the yard. Fran held the door and watched him join the other two, who were wrist-deep in the hens' corn feed. It made her think of their visits to Ralph, when Sid had mentioned that what else made him feel safe was the smell of the seed in the Canary Club shed. Their chatter seemed to have helped the lad and she smiled, thinking also of Viola, for her mam might not have to do too much matchmaking there.

She watched as the three lifelong marrers threw grain through the wire, then stood just watching the hens clucking and pecking, before heading for the gate. As Norm lifted the sneck, she heard Sid say, 'Aye, but you can't blame the lass, with Bob being a beggar and writing to say she could help make the divorce quick and easy if she'd be snapped in bed with someone, rather than he and the pregnant nurse do it, for what if the bairn ever found out. She said no to him, course she did. Told him to sort it. She's still into work every day, and anyway, do we really know if she's having a drink or two?'

Stan held the gate open. 'But the mams say she is, so where does the money, and the booze come from? The pubs aren't supplying it, for Mrs Oborne asked, nor the bottle shop, and she wouldn't go near that Norris, not after Mrs Bedley's do, surely?'

The gate shut, the sneck dropped and latched. Fran shut the back door and leaned against it, horrified, looking at her mam. 'Beth's drinking? Bob wants her to be photographed in bed with someone? We didn't know any of it. How bliddy dare he? All this talk of cigar smells, canary-seed smells, and I was walking close to her and I never noticed the smell of booze. What's the matter with us?'

Her mam shook her head. 'You've had the excitement, the wedding, and then there's the tea to bake for, and your factory work, and doing your bit for Ralph and Sandra. If she didn't tell you, how would you know?'

'But the bus . . . They all know, don't they, Mam?'

'Aye, they do, but they thought why spoil your special time, eh?' Her mam smiled wearily. ' 'Tis all right, her mam is there for her, and the last bit of power the lass has is to get up for work and not breathe a word to you. She needs that vestige of pride left to her by that man so she can spare you the worry.'

Her mam told Fran then that the lads had feared Beth was in with Norris Suffolk, but felt sure she wouldn't go to him, so it must be some other black marketeer. 'I wonder if she buys the drink to spend the allotment money as a way of getting back at Bob?' Annie mused.

She stared into the distance. Then said, 'Oh Fran, don't let it spoil this time, and don't tell her you know, the poor wee bairn. We mams are doing what we can. By, even Ben has chatted to her and walked with her, for he's a good lad. It breaks my heart, for she talks to her mam of the shame she's brought to the house, and she says it's her doing – something about it's payment for dropping Stan. And why should you girls guess when she chewed a bit of the dried-mint stem each morning in the scullery?'

Fran shook her head. 'Well, our shame is that we didn't guess. But you're right, she's struggled on, so I'll pretend I know nothing.' She sat at the kitchen table, then checked the clock. 'Where is Ben, anyway?'

Her mam shook her head. 'Where d'you think? Round seeing his hero, of course, showing him his latest cross-word setting and talking clues, I reckon.'

Fran smiled, wishing it was she who was there, but her mind kept taking her back to Beth, and she took herself out to the hens, where she gripped the chicken wire, resting her head against it, then looked up at the sky. 'Oh Da, what's to be done?'

She could imagine him sucking his pipe, deep in thought. Then he'd look up, and what would he have said? She waited a moment as the hens fussed, and finally she could almost hear his voice saying, 'Accept her gift of silence. But don't you dare move far from her in case she falls.'

Aye, that was good enough. For if that lass fell she'd be caught, but not just by her; she reckoned the lads would be there quick as a wink.

She patted the wire, knowing the hens would go into the coop to roost when they were good and ready. She made her way inside, looking up at the airer and her mam's outfit, then at her own dress. And there, hanging at the other end of the airer, was Ben's suit. He'd be too tall for it soon. She nodded. Time moved on. Why, tomorrow she and Davey would be man and wife and that would make them grown-up, and again she felt uncertain. Beth? Davey? Marriage? What if it went wrong? What if he wanted to divorce her?

Her mam was smiling at her. 'Oh, little Franny, I remember how strange it felt to be marrying your da. Suddenly it was here, that day, the day that would change my life.'

Fran nodded. 'Aye.'

'But you'll still be at home, for now. Here, where you've always been. 'Tis Davey who will move to us, just as Stan moved to Sarah's. He said he still thinks of here as home. It just takes time.' Her mam brought her a cup of tea, and sat down herself.

Fran thought of her dress, thankful to Mrs Oborne, and to Mrs Iris, who couldn't be at the wedding as she was on shift. She thought of the lads bringing down the bed, lads she'd known since she was a bairn, and of Davey. Davey who'd had a year of life before she was born, but from that moment on they'd been two halves of a whole.

She thought of one particular fitting in the sewing workshop when they'd all stood together, pinned, with the material inside out. Beth had hugged her, and the pins had pricked them. They'd laughed. Beth had said quietly, 'You look bliddy lovely, our Franny, and you know, don't you, that your Davey will never let you down. Don't you dare think what has happened to me will happen to you.' She had added, 'I should have married a Massingham boy, not someone I barely knew. You know that Davey is your world, he always has been, and you his.'

'One day you'll be happy again,' Fran had replied. 'Trust that, trust us, for we'll look after you.'

Beth had just nodded and Fran had worried, she remembered now, for she had smelled something on the lass, so had that been . . . ? Perhaps she was just being wise after the event. She stared at the range, the firebox full of coal, the flames flickering. Now, as she drank her tea, and then swirled the dregs around, she wondered if perhaps she had missed it on purpose, because it was easier?

Her mam leaned forward, reaching for Fran's hand. 'Don't you dare mither about Beth. Divint take that power from her, you hear? Not today, not tomorrow. Leave it until your Davey has gone, d'you hear, and she invites you into her world.' Her mam shook her hand. 'You hear me?'

Fran nodded, hearing her orders, hearing also what she had thought her da would say.

Her mam said, smiling now, 'Taking the lad into Newcastle, eh? Where will they really go, d'you think?'

They looked at one another and, laughing, said together, 'The Rising Sun.'

Chapter Twenty-Three

Fran woke in the double bed, the sheets crisp and clean. It was Thursday, 2 April 1942, Miss Frances Hall's wedding day. She pulled the sheet up and over her head, playing tents as she had done as a child. She thought of Davey, here with her, and instead of the excitement she'd expected she felt fear, again.

Had Sarah felt like this? She hadn't said even when Fran had hinted at how she felt yesterday evening as they'd set out the jam jars and daffodils on the tables at the Miners' Club hall. She lay, listening to the sounds of her house, but that didn't settle her as usual. She made herself breathe as her da had taught her, in for four, out for four, imagining him in the kitchen, standing in front of the range, wagging his finger at her. 'If you're ever in strife, you keep your head, our Franny. If you lose it, then do your breathing. It's saved more'n one pitman.'

But it divint save you, Da, she thought. She kept on breathing, and gradually the sounds of the house calmed her and she accepted she'd be here tomorrow, and the next day, and for months, perhaps years, as this was still her home until Davey was back from the South and the war was over. By then she'd be used to being Mrs Bedley and Davey'd go back to the pit, and they'd have their own bairns, and a colliery house until he got his magazine up and running. Maybe her mam would be living with *them*. Unless her mam remarried.

She sat up at the thought, startled. Her mam and a man?

Howay, no. But a small voice said, Why not? It wasn't something she wanted to think about. She flung herself out of bed and a second later Annie called up the stairs, 'Howay, our Viola, up and at 'em. Give our Ben a call from the bottom of the attic ladder, will you, pet?'

Fran had forgotten Viola had arrived last night to get an early start on the day. She was shrugging on her tatty old dressing gown when her mam rapped on the door. 'Fran Hall, soon to be Fran Bedley, up you get too. Remember, Mr Massingham is sending the car for you and the lasses, whilst us mams are going on the bus. Thanks be to God the sun is shining, eh. Stan and Davey are being taken in a taxi, and if it doesn't come, they'll have to pedal like the wind to get there in time, so I hope their hangovers aren't bad.'

Fran was laughing as she headed to the kitchen. At the same moment, Viola called from the landing, 'Howay, our blushing bride. Wait for the one who'll be walking along in your wake, always the bridesmaid, never the bride, eh.' She rushed down the stairs. 'I'm so excited, so bliddy pleased to be part of it all.'

Ben had just jumped down the last few steps of his attic ladder and called, 'Language, Miss Viola Ross, if you don't very much mind, or you'll feel me mam's hand skelping your good ear, for you're one of us now.' He hurtled down the stairs as the girls hurried into the kitchen, shouting as he caught them up, flinging himself into his chair at the table. 'Aye, you're one of us, in spite of living the high life with the nobs up at the Hall. What's more, Ralph will be back any minute.'

Annie came in from the kitchen and skelped his ear as Viola blushed. Fran shared a look with her mam. Ah, she thought, as her mam raised her eyebrows. Fran wondered if Viola was soon to become more of a nob than a Massingham village lass. She hoped so, for there was that certain look in her eye at any mention of the lad, and it was Viola's hand that Ralph had squeezed first, and Viola he had looked at when he came to.

'Stop showing off, you daft lad,' said Annie. 'You may be close to thirteen, but you're still a bairn, and don't you forget it.'

Ben crossed his arms, slumping back in his new shirt and suit trousers, and sighed. 'How can I forget it, with you lot going on? And I'm even wearing a tie, for the second time in a month, and the shirt rubs me neck.'

Annie brought out scrambled eggs on toast for all three of them, but she held it away from his reaching arm. 'We're not going to hear another word from you, lad, less it's a nice one, are we? And divint forget to do your teeth and rub a flannel over your face.'

Fran was trying to hide her laughter along with Viola, who said, 'Or you'll get no kisses from any girls at the wedding tea.' The women exchanged looks.

'There'll be nowt of that, I'll have you know,' Ben grumbled, 'and what's more, I'll be a little ray of sunshine, that I will.'

Annie laid his plate before him, then hurried back into the scullery, bringing out her own. She snatched a look at the clock. 'Heavens, quick, quick, 'tis seven o'clock. We need to leave at ten thirty to be there at eleven, or your Davey'll be left standing at the altar, looking gormless with Stan, who'll no doubt realise he's lost the ring.'

They were all sniggering now, Ben most of all, as they gobbled up the eggs. He finished, laid down his knife and fork, and made for the back door. 'I reckon our Fran'll need a good three hours to make herself look beautiful, but I'm first in the netty, so that's that.' He was out of the door like a shot.

The three of them looked at one another and laughed till

they felt exhausted. Fran pictured herself here, at this table, with her man, and with these people she loved, and knew it was all right. Suddenly, she couldn't wait, and the happiness exploded within her.

They dressed in old clothes, bustled to the Miners' Club hall to meet up with the co-op, who were sorting out the tea, though after an hour they sent the girls home to get ready. Fran tried to ignore the fact that Beth was so pale, even though she still helped, and laughed, and Fran could have wept, for how could she, when the poor lass's life was in shreds?

At ten thirty, when the girls were waiting in the kitchen, dressed, with some lippy and with their hair washed and gleaming, they heard a car horn at the front. Sarah gripped Fran's hand. 'You look a picture, our Fran. A right picture, a real princess. Look how it fits.' Viola insisted she do a twirl, a spin, and thought Mrs Oborne had done a beautiful job, for you couldn't see the stitches at all.

Sarah turned to Viola. 'You in your green, and Beth, that blue suits you to a T, and here I am in me pink. By, a fine gaggle of women we are, eh?'

Beth whispered, as though she was quite suddenly too tired, 'Sarah, that pink was made for you, and Viola, the green is so good with your dark auburn hair, isn't it, Mrs Hall?'

Annie was nodding, tears in her eyes. 'You are all so lovely. I'm proud of you.'

There was another hoot, and Fran picked up her bouquet of late daffodils. There weren't many left on the verges, but enough. They lifted their hems and rushed to the front door, waving goodbye to Mrs Hall, telling her how elegant she was in her lilac.

Ben was opening the door, ushering them out. 'Mam has

to get going an' all, out to the bus up the back alley, so get in the bliddy car.'

'Language,' they all yelled.

Sarah cuffed him, while Fran whispered, 'If me hands weren't full of the posy, I'd wallop you good and proper.'

The girls clambered into the car, with Alfie, smart in his grey uniform, holding the door, and Ben leaping into the front passenger seat, fiddling with his collar and moaning at the tightness of it. 'Bet that little silver mascot on the front of the bonnet didn't expect white ribbons tied to her,' he muttered.

Alfie looked at him, his uniform cap set straight, not at its usual jaunty angle. 'She's called Spirit of Ecstasy, lad, and she'll do as she's told, and if you don't, you'll be the one polishing her next time.'

The girls laughed. Fran called, 'Don't you go being a right pain, our Ben, just because you're in your suit. Alfie has orders to grab your tie and pull it tight if you get out of hand.'

Ben grinned at Alfie. 'You wouldn't, would you, for you'd have to take your hands off the steering wheel, and your boss would pull *your* tie tight if you wrote off the car.'

'It's more than a car, lad,' said Alfie. 'It's a Rolls-Royce, silent as a gentle breeze. The only noise is you, so shut your gob.'

Ben sank down in his seat. 'You know our lasses will all start calling themselves Ecstasy Spirits after riding in this. Especially looking so grand in their kegs.'

The girls exchanged glances. Beth said, 'Well, someone's noticed, even if our Alfie hasn't.'

As Alfie drew away, he said, 'That's because I'm speechless at all the beauty around me.'

'You've a smooth tongue, our Alfie,' called Sarah.

Alfie laughed quietly, saluting the pitmen's wives who were waving from their doorsteps. 'Well,' he said, 'who wouldn't be right gobsmacked to see all this beauty on the doorsteps waving at little old me.'

'Slap him, Ben,' demanded Viola, as they waved back to the neighbours until they turned onto Main Street and set off for St Oswald's.

It was then that Ben turned. 'They'll be dressed up in their kegs at the Miners' Club hall for the tea, or so Mrs Wainwright of number ten told me this morning. They're getting there early, putting the urn on, and this and that, or so they said.'

Fran sat next to Sarah. 'Best if the Reverend Walters' sister makes a few windy pops on the organ, and then no one will hear our shoes. The blessed things don't squeak anywhere else, so it must be those flagstones. Too much polish?'

'D'you remember Ralph winking at my wedding and wondering if we had mice in the church?' Sarah asked. 'He was nice that day, it sort of crowned the difference in him, made it public somehow. How's he doing, Viola?'

Viola smiled, blushing again. 'We hope he's coming to the wedding. He's been telephoning every evening while he's been getting himself functioning again. Sophia thinks he sounds as good as new and is so excited to be seeing him, but we haven't told the children, in case he can't get here. Eva's missed him more than anyone, it seems to me. She loves him so much. He spent time with them all when he was recovering from his septic cut.'

And you aren't backward in wanting to see him, I reckon, thought Fran, and knew that Viola could do much worse, for Ralph had finally proved himself a good man. She stared out of the window, and in the reflection she saw the kirby grip, falling—

She turned away. No, not today, not ever. That was over, and she was home, her mind had healed, and her memories.

She said finally, 'I hope he's really better.'

'Aye,' said Viola, 'I reckon some of what's ailing Sophia has been her worry over him. He's her lad, after all.'

Fran looked down, for Beth was grieved too, and hers was a running sore. Fran still couldn't bear that she had not seen the pain and struggle of her friend. Sarah must be thinking much the same, for she reached for Beth's hand and squeezed it. 'You look so lovely, Beth, and you're so brave.'

Beth looked round at them. 'Aye, well, 'tis what it is, and today you'll be at the church, our Fran, happy as Larry, and it will be a grand do, like Sarah's, and then there's just Viola to sort out.'

'I'll say this once, and once only,' Ben called back to them, 'that Bob's a disgrace and a fool, for you're a bliddy diamond, and I'm saying that to your face, our Beth.' He looked at her. Then turned to the front.

Fran heard Alfie whisper, 'Put a sock in it.'

'No I won't,' muttered Ben, 'for I want to punch him on the nose, so I do. So, you just concentrate on your driving, why don't you.'

Alfie flung a packet of Woodbines and a box of matches at him. 'Put a Woodbine in that big gob of yours, light it and give it me back. But don't make the end all wet. And for the love of Mike, shut up, for you'd have to stand on an orange crate to reach his nose, you daft bairn.'

There was silence, and then Beth began to laugh, high-pitched, but at least it was a laugh. Relieved, the others joined in, and as they petered out Fran slipped her free arm through Beth's, whispering, 'The lad's right, you're a dia-mond, and that's all you have to remember.'

Sarah was saying, 'By, the mams looked right smart, don't you think? Though their shoes are a size too big so there's room for the feet to swell.' There was more laughter and Beth joined in, and again they were four marrers, excited at the thought of the wedding.

'Penny for them?' Fran murmured to Sarah, who was looking thoughtful as Alfie checked his watch.

'We're all right for time,' he called.

Sarah smiled. 'Penny for me thoughts, eh? I were just thinking who'd have known that a parachute could make a bride look so magical, and some cotton material make the bridesmaids a sight for sore eyes. For we are, Beth, and you too, Viola. Beth, you look a picture with your hair up like that, caught up in that silver-looking slide.'

'Aye, where'd you get it?' Ben asked, as Alfie seemed to glide on air round the bend.

Beth flushed and said, 'Oh, just an old one I found.'

'I don't remember you ever wearing that, our Beth,' said Ben. 'Where've you been hiding it?'

There was a long silence, and finally Beth muttered, 'It was in the back of my drawer.'

'Right,' called Alfie. 'We're on schedule. I'll take you to the top of the church hill, then charge off for the Massinghams. You tuck yourselves in the vicar's robing room, though to call it that makes him sound like the Pope.'

He braked in front of the church. 'Let the beauties out, our Ben. And don't you dare go down the aisle till 'tis five minutes past eleven. Got to be late and give our Davey a scare – 'tis obligatory.'

The white ribbons were fluttering in the breeze as Ben opened the back door, bowing and beckoning them out. As Viola was first to leave the car, Sarah whispered to Fran, 'Be grateful the ribbons are only on the cars, for in times gone by they'd have decorated your bed and we'd all have a good look with you two in it.'

Beth clambered out next, holding her dress up with one hand.

'Take my hand, Beth,' said Viola.

'I meant to say,' called Alfie, 'the mams have left the bridesmaids' flowers in the robing room. They probably pinched them off the altar.'

'Shut up,' Beth and Viola shouted together and Alfie laughed.

'Bring the saxophone when you come, Sarah, if you would,' Viola asked.

Fran was easing herself out now, carefully gathering up the silk, but she called out, 'Nobody get any ideas about coming into the bedroom, or I'll have to belt you all.'

The wind was tugging at their hair, the sun catching Beth's silver slide. She'd have seen the new girl's kirby grip if it was silver, Fran thought. She brought up Ralph's face, his voice and that was enough.

Sarah was standing beside her. Ben shut the door with a tiny click. The mams were at the church door, which meant Bert's busload were already there. Annie beckoned. 'Quick, quick, out of the wind.'

They hurried past them into the entrance lobby. Fran glanced to the right, along the nave to the altar. Davey was already sitting in the front pew, with Stan. As Alfie eased the car down the hill, Fran swung round, seeing more people straggling up the hill.

He mam turned her round. 'By, look at your hair, 'tis blowing amok.'

'Have you any hairpins?' Mrs Bedley asked.

Ben held open the robing room, or vestry, which led off the lobby and gestured them in as though he was a policeman. 'I need to remind you Mam, your job is to greet; the girls are to hide,' he announced.

Beth hurried into the pale light of the vestry, glad she'd be hidden from those who had finally reached the church and were chatting to the mams. Once the girls were in, Ben closed the door. Beth wanted to lean against it, or against something, because she was weary with holding herself upright. She stared at the motes dancing in the light from the high, narrow window. She breathed. Yes, breathe, and now she smelled the ancient, tatty prayer books that were piled on every available surface.

She fixed on those on the shelf by Walters' desk, thinking of the hands that had held them. The books were so worn they seemed imbued with the prayers that had been repeated, prayers that had sunk into the very pages, into the stones of the church and probably the old oak pews.

In that moment she smelled the chrysanthemums that the co-op and the other women decorated the church with at Harvest Festival, at which the choir had sung. A choir they had joined when at school. Why had they left? Work, and the war? They should join again. Was that why Bob had left her – payback for failing the vicar? Or only for failing Stan and the gang and choosing Bob? No. Don't.

She saw the shafts of light coming through the stained-glass windows onto the church lectern, she heard voices raised in hymns, and now a quiet calm fell on her, because the world went on, no matter what people did. She looked around and up at the plain glass window, through which the bright morning light shone onto her marrers, those she had known for years, and would continue to know, just as the co-op continued, and the pitmen, Marrers and the Massingham people. As Fran tidied Viola's hair, and Sarah fiddled with Fran's, Beth smiled and her shoulders dropped. She breathed in easily, and out again. She sent a message to her da. 'Tis all right, Da. When I opened his new letter this morning, I felt I could not go on, I wanted to be there with you, away from it all. I miss you, Da, and I need you, but I still have my friends.

She moved closer to Fran and said, 'Aye, lass, let's get

287

this deserter back in place.' She tucked away the dark chestnut strand that kept escaping – but it wouldn't stay. So, she removed her slide, and clipped the hair into place with it. 'There, you look right tidy, and not as though you've been dragged through a hedge backwards.'

Fran smiled and smoothed Beth's auburn curls. Viola complained, 'If we could have long hair, then we'd look elegant for weddings. It could be down and flowing, or up in a chignon and smart.'

Fran grunted. 'I divint want me hair catching in any machinery and me ending up scalped and bald like that lass Esther, but you grow yours, you daft thing, but be aware that Eva might pull it, if she is displeased.'

Sarah turned Fran around, stepping back to check her. 'Aye,' she said. 'Our hair's barely streaked and our skin's not really yellow, is—'

'Not the Factory today,' called Ben through the door. The girls hushed. Ben called again. 'The church is filling up with people, and I reckon I should hold out a collection plate and nip off to buy a few beers with it.'

'One more word out of you,' said Fran, 'and you'll spend the wedding locked in here. And stop listening – we could be talking secrets.'

There was no reply. Then Ben said, 'Aye, Bert, choose left or right, 'tis no matter. Been having a quick fag, have you, after parking your bus nice and neat, I hope?'

'You mind your own business, young 'un,' growled Bert. 'Or you can go down there yourself and look after it.'

The girls waited. Finally, Ben said, 'Howay, Bert. I'm to give our Fran away, and if I don't we'll be stuck with her for ever, so I canna do that.'

The girls smothered their laughter and Bert muttered, 'Ah well, that'd be punishment enough for a cocky young bloke, I reckon.'

At that Fran called, 'I heard you, Bert Evans. No special sandwiches for you, my lad.'

There was silence, then Bert said, 'You could have said they were in there, you little varmint.' He raised his voice. 'You just get yourself down that aisle, our Fran, quick march, then we can get on to the important stuff at the club, eh.'

As they laughed, Beth pictured Ben standing with the brass collection plate in his hand, and now, in that moment, she allowed herself to think again of the letter she had received this morning, signed, as a final insult, by both Bob and his nurse, Heather, in which they'd informed her that a divorce had to be heard in the High Court. They had gone on to say that this was beyond their means.

Heather had written a section: *Without a divorce we cannot have the allotment which is a wife's due, so woman to woman, I ask you to be honest and send it on to us to make it easier when our bairn is born.*

Then it had reverted to Bob's handwriting: *It's not unreasonable, is it, for you to pay half the divorce costs, or give me back my own pay each month? I thought you would have done this of your own accord by now, for you earn good money at the Factory, and there's your singing.*

She had read it again. Bob? Bob had written this to *her*. Heather, too, and both had signed it. Beth moved to the shelf containing the prayer books. The spines were tattered. Were they spares to be used if necessary, or to be thrown out? She refused to think of herself in that way. Thrown away, eh, and expected to pay for the privilege. No, no Bob here, in this room. She reached out and laid her hand against the spines, holding the image of the work-worn hands that had gripped them.

Viola came to stand alongside. 'A lot of prayers have been said here, in this church. We're so small, aren't we, Beth, so bliddy small, and people come and go, and these stones breathe us in, and we know that we have lived, and so have all those that have gone before, and we will somehow go on living until we don't. Simple as that.'

Beth dropped her hand. 'You understand.'

'Oh aye, I've had me house on top of me, bricks digging into me, darkness, soot in my mouth, crunching between my teeth, till a distant voice said, "We're coming for you." Then another said, "Take my hand, let me lead you out." I thought it were an angel, or God, and it might as well have been, for the bricks were shifted, and this grimy, calloused hand came down. I reached up, his hand closed around mine, and out I came, into the darkness of the blackout, though fires were burning. "Who does this lass belong to?" he called. And no one answered, for those I belonged to were gone.'

Both girls stood in silence. Viola squeezed Beth's hand. 'Then, bonny lass, there I was, under another load of bricks in Scotland, and when I was out of hospital, there you all were, and your mams, and you all took my hand, led me into the warmth of Massingham.' Viola leaned closer now. 'So, you need to let us take your hand, pet, firm, like this.' She held up her hand clasping Beth's. 'Let us walk you out of the gloom, eh.'

Beth touched the spines again, with her other hand, pressing it against the rough, worn edges, harder and harder. She would tell them about the letter, another day. She would tell them she had started drinking and couldn't stop, and it was only now she really understood Mrs Bedley. But not on Fran's happy day. And she would pay the allotment, of course she would. She had already decided because it wasn't her money, and the bairn would need it, after all, none of this was its fault.

She turned to all three because she knew they were standing quite still, waiting. 'I know you're all beside me, or I'd not be here today, looking like a princess and putting you all in the shade.'

Fran went to hug her. Beth put her up hand. 'Your mam'll kill you if you crease that dress, not to mention Mrs Oborne, who'll have all our guts for garters.' They just nodded at one another, and Beth said, 'Hear the church bell.' They listened to the chimes . . . nine, ten, eleven. 'Let's gather up the bouquets,' said Beth, 'for we have to make sure our Fran gets wed.' The door was ajar, and Reverend Walters' sister was playing, but it wasn't the 'Wedding March'.

'Wait,' Ben ordered, slipping into the room. 'Wait till the squeaking starts.'

The girls looked at him. He winked, and then they were all laughing, and this time Beth's laughter was real.

The 'Wedding March' began. ' 'Tis time.' Ben beckoned them out.

They stood in the lobby, checking one another for the final time. Ben suddenly seemed pale and nervous, and such a young boy, and as Fran stood with him, she ruffled his hair.

'Oh divint, Franny,' he complained.

Viola whispered from behind, 'She's in such a rush to get to her Davey, 'tis unseemly.'

Ben and Fran linked arms, and Fran whispered, 'Breathe in for four, lad, and out for four.'

He looked at her. 'Like our da always said. By, Franny, you look right pretty, you do.' He stood on his toes and kissed her cheek. She squeezed his arm, then they gathered at the head of the aisle, with Fran looking towards the altar, to see if Davey was standing with Stan, ready to marry her. Instead she saw the Massinghams, who were tiptoeing up the aisle. There was a murmur of surprise as they passed the guests, who turned to one another, whispering.

The 'Wedding March' stopped to allow the Massinghams to take their place. Fran whispered, 'So Ralph didn't come.'

There was a heavy sigh from Viola, standing behind them. Ben said, 'Just wait, girls. One thing at a time.'

The 'Wedding March' started again. 'Shouldn't we go?' asked Beth.

Fran shook her head. 'Bit of a log jam. Let them get seated. I need a clear run to get at me man.' Alfie, who had been leaning against the back wall by the doorway, sidled up. 'We got stuck behind a bliddy tractor. I'll swing for Farmer Norton's lad. Would he pull over? The boss weren't pleased.' His whisper was loud. The back rows turned, laughing.

Fran said, 'It doesn't matter. Davey's not going to escape.' Alfie returned to leaning against the wall.

Behind her, the girls were laughing just as she was.

'Now?' she said, as the Massinghams stopped at a pew several rows from the front, but then there was movement in the evacuee children's pew behind theirs and a small fig-ure burst from it, squirrelled through the Massinghams and shouted, 'It's Mr Ralph – oh we hoped you might. Oh, Mr Ralph, I missed you so.'

'Oh,' breathed Fran as the Massinghams parted, and there was Ralph, laughing, beside Professor Smythe.

'Oh,' echoed Viola.

'There, just another surprise for you,' said Ben.

Eva hurled herself at Ralph, who staggered back, using his walking stick to recover, and held her close. The organ seemed to hiccup, then squeak and wheeze as the 'Wed-ding March' stopped again. The congregation grinned.

Sophia tried to wrestle Eva from Ralph, but he said into the quiet, 'Little Eva, I've missed you, but now I'm much, much better.' Professor Smythe took Ralph's walk-ing stick, leading the way to their pew as Eva still clung to Ralph, her arms around his neck. Her voice was clear in the hush.

'Oh, Mr Ralph, oh, dear Mr Ralph. I eat nice with me

knife and fork the blacksmith made like you asked him to. And I did tell you when you were asleep, well, we all did, that we're still learning our times tables. Mr Ralph, we were right worried, and so glad when you woke. Viola was an' all. We know she was because she sang a lot. Sophia did too.'

He was stroking her hair and turned, looking along the nave at Fran and Ben. He shook his head and called, 'Oh dear, Fran, I'm so sorry, and you look quite lovely – you all do.' He seemed to be looking over Fran's shoulder.

'That child,' whispered Viola, 'talks too much, and most of it's nonsense.'

The children were creeping from their pew and clustering around Ralph, only to be hushed and herded back to their seats by Sid. Fran heard Ralph say, 'Davey, I'm sorry to hold things up, but Fran would wait for you for ever, you know that.'

The laughter throughout the church was warm. Ralph limped into the pew, still carrying Eva. He stopped, untangled himself and sat down with the bairn beside him, but Eva wasn't through yet.

'Don't you leave us again. We were so miserable because you're so nice now, Mr Ralph. I reckon we love you.'

Sophia turned and mouthed 'So sorry' to the congregation and to Vicar Walters, who was standing with Stan and Davey, but there was no need, for all were grinning fit to burst.

Behind Fran, Sarah said, 'The prodigal son returns, though not quite tickety-boo, with a bliddy big scar on his forehead and half an ear missing, but looking surprisingly well. 'The Carlyle unit did him good, obviously.'

Smythe was taking his place, the Massinghams too, and the 'Wedding March' was being banged out yet again. Reverend Walters was beckoning them forward. He shouted to her – not, she thought, as a vicar should: 'Davey's champing at the bit, so come at a gallop, for the organist might run out of wind.'

They laughed their way up the aisle, Fran's eyes on Davey every step of the way, her blond, blue-eyed boy, so like Sarah. And beside him, her big brother, so dark, just like her. She grinned at Stan, he winked, then turned to the front, but Davey just watched her as she watched him, and she so wanted to toss aside her bouquet and run to reach him. Finally, they were there, and Davey took her hand, kissing it. He was pale, obviously hungover, and she leaned into him, whispering, 'By, lad, you're in need of the hair of the dog, I reckon.'

Reverend Walters smiled, then looked over their heads into the nave. 'Dearly beloved . . .'

Ralph watched as Fran and Davey kissed one another at the end of the service, now man and wife, while the three bridesmaids hurried to the spot beneath the hymn board. Mrs Hall drew out a saxophone from beneath the bride's family pew, and handed it to Ben, who passed it to the vicar, and then to Viola. Ah, Viola, who had held his hand, squeezed it, talked to him, whose very touch and sound had drawn him back so that he woke into a great sense of safety. The sense had actually been a scent, Sister Newsome had told him, for even the girls had puffed at the cigar. But nonetheless, it *was* an awakening into safety.

'Look at these women, they're just like a well-oiled machine,' whispered Reginald Massingham, poking Ralph over the head of Eva sitting between them. 'These women, young and older, are terrifying.'

Ralph smiled. 'Indeed.'

Professor Smythe, who was sitting on Ralph's right, asked, 'Are what?'

'Terrifying, Mr Massingham said, Professor Smythe,'

Eva explained. 'Do you reckon you need an 'earing aid for your lugs?'

Ralph bit his lip, feeling the laughter building. Professor Smythe merely raised an eyebrow at him before answering, 'Do you know, I believe I might, young lady. Whisper and let's see if I pick it up.'

But before Eva could do so, Viola was raising the saxophone strap over her head and beckoning to the child, who now clambered over Ralph's legs, carefully, and Professor Smythe's, less carefully, and ran up the side aisle to the girls.

'Clearly here I am, deaf and worthy of not very much except to be trampled on,' whispered the professor. 'I'm so glad I came, quite a boost to the morale, eh? So glad too, dear boy, that you and I got to talk a fair bit at 'the Carlyle' when I spent a few days there. Oh yes, we sorted out this and that, and just how to go about snaring our bête noire, eh, our ghastly little tyke? We will triumph. You and I will get our man.' Smythe's voice was a mere whisper. He added, a little louder, 'I am so pleased you came out of the dark tunnel, dear boy. Not for any other reason than you deserved to – grand effort with the bus.'

Ralph swung round to stare at him. 'Really?' he whispered.

'Indeed.' The tone was robust and genuine.

Ralph turned back, seeing Eva standing with Viola, facing the congregation. Eva saw him and shouted, 'Don't you leave, Mr Ralph. Don't you dare leave, even if you need a rest. You keep him there, Professor, you hear me.' She shouted again: 'Did you hear me?'

It was a real question. Professor Smythe stood, saluted and said, 'Loud and clear, Miss Eva, loud and clear.'

Eva turned to Viola. 'We thought he might be deaf, you see. He's old and dithery, aren't you, Professor Smythe?'

The professor said to Ralph, as he sat down, 'Dear Lord,

next she'll be asking me how old I am, and when am I going to die.' There were ripples of laughter through the church as this was repeated down the pews.

Viola, however, was hushing Eva as she crouched beside her. 'Have you remembered the words, Eva?'

'Course I have, Miss Viola.'

'Good girl.'

It was then that Ralph thanked God yet again that Viola was the evacuees' governess or Sophia's helper, or whatever name they'd given her, and they'd be under the same roof, for he wasn't sure he could exist without her, and he couldn't understand how love could come so suddenly. So it must have been for Sophia and his father. He looked down and moved his leg. His calf muscle was improving its function, and though part of his foot was numb from nerve damage, he felt much restored and able to work, and listen, and forage, as Smythe had put it.

He let himself think of Sister Newsome's words as she'd told him he'd sacrificed himself for all the Factory girls on the bus. But how could he not do that, when he had killed the fathers of two of them?

Eva was singing 'Cheek to Cheek' along with the saxophone, her hands clasped together, Viola's remaining fingers strong and able on the saxophone. Eva's eyes were closed and her voice steady.

The other bridesmaids were singing with her now, but Ralph stared at Eva. Orphaned Eva who seemed to love him, and who had moved him almost to tears when he'd heard her voice: 'Mr Ralph . . .' Eva with her parents beneath bricks. Eva who would go who knew where when the war was over? Well, not a bloody orphanage, if he had anything to do with it. He'd keep her with him if it was too much for Sophia. If he didn't die falling foul of Swinton, that was, for he was more determined and able after his survival in the car wreck to seek restitution for himself, and prison or worse for Swinton, and whoever the big boss was.

The song ended, and there was no applause for it was a church, after all, but Ralph silently clapped Eva, who was looking for his approval, and then he mouthed to Viola, 'Bless and thank you.' Viola blushed, but from the heat of his face, he was doing so too.

Fran and Davey walked down the aisle to the sound of handbells, which the children were ringing, having scooted along a side aisle to stand near the font. Davey whispered, 'Eva seems to think a wedding without bells is no wedding at all, so they arranged to get them from a handbell club or something like that. Or rather, our Viola did. They weren't having any truck with no church bells just because there's a war on.'

Fran was grinning, for wedding bells were wedding bells when all was said and done, and perhaps they might forget to throw the confetti they'd made, and which the vicar deplored. She waved to Cyn Ellington, Simon Parrot and Mr Swinton as she and Davey progressed along the nave.

Davey was waving to someone standing at the back, next to Alfie. As they neared, he stepped to one side, pulling Fran with him. 'Fran, remember me talking of Daniel? Well, here's the reprobate in person, and Daniel, this is Fr—'

'I think you mean Mrs Bedley,' Daniel interrupted. He smiled at Fran. 'We'll talk at the wedding tea, for I have much to tell of your crossword husband, absolutely all of it bad.' He winked, and now Davey was pulling her along to the door.

'Don't listen to a word he says.'

Chapter Twenty-Four

Fran stood in the porch in much the same way Sarah and Stan had a month ago. This time the trees were well in bud, though the wind was the same. It rustled her daffodil bouquet just as it had Sarah's, though that had been made up of snowdrops and ivy. She looked down the hill. Bert's bus was there, waiting, but not Cecil's, for he was taking delivery workers to the aft shift, then returning the fore shift. Valerie would be on that and Maisie, with a few others, all of whom would join them for the wedding tea.

Davey kissed her cheek. 'I miss everything about my home, but one day I will come back.'

Stevie was setting up his camera and called, 'Best you take your missus for a toddle round the graveyard, Davey. The confetti will be thrown when I take the photos. Sorry, Vicar, but the evacuees have been making it for days and we can't disappoint them, can we?'

Fran waved her bouquet at Stevie and smiled an apology at the vicar, who grinned, calling out, 'Never fear, I know when I'm beaten. Mr Massingham's given my nephews ten bob to sweep it up.'

Waving to Mr Massingham, Fran replied, 'Thank you so much, Reginald, and Stevie, we're off to tell our Betty all about the wedding. Give us ten minutes.'

The bridesmaids called from behind her, 'We'll catch you up. Mildred's just pinning up Beth's hem – she caught it on a pew.'

As the newly-weds set off down the path, they heard

Stan call, 'Howay, Mildred, you be careful with them pins. Divint want you jabbing left, right and centre. Ouch.'

Davey laughed. 'She's skelped his ear.'

They reached Betty's mound, next to Fran's great-grandma's headstone. They both stood by it, and as the bridesmaids caught up, Fran lay several daffodils on Betty's grave. ''Tis so small,' she whispered, as she always did, then added, 'We'll get that headstone, so we will, Betty, and for Da. Just you wait and see.' She turned to put a single daffodil on her da's mound.

She had held back two. 'For you, Davey, for your da, and Beth's.'

Davey nodded. Fran laid one daffodil on his da's, and one on Beth's da's. 'Marrers together,' he murmured.

Stevie was calling them back. The four girls hesitated and looked at one another.

'Race you,' yelled Fran.

Davey nodded. 'Eat my dust.' But the girls were away, running along the gravel path with Davey behind, yelling, 'False start, I weren't ready.'

Ahead, Stan, Norm and Daniel were cheering them on, with Sid, his hands cupped round his mouth, yelling, 'Stop being a big girl's blouse, Davey, lad, and put some petrol in your tank, you soft desk-worker.'

Davey drew alongside Fran, panting and calling out, 'Petrol's on ration, you dozy bugger. But you're right, sooner I get back into the pit the better, for I used to be able to wallop you, no trouble.'

They all arrived together to find that Stevie had turned the camera round and had taken a picture of them, five abreast, cheering themselves over the imaginary line, the girls holding their dresses up to their knees, showing their socks and sensible shoes.

Norm stood with his arms wide. 'By, it were the socks

that did it. Socks and sensible shoes. 'Tis a sight to carry to me grave.'

Annie was shaking her finger. 'Decorum – is it too much to ask on your wedding day, our Franny? And high time you threw that bouquet.'

Stevie had turned his tripod around again. 'Aye, come and stand in front of the church, everyone, and behave yourselves just for one bliddy minute, then I'll take a few pictures and we can get to the club for the important stuff.'

'Stevie,' warned Mildred, 'this isn't the Rising Sun, so language. Fran, no throwing the bouquet till I tell you, same for you bairns with the confetti. Don't listen to this old fool.'

Stevie pulled a face and disappeared under the blanket, while Daniel sidled up to Davey. 'I see why you love this woman, Davey. And all of them.'

Mildred had taken over the organisation and had the smaller ones in front and the taller ones behind, with two bridesmaids on each side of Fran and Davey, then the mams, Ben and Stan divided up similarly. She signalled for the confetti to be thrown. After ten minutes it was all over, and Mildred ranged the bridesmaids behind Fran, waving everyone back, then said, 'Throw the bouquet now, Fran. I could do with some of my elderberry wine, cos I'm cold to me vest.' Fran grinned, and threw it over her head.

She turned and saw that it had fallen on Beth, who grabbed it. Someone called, 'Oh aye, she's already gone through one husband, so throw it on, lass.'

Fran saw Mrs Pritchard from Leadenhall Terrace, a few houses along from number 14. She also saw the vicar's sister hush her and whisper. The flush rose on Mrs Pritchard's cheeks, and her hand went to her mouth.

Beth paled, but merely threw the bouquet, which caught on her hair and flicked sideways. Viola caught it with her good hand. Everyone clapped and now it was Annie who took control, standing with Beth and telling everyone to hurry down the hill, because once Bert got to the bus it would go. 'Bert is ready for his sandwiches. You'll have to stand, for we're short of a bus.'

'And I hope them pheasant ones have been put aside for this worker, I do an' all,' yelled Bert.

Mr Swinton patted Bert's shoulder. 'If I know these girls, they'll have checked that the sandwiches have your name writ large.'

The two of them walked on down the hill, and Bert could be seen offering his cigarettes to Mr Swinton, which was such a rare occurrence that Fran and the bridesmaids gaped, while Mrs Oborne called, 'By, that's a bliddy miracle.'

Her husband said something to her and she turned, trying to locate Reverend Walters, who was nearby, chatting to the Massinghams. ''Scuse me language, Vicar, but you have to admit 'tis a rare event for our Bert to offer up his cigs to anyone, let alone Swinton.' She was pointing at the two older men.

Reverend Walters looked up at the sky. 'Indeed, Tilly, whatever next. Might pigs fly?'

Ralph, Professor Smythe and the Massinghams were chuckling, looking from Tilly to the vicar and then watching those on their way down the hill. Eva came to stand with Ralph, holding his hand, while Viola sorted out the other children. Fran felt that she was looking at a close family.

Alfie stopped Fran and Davey as they started to join the crowd. 'Oh no, you don't. Our Professor Smythe is taking the Massinghams and you're to come with me and the bridesmaids. One can take the front because Ben's off with Stan and the marrers, hitching a lift on the bus. It'll not only be standing room, but lots sitting on the laps of others. Right cosy, I reckon. Others are going back on their bikes, so will build an appetite. Hope you've catered for it.'

They walked down the hill, and Davey held Fran's hand as he said to Alfie, 'Course they'll have done. They know the Massingham appetites like the backs of their hands, you daft beggar.'

Alfie laughed, and dropped back to chat to the girls, while Davey and Fran walked ahead. She leaned into him, loving every breath he drew, every word he said, and wondered how she could ever have felt uncertain or scared.

She and Davey slipped their arms round one another. He muttered, 'I were nervous. Sort of frightened at the change, even though I love you more than life itself. I think I'm scared of the night-time, of doing it right.'

Fran leaned even harder into him. 'I was too, but not now.'

They walked on, and were nearly at the car when she muttered, 'P'raps you should wear them drawers that foiled Daisy's little lie that you'd had your way with her – the ones with the saggy elastic that you sewed tight to keep them up. Aye, do that, then nowt can happen, we'll just slee—' She couldn't say anything for he'd spun her round and lifted her into his arms, hugging her till she could scarcely breathe.

He put her down, and they walked on, laughing together, before he said quietly, 'Aye, well, our lass, happen you're right, 'tis always a thought.'

Ralph listened to the girls singing 'Night and Day' once the speeches were over, the tiny cake beneath the cardboard had been cut and the scones with the Women's Institute jam devoured. Bert had stuffed himself to the brim with pheasant sandwiches. Mrs Oborne was fanning herself, her

302

colour heightened as she spoke to Reginald Massingham. Colin, her son, was deep in conversation with Norm.

Finally, Ralph looked at Fran, who, in just a month, looked different, more grown-up, more a woman, or had it been happening for a while? He looked at Viola. Ah, Viola, who was rather wonderful. He hoped she was able to move her fingers more, and was in less pain.

He felt an arm link with his and knew it was Sophia. 'A happy occasion, dearest Ralph,' she murmured. 'These two so as one, and you, though in pain from your leg, are relaxed. You have survived and come home to us.'

'Home?' he mused. 'Yes, that's just how I feel, looking around with your arm in mine, and do you know, dear Sophia, I think I'll feel that at Auld Hilda when I report for surface duties. I can't return to the face until my leg is just a bit more use than it is, but even that will be a normality.'

She shivered. 'I do so wish you wouldn't go back down.'

He said nothing for a moment, then, as the girls finished, and the clapping began and she disengaged, he said, 'I must, the pits have lost so many to the war and we have to keep the coal coming. At least I know pretty much how to do it now.'

Ralph saw his father detaching himself from Mrs Oborne and smiling as he headed towards them. Just then, Eva bobbed up at Ralph's side and fixed Sophia with an unblinking stare.

'Sophia isn't well, Mr Ralph. See, she's pale, and a bit pukey.'

Sophia shook her head. 'I am just tired, little bossyboots. It's been a bit of a time.'

'Aye,' Eva grumbled, 'maybe she has the squits an' all. But she wouldn't tell us, and we wouldn't want to hear neither. You could ask her, though.'

His father called out, to Ralph's relief. 'I think that's

quite enough from you, young lady. Viola's looking for you to sing a solo.'

Eva ran off. Reginald grinned at Ralph, then Sophia, who waved towards the revellers, saying, 'Off you go, too, Ralph, and revel.'

'But, Sophia, what about . . . ?'

She just continued to wave him away. 'Tiredness, darling boy, causes all sorts of mischief, and now we have the wonderful Viola, so all is well, and will become even better.'

Ralph nodded. His father waved him away too. 'Yes, and I am home more often for a while, so I am the overseer of all things domestic.'

Sophia raised her eyebrows, and then burst into loud laughter. Ralph wandered around, smiling and chatting, but falling silent when Eva sang, 'A-Tisket, A-Tasket'. The lump in his throat made talking out of the question, and as the post-song chatter escalated, he slipped through the outside door, shutting it quietly behind him.

Standing on the step, he welcomed the cool breeze, breathing in the coal and sulphur, nodding to himself. Yes, he was truly home. He looked to the right, towards Auld Hilda's pithead workings – such an ugly old bitch, but again, home.

He picked his way through the weed-strewn grass and leaned back against the nearby storeroom brick wall, lighting up his cigarette, so glad that Sophia accepted his need to stay in the pits and help to win the war. He was an honest man at last, doing a worthwhile job. But the extent of that job was his secret. Well, except for Smythe and his right-hand man, Yeland, and of course, his father . . .

He heard Beth's voice then, almost shouting: 'Norris, what are you doing here? I said I divint want any more drink. I'm trying not to—'

'More to the point, what are you doing outside when the

others are tripping the light fantastic? Heard anything from that husband of yours? A girl like you divint deserve that sort of thing. And where's that slide I gave you?'

'Oh, 'tis in Fran's hair, to keep her neat.' Beth sounded exhausted. 'I needed fresh air, and quiet. Not you.'

Norris's voice took on an edge. 'You let her have the slide I gave you? That's plain rude.'

Ralph moved as silently as he could to the corner, lifting his stick so it wouldn't scrape against any of the half bricks lying in the grass. The name was familiar. Hang on, wasn't that the black marketeer . . . Was he the one who'd supplied Mrs Bedley? He cringed, for Maud Bedley had been trying to come to terms with Tom's death in the roof fall that he, Ralph, had caused.

He made himself pay attention, seeing the girl reaching out, coming down the path to Norris Suffolk. But no, she wasn't reaching out. Her hand was flat – stop, she was saying. But Ralph was damned sure this bugger wouldn't let a customer go.

Ralph pinched out his cigarette, as Smythe had taught him to do when he'd come to 'the Carlyle'. 'Smoke alerts them,' he'd said. He moved slightly, to give himself a better line of sight, risking a look. Norris was slipping Beth a tin hip flask, folding her hand over it, saying, 'This'll make you feel better. You're too lovely a lass to be miserable, and with a grand voice an' all. I've contacts, you know.'

Beth pushed the flask back at Norris, but her mouth was working. Don't, Ralph wanted to shout. Please, please don't. Beth was backing right up to the wall of the club, but Norris was going with her, smiling, his black hair flopping over his eye.

Beth snatched the flask, gulping down its contents. Norris crowded her, his arms on either side of her, his hands pressed against the wall. 'Plenty more where that came from, and while you have the wives' allotment – what is it, one third of his pay? – why not spend it?'

Beth just shook her head. 'I have to pay for the divorce, he says, or send him the allotment. I got the letter this morning. I was always going to send it. He should know that.'

Ralph could hardly bear the anguish in her voice.

'Ah, but you get good money where you work, and besides, your mam has her rugs.'

Ralph was shaking his head, whispering, 'No, no, Beth. Don't let him into your life.'

Leaning back against the wall, Ralph looked up at the sky, hoping Beth's father, Tubby Smith, was on his cloud. He found himself whispering, 'Help her, Tubby. Don't let her get involved with Norris, not now, not ever.'

He waited, listened, but everything had gone quiet. Had Norris left? He risked a look. Norris was kissing her. Ralph closed his eyes. Someone had to intervene. He flexed his leg, grateful for the strength he had worked towards. The door was opening and Norris stepped back, snatching the flask from Beth, who looked confused and full of misery.

Ralph saw Sid standing outside the door, letting it shut behind him, staring from Norris to Beth, who was wiping her mouth. Was she wiping away Norris, or the booze? Glenn Miller drifted out from the hall.

Norris was backing along the path towards the road, tipping his cap. 'Just having a word with the prettiest bridesmaid in Massingham.'

Sid was shaking his head at Norris. 'Aye, and I believe in Father Christmas. What's that you're holding in your hand? Why, a flask – one you've just given to her to pour down her bliddy throat, eh?'

He was striding after Norris, who was increasing his speed, but Sid lunged, grabbed Norris by the lapels, swung him round and hauled him out through the gateway and onto the pavement, calling back at Beth, his voice gentle, 'You get yourself inside, bonny lass. No need to mention any of this to anyone, eh? Don't want to spoil the party for this lump of—'

'Big mistake, sonny,' Norris ground out, his mouth hardly moving. 'This is different to the Bedleys' backyard, for you've not got Stan leading the charge.'

Ralph saw Sid hang on to one lapel and snatch the flask from Norris's other hand, sniffing, then dropping it onto the ground, grinding it beneath his steel-capped boot until it was flattened. 'Aye, it is a mistake for *you*, you bastard.' He gripped both Norris's lapels again and all the beggar did, Ralph saw, was to sag like a deadweight.

Sid shook him and still Norris just sagged, a stupid grin on his face. 'Ah, that's a girl's response, because it's hard to hold you up and slap you at the same time.' Sid's voice was low, but so furious that it carried on the breeze. 'Don't even think you can try and get that lass in the palm of your hand, like you did Sarah's mam. Making money from them with your rising interest on the bill. What then? How would you expect her to pay it off? You lay a bliddy hand on her ever again, you even look at her, and I'll rip your throat out, and no, I divint need Stan for that. You were told back then, in Mrs Smith's yard, to sling your hook, and now I'm telling you again.'

Sid was so close to Norris that their foreheads touched. 'So, don't you bring your filthy bootleg brandy and whatever else anywhere near her.'

'She was keen enough to take a silver slide from me, for which a man expects a little something.'

Sid shook him. 'For a start, the silver bliddy trinket is painted tin, and if you want it back, I'll post it in your gob, got it?'

He let him go, Norris staggered back, then forwards, and fell onto one knee. For a moment nothing happened, and then Norris lifted an arm. To do what? Ralph wondered. Was he asking for a hand up? He'd more likely get a punch on the nose. But no, Norris was gesturing to someone or something out of sight. From behind the hedge that divided the club from the road, Ralph heard car doors slam. Two men appeared, heavily muscled. Norris scrambled to his feet, dusting himself off.

Stepping back, Sid looked from the men to Norris, then glanced over his shoulder before assessing the three men again. Ralph saw that Beth hadn't moved. Sid's voice was calm and gentle as he kept his eyes on the men. 'You get inside like I said, our Beth, right now. Don't say a word to t'others, and if you've never done anything anyone's told you before, do it now. Leave me to deal with this.'

Sid's fists were clenched, he was settling his weight, with no sign of fear. Of course not; he was a pitman. 'You go in, bonny lass,' he repeated. Beth wiped her hand across her mouth again, and at last almost slid into the hall.

Ralph looked again at the tableau. Three to one, eh? Hardly fair odds. He flexed his leg. It would hold him up, because as Smythe had said, it came down to balance, and that was what some of the exercises in rehab had been all about. He also had the walking stick with the heavy lion's head. A gift from Smythe for those tricky moments, as the old boy had said, meaningfully.

'You're a bliddy coward, Norris,' growled Sid, 'bringing your monkeys with you. But it'll do you no good.'

Ralph waited, for any minute now the men would make their move. He looked at their faces, their eyes, the balance of their bodies, as Smythe had taught. For a moment no one moved, and then Norris and his men shifted their weight . . . Sid caught Norris with his boot as he came at him from the side, and punched the bigger of the other two while the third brandished a blackjack, swinging it wildly.

Ralph reached Sid, standing full square at his side, his walking stick across his body, muttering, 'Can't even have a pee in peace.' He swung his stick, lion's head first, catching Norris's neck. Always guaranteed to put someone out of action for a few valuable moments. He threw the stick behind him and turned to face the other two. 'Better odds, eh, Sid?'

Sid was dodging the blackjack, looking for an opening. 'Bliddy hell,' he gasped, 'and like a puff of smoke you're here, our lad.' He hadn't taken his eyes off the others for a moment.

The blackjack missed Sid, leaving the thug off balance. Norris came at Ralph. Ralph couldn't kick out with his leg, but he could punch, and did. Beside him, Sid did the same. The blackjack was dropped. Norris staggered to his feet, drawing out a knuckleduster from his back pocket.

Ralph dodged back, his leg failed him and a steel punch clipped his cheek, just catching his eye. Another punch went for his ribs. He blocked it and punched quick and fast, as he'd learned at school in the boxing ring. He picked up his stick, whipping Norris's feet from under him. Sid dispatched the other two. All three were making the road untidy, but then they groaned and stirred. Ralph flexed his hands – no damage, they just ached.. He blessed his fitness instructor, Smythe's advice and boxing.

Sid touched the men with his boot. 'Up you get, you load of rubbish, and get on home.'

The men groaned, scrambling to their feet. Sid was barely panting, though Ralph was trying to get his breath. Glenn Miller was still playing.

'Don't leave this bit o' nonsense here,' said Sid. 'Take him, throw him in the bliddy beck for all I care. Do it now.'

The men hauled Norris to his feet. 'Take that flask as well,' said Ralph. One of them picked it up.

'Never, ever go near Beth Jones again, Norris, or you won't be getting up, you won't even be found. Do you understand?' said Sid.

Norris just groaned. Ralph nodded. 'We'll take that as a yes.'

Ralph and Sid grinned at one another as Norris was helped to the car and tipped into the back seat, swearing bloody murder. Without looking back, the heavies opened the door to the front seats, almost fell in, started the motor and drove away.

Sid and Ralph watched whilst a few hundred yards behind them Auld Hilda's winding gear still sang, its song mingling with 'In the Mood'. Sid offered a Woodbine to Ralph, who thought for a moment, then brought out two of the cigars his father had left on his hospital bedside table. 'You like cigars, don't you, Sid? Don't know who told me, but you had one at Christmas with your grandpa. Well, let's have one now.'

Sid lit them, properly, the flame not touching the cigar. Ralph muttered, 'That's right, your grandpa taught you.'

'Something went into your noddle in hospital.' Sid laughed. He exhaled into the night air. 'We were talking about what made us feel safe. Howay lad, we'll have the ARP warden shouting the odds any minute now with this big beggar of burning ash.' They stood quietly for a moment. Sid nudged him. 'Strange thing is, you know, Ralph, the netty's right at the back of the hall.'

'Ah well, it was something to say. I just fancied some fresh air, but it sounded a bit feeble.'

The two men stayed where they were, quietly smoking. Ralph's leg and hands hurt, but nothing else. 'And Beth?' he asked, finally.

'Bob's got a pregnant fancy woman in Grimsby,' Sid muttered. 'He wants a divorce and the tongues are wagging. I reckon our Beth's thinking that she's brought shame to her mam's house.'

Ralph had heard what Beth had said to Norris, and repeated it. Sid merely said, 'Help pay for the divorce? Or give up the allotment on his pay? Shame that Bob's not here, for I'd have pulled his head off and stuffed him in the car with the other three.'

'She needs her friends, and someone who cares more than Bob ever did. I heard your voice tonight. Be the one who's there, eh?'

Sid tapped his cigar. 'Oh aye, it'll be me, bonny lad. No one will hurt her any more than she is hurting now, I'll make sure of that. But I reckon you can be my flank man, eh? Nifty bit of fighting – where'd you learn?'

Ralph examined his own cigar as Sid jerked his head towards the door. As they headed for the hall, he said, 'You'd be surprised what fitness exercises bring out in a man.'

Sid laughed. 'Screens tomorrow, then?'

Ralph nodded. 'Aft shift for now. When my leg's a bit stronger I'll be back on the face, that's if my place on your team's free?'

Sid pulled the door open. 'Ready for some scones, eh?'

'A beer more like, though a sip of that brandy that's soaking into the road would've been good.'

Sid laughed. 'Aye, bonny lad, you can always give the tarmac a good lick, eh?'

They entered. Bonny lad, eh? Ralph thought. None of them, not Stan, Norm or Sid, had ever called him that before.

'You'll be welcome back at the face with us, man,' Sid said quietly. 'But best brush the confetti out of your hair first.'

Ralph laughed, because he really was home if he was to

be welcomed, not just suffered. They walked towards the laughter, the singing, the dancing, and here was Eva weaving through the groups, calling, 'Mr Ralph? Oh, Mr Ralph, there you are. I'm going to sing with the girls again, so stay in here now, you hear me?'

She reached him, panting, her eyes alight, her plaits swinging, and grabbed his hand. He winced. She peered at his grazed knuckles, and then up at his face. 'What you been doing, Mr Ralph? You've a cut eye, and your hand is sore.'

'Tripped over my walking stick,' he said.

Nearby, Sid winked and gestured to the table where the lads were sitting, their chairs turned to face the girls, who were getting ready on the stage. 'Sit with us?' Sid mouthed to Ralph. To Eva, he called, 'We'll all be listening, lass, so you'd best hightail it.'

Ralph watched her weave her way back, her pigtails swinging, then replied, 'I'd like that, Sid.'

Chapter Twenty-Five

Ralph walked to the table with Sid, then hesitated. Would he be welcomed by the others?

'Sit yourself down,' said Sid. 'Divint hang about like a bad smell, lad. No way you're using that leg to get us to pull your bliddy chair out. Nowt wrong with it, seems to me.'

Stan looked surprised and raised an eyebrow.

'Mithering away like two auld women on the step,' Norm said, 'instead of breathing in the cigarette smoke in here.'

Ralph murmured, waving his cigar, 'I had to take a break. Makes me cough when it's smoky.'

Norm and Stan burst out laughing. 'Cigar, eh?'

Ralph nodded at them. 'Father left them by the bed. Anyone else?'

They waved away the idea. 'Had enough of that puffing over a sleeping beauty,' Stan said. 'One I reckon would have opened his eyes sharpish if there'd been a pretty princess hacking her way through the thorns to give him a kiss.'

Ralph looked around, seeing the Massingham people, and on the co-op table his family – Sophia, Reginald, even Professor Smythe – talking nineteen to the dozen with the mams. Over on the stage Viola was warming up the saxophone as Eva jumped up and down. The evacuees sat on a table close to the co-op. Probably so that one or other of the women could clip their ears if they got out of control. Ralph grinned.

He dug his hands in his pockets, his walking stick

hanging from his arm, just like his grandfather's portrait in the study. He looked around, knowing that all the Massingham people had such families and now and in the future, they were his responsibility, just as his father had always said. As he concentrated on Stan and the marrers, he realised that not only had he come to understand his father's decency and honour; but also, he acknowledged the Massingham family's tradition of compassion and commitment, mirrored by all these here.

He had to swallow hard against his tears, which had come readily in the first day or two after his 'second coming', as Sister Newsome called his recovery. When he wept, Sister Newsome had said, 'Young man, you have survived a good deed. Let's face it, it's not every day a youngster avoids a bus by driving into a tree. So, the obnoxious little brat has cast his skin. Focus now on what is to come. One step at a time, feel the ground beneath your feet, the sun on your face.' Dr Wilson had then sent him on to 'the Carlyle', an establishment in which Professor Smythe had an interest, the doctor said. Well, yes, thought Ralph now.

Norm was calling him now. 'Get your arse sat down, lad, you're making the place untidy, and what were you two up to out there, really?'

Sid winked at him as he sat. Ralph said, 'Oh, we chatted, and maybe had a bit of a twirl. Glenn Miller deserved some fancy footwork, indeed he did.' Sid roared with laughter, but Stan quietened him, because the girls were starting to sing. For a moment they listened to 'Over the Rainbow', but then Sid took a couple of tankards of beer from the tray Mrs Bedley was carrying from table to table and whispered, 'Ta, Mrs Bedley.'

She moved on as Sid put one of them down in front of Ralph. 'Wrap yourself around this. As a pitman you've a right to a glass of Stevie's best, not the stuff he keeps for the common herd. Besides, it was you who paid for all the booze, like you did for Stan and Sarah's wedding tea, so 'tis your right.'

Sid lifted his tankard to his lips, and Stan's gaze settled on his knuckles, then on Ralph's, but he just nodded. 'Over the Rainbow' came to an end and now Beth sashayed to the front and Eva joined her. Ralph found himself tensing, but Beth looked far from drunk.

'The girls thought a few cups of tea would help the lass,' Stan whispered. 'And food. She hadn't eaten all day, or probably the day before and the one before that, so they forced it down her. She'd had a glass or two on an empty stomach, 'tis all.'

Eva and Beth sang 'Keep the Home Fires Burning'. Ralph's gaze was fixed on the child as her marvellous, clear voice soared in harmony with Beth's contralto, then the duo fell silent as Viola's saxophone took over. It was Viola he watched now, that poor hand, and ear, her beautiful face. He touched his own ear, the scar down his forehead. Beth and Eva sang again, shredding the souls of those sitting or standing. When they reached the final two lines, Fran, in her bridal gown, and Sarah in her pink bridesmaid's dress joined in from the floor, and Viola's saxophone was a whisper as the song drew to a close.

There was silence, and Viola stroked Eva's hair, while Beth hugged the child to her. Still the silence continued, and no one moved. The girls bowed as one. Ralph stood up and started clapping. 'Bravo.'

It seemed, then, that everyone was on their feet, and Davey wove his way through the tables onto the stage. He led Eva to the centre. 'Ladies and gentlemen, a star of the future: Eva Harrison, a right handful of a bonny lass. Your mam and da will be so proud as they look down.'

Eva bowed as the girls joined the clapping, and Ralph

knew that his love for this incorrigible child was set in stone. Stan turned, grinning. 'Howay, lad, she's a special lass. Best you take good care of her, eh.'

As the clapping died, they heard Eva turn to Davey and say, 'D'you really reckon me mam and da can hear me up on their cloud, Mr Davey?'

Ralph made his way towards the stage, arriving at the same time as Sophia. 'Of course they can, little Eva,' he called.

She came to the front of the stage and jumped. He caught her.

'I knew you'd catch me. I know you always will.'

Ralph put her down and led her to the co-op's table, with Sophia taking his arm. 'Anyone here would,' he said, quietly. 'You're quite safe in Massingham. Trust me.'

Behind him, Ben put on a record: the 'Sweetheart Waltz'.

Davey pulled Fran closer still once they reached the floor. He led her into a waltz, and neither of them wanted the day to end as long as they were here, dancing, laughing, and together. For tomorrow he would leave.

As they circled the floor, they neared the co-op's table where the Massinghams and the professor still sat, and Davey whispered, 'I need to make good the mistake I made at Sarah's wedding tea, lass. Just a word with the professor, eh?' He spun her round, and Beth's slide fell from Fran's hair onto the floor. While she picked it up, Davey slipped between the tables reaching the professor, who was in full lecture mode, telling Mrs Oborne about the ancient Greeks.

Tilly Oborne nodded towards Davey. 'Eh, bonny lad, the professor looks at me and sees an old bag, and tries to make me feel better by battering me with facts on a load of Greeks who're even older.' She winked.

The professor spun round. 'My dear boy,' he said, rising.

'Such a pleasure to be here again, at the celebration of another son of the coal, one who is toying with things other.'

Mrs Oborne shouted across, 'By, he means he's right glad to be here with us sparkling souls.'

It was the professor's turn to wink at Davey as Fran caught up. 'That's it, in a nutshell. I think, dear Mrs Oborne, you simply must come to Oxford with me. I need you to teach my young show-offs how to grasp the nub of things.'

Mr Massingham roared with laughter, slapping the table. 'Best not, Auberon, old man. She'd sort them out a little too much, I reckon, and ears would be skelped within the first hour.'

Professor Smythe shook Davey's hand, and kissed Fran's. 'I can only think that would be good for the little smart alecs.'

Davey leaned in closer. 'I have come to say how glad I am to hear from Sophia that your son is safe. Last time we met, at Stan's wedding, I didn't even know he was missing and dropped a bliddy big clanger. Stan tells me he's a POW, bloodied, but unbowed.'

Again, Mrs Oborne involved herself. 'By, that one of your clues, Davey Bedley? Bloodied but unbowed, indeed.'

Fran grinned as Mr Oborne muttered, 'You're not having any more elderberry wine, lass. That tongue of yours is taking flight.'

The professor smiled around at everyone. 'I do so love being up here, it reassures me that the world hasn't gone completely mad. What's more, I think we should all have a Mrs Oborne living near us, because I could do with absorbing some of her verve.'

Bert was passing and held up his half-pint of beer. 'Then take her, Professor, for the love of God, take her. Give us some peace.'

The professor caught Davey under the elbow. 'I'm wending my way to see young Ralph. Nasty mishap; a grand attempt to save lives, eh?'

Without quite knowing how, Fran and Davey found themselves being propelled towards the lads' table, but Davey extricated himself firmly, gripping Fran's hand and saying, 'You go on, Professor. I'm dancing with me wife while I have the chance.'

Ralph stood up when he saw Smythe on his way. Was he the only one who could see the sharpness of those eyes belied the befuddled persona? They met halfway.

'Well, young Ralph . . .' The professor shook his hand and then waved expansively around the room. 'We do keep meeting at these weddings. Any more on the horizon? A chance to chat with all and sundry.'

Together they surveyed the guests, but both were really checking up, as Ralph always was now: who was listening, who was in a group? Who was a stranger? Who was asking too many questions?

Smythe brought his drink to his lips. 'Be interesting to hear if young Swinton knows you're back on the scene. No need – after Carlyle – to ask if you are still up to staying deep in it all.'

Ralph dug his hands in his pockets, the material rasping on his grazes. 'No need at all.'

The professor smiled, then laughed, just as Ralph did as he played this game of subterfuge in order to protect his people and his country's present and future. It was, as he recognised at last, his duty.

'Right you are,' said Smythe. 'Go boldly, but carefully. You'll have a black eye in the morning after your shindig. Interesting, what window-peeping reveals. Norris Suffolk is a bad lot.' He raised an eyebrow. 'Another time, laddie, protect the face. So sad, to trip over your stick. Leeches – should you fear for your princely looks.'

Ralph winced. 'No leeches. My princely looks will have to wait until nature takes its course.'

Smythe nodded. 'Be ready with an answer if Swinton gets in touch. Be fascinating to see if he mentions the boxing bout. Remember, report anything, big or small, and enjoy being back in the land of the living.' He raised his voice. 'So pleased you have made such an excellent recovery.'

The professor stepped closer to Ralph. 'I mean it. Enjoy life. Not sure if Yeland and I promote that enough. Feel the ground beneath your feet, the breeze on your face. Keep your friends close, but not too close, never lose control, never drink too much or say too much, but feel, and live. Oh dear, I'm waxing lyrical. One doesn't realise until one stands up that there is quite a kick in Stevie's elderberry plonk. He should start a separate business after the war.'

He walked away and Ralph strolled back to the table, thinking that Sister Newsome and Smythe must have come from the same mould. He stopped. Dr Wilson had sent him to the Carlyle Rehabilitation Unit, in which Smythe had an interest. Sister Newsome was married to Dr Wilson ... Well, well, wheels within wheels. Ah, so he really wasn't alone, because he himself, he suspected, was part of another cell, one on the right side this time.

Ralph didn't sit down. Instead, his leg barely troubling him, he headed towards Viola, sitting with Norm. She looked up, surprised, as he stopped by her side. He said, nervousness making his voice high-pitched, 'May I have this dance, though I have two left feet?'

Daniel, who had been loitering, took over Ralph's chair, saying, 'Well, if you're on the move, I'll keep it warm for you, having given mine to Sarah.' Before he sat, though, he called to Davey and Fran, who were approaching from the dance floor, 'I say, your mother has been telling me how you tried to climb the Christmas tree and brought the whole lot down.'

Davey shook his fist. Fran laughed. 'Oh aye, I remember that.'

'Me too,' called Beth. 'He were stuck under it, and his mam came down after midnight to see what the noise was all about.'

Sarah joined in. 'Aye, there were pine needles everywhere, and in him an' all.'

Daniel sat back. 'Grist to the mill. Colin and Martin will be agog.'

Fran shrieked with laughter, leaning against Davey, who said, 'One more word, young man, and I'll set our Fran on you. Just to show I mean it, I'll throw you in the beck tomorrow.'

As Ralph began to lead Viola away towards the floor, Davey called after him, 'You coming too, Ralph? You're on aft shift like this lot, so there's time, eh?'

Viola was looking up at him. 'Are you well enough, just back as you are with a dicky leg?'

Sid's snort could be heard yards away. 'Oh aye, Ralph's leg's right enough. I reckon 'tis a whopper he's told the hospital.'

Ralph grinned. 'The beck sounds good. I'll rent Alfie's bike again, even though his charges are exorbitant and his saddle worse. It'll tie in with the exercises I've been doing.'

Smiling, Viola grabbed his arm, leading the way to the dance floor, and Ralph allowed himself to feel happy.

Ben was just putting on another record. Maisie, Beatrice Adams' daughter, yelled, 'Howay, lad, make it a waltz. Canna be zipping around doing another foxtrot. My feet are throbbing and it isn't good for my old mam, and Mr Swinton neither.' Everyone laughed.

'Mind your manners, young lady,' said Mrs Adams.

Ben just shook his head. 'Right away, Maisie. Got a waltz, have you, William?'

William nodded. 'I reckon so.'

As the music started, the needle jumped every few seconds, but what did it matter? Ralph held out his arms and Viola stepped into them. She laid her damaged hand on his shoulder, and he slipped his arm around her. He could smell lavender in her auburn hair. He could see her burned scalp, her damaged ear, and thought she was the most beautiful girl he had ever seen, and the bravest.

The music seemed to have staggered beyond the scratches and now the big band sound flowed, which was more than could be said for his heart, which was flipping about doing a dance all its own at the nearness of her. She was looking at him, her eyes alight with – what? Laughter? Fun? Could it be enjoyment?

Swallowing, he listened to the music, hardly believing she was here, in his arms, but he couldn't gather his wits. How the hell did a waltz go? Think, man. Forward with the left, side step, back with the right. Or was it forward with the right? He did a sort of hop, and off he went, forward with the right, and stepped on Viola's foot. 'So sorry.'

He tried again, feeling the sweat running down his back at the touch of her injured hand. She'd think him a fool. He searched her face, but she was just waiting, her eyes still alight.

Again, he stepped forward, with the left this time, and not a stride, just a step, groping for something to take his mind off it, focusing on – and there it was, the fitness bike at the Carlyle, the pedals, the saddle, the wheels going round and round, his leg growing stronger, his mind keener.

He approached a turn without stumbling, and asked

how she liked working at the Hall, with all the children to care for? His hand tightened on hers as he manoeuvred round. He trod on her foot.

'I like it very well, thank you Master Ralph.' She gave a sort of bob.

Ralph closed his eyes and felt the heat rising up his neck. 'Oh no, I didn't mean boss to ... No, not that either. Oh, God ...' He trod on her toe again. 'Oh God.'

She was laughing up at him, and he wanted to kiss her mouth. 'I were teasing,' she said. 'Stop worrying, listen to the music, Ralph. Move to it, lad ... Listen, feel,' she breathed, drawing closer, and slowly his shoulders dropped, his hands opened. It was only then that he realised he'd been squeezing her hand.

'Oh Lord, so sorry.'

'Hush,' she said. ' 'Tis only a dance.'

But it wasn't, not for Ralph, for this red-haired girl was special and made his heart twist and leap. Was this what love was? He didn't know. Should he even question what it was? Perhaps not. They danced on until the song ended. He stood still, but didn't release Viola, he couldn't, but neither did she try to leave. She just said, 'Our Ben might launch into a samba.'

'Then I'm lost,' Ralph muttered, keeping his eyes on the stage as William brandished another record. Please, another waltz, Ralph willed. It was, and off they went again, and this time for Ralph and Viola there were no damaged feet, and he managed to talk of the joys of spring, the Australian troops who were forcing back the Japanese in New Guinea, and the Indians in Burma who were falling back against the Germans.

Then she raised an eyebrow, and he fell silent and 'felt' the music.

He danced on, her hand linked with his, her other resting

on his shoulder, feeling the warmth she gave him, the music, and finally the happiness as she looked up, into his eyes. As she did, something passed between them, and they nodded at the same time, and she touched his cut eyebrow and the scar down his forehead with the two fingers of her damaged hand, and he thought his heart would melt and knew he'd give his life for her. Of course it was love, but did she feel the same? Why would she?

They paused, still standing together as the record was changed yet again, and this time it *was* a samba.

He dropped his arm, releasing her, expecting her to disengage in turn. She didn't. Her other hand still lay on his shoulder. He said, 'Will you come to the beck tomorrow?'

She nodded, and only now did they move to the side and stand – together, but not touching. 'Oh aye, I've the morning off for it, and I reckon our Alfie knew you wanted to hire his bike, for he was pumping up the tyres. Lord knows what I'll do for one, though.'

The samba dancers swirled and twirled, with Eddie Corbitt, a pitman friend of the Hall and Bedley fathers, dancing with his lady friend, as he called her. Mr Swinton was bobbing about with Mrs Adams, not doing a samba by any stretch of the imagination, but what did it matter, for they were talking non-stop just as he remembered them doing at Sarah's wedding tea.

Ralph looked at Viola and found some words. 'Alfie's has a crossbar. I'll pedal, you sit.'

Davey spoke up from behind them. 'Don't be so daft, the lass won't be safe with you swerving about. Our Maisie'll lend you hers, I reckon, but Ralph'll have to cycle you down to the corner shop. The rest of us'll meet up there, and we'll go off like a gaggle of geese.'

He dragged his mam past them and onto the dance floor, where they showed the rest of the room just how to do a proper samba. Ralph stared. Viola said, 'The co-op ladies are formidable. There is nowt they canna do.'

It was then that Ralph noticed Eva, Abraham and Tommy watching the dancing. Eva swayed to the music, but her face was sad. Was she thinking of her parents? He couldn't bear it and turned to Viola, taking hold of her hand. 'Please, help Sophia look after Eva. She's sparky, but underneath she is scared. If I'm ever not here – if something happens – Eva is special, well, they all are, and I'm having none of them in an orphanage when this bloody war is at an end. Well, those without parents, because the others will go . . .' He stopped just as the music did.

They stood together as the record changed. This time it was a quick step. Viola turned to him. 'Of course I will.' They smiled at one another. 'Besides,' she said, 'you'll be on the surface yet awhile. I daresay you're thinking of Mr Bedley and Mr Hall, but it's not often a roof comes down.'

Those words, he thought, that image. 'Let's return to the table, eh?' His tone had changed, he knew it had, but he smiled and so did she, though her eyes shadowed. He picked up her hand, kissed it. 'The war has taken too many people. Your parents, Eva's. It's so sad.'

Her face cleared, and she gripped his hand, not allowing him to disengage. 'Aye, it is that, lad, but the music plays on, and we just have to dance.'

Chapter Twenty-Six

Friday, 3 April

Davey woke in the darkness of the Halls' front room, rolled over and gazed at Fran as she slept, feeling thankful, and loved, and remembering last night. The feel of her in his arms, his lips on hers, the confetti in the bed, on the carpet, in her hair and his. He'd begun to laugh. She'd said, 'Howay, lad, are you thinking what I am?'

'Confetti?'

She'd drawn away, just a bit, raised herself on her elbow, looked down at him and nodded towards the trail of discarded clothes leading to the bed. 'Not confetti. You, sewing yourself into your drawers.'

'Oh, for the love of Pete, don't go on.' But she was laughing so hard she had to sit up, so he joined her, and she was trying to hush him, and herself. Finally, she gulped. 'Aye, but it kept that Daisy at arm's length. But poor lass, her lad's gone, the bairn's due, so she must be at her wits' end. Or hang on, is the bairn born by now?'

He'd shrugged. 'Born I reckon, or it will be the biggest bairn there's been, almost walking out. I'll ask Daniel, his da should know.'

She'd slapped him, he'd grabbed her arm and kissed it, and again, right up to her shoulder, and then . . . Oh, then . . .

Thinking about it now, in the early-morning gloom, he smiled because everything had happened just as Stan had said it would and he'd felt Fran and he really were one person, and she, his lovely Franny, had whispered, 'Don't you ever leave me, Davey Bedley, or I'll hunt you down and drag you back, cos you're half of me from this minute.'

He smiled, watching her now, drinking in the first morning of their life together. Outside there was the distant sound of the fore shift heading for the pit down the back lanes. He lay facing her, the confetti scratching him. 'I'll have to speak to our Viola about all this making of confetti,' he murmured. 'It gets bliddy everywhere.'

He kissed her, and she kissed him and he knew that he had never been so happy, and that it could only get better.

At eight the same morning, Ralph felt the pull of his calf muscle where it had been stitched, but that was all, and he hoped it would withstand not only the cycle ride to the beck but the aft shift at the pit. Well, it ruddy well must. He used his stick crossing the hall, but didn't really need it. Then down the stairs to the kitchen, seeking Viola and a cup of tea, in that order. He could see through the half-glazed door that she was busy feeding the five thousand. He entered, but no one looked up from their seats at the table except Viola, who stood holding two plates of scrambled egg and toast. He smiled, she smiled back, but her eyes didn't quite meet his. His spirits sank.

The children drooped with tiredness because the festivities hadn't ended until nine in the evening. Ralph was fairly certain that during that time some elderberry wine had found itself into mouths that had no business snaffling it from the buffet table, just as they had after Sarah and Stan's wedding.

Tommy, in particular, was pale. 'By, I could've stayed in bed. Me 'ead hurts, so it does.'

Viola placed one of the plates in front of him, and the

other in front of Abraham. 'This might help. Or is it a cycle ride to the beck for you all?'

Ralph hoped they'd say no, for he wanted time with Viola. Tommy pushed the plate away. 'I divint feel quite meself, our Viola. I reckon, if you don't mind, I'll get back to me bed for a bit.'

Eva followed him, though first she came to Ralph. 'Mornin', Mr Ralph. You'll have to go to the beck on your own, me tummy feels funny. I feel like Sophia looks of a morning.'

Some of the children managed a bit, others none. 'You'll have it for your tea, remember?' Viola warned.

They said nothing, just followed the others out of the door and back up the stairs. Ralph whispered, 'I do declare they must all have had more than a drop of the hard stuff.'

Viola disappeared into the scullery. 'Sophia's upstairs sorting out some washing, but she'll keep an eye on 'em. She was in bed good and early, and will be the better for it.'

In the quiet of the kitchen, Ralph leaned against the table and flexed his leg, then collected the plates. Viola carried a half-empty bottle of elderberry wine as she came back from the scullery. 'The hair of the dog, from the co-op. It was all that was left, and is for the beck. Fran and Sarah are bringing the remains of the buffet, what there is of it. We must leave for home by eleven, because everyone, even the blushing bride, has to be back for the aft shift, and the groom and Daniel for the train.'

He waggled the two plates he was carrying at her. She laughed. 'Oh, I can't do it to them. We'll put it in the hens' mash, eh.' Again, their eyes didn't quite meet before she dashed past him and up the stairs to check that Sophia and Reginald were up and about, and that the bairns were back in bed, sleeping off their hangovers. Ralph tipped the wasted food into the mash bin, washed the plates, leaving them on the rack, then made his way to the garage. The bike was ready, and he left a ten-bob note on the work-bench, calling loudly, 'Thanks, Alfie.'

There was only a groan in reply. Ralph grimaced in sympathy and pushed the bike to the top of the basement steps, and out she came – Viola, beautiful Viola. wearing her mac, with a scarf around her neck and carrying a bag over her shoulder and a folded blanket. 'It's to pad out the crossbar,' she said. She heaved herself up, using his arm. Use the whole of me, he longed to say. He rumbled across the cob-bled yard, keeping her safe in his arms as her glorious hair escaped from beneath her woollen hat.

He angled his leg to steer clear of hers – there was barely an ache – and off they went, down the drive. Neither said anything, but she leaned stiffly against him and he could smell the lavender water. They swung left out of Massingham Hall's wrought-iron gates and passed daffo-dils and sheep, who took no notice of them, but instead bleated to one another. Lucky them, Ralph thought, because he had no words.

As he pedalled, Viola relaxed and laughed, ducking as startled pigeons fluttered from the ploughed fields.

She rested her good hand on the centre of the handle-bars. 'I enjoyed the wedding tea, did you?'

He wanted to say it was heaven, the best moment of my life. Instead, he said, 'Yes, it was quite perfect.'

'Fran and the co-op planned it so well. Did you know that they found the parachute silk in a trunk in your attic?'

'I did.' It was all he said as he puffed up an incline, drenched with shame, because his father had told him on his return from the wedding tea how Mrs Hall had found his old BUF uniform and had enabled the burning of it – with no recriminations, for it had been the uniform of a boy.

They swung towards Massingham, and his mouth was

dry. He made himself remember Auberon Smythe, and focused: acceptance of a wrong done, atonement undertaken.

'Penny for them?' she asked.

He dragged himself back to the present. 'Not worth a farthing, Viola.'

She was leaning against his chest, more relaxed now, and began to sing 'All or Nothing at All', and all he could think was that he'd take anything she felt she could give, and if it was nothing, then so be it.

They cycled in convoy to the beck, led by the new Mr and Mrs Bedley, with Viola pedalling happily on Maisie's bike alongside Sarah and Beth, and sometimes alongside Sid and Ralph, who talked together quietly.

Stan cycled with Ben, Norm with Daniel, who was grateful for the loan of Simon Parrot's bike. Beth watched and listened, and remembered the feel of Norris's mouth on hers, his searching tongue, and though she'd tried to wash her mouth out with salt, somehow he, it, was still there.

Once at the beck, Beth leaned her bike against Viola's and they unpacked the sandwiches; everyone had slept late and there'd been no time to eat breakfast. The lads made up the fire on top of the blackened earth, which, even after the long winter, still bore the scars of the many they had lit over the years.

Beth spread Viola's blanket, and Fran hers, which her mam had insisted she take. They all sat close and each took the merest sip from the bottle of wine, as it was too early. But it was a wedding breakfast, Daniel had insisted, toasting them all. The group split up, with Ben and Stan having a race across the bridge to the oak tree from which the rope swing hung. Fran called across, 'Divint you dare try it out, either of you. The water'll be bliddy freezing.'

Everyone, including Ben, yelled, 'Language.'

Daniel laughed and said to Davey, who was sitting across from him as sparks crackled into the air and the heat of the fire warmed them, 'I can see why you miss it all so much.'

Davey kissed the top of Fran's head as she leaned back against him, laughing at Ben and Stan hurling twigs from the bridge onto the beck, then crossing over to see whose had won.

Daniel finished his sandwich, then slapped his hands free of crumbs. 'I'm sorry to change the mood, Davey,' he said, 'but I need to ask if Daisy has been in touch with you, or Fran? If I remember rightly, you gave her the fourteen Leadenhall address, but you've said nothing about a letter from her. She's gone missing you see, with the babe.'

'What?' Davey gasped.

The others stopped their murmured conversations and Ben straightened up on the bridge, calling, 'What's up, Davey?'

Daniel repeated it. 'But how old's the babe?' asked Fran.

'Three weeks.'

Viola rose into a kneeling position. 'Oh no, but surely she won't have hurt him?'

'It's a her, actually, and who's to tell? Why the hell she couldn't have just stayed in the home, I do not know. She's so contrary.'

Viola turned to Ralph. 'I can't imagine what it must be like to give up a babe. Awful for her, awful for everyone at the home. So worrying. I doubt she'll know how to look after it properly.'

Davey threw a shoot of grass at Daniel. 'No, we've heard nothing, and why the hell didn't you tell us sooner?'

'It wasn't the time or place.' He waved his hand around at the group, who were all looking thoughtful or talking quietly. 'Dad just hoped you might have had a letter, with an address. Perhaps of her parents' home?'

Sarah spoke for all of them. 'Oh, that's a point. She'll have gone home, of course she will, taking the baby, and the parents' hearts will melt . . .'

Daniel shrugged. 'Dad got the police on to it pretty smartly, to keep an eye out, but there's a war on. He's trying to get the parents' address from Bl—Well, where we work. The one she gave the mother-and-baby home was false. She always said she wouldn't go to her parents – bit of history there, it seems.'

The bottle came around again as the lads put more wood on the fire. They all took the merest sip again, except for Beth, who waved it away.

'Have some, Beth,' said Viola, 'it's only the tiniest sip to warm us. Oh dear . . .' she faded, looking embarrassed, perhaps thinking of Beth's secret drinking. Sid and Ralph shared a glance but said nothing. It wasn't theirs to tell.

Beth poked the fire with a stick and finally answered, looking at the flames, not at them. 'Aye, you see, I've taken to drinking and I want to stop, and 'tis hard, for Bob makes it hard. I just get a handle on it and then another letter comes, like just before the wedding. He wants me to pay half the cost of the divorce because it has to be heard in the High Court, or summat like that, or to send them the allotment from his pay that we wives get each month. It's right that I do send that to them, for the bairn'll need it. I know me and mam can just manage without it, especially now I won't buy any more off Norris.'

Sarah said quietly, 'Oh, poor Beth.'

Beth shrugged. 'I were upset that Bob could be as he was, for the letter were from them both, and I felt so damned alone. I said to Norris I didn't want more, but I gulped it down because it stops me thinking. I . . . I let—'

'You did nowt,' Sid burst out. 'It's that Bob who's a bliddy bastard. I'll bliddy take myself to Grimsby and sort him out, so I will.'

Sarah and Fran reached out to her, but Beth stood up, waving them down. 'I'm all right, really I am. I've written I'll send the allotment money but pay for nowt else, and I'll read no more of his letters so I can sort myself out. Mam said it weren't fair for me to suffer, but maybe it is, for I made you suffer, our Stan. Things get paid back, eh?' She headed for the path, calling back, 'I'll go and fetch a bit more firewood. You stay here, make the most of your time, for we have to go in half an hour.'

She walked off. Sarah rose, but Ralph was up before her, his hand out. 'Sarah, you stay with Stan. I'm an outsider, and sometimes that's better, eh?'

Fran and Sarah looked at one another. 'I reckon the lad is right, you know,' said Fran. 'It's like telling secrets to someone on a bus because you'll never see them again.'

'Don't be so bliddy daft,' Davey laughed. 'You only go on the Factory bus and you know everyone on it, inside out.'

Sid was getting up. 'Best I go too.'

Davey picked up Ralph's half-eaten sandwich and threw it at him. 'Best you don't. Let Ralph see what he can do, for perhaps he knows more about these things. You know, the law and divorce and so on. We know nowt, and we're too close.'

'All I know is that when Ralph was being foul, I couldn't talk to you all,' said Fran. 'Don't you remember? I carted myself off to St Oswald's to chat to whoever it was looking down.'

'But—' said Sid.

This time it was Stan who waved him down. 'I reckon our Franny is right. Let's see how Ralph manages, eh? If he makes a pig's ear of it, we'll send the next man in.'

'Sounds like a military campaign,' muttered Ben.

Stan nudged him with his toe. 'Aye, well, dealing with women is, lad.'

This time the girls threw bits of sandwich.

Beth rushed along the path, cursing herself for bringing it all up, but she was fighting not to drink, and if word got around about Norris being outside the Miners' Club yesterday . . . And what if someone saw the kiss, other than Sid? Had he actually seen it? She couldn't remember.

Anyway, she had to tell. Or did she? She didn't know anything any more, only that she hadn't drunk anything before the elderberry wine, and that was a sort of victory.

Just keep walking, she told herself. She continued along the bank, where the beck was shallow and the water ran over stones, splashing and tumbling. But as she reached the drystone wall where the hawthorns grew high and straggly, it ran deeper, and slower, and was soundless . . . which was when she heard breathing, and footsteps.

She spun round. It was Ralph, catching up, his walking stick under his arm. She stopped. Waited.

He reached her. 'I'm the emissary, or perhaps the messenger.'

She said, 'I know what an emissary is, Ralph,' she said. She wasn't cross or insulted. She wasn't anything.

Ralph tucked his walking stick under his arm. 'Of course, you do. I was just talking for the sake of it. The path's widening, perhaps I may take your arm?'

He did so without waiting for permission and eased her onwards, and it was what she wanted – to be led – because she had no idea what she should be thinking or doing. She said, 'I heard Mrs Pritchard at the wedding tea. She were saying to her friends that there was no smoke without fire, that I had changed my mind from Stan to Bob, so who knew what I was doing with who now. She said maybe it was Norris, so she must have seen me meeting him for me booze. I have to thank you for helping our Sid, for I waited, and watched through the window of the cloakroom, just for a moment. I knew, with two of you, it would be all right.'

Ralph pushed her on, but she wanted to stop, for his leg must hurt.

'Don't fret about my leg. It's remarkably fine. The walking stick is "just in case". Mrs Pritchard is a fool. You were very young when you were with Stan. Then you met someone else. It was bound to happen.' He wondered where he was getting all this from.

Did it matter? It was just there, in his head, then his mouth, and actually it seemed to him to make sense.

Beth remembered the cornfield where she lay with Bob and they did what they did, and it had been what she wanted. 'It weren't right, though, what we did behind Stan's back.'

She felt Ralph pull her to a halt, her ankle twisting on a large embedded stone, his fingers digging into her arm.

'Oh Lord, Beth Smith, for you *are* Smith, not Jones. Do you think you are such a special person that a mistake is unforgivable? Don't keep reliving it, rethinking it. If you do, it digs in. You've had a boyfriend, knew he wasn't for you, but neither was the new one, the husband. It's his loss. There's fear, grief and anger: at him, at yourself, at the whole damned world. You think you cannot control anything. But you can. Feel it, face the misery, but only for a moment, then take a step forward, shedding it as you go.'

They were in the lee of another hawthorn hedge that provided a bit of a barrier from the wind, but only a bit. Ralph continued. 'I don't know where I'm getting this, but I reckon it makes sense. Yes, shed it.' He pointed back to where the smoke from the fire was rising. 'I rather wonder ... Look, it rises, it disappears. It's gone. Move on. Thinking is overrated. Living isn't, so live.'

She just stared at him. 'You *know*?'

He grinned. 'Remember me, the horrid lad who smashed a precious papier-mâché football, who made Fran's life a misery. Well, that *was* me. My mother died, I was frightened, I missed her, got angry instead, sank in the memory of the loss. I didn't want to see that Sophia and my father loved me. Even when we're older we still make mistakes and relive them. Sometimes we learn from them, other times we just curl up and—'

'—want to die.'

'Oh yes. I suppose it was a bit like that when I was out for the count. I came round. I was told – later – to really live. So why don't we both do that?'

Ralph was looking across the beck, so deep and slow and slumbering. Beth stood by him, and his arm was round her shoulders. He whispered, 'Be angry with Bob and Norris. Not yourself, not any more. Forgive them, or forget them, not sure if it matters which.'

'You had a car accident and it made you come to your senses,' said Beth, 'but, Ralph Massingham, I'm not going to ride me bike into a tree to change meself.' She bobbed a curtsy, and though her tone was strained, she was trying.

Ralph laughed. 'I'll push you in the beck and haul you out, telling you it wasn't your mistake that put you there. Heavens, girl, you pulled Mrs Bedley round. What else do you need to do to feel proud?'

He passed over his handkerchief. 'Your nose is running.' She blew it, offering it back. He grimaced. 'You can wash that and return it when you're on track, eh? And if you ever want to talk, I'm the master of mistakes. Also, you have your gang, your work ...' Ralph looked at his watch. 'Speaking of which, the aft shift is looming.'

As they walked back, Ralph said, 'Will you let me pay for the divorce, just to set you free?'

She shook her head. 'No, for that's someone else setting me free, and that's no way to sort it. You'll be there to talk to, and that's enough. You see, my marrers are happy being in love, so I canna disturb them.'

As they approached, Beth slipped from beneath his arm. 'Maybe you'll need someone to talk to as well, so don't you forget me, eh?'

She walked ahead and he called, 'Don't forget to look at who is in front of you. Someone who isn't in love with anyone else.' This last he whispered, for Sid had come to meet them.

Chapter Twenty-Seven

The co-op toiled along the incline that marked the final fifty yards of Massingham Hall's drive, with Maud Bedley muttering, 'Why did we say we'd come? Clearing the hall all morning, and proggy-rugging all afternoon with this set of scamps? 'Tis Good Friday, and they were in school this morning for Bible stories and such like, so I'm hoping they'll be awash with goodness.'

'On that happy note . . .' puffed Annie Hall as she led the way into the garage yard.

Coming along behind her, Madge adjusted her royal blue eyepatch, stopped with a squeal of brakes and cheered. The others dismounted, staring at her. 'Listen,' she called, 'I've just remembered 'tis only the lasses, for our Alfie is to take the lads to the field for footie.'

Alfie looked up from polishing Ralph's repaired roadster, which was back in the garage. 'Too busy, I am. You tell them that.'

'Not a chance, lad,' Madge almost sang, wheeling her bike to the far end of the garage. 'No Rolls-Royce?' she asked.

'Mr Massingham's taken Sophia to the doctor.'

'Why? Is she badly?' It was Annie. She gripped Maud's arm.

'Reckon so. I heard a bit of a kerfuffle, and the next thing the boss was helping her out to the Rolls and she were bleeding from her forehead and as white as a bliddy sheet. Mr Massingham didn't look much better. Fair shook me.'

Annie Hall and the others looked at one another, then at

Alfie. 'Why didn't the Massinghams send you down for us? We'd—'

Alfie was shaking out the cloth and hanging it up on a hook above the workbench. 'No, no, Mrs Phillips is here, and has an iron fist in an iron glove, cos she don't know the meaning of velvet, and Viola's here too. But I reckon Mrs Phillips would like to get on home, if you can take over. And don't you be worrying, I were only joking, for I'll grab the lads and run them ragged on the back field soon as I've done with this. But I reckon they'll not be wanting to do much till Mr Massingham gets back, and I don't want to neither.'

It was only then that they saw the worry on the lad's face, and knew it was reflected on their own.

'Quick, quick,' ordered Madge, unloading the proggy and hooky frames from the trolley. They each carried two, and scurried across the cobbles and down the steps before bursting into the kitchen. The heat from the range was welcome, and its gurgle and hiss were clear as day in the unnatural silence. The bairns had their heads down, but as the women entered they looked up, Mrs Phillips too.

'By,' Mrs Phillips said, 'am I right pleased to see you. Is that Alfie on his way with the football?'

Annie nodded. 'In a minute or two.' She heaped her frames in the corner of the kitchen.

'What's eleven times five, Eva?' Melanie called out.

'I don't bliddy well care.'

Annie and Madge said together, 'Language, Eva.'

Eva stuck out her lower lip. 'I don't bliddy care about that either, for Sophia fell and conked her head on the bliddy table. She bled, she did. It were red against her white skin.'

Maud and Audrey took everyone's macs to hang in the corridor, while Annie approached the table. 'That's quite enough language, Eva. Tell Melanie what eleven times five is, if you please.'

Eva drew in a deep breath. ' 'Tis fifty-five. Remember the sounds. Eleven times five is fifty-five.' The bairn beat the time on the table.

Madge took it up. 'So twelve times five is . . .'

The children looked up and finished it for her. Normality returned, and heads went down to their exercise books again.

It was only then that Annie went to Eva and placed a hand on her shoulder. Her heart melted as the bairn rested her head against her arm. 'Sophia is very tired,' Annie murmured.

'It's us, isn't it?' muttered Abraham. 'Will they send us to a home, those of us with no one?'

Just then Viola came running down the stairs, entered and shut the door behind her. 'Sorry not to be here. I was just sorting out Sophia's bed, because she'll go up the minute she comes in, and don't be silly, Abraham. I heard the end of that, and if Sophia and Reginald can't manage just at the moment, then the rest of us will sort it out, won't we?'

Annie and the others looked at one another, and without missing a beat Maud Bedley nodded. 'Oh aye, we'll fight over you, that we will, cos we'll want all of you.'

The afternoon drew on. The boys played footie, the girls continued with their rugs under the eagle eye of the co-op, and then they made scones, which came out of the oven as the boys tumbled in. Still, Sophia and Reginald did not return.

After a couple of hours they heard the hoot of the Rolls-Royce as it entered the yard. No one moved; everyone waited. At last they heard footsteps and voices, and the door opened. Annie's breath seemed to catch in her chest.

Sophia entered, a plaster on her forehead, and an amazing smile on her face. The women looked at her, then at one another. The bairns scrambled from their stools and clamoured around her. Reginald came into the kitchen hot on his wife's heels, and the boys gravitated towards him, standing as though blocking his way.

'Well?' Abraham demanded, his hands on his hips. 'What's amiss?'

It was Madge who said, 'Aye, took the words out of me mouth.'

Sophia looked at Reginald, who nodded, and then she frowned, focusing on the children. 'What I have to tell you is a secret, and must remain one until we have told Ralph, for his life will be changed.'

The co-op looked at one another. A smiling Sophia; Ralph's life changing?

'We can't keep a secret if you don't tell us what it is, Sophia,' said Eva. ' 'Tis no cause for you to smile, Mr Reginald, for we're nearly peeing ourselves with worry.'

Reginald laughed aloud then and put his arm around Sophia. Annie knew instantly, just as the other co-op women did, and why on earth hadn't they seen it before? Viola was smiling as Madge breathed, 'A . . .' She stopped, frowning. Annie understood, for what if the news wasn't what they thought? After all, Sophia was coming up thirty-nine, so why now?

Reginald drew Eva to him and held her hand. 'We're all to have a baby.'

The bairns looked at one another, and then at the couple. Tommy said, 'That means you did – you know, that *thing*.'

Sophia flushed.

Abraham muttered doubtfully to Stephen, 'Aren't they too old?'

Madge was pulling out a stool. 'Sit yourself down – no, not you, Eva, I meant Sophia. You're no spring chicken for this, so all this bliddy rushing around must stop.'

As Sophia moved to the stool, Alfie came in and approached Reginald, his arm outstretched. 'That's a relief, and 'tis as well you have Viola. Better make her an offer so she doesn't do a runner back to the Factory, now there's to be another, eh?'

Reginald Massingham nodded and shook Alfie's hand. 'Thank you for your sage words of advice. Now, has anyone put the kettle on? Especially if the mother-to-be is so dreadfully old.'

Sophia slapped his belly with the back of her hand as Viola reached for the kettle. 'It's been simmering nicely, Mr Massingham, and I have no intention of leaving you all, so my agent can sit down and keep his big mouth shut. Though he may have a cuppa before polishing the car.'

As Reginald followed his wife to the table, and the women plied her with questions about the expected arrival date, he suddenly paled. Madge was nearest and gripped him by the arm, hissing at Alfie to take his other side. 'Bliddy hell,' she added, ' 'tis the pregnant woman who usually needs smelling salts. Man up, Mr Massingham, for the Lord's sake.'

Again, the room fell silent, but then the women started laughing as Reginald was led to the stool and made to sit. Sophia murmured, 'I'm the one who's supposed to have the vapours, darling.'

Annie hurried to the pantry and brought out the cooking brandy. Sophia shook her head. 'Oh no, I think only the best. Perhaps, Maud, you'd fetch the decanter from the side table in the living room upstairs.' The two women looked at one another, and in that look was a wealth of meaning, for Maud had been discovered by Sophia at that side table not so long ago, when she had been battling her need for alcohol. Sophia, however, had decided to believe Maud's protestation of innocence, though both had known it was a lie.

Maud nodded, for there was no chance that she would have a nip, not after Beth had been so steadfast in her support. She hurried up the stairs, across the hall and into the sitting room, grabbed the decanter and headed back, not in the least tempted, because she had finally accepted her pitman husband's death.

Meanwhile, Viola had found a glass for Reginald, but Sophia was insisting that all the adults had a nip too, excluding her, for it was the last thing she felt like, she confessed. At the same time, Viola brought out the jam she had been saving for each of the children's birthday teas. What could be more fitting for such an occasion? she thought. But instead of being excited, the children had grouped themselves by the back door, whispering, their shoulders hunched. As the adults watched, Sophia went to them and crouched down. 'Whatever's the matter?'

It was Abraham who was pushed forward as Tommy whispered, 'Tell 'er.'

Eva pulled him out of the way. 'If you have your own bairn, why would you want us? And if we go with the co-op we'll be split up, because they have small houses. So it'll be an orphanage, 'cept for those who can go to their mams.'

Sophia stood up, staring helplessly at her husband. Reginald was still white and shaken, but rallied to say, 'Look, it will make no difference. We love you all – the babe will just be part of everything, and we will need you to be their sisters and brothers. Some of you will go home when the war is over, some will stay. Those who go will come back whenever they want, for what will the babe think if their brothers and sisters disappear?'

'They'll think we're under bricks,' whispered Melanie.

Annie gripped Maud and Madge's hands, and somehow kept her smile. It was Audrey Smith who leaned back from the stool, her whisper little more than a breath. ''Tis now I wish I could see inside their heads, so we can make sure we heal them.'

When the co-op cycled down the drive at the end of the afternoon, leaving Viola to sort out the children's evening, Annie called to the other three, 'I'm going to St Oswald's. I will see you tomorrow, ladies.'

She set off, for she had to see Betty to tell her that she hadn't forgotten the weight of her in her arms, that though she helped with the evacuees, and would soon help with the bairn too, her own sweet Betty would always be with her.

From behind, she heard the others calling, 'Hang on.' She looked over her shoulder: they were pedalling after her, with Maud yelling, 'D'you think we would leave you to go alone? Betty needs to know we *all* remember and miss her. By, we all miss our wee bairns now they're grown. 'Tis time there's a new one amongst us. Too many men away, not enough little ones. Even your Bobby, Madge, is growing fast, and into a higher class at school.'

So, the co-op cycled on together, as they always did, Annie thought, and the comfort it gave her, and them all, was more than words could explain.

Ralph returned to the Hall at about eleven o'clock, after the end of the shift. His lamp shone a miserable slit of light, but he could do it blindfold anyway. He couldn't believe how quickly he'd got into the rhythm of sorting the coal on the screens, how much he'd missed the company, how good it was to see the lads clomping across the yard to the lamp-house. His leg had stood up well, while the cycling of the morning had been good exercise and he should make sure he kept it up. Standing at the sorting screens was just something he had to become used to again, though it made him

343

realise that hacking at the face, and crawling down low seams, would be a completely different story.

He was panting hard by the time he reached the top of the drive, and he swept through the entrance of the garage yard with sweat running down his back. He leaned the bike against the wall and patted it, knowing his hand was shaking, just like the rest of him, but it was tiredness after a good day's work, and felt good. 'Well done, you. But I think I need to hand you back to Alfie, for I'll be giving you too much of a run every day, and one day you, or I, will break down. I've got to buy my own two wheels, that's all there is to it.'

There was no sound from Alfie's flat as Ralph limped across the yard towards the kitchen. Sophia always left the light on for him, and he realised he hadn't worried about her today as he'd sorted the coal, but now it all rushed at him. She was just too tired to deal with all these children, so they really did need another person to help.

He headed down the steps, through the back door into the boot hall, and eased off his boots, leaving them on the newspaper. He entered the kitchen quietly, heading to the bathroom in the butler's quarters, sluiced himself off and tidied up, then slipped into the pyjamas, slippers and dressing gown left out by Sophia, bless her.

After he checked the range had been banked up, he headed up the stairs, went through the green baize door, and was about to pad across the hall when he realised the lights were on in the sitting room. Was someone up? He double-checked the clock on the side table. Just gone eleven thirty. It must be his father.

He peered through the open doorway to see Sophia sitting on the sofa with his father, her head on his shoulder, his arm around her. There was a plaster on her forehead. He closed his eyes. Oh Lord above, what now? The fire was glowing with tired embers. He entered and they looked up at him, straightening, as though bracing themselves. Immediately, he knew it was bad news, but what?

Making his way round the sofa, he sat down opposite them, leaning forward, but his father rose and stood with his back to the fire, gesturing to Sophia to remain seated. This was what always happened when Ralph was in trouble. It was Ralph who rose now, looking from Sophia to his father. 'What's wrong. What have you . . .'

His throat was dry, not only from coal dust, but fear too.

Sophia sprang to her feet. It's like a game, Ralph thought. If I sit down, will they?

'What?' He knew he sounded fierce. He tried to smile, but failed.

Sophia stood in front of her husband, facing Ralph, wringing her hands. 'We have learned . . .' She stopped. Began again. 'It doesn't mean we don't love you any the less . . .'

Had she found out that he had killed Bedley and Hall in Bell Seam? Had his father explained that Ralph was trying to make amends?

Reginald took over, his eyes on his son, shaking his head in warning. 'Let me, darling. Ralph, you are to have a brother or perhaps a sister. There.'

Ralph looked from one to the other. 'What?' It was all he could find to say. His mind was racing. Were they adopting one of the children? How could they choose one? Eva, Abraham, Marty? 'How can you choose just one?' he asked. 'It'll have to be all the orphans.'

They looked at one another, confused. Ralph continued. 'Really, it can't just be one, it would be too hurtful. I'll help pay for them, but Sophia, you're too tired—'

'Oh, for the love of God,' his father barked. 'We're pregnant.'

Ralph let the words hang there, in front of him, and all he felt was utter relief. Sophia wasn't ill. Not at all. And then anxiety took the place of relief. 'But Sophia, you're—'

She put up her hand. 'Stop. Other women have babies in their late thirties, of course they do. So can we please not discuss my age.'

Ralph laughed, for in that moment he remembered that's how Sophia had ticked him off when she was his nanny. Up would go the hand, like a policeman. He strode to her and took her in his arms. 'You will be an exemplary mother, just as you were a nanny. But forget about me – what about the children? How have they taken it?'

Sophia was patting his back and his father had made his way to the drinks table and was pouring brandy for Ralph and himself. He left it to Sophia to explain that they'd had to calm their fears of rejection.

Ralph took his brandy and saluted Sophia, and then his father. 'Couldn't be more delighted, but only if, Sophia, you don't do so much. I know we have Viola, but is that enough? Shouldn't we try and find someone else, because the co-op will do what they can, I'm sure, but you'll need another person to be here all the time. Besides, we only pay the little the co-op will accept for their help, and simply can't impose more.'

He sipped his drink and his father nodded. 'I agree. The baby will be born in about seven months, so we need someone as soon as possible. Alfie is putting out feelers, and the co-op too. So, I think we can rest assured that everything will be resolved.'

The three of them stood smiling at one another.

'Are you sure you don't mind, Ralph?' asked Sophia.

'Quite honestly, Sophia, what's one more hooligan?'

His father shrugged. 'But it will impinge on your inheritance – I have to say that now.'

Ralph knew that, of course, but if he couldn't make the pits and factories work, then he deserved to be poor. He simply had to keep everything running properly, in the real Massingham manner, once his father was no longer able; not just for the family, but for the community. He had been thinking in terms of a co-op, some sort of workers' shares in the business, but with a strong management core. That might work, but that was for the future. And that future must include not just the new baby, but those of the evacuees who needed a home.

Sophia was kissing Reginald's cheek. 'Don't be long, you have meetings tomorrow, darling.' She kissed Ralph and almost floated from the room. Ralph and Reginald watched.

His father raised his glass again. 'That's what you need, lad. A good woman.'

'Ah yes,' muttered Ralph, 'but sadly, they don't grow on trees, especially when I am what I am.'

The telephone in the hall was ringing. His father raised a finger; his eyebrow lifted in enquiry. Ralph grimaced. 'I'll take it. It's bound to be you-know-who.'

'I'll go on up. The less I know the better.' While Ralph hurried for the telephone, his father replaced his empty goblet on the table, then crept past as Ralph lifted the receiver.

Ralph put his hand over the mouthpiece and called softly, 'Night, night, Daddy. Get as many hours in as possible, for soon you'll be up on and off throughout the night, and let's face it, *you're* not in your late thirties.'

His father's laugh drifted back down as he climbed the stairs. 'Enough of your cheek, sonny.'

'Hello,' said Ralph, 'Massingham resid—'

'It's me, Ralphy boy. You're better, then? On your feet, stick to hand when needed, and just in time for the wedding. All recovered except for that cut in your leg, which must be well healed by now. Been doing some exercises, I hear.'

It was the call Ralph had been expecting. He played along because Smythe's lot would be tapping the line. 'Hello, Tim. Yes, back at work. Had to get my body fit, and someone mentioned a bit of a bruised brain, which had to settle down, if you see what I mean. Well, of course you don't know what I mean, but any doctor will tell you.'

Tim's tone was cold. 'Aye, and I'll make it me business to find out. But there're other things to sort now you're back. Someone who used to blab about the Factory has been – shall we say – corralled. So, you're going to have to listen long and hard, find another Factory girl who'll be a source of information – one under stress will do. I heard there was one, until you and Sid used your fists. She's on her feet now. That's one possibility down the spout. Find another.'

Ralph sighed. 'I'll keep my ears and eyes open.'

'It's late,' Tim muttered, 'and I'm too bliddy tired to think, but do that. You're on the surface screens, but you can still hear things, and from Stan and his marrers. Pit and Factory – those are your areas, so get on with it.'

Ralph's grip on the receiver tightened. 'Yes, I'm doing so, but any reason for the rush?'

Tim, his voice cold, muttered, 'I reckon your brain's still bruised, for you know better than to ask questions. Just do as you're bliddy well told.'

Ralph wondered if he could grip the receiver any tighter. 'Sorry, like you I'm tired.'

He heard Tim breathe, 'Got to go. I'll keep in touch.' The line went dead. Ralph replaced the receiver, rubbing his hands together, then wished he hadn't, as the blisters from the shift set his teeth on edge.

Ralph checked behind him and up the stairs, but for safety's sake he carried his brandy into the study, closing the door. He snatched a quick look at the clock. Well, Smythe had said day or night if he needed to speak to him or Yeland.

He asked the operator for the number. Yeland answered at the first ring. 'Ralph?'

'That you, Yeland?'

'No, it's the Fairy Queen. What can I do for you, Ralph?'

Ralph relayed the conversation, adding, 'I know you'll hear it in due course, or perhaps listened as it happened. Either way, I asked a question. I could have kicked myself.'

'Yes, we heard,' said Yeland. 'Don't worry, he'll expect you to be a bit dozy. Interesting that he knows that someone has been warned about blabbing. We know who it is. Interesting, too, that he knows about Beth. Someone in Massingham has eyes on you all, but who?'

Yeland was speaking to someone else, quietly. Ralph couldn't make out the words.

'I'll get back to you,' Yeland said. 'Don't know where, don't know when, as the song goes. Aft shift, aren't you? Keep going. You're doing fine.'

'I will.'

Click.

Ralph carried his goblet into the sitting room and poured another brandy. He watched the glow fading from the embers. The loose mouth could only be Amelia. So, someone in the cell had eyes on things in the Factory, and in Massingham. He was pleased the curtains were drawn.

Chapter Twenty-Eight

One week later

At four o'clock in the afternoon, Ralph was talking to his father in the study when the telephone rang. They looked at one another. Ralph sighed. 'I do hope it's not Tim.'

His father shook his head. 'It's too early, surely. The little beggar usually phones about nine, or later.'

The telephone was still ringing.

As his father went to answer the phone, Ralph leaned back in his chair, trying to look relaxed, for he'd no news for Tim. He couldn't hear anything on the screens, only lip-read, and there'd been no snippets, anywhere. Besides, if there *was* anything of real interest, he'd pass it to Smythe, not Swinton. Tim would only receive useless fragments.

'Ah, it's you, Auberon,' said Reginald. 'Yes, yes, Sophia is fine, blooming, in fact. Well, we think in the autumn.' There was a pause. 'Indeed, we will have to keep the little rascal well wrapped and the others under control, but don't you worry, we have Viola, and we're on the hunt for another lass.' His father paused again, then laughed. 'The co-op are on the case, God bless them. Yes, he's here.'

Ralph took the receiver from his father, who rose, but Ralph waved him down, saying, with his hand over the mouthpiece, 'We have no secrets. Do stay.'

Auberon was saying, 'Are you there, Ralph? Just a quick call, since Yeland and I thought you should know the result of our own investigation into the roof fall And don't panic, this is now a safe line. Just to say we have news that will be welcome to you, but in solving one issue, it opens the way for a bigger question. It seems there were two charges laid, yours and one other. Clearly, you could not be trusted to bring the whole lot down, for your charge wouldn't have troubled a gnat's house, but by having you commit the act, or at least thinking you had, Tim Swinton knew he'd have you over a barrel. The bonus of two surveyors being there, when it was thought they would work at night must have been a delightful additional gift for such a worm: Ralph Massingham, the murderer of two men.'

Ralph listened, trying to make sense of what Smythe was saying, but the man was rattling on. 'But no, it was a further charge two props along that was the widow-maker. This charge was laid, we assume by a pitman who actually knew what he was doing. It is he who is culpable. On his shoulders lies the tragedy. You were but a pawn in the game, a foolish one it must be said, but you are not a murderer.'

Ralph was staring at his father, trying to absorb the words. He heard Auberon say into the silence, 'Are you there?'

'Yes.' It was all he could say, but then his mind raced on, and he added, 'Nonetheless, I was prepared to commit sabotage, I knew—'

Auberon's sigh was heavy. 'Oh, do grow up. You intended to bring down the roof, yes. They knew it was unlikely you would succeed – perhaps the timing would be wrong, the fuse wire too long, too short, or you would panic and not do it at all. So, they left the materials for you, as they said. You didn't have the experience to know it would do little more than go pop, for there was barely any explosive in the stick of dynamite, our experts decided. I repeat, someone else did the deed. You were the sacrificial lamb should anything go wrong and questions be asked.'

'I see, I see.' Ralph did, at last. It was not he who had killed those two fine men. Yes, he was guilty because he could have, but, in fact, he hadn't. What's more, he was attempting in every way possible, even risking his own life, to destroy those traitors who would damage Britain. He stared at his father, who was looking at him intently. Ralph asked the question that begged to be answered: 'The question is, who did?'

'Indeed. We have a name. Just a floating name, which might be something, it might be nothing, but keep your eyes and ears open for anything you hear about an Eddie Corbitt.'

Ralph felt his mouth drop open.

'Have a good evening, Ralph. A really good evening. Put me back to your father. Ears open, now, and mouth closed, for I took a gamble in telling you this, knowing you might feel you could walk away from us.'

Ralph laughed, feeling a million tons of grief lift from him. 'You'd let me do that? Besides, there's no way I'm walking away from these beggars. They must be stopped.'

Smythe said quietly, 'I can't answer the first part, but I am pleased to hear the determination in your voice. Your father, please. I will tell him the news, if that is satisfactory?'

Ralph smiled at his father. 'Thank you. More than satisfactory. Here he is.'

He handed over the receiver and hurried from the room, across the hall and down the stairs into the kitchen, because there was now someone he could see, talk to, kiss, walk with, eat with and not just long for, because he had killed no one.

Viola was there, helping Sophia to clear the dishes while the children did their homework. He grabbed her hand, and dragged her out of the back door.

'Mr Ralph, what are you doing?' called Eva.

'Not now, Eva. I'll talk to you later. I have to ask Viola a question.'

Viola was laughing as he pulled her up the steps into the late-afternoon sunlight of the yard. He turned, holding on to her hand. 'I've not asked you out. I just felt I couldn't. I had . . .' He shook his head. 'It doesn't matter, but Viola, can we go to the Rising Sun for a drink, or spam fritters, or some other delight? Just the two of us, no children, no marrers, just us.'

He waited for her answer to the question he felt he could now ask. Yes, he'd wanted to bring the roof down – then. He would rather die than do such a thing – now. But someone else had, not intending death, but it had happened. He, Ralph Massingham, would carry his mistake for the rest of his life, but he would spend that life making restitution.

But Eddie Corbitt? He brushed the thought aside – for now. Only for now, because Viola was smiling at him. She reached up and laid her hand on his face. She said, 'We laid our hands on your cheek after your accident, to let you know we were there and you were not alone. And you're not now. For I'm here, and yes, I'll come for a drink, but I just want to know why the bliddy hell you've left it so long?'

He kissed her then, and her lips were soft and he knew that she was the person he could never be without. It was then they heard the whistle, and sprang apart. Alfie whistled again and called from the garage, 'In front of the bairns, too.'

They turned from him to the steps, and there they all were, with Eva in the lead, her arms crossed, shaking her head. 'You took your time, Mr Ralph.'

The three girls had been on the fore shift again, which they preferred, and the bus was quiet by the time they arrived back at Massingham at four. The bus juddered to a halt. 'All disembark from the *Skylark*, if you please.'

353

Mrs Oborne heaved herself up, the right side of her face still sore She'd been in the detonator workshop when a detonator had been dropped. This time, miraculously, no one was really hurt, it was just a bit of a flash.

They'd heard the bang in the pellet section, and had waited. Miss Ellington had nipped in with the news that all was well, though Tilly looked as if she'd had a bit too much sun on her left side. Fran had stepped back, relieved, and brushed aside a strand of her streaked hair that was catching her face, near her eye. The SO Miss Jenkins had shouted too late, 'No, Fran.'

Fran had hurried to the water tank, annoyed with herself for such a basic mistake. Miss Jenkins was ready and bathed her eye and cheek clear of chemicals, then patted her dry with a threadbare towel. They stood together as Mr Swinton entered and saw them both. He'd called, 'You all right?' Fran had nodded and resumed her place. It was all in a day's work, and, what's more, a timely reminder to concentrate.

Back in Massingham now, everyone queued to leave the bus and Mrs Oborne took her place at the end of the slow-moving crocodile. She glanced at the three girls still sitting on the back seat with Cyn Ellington.

'Are you waiting there till Bert takes the charabanc to the depot?'

'No,' said Beth, 'just waiting for the hoi polloi to leave a way clear for the princesses.'

Tilly Oborne laughed. 'That'll be the day. Off you get or have your ears skelped.'

Fran was up in a minute and hurried towards Tilly, hugging her. 'I love you,' she said. 'We all do, and you need to get a bit of a tan on the other side, to even things up. It's a great life if you don't weaken, eh?'

For a moment Mrs Oborne rested against her, and Fran

felt her trembling. She hugged her tighter. 'You need a drink of elderberry,' she whispered.

Mrs Oborne stepped away. 'Howay, I need to bathe in it, like Cleopatra,' she said, heading down the aisle at a trot.

They followed, Beth calling, 'That was asses' milk.'

'I have me own version,' Tilly yelled. She drew level with the cab.

'You take care of yourself, our Tilly,' muttered Bert. 'At least it weren't your arse.'

At that, the girls grinned at one another, for this was their world: narrow squeaks, worse ones, and the worst. This was almost nothing, so it was a good day.

Mrs Oborne clipped Bert's ear, and then again. 'That's because I can skelp you,' she said. 'For you're a gentleman and canna skelp me back when I'm a wounded wee lass.'

She eased herself down the steps. Bert looked at Fran. 'You take care of her. Best bliddy harridan in Massingham, she is, and bliddy lucky into the bargain.'

Fran squeezed his hand. 'She was, and is, the best.' They both laughed.

Stan and the marrers were waiting on the pavement and it was only then that they realised Cyn wasn't with them. 'She'll come. Dropped her pass,' said Beth. Sarah walked into Stan's arms, while Norm and Sid pulled Fran and Beth into the bus shelter, handing out cigarettes. Fran drew on her Woodbine, longing to be held by Davey, and Beth no doubt by Bob the Bastard.

Finally Cyn came down the bus steps.

'Hurry along, if you please,' called Fran.

Cyn beckoned them over. 'Well, you could have gone ahead. You know Simon's expecting us. It's spring. There is work to be done on the allotment. So, let's not dawdle, eh?'

'Oh do let's dawdle,' Beth said. There was laughter. There always was. Fran and Beth walked ahead, following Cyn, with Sid and Norm talking about nothing much behind them, and Sarah and Stan murmuring Lord knew what as they brought up the rear.

Fran was thinking what bliss it must be to have a husband at home with you, not miles and miles away, when Cyn raised her voice. 'A suggestion, girls. The Massinghams need help, especially when that bairn comes, so if one lass has half a left hand and t'other, Sandra Young, is missing some of her sight, the two seem well matched. In other words, they'd work right well together. Think on, and it would be something to offer Sandra when we get her signed off from the Factory. Tell me your thoughts on it, and on who is to talk to the Massinghams. Let's not dilly-dally, for I don't want them to fill the post and Sandra to have no money coming in if she's not up to the sewing shop.'

They were nearing the allotments, and already beanpoles were up on some plots, but not their das'.

'I'll tell Mam,' Fran said. 'She's been a bit down what with the Massingham babe coming. It's reminded her too much of Betty. She'll be glad to have some organising to do.'

Simon Parrot came to the door of the Canary Club. 'Howay, I've me own beer on the go, lads, and I reckon a taste of elderberry wine'll go down a treat.'

The shed was dark and Sid sat on an upturned barrel, smelling the bird seed, and it was as it had been most of his growing years. His father had kept pigeons before he'd been a member of the Canary Club in its early days, but then the black lung had taken him. It was long ago, while Sid was still at school, and the wedding photograph his mam kept on the mantelpiece didn't remind him a bit of the ailing man he'd known.

He watched as Cyn handed the girls bitty glasses of wine. There'd been no more from Bob after Beth'd sent her reply promising to send the allotment monthly, but he, Sid Barratt, could still see her pain, even though she was moving forward, as Ralph had said. He grinned to himself, for Ralph, the daft pillock, took his new walking stick to the pit, hooked over his arm as he walked up the slope to the screens, just to give everyone a good laugh. He fitted in and could even lip-read now, he'd said as they wheeled their bikes out of the pit yard one day. 'Well, I bliddy have to,' he'd said. They'd all swung round and looked at him.

'Bliddy?' asked Stan.

Ralph raised his eyebrows. 'Well, hard not to come down to everyone else's level when I'm a pitman amongst pitmen.' They'd beaten him about the head, then kicked his arse. He'd cycled away, calling back, 'Read my lips,' then mouthed, 'Pillocks.' They'd chased after him, but were laughing too much to go more than a few yards.

Sid dragged on the last of his Woodbine. It was strange because now everyone, mostly, forgot the lad was the boss's son. He was just one of them. What's more, Sid knew that he'd stand side by side with them from now on, as he had against Norris.

Sid took a beer from Simon. It was home brew, and strong enough to blow your head off.

'When you've wet your whistle, lad,' said Simon, 'you and Norm help the girls sort out the seed. Just see if you think there's too much red millet, for it gets stuck in their crop. Our Stan's too caught up with the missus to help.' Simon winked. 'Then we need to get on putting up the beanpoles.'

'We can help, eh, Fran?' Beth called across.

Fran nodded. 'Da would have had 'em up by now, so he'll be mithering.'

'I meant help with the seed, for heaven's sake,' said Beth.

There was more laughter.

Beth and Fran moved to sit either side of Sid, running their hands through the seed, and Sid felt happy, for he was here, with Beth, and Norm was there too, ignoring the seed, but instead prattling about the spuds needing water and double digging or some such, though what the hell was double digging?

Sid asked, and was told, once Norm had dragged his hand across his mouth, wiping it clean of the last of the beer. Sid thought of Beth doing just that after Norris's kiss. He looked down and saw that her hands had stilled in the seed, and she was also staring at Norm. Inching his hand towards hers, Sid entwined her little finger and ring finger with his. Her wedding ring was gone. He squeezed. She did nothing. Perhaps it was a cheek of him?

He moved his hand, but she snagged her fingers with his, momentarily. Then released them.

He glanced at her. She at him. He whispered, 'It's in the past.' She nodded. Fran was peering at the seed, checking for red millet as the two of them dug their hands in again, but all the while, Sid could see Beth's slight smile in his mind's eye.

'Sifted to death, you three,' called Simon. 'Time for the real work.'

'Not sure I signed up for this,' muttered Sid.

'If you're one of us, aye, you did,' Beth said.

There was laughter. They all downed their drinks and within five minutes Sid found himself with the spade, learning just what double digging was all about and wishing he'd kept his big mouth shut. It wasn't until he looked up and saw Beth laughing at him, dragging the dead runner beans from the poles, that it was all worthwhile. He said, 'The first big juicy worm I find will be down your neck, pet, if you think there's owt funny in this.'

Beth's laugh was louder still. 'You and whose army, our Sid?'

He said, quietly, 'I reckon I'll get me squaddie, Ralph, at me side, and we'll take you on, lass, no trouble.'

At that her gaze softened, her laughter grew quiet. 'Oh aye,' she whispered. 'I'll never forget that it were you, Sid, who saw that beggar off. Ralph helped, but it were you, and it changed how I felt, just as Ralph did later with his words. But it were you first and foremost. I didn't see it at the time, though.'

He stopped with his boot on the spade, and she with a beanpole in her hand, and they just looked, and he felt he could reach out and touch the warmth of her gaze.

Fran, Sarah and Beth walked back to Beth's house, though the other two would go on to their mams' after they'd checked that she'd had no more letters. The lads were still working nearby at the allotment, just in case she had and they were needed. The girls' boots clattered on the cobbles.

Beth lifted the sneck, collected the key from the old pigeon loft and let herself in. She removed her boots, while Fran stood in the doorway on the newspaper, Sarah at her shoulder. The kettle was on the side of the range but could be heated quickly for a cup of tea. Beth didn't bother to argue that she was strong enough to cope if she had another letter about the divorce and how to pay for it, but trotted through to the front door. There were two letters. One was a bill, the other was in Bob's handwriting. She brought both back to the kitchen, and when Fran and Sarah saw it, they removed their boots and joined her.

'I told him I wouldn't read any more of his letters,' she said. The envelope was cool in her hands; his handwriting was looped, and written in the same royal blue ink. Was he apologising and asking to be forgiven? What would she say? That's what she had lain awake trying to work out all week.

She faced the answer now, staring at his handwriting, for it was no. She could *never* like him again. Neither, she knew, could any of them. So, when she had got out of bed, she had realised that if he ever came back, the choice would be between her world and Bob. She looked around the kitchen. There was no room for him here; too much had been said and done.

Fran leaned forward. 'Open the bliddy thing, for 'tis driving me mad. Does he want to come back? Or is he up to mischief again? Come on, Beth. Open it.'

Beth shook her head. 'I said I'd not reply to owt he wrote. I said to let a solicitor handle the papers. So, it is only *that* envelope I will open. I divint want him back. He wouldn't fit, not here, not with us, or so I have come to feel.'

They turned at a tap on the door. Sid entered. 'I came to help. I heard what you said. I have a place for this letter, if it's what you really mean, bonny lass. Might as well give the worms something to do, if I'm not to stuff them down your neck.' His voice was quiet, but firm.

Somehow Beth wasn't surprised to see him, but the other two were, and they stared at Sid, open-mouthed. Beth looked up at her wedding photograph on the shelf. Then down at Bob's letter.

She put the letter in her pocket and put on her boots. Sid held the door open. The two girls booted up and came too. They walked across the yard and into the back lane. Sid led the way, back to the allotment. No one spoke. They tramped past Mr Oborne's, and Mrs Adams', until they reached their fathers' plots.

Stan, Simon and Cyn waited, standing by one of the double-dug rows they'd been working on. It was on Beth's da's plot. Sid pointed. 'Into the trench then, if you're sure.'

She looked at them, these friends, these marrers, these people who were part of her world and were her mainstay, her life. She looked finally at Sid, his freckles, his Woodbine in the corner of his mouth, his cap slanted over to the side, and smiled. 'Aye, I'm sure. Might as well do the soil some good.'

Stan realised then what was happening, and nudged Cyn and Simon. Fran squeezed Beth's hand. Sarah linked arms with her. They walked almost to the trench. Beth took one more look at the royal blue ink, the sloping writing, and couldn't bear to hold the envelope any longer, so tore it into shreds and let the pieces flutter into the trench. Stan pulled the spade out of the earth and handed it to Sid.

'Best cover it, lad.'

Sid dug in the spade to start the second trench and tossed the topsoil into the first, burying the shredded letter. He dug in the spade again, pressing down with his boot. Then Beth shouted, 'No. No, it's my job.'

She took the spade and dug and dug until she had finished the whole row, tossing the soil into the first trench each time. Sweat poured from her; her hands were sore from heaving the spade. She stood back. There, she thought. That's what I'll do with your madness every time from now on, do you hear?

Sid came and took the spade. Their hands touched. He looked at her. 'I'm right proud of you, lass. We all are.'

She pushed back her hair, looking around. Fran and Sarah were smiling, the lads were nodding. Cyn Ellington came and put her arm around her. 'Well, bonny lass. That's shown the toerag, eh?'

Before too long, the men had completed the digging and the beanpoles were in place, tied with twine by the girls. Down in the earth, thought Beth, were her husband's last words to her. She breathed in, then out, here on the allotment where her da had dug with Mr Bedley and Mr Hall, the three plots side by side. She and her marrers were together, as they had been since childhood. A childhood of which Bob had not been a part. A gang of which he had not been a member. The pain wasn't a pinprick, but neither was it a stab. It was just pain.

She looked around. All this was enough, all this was her present and future: the slag heap shimmering, the Factory with Swinton as foreman, the co-op, her friends. Aye, they were enough, but Bob had been her husband, and she had thought he loved her. She stared up at the sky, to her da, in the gloom of the fading day, a day on the cusp of evening, and realised that perhaps Bob had never cared, not really. Had she known him, really, or he her, ever? She looked around again, and there was Sid dusting off his hands, nodding at her. Yes, there was Sid, whom she hadn't thought of as a man – just part of the gang. But he was a man, and he had the kindest of eyes, a redness to his hair, and those freckles . . .

They walked home and were so late that Fran realised their mams would skelp them, but more than that, Davey would be telephoning any minute. She yelled as much to the girls, and together they ran, leaving Sid and Norm to go on to their own homes, and Cyn and Simon to do what they would.

The telephone was ringing in the telephone box, and magically there was no queue to sigh and roll their eyes. There were just the deepening shadows of the houses along the street, and the trees with branches like bare fingers against the darkening sky. Fran snatched up the receiver while the other two pressed their faces against the glass, pulling grotesque faces. She laughed and turned her back, listening to his precious voice.

Fran talked, laughed, and briefly mentioned the burial of Bob's letter. Davey cheered. The girls were tapping on the glass now.

'Go away,' Fran said, waving them off. Davey was telling her that Daniel had heard from his father, and that Daisy's parents had not seen anything of her, nor had anyone else. He paused, then said as an afterthought, 'Though there's a vague police report that someone perhaps answering her description bought a ticket for a train heading to the North.'

'What? Has she family up here?'

She imagined his shrug as he said, 'Who knows? 'Tis the bairn I worry about.' He added, 'I gather her parents would insist on adoption. But 'tis none of our business, thank heavens.'

Fran remembered Sandra Young now and told him that it was possible she would work at the Hall, with Viola and Sophia. He said, 'Aye, Sophia'll need it at her age.'

'For heaven's sake, she's not ancient,' Fran shouted. 'It's only because Reginald is older that you think that. Besides, the co-op'll take care of her.'

'Aye, but the thing is,' Davey said, 'I know some families have millions of bairns, but they're not all a similar age.' He paused, then said, 'Oh Fran, never mind Sandra Young heading to Massingham Hall, why don't you do it? Anything to get you out of the Factory.'

She shook her head. 'That's what I heard Stan say to Sarah, and there's nowt chance of it happening with either of us, or our Beth. There's a war to win. It'd be like running away and leaving others up to their eyes in it.'

Their trunk call was running out of time, and he was yelling, 'I'd rather you ran than were—' The line went dead.

She replaced the receiver, pressing down on it, wanting him here and in her bed of a night, holding her till the dawn. But he wasn't and that was that, but one day he would be.

She opened the door, and the three of them walked home first to Sarah's, where Stan was waiting, then to Beth's, where they saw Sid leaning against the wall near her yard gate.

'Howay, lass. Thought maybe there'd be a cuppa going spare.'

Fran grinned, turned and headed for her own back lane, sauntering down it and in through the gate, resting her head against the hen's chicken wire, telling them it had been a good day, a lucky day, just a bit of suntan for Tilly, nowt to speak of. She heard her mam singing in the scullery, opened the back door, removed her boots on the newspaper, and tucked them next to Ben's outside, under her da's old chair.

'Howay, Mam. I'm home.'

The singing stopped. 'Sit yourself down then, lass. We'll have a cuppa.'

Ben looked up from the crossword he was setting, winked and said, 'Best wash your hands, our Franny, or she'll skelp you.' They laughed together.

Welcome to

Penny Street

where your favourite authors and stories live.

Meet casts of characters you'll never forget,
create memories you'll treasure for ever,
and discover places that will stay with
you long after the last page.

Turn the page to step into the home of

ANNIE CLARKE

and discover more about

The Factory Girls . . .

Hello my dear friends,

I do love a good wedding. In fact, I love anything that lifts life a little: any excuse for a celebration, mum used to say. So what could be better than to have a couple of our girls getting hitched, and a bit of a celebration 'tea', a singsong. I love having a singsong in my novels, as I have such a foghorn of a voice, I am for a moment, transported into someone who has a voice that can soar and swoop, and bring an audience to their feet.

But clothes? Oh clothes in wartime, with strict rationing . . . Such a problem.

Then I remembered a photo of my mum and dad. They were married in India having met on a convoy over during the war. My dad was a pilot in the RAF and mum a military nurse. I've probably told you she was destined to nurse in Singapore but it fell while they were en route. So that 'squadron' of nurses went on to India with the convoy. Sadly, some of her friends were on an earlier convoy and fell victim to the Japanese.

So, there were mum and dad, having met on the boat, deciding to marry, and setting a date, but – arghhh – no frock. So, with Dad in the RAF, parachutes were available. A lovely frock ensued. And a wedding, and a reception at which they partied into the early hours. In the image you can see how terribly hot it was, the men sweated through their uniforms, but there was mum, elegant as ever on the day she changed from Annie Newsome (or Sister Newsome in my novels and as she was) to – eventually – my mum.

In my mind, the frock was already a solid starting point for the next stage of the Home Front girls. I just needed to think of the rest of the story!

I seem to write a great deal about communities, friendship, loyalty, endurance, love, and the odd fly in the ointment. Mum's pit village abounded with all these virtues. Here, in

Mum and Dad on their wedding day

North Yorkshire where we now live, we find the same: the goodness of people, the humour, the endurance.

When my editor told me that Fran's dress for the cover photoshoot was actually a heritage dress, made from parachute silk, and dating back to the war, I was absolutely thrilled.

In the fourth book, coming in October 2020, there is to be a pantomime. Who I wonder, is going to be the back end of the cow, who will be the nasty step-mother, and who the lovely fairy? Be still my beating heart.

Will there be another wedding, or perhaps an engagement? A baby or two? Now, let me see where my characters take me. Careful, they're behind you. Oh no they aren't. Oh yes they are . . .

Annie x

Turn the page for a sneak
peek into my new novel

Christmas on the
Home Front

Coming October 2020
Available to pre-order now

Early October 1942, Massingham pit village

Sarah, Beth and Fran congregated in the Halls' kitchen, standing in a line as Fran's mam, Annie Hall, handed a pair of knitting needles to each of them. Each pair had been stabbed into a ball of pale yellow wool. It was wool that Annie had pulled out from three tattered and tired baby coats she'd bought at the 'Jumble Sale for the War Effort' last week at the Miners' Club.

It was mid-morning, on Monday, and unfortunately the girls weren't due to head for the munitions factory bus until just before twelve, though the three of them wished it could be sooner.

Annie pointed her forefinger, a sign that she must be obeyed. 'I warned you yesterday I'd be up and at you this morning, for 'tis more than time you got to work on cardigans for Sophia Massingham's expected babe. You promised a while ago, but cardigans . . .' She raised her eyebrows and looked at each of them in turn. 'Came there none, as the Vicar's sister would say. Meanwhile, I say the bairn'll be walking before you three cack-handed lasses get round to producing owt. You know right well the babe is due at the end of the month, not earlier as the doctor thought. So at least you have a while longer. You've to knit, knit and knit again, lasses, for you're in a race against nature. Winter will soon be upon us and woollies will be required.'

Fran, Beth and Sarah shared a look but knew protests were pointless, not that they really wanted to demur, for they loved Sophia and Reginald Massingham, the enlightened owners of the pit, and the village, and lord knows what else.

Fran ran her fingers over the wool, remembering how

Davey had laughed last night when he telephoned her at the public phone box as usual, and Fran had told him of the lesson planned for the next morning. Her husband of six months had said, 'Knitting for the babe at last, eh? Well, you've put it off for so long on the pretext of no time, or too much work so I'm not surprised your mam's cornered you. I mean work? What work?'

Fran had laughed, 'I reckon when I next see you you'll pay for that remark, young man. You who sit at a desk throughout your shift and fiddle about much as though you're playing around with crosswords.'

Now, in the kitchen, she still felt the longing as her friends and mam chattered around her, and remembered almost moaning, 'Oh Davey, I just wish I was knitting for our own bairn, lad. I need something of you, for I miss you so much.'

Davey had been soft as he replied, 'It will be one day lass, just wait and see.' Silence had fallen between them, until she remembered something to lift their mood. 'Davey, oh Davey, Eva's come up with an idea, the little madam.'

Davey had sighed, though she could almost sense his smile. 'Oh lord, not another idea. She's full of them. Tell me, make me laugh.'

So she did, explaining that one of the orphaned evacuees, Melanie, had been adopted by an aunt and was off to live in Wales just before Christmas, and that Eva, in spite of being heartbroken, was trying to plan a farewell party to see her off. 'Typically our Eva has everyone else doing the work, starting with Stan, Sid and Norm finding a Christmas tree to her liking.'

Davey had laughed, spluttering, 'Oh aye, and then there'll be the Proggy Makers' Co-op dragged in to do the eats because Sophia will be busy with the new babe, and you, The Factory Girls group will have to s—'

Fran had interrupted, 'Are you a mind reader?' At that point the telephone box door had opened, and Sarah yelled to Davey, 'Talk quickly, older brother, it's too cold for me and Beth standing here waiting on her ladyship. 'Tis fine for you down in the South.'

Whereupon she and Beth had crowded in, as Fran repeated what he'd said. Beth shouted, 'Aye, spot on, our Davey. Eva's making a list of all that's to happen, and ticking it off when I swear she hasn't even asked anyone—' Sarah had snatched the receiver, sharing it with Beth. 'Aye, I reckon the co-op's been giving her lessons on how to be bossy.'

Now, in the warmth of the kitchen, Sarah was nudging her, waving her knitting needles and wool, saying, 'Remember Davey's phone call, and us telling him about Eva keeping track of everyone's jobs when—' They all sniggered as Beth interrupted, 'Aye, but the difference is, we did actually agree to knit these cardigans, t'isn't just your mam making it up. So, we should get on with it.'

'Oh, who's trying to be favourite,' Fran chanted. Beth held up her hand, and continued, 'At least your mam's shown thought and chosen lemon wool to match our skin colour.'

They burst out laughing though Mrs Hall muttered, 'Don't remind me of those dreadful explosives you work with, please. You know we mams spend our time doing our best to forget them.'

Sarah stopped laughing and was pulling the ball of wool from her needles, deep in thought, then she looked up. 'With us talking of making things up, I found meself thinking of that Daisy who made such a habit of fibbing. Did Davey say if any more has been heard about her whereabouts? It was Scotland last month, wasn't it? It's the babe who worries me, I can't imagine how the wretched girl will cope alone.'

'No, nothing more, and even that sighting was a "perhaps",' Fran answered, not wanting to think about Daisy in any way, shape or form, for she'd been such a nuisance at the Bletchley Park decoding establishment, accusing both Davey and his marrer Daniel of forcing themselves on her. No one could understand why, until it became apparent she was pregnant, and wanted someone to share the responsibility of the baby, which was in fact her boyfriend's. Poor bloke, he'd been shot down during an air battle. Davey, soft as he was, and Daniel too, had felt pity for the pregnant young woman and got Daniel's father, a vicar, to find a place for her in an unmarried mother and baby home. From there, she had disappeared, taking the baby with her.

It was her mam knocking on the kitchen table who brought the girls to order. 'Attention please, we haven't all day, so sit down, the three of you, and watch close, for I'm sick of showing you how to do this. By, t'isn't as though you know nowt about knitting for you learned at school. 'Tis such a simple thing but to make it even easier I'm showing you how to cast on using your thumb. I've decided I daren't let you loose with the two needles, for it seems to me you leave your brains behind at the very sight of a ball of wool.'

Fran was laughing silently, as her mam took her place at the head of the table, while they sat down. She watched as she wound a strand of wool around her thumb before looking at each of them in turn. 'Watch close, because while you do, I have to tell you that we must help Eva, and obey the ticks against our chores. And 'tis your chore that's becoming larger.'

The girls groaned, but watched Mrs Hall. 'Eva wants a bigger group of singers around the Christmas tree, which she insists is to be set up in the sitting room at the Massingham's. So you need to recruit about four or five others to join in though it doesn't matter whether they can sing, for the bairn's'll join in, and drown all out. Watch carefully now.' Annie Hall shook her head, causing a strand of grey hair to come loose from her bun, and fall across her eye. She blew it off her face.

Beth copied Mrs Hall, winding the wool round her thumb, saying, 'But that's all very well, Mrs Hall, for though Eva's ticked us off on her list as certainties, we haven't agr—'

Mrs Hall rode over her. 'Agreement's nowt to do with owt and it'll do you all good to be involved in a party. For a start it'll take Fran's mind off mooning over Davey, and calm you, Beth, when you get to thinking about not hearing from your Bob over the divorce he wants. And what about our Sarah, still swooning over our Stan, though they've been married – what – seven months? If he's there, then she'll be, so might as well give her some'at to do.'

Fran raised an eyebrow. 'I'm mooning, eh?'

'Concentrate, Fran.'

Fran laughed, loving this woman. Sarah said, 'Tell you what, Mrs Hall, let's just get on with knitting because you know very well we'll do as we're told, or you'll be sure to strangle us with the wool.'

Beth nudged her, as she struggled with the stitches for a moment, saying, 'Aye, but Mrs Hall knows we have to make a bit of a fight of it, or 'tis no fun.'

Annie Hall looked up from her six cast-on stitches, waving them in front of the girls and checking theirs, before nodding. 'Good, keep going, and while I think of it there's a piano in the ballroom. Perhaps we can bring it through to the sitting room, then the vicar's sister can accompany you. Even if it's a bit out of tune it'll be better that the organ and all her puffing and wheezing. Just one squeak from her tubes and it'll set everyone off.'

Fran muttered, struggling to push the needle through

the wool which she'd wound too tightly round her thumb. ''Tis the organ's tubes, Mam.'

The girls all grinned, and Mrs Hall too. 'Aye, well, that's as maybe, but to help you out I'll talk to Sophia about the piano, and then maybe suggest it to Eva. Though she's so sharp it wouldn't surprise me if she's been on to the idea without the help of any of us. As long as she has a labour force she reckons everything is possible. Mind, she'll not put up with any forming of a union to question her thoughts on what needs to be done.'

Sarah muttered, making another stitch, and nodding towards Mrs Hall. 'Wonder who she reminds me of, our Fran? And aye, you have to live with her.'

Fran was making another stitch after loosening the wool, but muttered, 'Aye, 'tis why I'm such a wreck and moon over someone else.'

Mrs Hall took no notice. 'I reckon the co-op can bake a few tarts, there'll be some apples stored up at the Hall and I'll think of more things, but I reckon our Eva will have sorted what she wants already, so why am I bothering?'

Again they all laughed and continued casting on, Fran created a fourth stitch, then a fifth as her mam continued, 'Now, the pattern says thirty stitches, so keep at it. This will be the back.'

The girls, as one, looked at the clock above the range, but no, it wasn't nearly time to leave for the bus. They groaned, and worked on until each had thirty stitches on the needle. Mrs Hall nodded, 'Aye, that's grand. 'Tis the most difficult part, until you come to the armholes that is.'

The girls sighed. She continued, 'So we will now knit one, pearl one for the rib. We want the wee mite to feel welcome, divint we, and a few nice cardigans isn't too much to ask, is it, eh?'

The girls sighed again, and did as they were told, for this

last comment was just another example of the co-op's nice line in emotional blackmail.

Mrs Hall mused, 'Maybe you'll work on it as you take the bus to and from the factory, and even during the meal break?'

Fran said, 'Oh aye, just think of the guards finding these metal needles as we go in. They'll have them off us quick as a wink, and give us a tongue lashing into the bargain.'

'Then I'll be down there, frisking them, and taking the needles back just as quick, let me tell you,' Mrs Hall replied. 'Now, I'll remind you that there were rips in the coats I bought, so the wool, though 'tis wound into a ball, is broken. You'll have to join it. Divint even think of knotting it. You knit it with the two ends side by side, just for two, perhaps three stitches, and when it's finished, use your big-eyed sewing needle to thread the ends through so it doesn't show.'

She smiled at them, as though all the problems of the world had been solved. Fran pressed her lips together against a retort, which would have anyway died a death, because her mam was roaring on. 'Wait, I've an idea. I reckon if you talk to Bert, he'll keep the knitting in the cab of his bus, so you can still knit on the way to and from work, and we don't have to cause a scene at the gate.'

Fran broke off from creating a pearl stitch. 'Mam, did I hear you say "we". It's an "us", I reckon.'

'Aye, lass, but I'll be with you in spirit.'

Beth muttered, 'That's what we're afeared of.'

All four of them grinned as they continued working in rib; one plain, one pearl and Fran found her shoulders relaxing. She could feel the wool, the cool of the needles, and hear the click. The repetition was soothing, which is what her mam had always said. She smiled, for it pushed the absence of Davey into the background and that took some doing.

Sarah dropped a stitch. 'Oh no, look.' She held up her knitting. Mrs Hall came round the table. 'Watch, everyone.' They did as commanded, and learned now to re-capture the stitch, and it was Beth who said, 'By, poor wretch, it thought it had escaped, but let's face it, if it wasn't Mrs Hall, it'd be me own mam, or yours, Sarah, recapturing it, putting paid to its little game, just like they do to us.'

Mrs Hall gave Beth one of her looks as she handed the knitting back to Sarah. 'Two more rows, girls, then a cuppa, and perhaps "good girl" honey scones.'

Fran raised her eyebrows. 'You were that certain we'd fall in line that you've baked them already, you wicked woman?'

'Aye, well, you're good lasses, and all the effort is for the evacuees, poor wee bairns, for Eva will miss Melanie sorely when she goes back with her auntie. Better if Wales was next door, but it is what it is.' Mrs Hall ended the row, then pierced the ball of wool with the needles, leaving them on the table before heading for the range, where she perked up the simmering kettle, poured the water over the used tea leaves already in the teapot, leaving it to stew. She hurried into the scullery, bringing back scones, and placing them in the middle of the table. They were already split, buttered and thinly spread with honey.

Beth completed her row, just a step behind Fran, but Sarah dropped another stitch. 'I reckon this wool's got a life of its own.' She couldn't pick up the stitch, and dropped another into the bargain. Mrs Hall brought over the teapot, poured them each a cup, then went to Sarah. 'By lass, you're making a right dog's dinner. Give it to me a minute, and for the love of Mike, watch.'

She caught the stitches, slowly, checking that Sarah was

watching, and handed it back, just as Fran set aside her needles and sipped her tea, looking over at Beth. 'So, and you'll be sick of the question you're asked too often, I expect: nowt more from Bob then about the divorce he wants?'

Beth shook her head. 'Nothing, and if I do get a letter from him, I'll send it back to Grimsby, Return to Sender, much as he did to me, his wife. The only letters I'll open are from his solicitor.'

'How do you really feel, pet, now it's some months further on?' It was Mrs Hall asking as she busied herself wiping down the range. It was the question Fran wanted to ask, because her friend still hadn't regained the weight she had lost when Bob had left her.

Beth concentrated on finishing another row, mouthing rib one, pearl one, then laid the knitting aside as the others had now done, and reached for a scone. She took a bite, then looked up. 'A bit frit sometimes, for he was right horrid by the end, but you know that, and I'm with my mam, and me marrers and that's what's important.' She smiled at them all. ''Tis strange really, for though I feel a bit better about it, I'll be going along, doing something ordinary, and suddenly I remember something we did in the past. Or I see his face in a shop window, and think he's there, behind me, angry because I won't help him pay for the divorce. I mean, I send my wife's allotment from his pay to him and Heather for the babe, and 'tis enough. The divorce is his business to pursue.'

She looked around at them, and the scone in her hand. 'But you know what, I can kick him out of me head easier now, just like a football: wham, bang. What's more I make sure I miss the goal so he goes blasting away for miles.' She grinned, the others laughed, finishing their scones and licking their fingers. Mrs Hall tutted and brought out a damp flannel.

Beth mused, 'I'm starting to wonder if I ever really knew him, for he were off to war so quick, and then at sea . . . But, really truly, I mean it when I say I don't want anything more of his nonsense.'

She continued knitting, starting another row, knit one, pearl one, saying, 'Besides, that's the way it is, as our Fran says far too often, and drives us bliddy mad.'

Fran pulled a face. The others grinned. Beth said, 'If the wind changes, our Franny, you'll stay like it.'

'Talking of wind,' her mam called from the scullery. 'Check the back door is shut, would you, Franny. Seems to me 'tis rattling.'

Fran checked the door, but it was closed properly. She returned to the table. Sarah was head down, knitting, and Beth too. Fran took her place, picked up her needles, pleased with her efforts. The only sound was her mam pottering about the kitchen, the gurgling of the range, and the ticking as the warming plate cooled. It was all so normal, when out there in the world, Fran thought, the war was raging. She found herself wondering if Bob was away escorting convoys or something, because the first convoy had got through to Russia, or so the newspapers said. Well, she damn well hoped so, for it was time Bob concentrated on his job and did someone some good.

They knitted on, rewarding themselves with sips of tea at the end of each row so the sudden banging on the front door made Fran jump. She spun round, confused, then her mind raced. She froze, for the front door was for the police, or telegram boys, or authorities of some sort. Telegrams? *Oh no*. Fran felt faint, then threw down her knitting, and was up and out of her chair, rushing down the hall, her heart racing. 'Davey? Not Davey?'

Her anguished call must have galvanised them all, for she heard them tearing after her, her mam calling, 'No,

Franny. Let me.' Fran didn't slow, but still her mam reached the sneck ahead of her, pulling the door open, her arm out to hold the girls back. But there was no one there. Fran stepped out into Leadenhall Terrace, looking up and down the street. Beth, Sarah and her mam clustered around her.

'Bairns I reckon, bored for they're not in school in the mornings, which is the evacuees' time,' Mrs Hall muttered, slapping her hands together as though wishing it was their backsides.

Fran was almost crying, her throat thick. 'I thought . . .' Sarah hugged her. 'We all thought, lass.'

Her mam led the way back into the house, and slammed the door behind them, leading the way to the kitchen, but as they entered, they saw the coals burning brightly in the range's firebox, and felt a draught. Fran put up her hand, stopping them, for the back door was swinging in the cold wind. 'What?' She started to say. But her mam shouted, 'By, the bairns must have tricked us, got us to the front and come in—' She stopped. 'But not Massingham bairns, no.' They looked round checking, but what was there to steal?

Mrs Hall said, slapping her forehead. 'Oh, wait, it'll be Madge, she was coming to do some rug making.' Fran raised her eyebrows. All this and it was Madge? But . . . She looked from the open door, to the corridor. But no, for who knocked on the front door? Her mam was raising her voice, 'Come away in, Madge, take your boots off in here, and stop heating the yard.' There was no answer, just an odd mewling noise. 'A cat?' queried Beth. Fran shook her head. 'A cat can't open a door.'

Mrs Hall pushed past. 'If it's that bliddy tom of the Pritchard's after me hens, I'll have its guts for garters. He's a bliddy nuisance he is, like his owner. Yowls at the feathered ladies and gets 'em in a tizz so they stop laying, and I'm not bliddy having it.' She grabbed the broom from the scullery and almost ran to the back door, while the three girls stood back, laughing. Fran called, 'Oh Mam, they'll peck him to death if he ever gets in, bliddy old boilers.'

Beth pulled at Sarah's arm, sounding alarmed suddenly. 'I wonder, d'you reckon 'tis Bob? But why . . . ?'

Mrs Hall opened the door a bit wider, and Beth heard her gasp, and make what sounded like a groan as she almost threw the broom back into the room. Fran moved, leaving the other two. Beth felt herself shaking. She called, 'Is it him, Mrs Hall?'

Fran reached the door, as Mrs Hall looked as though she was tipping over onto the step. Fran reached back, grabbed the broom, brandishing it and flinging the door so wide it crashed against the wall, shouting, 'Get away, leave me mam, you bastard. Go—'

She stopped. 'Oh, what? What . . . ?' She felt faint when she realised what her mam had seen, and was now bending over and could hardly speak. She swallowed, and her voice sounded far away, even to her own ears. 'No, Beth, it's not Bob. Look.'

She watched as her mother reached for the bundle on the step, hearing her say, 'Oh, who'd do . . . Oh, I divint believe it, holy Mother of God.' Her mam's voice was a mere whisper as she straightened, carrying the bundle, looking helplessly at Fran.

Fran couldn't believe what she was seeing either.

The girls had gathered behind Fran, and now all three stepped back. 'What? Whose? Why?' Fran dropped the broom, and reached for her mam, who nodded. Fran felt the chill of the blankets as she pulled them down. Yes, it was true, it was a bairn, and it was pale and quiet, but moving, breathing, mewling.

*

Beth just stared as Sarah took the other side of Mrs Hall, helping Fran guide her to the table, and all the while the anger was building in her. Bob, her husband. Bob, his baby. Finally she rushed to the back door, through the yard, to the gate, looking up and down the back lane. 'Hello, hello,' she called. Why would Bob? He wouldn't, surely? There was no reply, no Bob. There was nothing but the usual Massingham noise; the singing of the wind in the pit head winding gear, the banging and crashing of the tubs bringing coal to the surface screens, the grinding of gears as lorries took the coal to the station. But then she heard it, a different sound, that of a car revving, a door slamming. It came from Main Street.

She flew along the lane, her feet bare, heedless of the freezing cold cobbles, seeing the car, dirty and mud covered, roar past the head of the lane before she was halfway to Main Street. 'Bob?' Instead of a shout, she heard little more than a whisper, for her voice wasn't working. She kept on running, her breath heaving in her chest, her feet slipping until she reached the road, looked to the right, shading her eyes against the glare of the sun. The car was in the far distance, taking the Newcastle fork.

'What on earth? Bob didn't have a car.' She turned, and ran towards the backyard, heading for the open door, stepping over the broom which still lay discarded half on the steps, half in the kitchen. To the right of the door, lying on the chair beneath which young Ben put his boots on his return from school, was a bag. She picked it up and carried it through to the kitchen table, where the girls were talking together, while Mrs Hall sat crooning to the bairn. The knitting needles were left abandoned on the table, the pale lemon wool too. She went to shut the door, but the broom was in the way. She felt such a deep chill in her heart, a chill far worse than that of an October day in Massingham.

Helplessly she made her way back to the small group at the table, staring at the babe, making herself be calm, making herself think, for this surely . . . Yes, she was right, this bairn was too big, seven, maybe eight months old and Bob and Heather's wouldn't be. She closed her eyes, feeling a moment of relief, but only a moment, for the babe was so wan, and thin, too cold and too quiet. And if not Bob's, then whose? She heard herself say, 'Who would do this? It divint make sense . . .'

She heard the sneck on the yard gate lift, then it slammed. Beth spun round. Was this the mother? Had the car returned? She held out her hand, stopping Fran. 'Let me.' She ran to the door, which was already open, and pulled it wide but it was Madge and Beth's own mam, Audrey Smith, who called, 'We've come to chivvy our Annie, pet. I know Madge was to work on the rugs here, but we met her, and decided it were best we take them to the Hall to help our Sophia, eh? She's so laden with the bairn she's almost past walking. Maud Bedley is waiting down the road.'

Beth stood gaping at them.

Madge pointed to the broom. 'What's amiss? Why are you looking so gormless, our Beth, standing guarding the door, like that, eh?' Still Beth couldn't speak. Alarmed, Madge stepped over the broom, and pushed past. 'Is it our Annie?'

Beth could see Fran standing at the table, carefully unpacking the bag, laying out baby bottles, clothes, nappies; the girls' knitting had been moved aside into a pile. Finally, there was a letter. Fran held it up. Beth's mam, Audrey, snatched it from her while Madge squatted by Annie's chair, pulling aside the blanket. Beth picked up the broom, leaning it against the wall, and shut the door. Madge muttered, 'By, this babe isn't thriving. I know it's cold, but even so, look, it's so thin.' Madge was rubbing the bairn's hands, blowing warm breath, while Annie Hall stood and moved closer to the range.

Audrey Smith said, 'It's addressed to you, Fran.'

'Aye, I reckon I saw that before you ripped it from me hand.' She took it back, unfolded the sheet of paper, and scanned it.

Fran was trembling, and she shook her head. The babe was mewling now, but weakly, and aye, it were like Pritchard's tom cat.

Mrs Smith said, 'For the love of God, lass, read it out.'

Fran had to read it twice to herself, because she couldn't understand the first time, or believe it the second. She looked up, staring across at her mam, who was rocking the bairn as she walked backwards and forwards. She looked around at the others, then let the letter drop to the table, saying, and meaning it. 'I'll bliddy strangle her, so I will.'

'Who?' shouted Beth as she made her way towards the others.

'Daisy.' The baby's wail was loud. Annie hushed her, rocking her as Madge picked up the letter and read it, her eye patch green today. Mrs Smith peered over her shoulder. Annie Hall muttered, 'If someone doesn't read the damn thing out, I'll be the one strangling the lot of you. Daisy? Oh, the one our Davey had the troubles—Oh, for the love of God. And someone put the kettle to boil as we'll have to sterilise these bottles, get something warm into the wee thing. Pan on the shelf in the scullery, Beth. Tip the boiled water in it, but keep it boiling, eh? Have we time to boil the milk and let it cool, or look, maybe the tot is old enough to drink it warm?'

The door opened, and in came Maud Bedley, Sarah's mam. 'I've given up waiting for you. The wind on the corner of Main Street got right into me drawers.'

Fran looked from the letter to her mam, who had become quite still, and was staring at her daughter. 'Mam?'

Mrs Hall said, 'If it's Daisy's, is she coming back for the bairn? Or is it forever?' She stopped. 'But 'tis the bairn we need to sort, nowt more, not yet.'

Fran just nodded, as Beth came from the scullery with the pan and poured in the kettle water. Madge had opened the vents on the firebox so the coals glowed red hot. Beth scuttled on more coal. 'Hush Beth, quietly, eh,' Fran called softly. She read out the letter then, equally quietly.

Fran, I know that you are a good person for Davey has talked a lot about you. I didn't want to have my baby adopted and because you are good, I know you will keep her 'til I am able to have her back. It will be good for your mother too, Fran, as I know her own Betty died, and guess what, my baby is called Betty too, to make it easier for you and your mother to be good to her. Don't try and find me. But please tell Daniel's father, for he was kind to me. I will come for her, one day.
Gratefully, Daisy.

Sarah sighed, 'Davey said she was devious, and I reckon he were only partway right, for she's very, *very* devious naming her Betty, if she bliddy did. For this little babe were born months ago. I bet she's called some'at else really. As though that makes any difference as to whether you'll keep the lass. But you divint have to, you know. This is blackmail.'

Read more from
ANNIE CLARKE

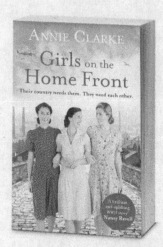

Hear more from

Annie Clarke